CONFIDENCE

A NOVEL

RAFAEL FRUMKIN

SIMON & SCHUSTER

NEW YORK   LONDON   TORONTO   SYDNEY   NEW DELHI

Simon & Schuster
1230 Avenue of the Americas
New York, NY 10020

First Simon & Schuster hardcover edition March 2023

SIMON & SCHUSTER and colophon are registered trademarks of Simon & Schuster, Inc.

For information about special discounts for bulk purchases, please contact Simon & Schuster Special Sales at 1-866-506-1949 or business@simonandschuster.com.

The Simon & Schuster Speakers Bureau can bring authors to your live event. For more information or to book an event, contact the Simon & Schuster Speakers Bureau at 1-866-248-3049 or visit our website at www.simonspeakers.com.

Interior design by Carly Loman

Manufactured in the United States of America

10 9 8 7 6 5 4 3 2 1

Library of Congress Cataloging-in-Publication Data has been applied for.

ISBN 978-1-9821-8973-0
ISBN 978-1-9821-8975-4 (ebook)

For Fig

I followed you, Muse! Beneath your spell,
Oh, la, la, what glorious loves I dreamed!

—Arthur Rimbaud, "Wandering"

Is there a good kind of hustler?

—Maggie Nelson, *Bluets*

PROLOGUE

IN PRISON, SMALL THINGS MATTER: A PENCIL, A BANANA, A PACKET OF RAMEN.
People studying for their GEDs got pencils; bananas were a rare commodity,
meaning you had to be rich or smart if you were mashing one into your oatmeal; and ramen was so warm and filling, gave the eater such a sense of reas-
surance that people would trade cigarettes for it, or pay you to take their GED
exams in exchange for five or six packets. You had to purchase the ramen
from the commissary and then it would be "released" to you in the chow hall
at the end of the meal. The inmates working in the kitchen would heat it up
and give it to you in a little bowl with a plastic spoon, and you'd be allowed
to take it back to your cell—or, if you were lucky, the TV room—to eat.
Plastic spoons could be snapped in half and given rigid edges, so you had to
be proven well-behaved to get to use one outside the chow hall. My cellmate
once made a gash in someone's forearm with the end of a plastic fork. He
wasn't allowed any utensils—instead he ate his food with his hands, which
worked, because most of the food was congealed into cakey spheres that were
easy to pick up and eat in a matter of bites. Unlike him, I had connections.
I was eating macaroni and cheese when everyone else was eating meat loaf,
brownies when everyone else was eating Jell-O.

Everyone was surprised by how well I fared in prison: it was kind of a
joke, *the little pretty kid is actually the meanest motherfucker in here.* But, really, I
wasn't mean, nor was I particularly pretty. I was just focused on doing what
I did best. I'd converted another inmate, Tyrell, to the magic of NuLife,
and together we'd become business partners, Synthesizing members of the
general population in exchange for loosies, ramen, drugs, shower privileges,

protection, and sex. We held weekly informational meetings in the library that we pretended were AA meetings, bribing the COs with low-quality molly and oxy to go get high in the stacks and ignore us. We'd rearrange the demeaning twelve-step circle into rows and Tyrell and I would stand at the front, his lanky form towering over mine. Our first meeting was on a Wednesday night directly after chow, in those restless few hours when people tried to get drunk or pick fights before we had to return to our bunks.

"What's NuLife?" Duke, who'd lost an eye in a botched bank robbery, wanted to know.

"NuLife is a way of turning matter into potential," I said.

Tyrell gestured to the four walls enclosing us.

"Take this library," he said. "The windows are barred. It's only books in the stacks that's supposed to be *safe* for convicts to read. You know what I mean by 'safe'?"

Blank stares.

"Unlikely to provoke restlessness, awareness of our condition," I chimed in. "Stifling independent thought. Prohibitive to freedom."

"But with the power of NuLife, you can be free anywhere," Tyrell said, nodding to me.

"You wake up every morning doubting yourselves and doubt yourselves until you go to sleep." I began walking up and down the aisles, watching the inmates' heads swivel to accommodate my movement. "You spend an inordinate amount of time living under the suspicion that you are frauds, undignified, unworthy of the special attentions and affections of others. On the outside, you labor in your jobs, assuming that if you make more money, you'll be happier, and then of course you're not happier. You deny yourselves bliss. You deny yourselves simple, beautiful, uncritical living. You hunger after *betterness*, and that hunger—even the betterness itself—makes for unhappiness."

This is when Tyrell played dumb. He let out a little laugh and pulled at the collar of his uniform. "So how're you planning to solve the problem of betterness?"

All eyes on me again, some bald heads gleaming with the ceiling's fluorescence, some tattooed arms folded. It was incredible to have an audience like this, phone-less and understimulated, more rapt than any audience I could have had on the outside. This was my milieu.

"Synthesis," I said.

A raised hand, this one from Al, who'd blown up a bar in which members of a rival gang were celebrating someone's birthday. When I called on him, he slouched forward, forehead wrinkled thoughtfully, hands squeezed between his knees.

"I was wondering—maybe I missed this—but what's Synthesis?"

"You didn't miss anything, Al," I said, and resumed my pacing. "It's difficult to explain exactly what Synthesis is. I won't even attempt to do it now. Suffice it to say that it rebuilds your memories and leaves you in a state of complete and uninhibited bliss. It gathers the shards of your self-worth up off the ground."

"My self-worth?"

"See, you have to stop thinking on a big, macro scale," I blazed ahead. "We all have traumas, right? But what are the *specific moments* that those traumas became most salient in our lives? You hate your dad? Okay great. But what was the *one thing* he did that made you hate him most? You're scared of heights? Makes sense—so am I. Synthesis takes you back to the moment when you got stuck at the top of the Ferris wheel, or when you were peering over the cliff's edge, or when you couldn't climb down from that tree. It asks you to take sovereignty over those moments."

"Sovereignty," Tyrell repeated slowly, like a schoolteacher. "Basically, like, ownership."

"You could say I'm the first beneficiary of Synthesis," I said. "I've undergone it myself, and by now I've watched countless people undergo it, and believe me, it's life-changing."

I didn't tell them about Orson: the little crack in his morning voice, his eyes meeting mine as we woke up, his smile anticipating my own, his hair matted from sleep. I didn't tell them about the Farm, about the hundreds of people sitting cross-legged awaiting his appearance, listening with rapt devotion when he finally took the stage. And I certainly didn't tell them about Orson being led away from me in handcuffs, shouting over his shoulder: *Just hang on, Ez! We'll be fine!* How could I tell them about any of that? They wouldn't have understood.

"After Synthesis, you're left with the memory and none of the pain," I said. "You're left with the opposite of pain, actually."

"Your self-doubt goes into *remission*," Tyrell said, clearly aware that he was introducing a new vocabulary term. "That means it stops being active. You get free that way. And then you keep up the cycle: you get better by giving back. That means you gotta bring more people to NuLife, you gotta get them to join up. The bigger the NuLife family, the more freedom to go around."

Duke looked skeptical. "How'd you get in here again?"

The question was clearly directed at me, but I acted confused anyway. "Me?" He nodded.

"I knocked over a 7-Eleven," I said. "I accidentally shot the clerk."

"*You* shot the clerk?" This came from someone called D-Red, who had spent two months in solitary for nearly killing a CO with a lock in a sock.

"Yeah, man," Tyrell said, stepping forward as though he were my counsel approaching the bench. "It's true."

"You don't look like you could even handle a gun," D-Red said.

"Nah, little homie can handle a gun," Tyrell insisted.

"This isn't about me," I said quickly. "This is about NuLife and the radical power of Synthesis. This is about taking you all from the un-Synthesized to the Synthesized state and helping you reclaim your bliss."

"Is this like finding God?" Al wanted to know.

"It's a little like that, yeah," Tyrell said. "But better."

"Who wants to try it?" I asked. "It's painless, and Tyrell here is one of the most gifted Synthesizers I've ever met."

A few raised hands. I waited long enough to elicit a few more.

"Great," I said. "We'll just collect whatever you got."

I walked up and down the aisles and they palmed me their contraband, some of which I tucked into the waistband of my uniform, some of which I swallowed on the spot. Then I nodded to Tyrell, who arranged two of the folding chairs across from each other and invited one of the willing to sit in the chair opposite him.

I took a seat in the back row as he Synthesized them, watching their trembling smiles and tears, applauding as each sprang from his seat to announce he'd been changed forever. Tyrell could elicit this kind of reaction without fail—he was better at it than me, even. But Orson had been the best at it. The way he'd lean forward and lace his fingers together, smile when the Synthesized smiled and sigh when the Synthesized sighed. He'd put a finger to his lips in thought and then say something spellbinding, something that could echo in your ears for hours or even days afterward.

There was nothing like it. There was no one like him.

PART I

ONE

IT WAS DIFFICULT TO BE ME IN 2007. I WAS, TO MY DISAPPOINTMENT, MUCH shorter than the average height. Our finances forced my parents to choose between a pediatrician and a dentist, which meant that I never got braces to correct the space between my front teeth or my right-side snaggletooth. I was desperately addicted to the internet, from the edgelording of 4Chan to the privilege-checking of Tumblr (though we didn't have names for edgelording or privilege-checking back then) to the unremitting capitalism of YouTube (we've always had a name for that). I made very little eye contact, preferring instead to study the textures of the ground and my shoes. This wasn't because I was shy—I actually *could* start a conversation with anyone willing to talk to me—but because my eyesight was so bad that at seventeen, I was halfway to being legally blind, and making eye contact meant showing whomever I was looking at the disturbing degree to which the lenses of my glasses magnified my eyes. The glasses were the worst thing about me, possibly the worst thing about anyone. I had begun wearing them at age two, and my eyesight had deteriorated in the intervening fifteen years so that I had 20/100 vision by the time I was a junior in high school and reading was only possible with bifocals. Pretty girls in ribboned pigtails and Aéropostale approached me in the hallway, asking with polite concern how I'd done on some trigonometry quiz or AP US history test. They did this as if being kind to me would guarantee them entry into a top-tier college. I told them—truthfully—that I'd received a 98 or 99 (I'd always received a 98 or 99), which infuriated them. I wasn't supposed to be self-sufficient, and I certainly wasn't supposed to be capable of outperforming them.

Things got worse when I arrived at Last Chance Camp, where even the younger prisoners towered over me, muscular, shadow jawed. The camp, which was really called Wellspring, was run by a former pastor, an ex–Navy SEAL, and a group of early-twenties "counselors" who were supposed to discipline us by forcing us to do hard work. It was located on a farm in rural Colorado, on land we cultivated by ourselves with only shovels and hoes as though we were medieval serfs. We would be awakened at 5:00 in the morning by the ex–Navy SEAL blaring a police siren from his Honda Civic as he drove down the gravel road behind our cabins. Then a lucky quarter of us would be placed on mess duty, making breakfast while the rest of us performed "inspection," which meant cleaning every inch of every cabin and standing outside while the former pastor and the ex–Navy SEAL inspected each of them. Both the former pastor's and the ex–Navy SEAL's names were Doug, so we referred to them by their last names: Mr. Kimborough (the former pastor) and Mr. Sledge (the ex–Navy SEAL). Kimborough would sometimes compliment us on our cleaning, but Sledge always found something out of place, some crumb or pocket of dust untouched by our washcloths and brooms, and for these small errors he would make us run three times around the entire property. This happened so often that I couldn't remember going to breakfast *not* sweating, too hot and dizzy to eat whatever warm mash those on mess duty had prepared. We would be worked so hard for the rest of the day that I should have had an appetite, but I never did. I typically ate a boiled egg or a rock-hard potato for lunch, and then I choked down half of whatever protein-rich mash was being served for dinner. Being rotated onto mess duty didn't help the problem, either, because I didn't know how to cook—no one did, really. I lost twenty pounds I didn't have to spare.

Last Chance Camp was supposed to be the final stop before juvie, but its price tag suggested that whoever went there had parents who could pay their way out of juvie. The cost was prohibitive for my family, but my dad insisted I apply for a scholarship after the incident. I tried to tank the essay but I was required to submit my transcripts, and there was no way to pretend that I didn't have a near-perfect GPA. This was because the material in high school was easy to master without taking notes or spending more than ten minutes glancing over a textbook. I was able to quickly diagnose each teacher's particular brand of laziness. If they were enamored of their own cults of personality, they'd assign massive tests that were worth half the grade. If they were timid and bored, they'd assign frequent quizzes that someone with a memory worse than mine might have needed to study for. And if they were bitter about their unglamorous work, as most of them were, they arranged the class so they'd have to do as little grading as possible: one big project that was easily bullshit-able, one big test that there was no need to study for. Last Chance awarded me a full scholarship, much to my horror and disappointment.

I landed at Last Chance because of a hustle. My family lived in an apartment on the border of a wealthy school district, and my parents had lobbied to let me attend the wealthy school instead of the overheated, overcrowded, and understaffed public school in our district. I was granted access to the kingdom, which meant that I was the only student wearing shirts with too-short sleeves, carrying a backpack with frayed straps, entirely without a car or a good-looking cell phone. I biked the five miles to school because the bus was a moving shark tank: if I was cornered, there would be no escape. I wanted at least half an hour of peace before I was surrounded at the school, shoved, elbowed, stared at. I ate alone in the cafeteria and was frequently the object of pity for kids of moderate social standing who had been taught by their liberal parents to mime empathy. They were worse than the Aéropostale girls because they thought they were being charitable. "Do you want my sandwich? Do you need me to buy you some milk?"

One day, I bought a $10 pair of white sneakers from the bottom of the clearance bin at the Payless in the mall. I brought them home, took my mom's sewing kit from its place in the utility cabinet we'd dedicated to everything we didn't have space for: a wrench, a discolored plunger, tattered washcloths. As my parents slept, I stitched the sneakers up to look like Adidases. It wasn't as difficult as I thought it would be: I'd been coveting other people's Adidases my entire life, and I had a surprisingly steady hand. This took several nights, and when they were finished, I wore them to school. I drew looks in the hallway and cafeteria and pretended to be oblivious to them. I ate the bologna and cheese sandwich my mom had packed for me and stared ahead as Hayden Pritzker and his friends swarmed around me.

"Hey, bruh," Hayden said. He was white but desperately wanted to be Black.

I looked up as though I'd just noticed him. He was flanked by Tyler Scarpone and Nick DeQuist, both of whom drove SUVs to school.

"Those shoes are tight as hell," Hayden said.

I looked from my shoes to Hayden to my shoes again. "They're limited edition," I said. "Like not in stores yet. I know a guy."

"How much they cost?"

I took a moment to think of a realistic number. "Three-fifty."

The three of them exchanged looks. That I should be wearing a pair of $350 shoes made little sense to them, but there I was, wearing them. The fact couldn't be questioned. Neither could it be questioned that they wanted them.

"So you have a hookup?" Tyler asked.

I nodded.

I had saved up $100 doing yardwork over the summer, which I then spent on ten pairs of white Payless sneakers. I spent a month stitching these sneakers up. I told Hayden that my connect was "laying low" in Hawaii, and that he'd hit me up the minute he got back. At the end of the month, I sold Hayden, Tommy, and Nick three pairs for the discount price of $300. I sold the rest to their friends.

"What else your hookup got?" Hayden lisped through his fake grill.

My hookup had XiX, the perfect blend of coke and molly that was really just my dad's ground-up Sudafed and sea salt. XiX sold for $40 an eighth and $75 a fourth. Hayden bought a fourth from me and invited me to his party, where he said he and his friends planned to snort the entire bag. I respectfully declined, making up some pressing homework assignment, and Hayden shrugged and said, "You still cool, man." The next night, a Saturday, he texted me: *i'm hallucinating off this shit!!!* I texted back: *just do little pinkie bumps*.

I told my parents that I'd picked up some "odd jobs" after school, raking the leaves and cleaning the gutters of families richer than us. What I really did was ride my bike to Hayden's neighborhood and look at the towering McMansions there, the lawn crews mowing grass and trimming hedges, the children speeding down the streets on Vespas. I rode down every street and around every cul-de-sac several times, waiting for an hour to pass until I could return home and give my parents $100. My dad was agog. He wanted to know how I'd made that much in a single afternoon.

I shrugged. "They tip well in that neighborhood," I said.

After a year of Adidases and XiX, I'd made $2,500, which I gave to my parents in installments of $100 and $200. No suspicion from administrators, who were too checked out to care about anything we were doing. I stressed that everyone take XiX in the smallest amounts possible—it was *so potent*—and because I'd become "that guy," people listened to me. Except for Jordan Pinkerton, who was desperate to impress her boyfriend, a soccer player who'd won a scholarship to Harvard and was known for being able to drink anyone under the table.

I was in gym class with Jordan on the day it happened. We all had to change into uniforms that were our school colors, the T-shirts gray and the mesh shorts primary blue. I had sold Jordan an eighth of XiX the night before, and she looked dazed. She may have been doing bumps or even lines throughout the school day, possibly to convince her boyfriend that she was as hard-core as he was. As we ran laps around the gym, I considered breaking out of our lackluster formation and asking her if she was all right. This was the first time that I thought I might have crossed a line, that these people who had so much more than me were still human. It was in that moment that Jordan developed a raging nosebleed. She stopped running, saw the blood forming dark crimson dots on her gym shirt, and fainted on the spot. When she woke up, she told the principal where she'd gotten the XiX. I was expelled. The Pinkertons agreed not to press charges on the provision that I served some sort of time, be it in juvie or somewhere else that would "straighten me out." And so I spent my summer at Last Chance.

There was a hierarchy at Last Chance and I was at the bottom. I tried not to reveal that I was on scholarship but I stank of it: my frayed shorts, my hole-filled Neutral Milk Hotel T-shirt that I wore twice before Kimborough confiscated it, my wrecked Converses. I was forced to wear thin white tank tops from a package of ten Kimborough bought for me from Walmart, and the fact that I had been the recipient of Kimborough's charity seemed to anger people, not because they were jealous but because I was a bottom dweller, always pitied and never feared, and because they were unaccustomed to having a person like me among them. They ignored me when we were forced to lug giant bales of hay across fields together or harvest yards of turnips or do seventy-five crunches as punishment for leaving bits of flaky, toxic shit on the chicken coop floor. After a month of this, they began to tolerate me: I didn't share their anger and embarrassment at having lost their Benzes and summer vacations to Mexico, but I was unobtrusive, a nonentity, and there would be no consequences for them if they talked shit about Kimborough and Sledge while I read a book in the background.

When I was seventeen I could still see well enough to read. My reading was a trait my parents admired without sharing it themselves. They described me to their friends as "bookish." Really, I just appreciated how static and parsable words were on a page, how little they demanded of me visually. I liked books that took a long time to read, which meant that I read a lot of Russian novels, and *The Brothers Karamazov* was my favorite. I was reading it for the third time at Last Chance, imagining that I was Alyosha, a saint surrounded by sinners. I especially liked the part where the Elder Zosima described his childhood: I was the sickly elder brother who inspired him to become a man of the cloth, or maybe I was Zosima himself, who Alyosha prayed both for and with. The book had as many examples of how to be good as it had examples of how to be bad. It stretched for miles in my head.

We were given one hour of rec time before dinner, an idea which had clearly originated with Kimborough because Sledge obviously resented it. The other Last Chance prisoners would kick around a half-deflated soccer ball or improvise a game of touch football and Sledge would stand cross-armed watching them, waiting for one of them to scream in frustration at a missed goal or kick someone in the shins out of anger and hopelessness. Then Sledge could make them run three laps around the property. But that rarely happened, because these games were played with little effort, their players so exhausted from the day that they seemed to be playing just to spite Sledge, to prove that he couldn't beat them. But I knew from my Russian novels that anything motivated by hubris can't be sustained: Sledge always found a way to punish people, whether it was for "poor form" (whatever that meant) or for giving him what he referred to as an "insubordinate look." Most of rec time was spent performing military-grade exercises to the point of dehydrated collapse. And even though I was never playing soccer or touch football—I was always sitting on the grass reading, trying to regulate my breathing as the scene in front of me escalated—Sledge would force me to join in.

"Get the fuck over here, Green," he said to me on a day when another prisoner had sworn after turning his ankle in the grass. "You're part of this."

I didn't protest: protesting meant we were given half portions in the mess hall for the next twenty-four hours. I left the book in the grass and assumed my place in the disgruntled herd of prisoners. We were told to plank for two minutes, and whoever dropped out of his plank would have to plank for an additional three minutes before moving on to the hundred crunches. I held my plank, my arms shaking, my glasses sliding down my nose, sweat dripping from my hair. I was close to Sledge—I could see the mud on his army boots—and then I could see two pairs of feet approaching his, one of which was sneaker clad and clearly belonged to Kimborough, and the other of which I'd never seen before.

"He's starting today," I heard Kimborough say to Sledge.

"Yeah, okay," Sledge said. "Who are you again?"

"Orson Ortman," a voice said.

"Time," Sledge barked at us. "Start the crunches."

I turned onto my back and saw him: lean, graceful looking, his hand at the back of his neck. His hair, orangish brown, shot from his head in a messy corona and he was watching us with a combination of interest and sadness. I couldn't tell if he was sad for us or sad that he'd soon be among us but there was a softness to his stare that suggested the former, that he was really genuinely feeling bad for us and would have liked to change our situation. He had a hint of a beard: Sledge would make him shave. I couldn't help imagining him shaving, wrinkling his nose to get a spot on the underside of his chin. I couldn't stop looking at him.

"Green!" Sledge said, and I began my crunches quickly, trying not to linger on the sit-up.

"This is Orson Ortman," Kimborough said. "He's going to be joining us for the rest of the summer."

"Don't stop your fucking crunches," Sledge hissed.

Kimborough cleared his throat. "Orson will be in cabin six. Please don't hassle him; give him a chance to settle in."

Sledge grunted at Kimborough's use of the word "please," and I tried not to watch as Kimborough and Orson walked away toward my cabin.

We marched, sweat drenched, to the mess hall, where we collapsed on benches and tried to summon the strength to get our plates and get food at the head of the room. I folded my arms on the table and rested my head on my wrists, taking breaths so deep they almost caught in my throat. When I looked up, Orson Ortman was sitting across from me.

"How'd you get here?" I asked.

He shrugged. "I just sat down. You were breathing so heavy, maybe that's why you didn't hear me." He extended his hand to shake. "Orson," he said.

"I know," I said. "Why are you here?"

"That's a long story."

"No, like—why are you here at this table with me?"

"Because I don't like crowded places. Every other table in this cafeteria—"

"Mess hall," I corrected.

"Right, every other table in this mess hall is full of people. I don't want to sit wedged in with a bunch of people." He extended his arms out to either side like a bird preparing for flight. "I like my space."

"There's space here," I said, resigning myself to generosity. It was a trait that didn't get you very far at Last Chance, but I couldn't help it: there'd been something captivating about him in those first moments I'd seen him, something worthy of investigation.

"Do you want me to get you a plate?"

I shrugged.

"I'll get you a plate," he said. "Just give me a second."

He sprung grasshopper-like from his seat and came back with two plates of brownish mash and green beans. The food was nauseating, as always, and I was almost too weak to eat it, but I wanted to perform normalcy. I drew a fork from the canister in the middle of the table, watching him.

"Is this meat loaf?" he asked, poking at his.

"It's always meat loaf," I said. "We have to cook it and there's, like, only one recipe."

He took a bite and grimaced. "*We* cook it?"

"Eventually you'll cook it. Maybe you're the one person in the world who knows how to make it better."

My head echoed with the sound of Sledge's voice. I felt the crust of the previous hour's sweat on my face.

"No phones here, huh?" Orson said.

17

"No screens of any sort." I lowered my face close to the mash, struggling to raise my arm from the plate to my mouth. "Didn't Kimborough tell you? We make calls on pay phones. The only good thing to do is read, really."

He nodded. "That's fine," he said, too chipper. And then he extended his hand to shake. "You should shake my hand."

"What?"

He kept it extended. "You should shake it."

"Dude, what the fuck?"

His insistence—the small smile, the way he nodded toward his outstretched hand—was both frustrating and inviting.

"I swear I'm going to stand up and leave this fucking table," I said.

He shrugged, his hand still extended. "You're too tired to stand up. I know that for a fact." His smile broadened.

"Jesus," I muttered, and took his hand in mine. I felt something between our palms and pulled away, frightened, but not so frightened that I would risk dropping it in front of the counselors, who were roaming the mess hall in their utility belts and too-short haircuts. When I opened my hand, I saw that he'd given me a perfectly rolled joint. I pocketed it immediately.

"I don't drink or do drugs of any sort," he said, as though this could possibly be an explanation for what had just happened. "I've always been pretty straight-edge. My dad just, you know, sits on the sofa in front of the TV the minute he gets home and drinks a six-pack. So I'm trying to be different."

And yet he'd just given me a joint. I was too shocked to speak.

"You seem nice," he said, and winked so quickly I almost missed it. "You seem reliable."

At night, the barn and the mess hall were locked: if we wanted to go to the bathroom, we had to use a latrine that stank from years of use at the edge of the property, close to the barbed wire fence that kept us pent in. The joint wedged in my right shoe, a book of matches I'd stolen from my bunkmate wedged in my left, I took our cabin's designated flashlight and switched it on. Pretending to test it, I shone it in the direction of Orson, who was asleep in the bunk across from me. He whinnied a little in his sleep but didn't snore, and when he rolled onto his back, I snatched the light away for fear I'd wake him up.

I saw poorly in the dark and was nearly drained of strength, so I had to walk slowly to the latrine, and even with the flashlight's guidance I tripped twice. When I got to the latrine I sat next to the hole, the putrid smell of which made me even more light-headed, and lit the joint. I rarely smoked, so I was dizzyingly high after two hits. The wood walls seemed to swell with the scent of the purplest, stickiest weed I'd smoked in my life. Within minutes I was no longer in the latrine, no longer at Last Chance—I was a numb and giggly spirit emerged from a bottle. I stumbled back to the cabin, laughing to myself, the tips of my fingers tingling. I buried the matches in a row of snap peas, thinking that maybe they'd grow into a match plant whose matches I would harvest and keep forever. Maybe I'd get rich from inventing the match plant.

The next morning at breakfast, I could tell Orson could tell that I'd spent the night high. He grinned and palmed me another joint, which I smoked that night. This went on for two more nights until I confronted him at breakfast.

"So why are you being so nice to me?"

He laughed. " 'So nice.' That's such a delicate way of putting it."

I made a severe face, but it was almost impossible to be mad at him. "Why?" I pressed.

"Well, I told you before that I like you," he said. "And I'm on scholarship, like you clearly are. And there's something, I don't know—there's something really innocent-seeming about you. I think people look at me and think, like, 'Oh, here comes this asshole, what's he gonna sell me now?' You don't give off that vibe."

I couldn't tell if this was an insult or a compliment, so I just nodded.

"I thought maybe you could help me," he said. And then he palmed me two pills of Adderall.

I had no idea how he was doing it, or why he was doing it given that he was so straight-edge, but he had the largest collection of contraband at Last Chance. Together, we sold it to our trapped, rich market: weed was $25 per joint, Adderall was $30 per pill, lighters were $35, pocketknives were $50. He even had a Game Boy somehow, which he managed to sell for $400. It seemed like everyone had sewn money into their clothes in anticipation of something like this—real money, rich kid money. It took us two weeks to clear $1,000, another two to clear $3,000. I didn't ask him where he was getting everything, and he seemed fine not telling me.

He never seemed to get tired, either. At rec time, he was the most energetic soccer player, running and kicking and jumping with a grace that seemed impossible to me: the grace of someone who's so accustomed to being in his body that his every movement is flawless, totally devoid of calculation. It was like watching a falling star rocket effortlessly through the sky. I felt lucky just getting to see it. He was untouchable, both as the source of the contraband and as a body in space, sinewy but clearly capable of winning any fight. And he read, too. White men who disagreed with other white men: Karl Marx, Niccolò Machiavelli, Marcus Aurelius. But the best writers, he told me, were the ones who wrote like the contents of a mind spilled onto a page.

"Toni Morrison and Virginia Woolf," he said as we stooped to clean the chicken coop of its biohazardous mess. "Have you read *Sula* or *Mrs. Dalloway*?"

I shook my head.

"Get them from the library when you get home," he said. "They're brains on a page. Gives you some insight into how we think."

I became respected—at first begrudgingly and then with enthusiasm—and prisoners began to talk me up during our rotations together, asking me in densely coded language what I was holding and how they could get some. I shook a lot of hands and gave a lot of careful high fives. The best times were when I was on work rotation with Orson. He ran his hand through his flame-orange hair, dripped sweat through his T-shirt, smiled at me as we labored. The first time we were put on the slaughter rotation, I shuddered at having to chop the heads off chickens.

"It's better than the pigs," he offered. "There you have to stun them and slit their throats."

It always surprised me what he knew: he was encyclopedic, terminally curious.

"But not cut their heads off," I said.

"Well, their necks are too big."

"But the head stays on," I insisted.

He grabbed a chicken, belly swollen and legs deformed, from the to-be-slaughtered pen. It was difficult to watch him hold it by the neck, let alone consider its neck being severed.

"Okay, think of it this way," he said. "We outrank Sledge."

"Outrank him?"

"Yeah. You're the lieutenant and I'm the colonel." He righted his posture and stood rigid, saluting me. "Lieutenant, I have received orders to slaughter this chicken at thirteen thirty-four."

"I think it's 'lieutenant colonel.'"

"I'm afraid it's not, sir. I am the colonel, sir, and you are the lieutenant, sir. This chicken is named Major Sledge, sir."

"Does that chicken outrank us? Or no?"

"I don't give a shit, sir," he said, still rigid. "Will you help me kill Major Sledge, sir?"

"Okay, yes, sir," I said, and took the squawking, disoriented chicken from him. I held the bird down as he axed its neck. We did this again and again and again, the heads falling to the ground, my stomach turning.

"Don't worry, lieutenant, sir," Orson said. "This is only going to last another twenty minutes and then we can just chill out planting soy beans or whatever, sir."

"Yes, sir," I said, biting my lip.

"Just look at my face, sir," he offered. "Don't look at the heads. Just look at me."

So I did. His brows knit with the effort of swinging the axe, but otherwise his face was placid, settled almost. It was unsettling to watch: he seemed indifferent to the brutality. Was this how he always was, or was he just performing for me? I looked away, to a corner of the barn just over his left shoulder, and felt some of the chicken's blood splatter against my shirtfront.

"That wasn't so bad, lieutenant, sir, was it, sir?" he said when we'd finished with the last chicken.

"No, sir," I said. "It didn't suck as much as I thought it would, sir."

When we were on a particularly tedious rotation, like lugging hay from the barn to the horse stable or planting seedlings in the high heat or cleaning up after the cows, Orson told me to talk about myself.

"I'm not that interesting," I said the first time he asked. "There's really nothing to know."

He scoffed. "You're not *interesting*? You're one of the most interesting people I've ever met."

My face reddened. I tried to focus on packing soil around the pea seed I'd just planted.

"Lieutenant," he said. "I want to know about you, sir."

I stood up, wiping dirt from my hands, and met his eyes. He was leaning on his shovel, grinning.

"What do you want to know?" I asked.

"Start at the beginning," he said.

So I told him about my parents. They'd had me young. My maternal grandparents were both alcoholics and my paternal grandparents were both dead. My mom and dad met in high school, knew they'd never be able to afford college, and got pregnant with me when my mom was in the eleventh grade and my dad in the twelfth. My dad had been kicked out of school for selling weed but had managed to get his GED through night classes.

My mom graduated, but just barely because she'd been so busy caring for me. They'd both had to take jobs to make ends meet, the same jobs they currently had: my dad hauling slabs of flesh through subzero freezers in a meatpacking warehouse and my mom serving ungrateful patrons eggs and grits in a diner. They moved into an apartment across the street from my mom's parents, whom they saw increasingly less as the parents' alcoholism worsened.

"Were the grandparents bitter that your mom got pregnant so young?" Orson asked as we shoveled three-foot piles of cow dung.

"I think so," I said. "My mom doesn't really talk about it. I think her dad gave her some money and then just kind of cut her off."

"So you went to this rich kid high school?"

"My parents fought to let me attend. They were determined to get me to succeed."

"So they're pissed right now."

I stuck my shovel into the dung and became acutely aware of the smell, stronger even than the latrine. "Yeah, you could say so."

Orson rarely talked about himself. I couldn't tell if that was because I was genuinely interesting—though I had my doubts—or because he just didn't want me to know about him. In my bunk after lights out, I squinted at his sleeping form in the dark and tried to imagine what his life had been like, where he lived, who his friends were, what he'd done to get sent to Last Chance. In my imagination, he was kicking a soccer ball on a professionally sodded field, or he was sitting imperiously in detention, smiling because he knew more about everything than his fellow prisoners. The possibility that his offense had been violent never crossed my mind. He didn't seem to have it in his nature.

Sledge caught us stopping work to talk on more than one occasion and split us up, making me run laps and Orson do two hundred crunches. As I ran, I thought about Orson, worried about him: was Sledge breaking his spirit? I knew Sledge couldn't break mine as long as Orson and I were together, but what if I wasn't enough to buoy Orson? What if the half rations we so often had to endure in the mess hall were weakening him? What if he started hallucinating from hunger and exhaustion, as a few of the other prisoners already had?

In the mess hall, sitting over our half potatoes and half mash, I asked him: "Is this too much?"

He looked at me, smiling. There was nothing in his face to suggest exhaustion, though it was clear he'd lost a considerable amount of weight since his arrival. "What?"

"Getting caught talking to me all the time. Getting in trouble."

He shook his head vigorously, straightening his shoulders. "Nope. It's all worth it, sir, lieutenant, sir."

"Seriously?"

"Yes, sir. Your stories are interesting, sir. They're like mine, sir."

I ate a bite of my mash. "What are your stories, sir, colonel, sir?"

He waved his hand at me, his shoulders softening out of colonel posture. "Honestly, I can't talk about myself. I can get really self-absorbed. It's like some dark triad shit."

"Try me," I said. "I can handle it."

His lips tightened. He looked from me to his plate to me again.

"I can handle it, sir, colonel, sir."

He sighed. "I'm here for hotwiring a car. They said I could either do two months in juvie or two months here."

My eyes widened. Hotwiring a car. It sounded almost glamorous when he said it.

Orson's father frequented a bar where they didn't cut him off until he was swaying on his stool. Whenever Orson could, he would go to the bar with his father and chat with the bartender, drinking Cherry Cokes, trying to keep his father from getting too drunk. There was a wide-shouldered, sideburned man at the bar named Richard Haley who owned a Jiffy Lube that had employed Orson one summer for $8.50 an hour. Haley had fired

Orson for taking an unscheduled smoke break. Because of this, Haley thought he was better than Orson and Orson's frequently drunk father, and he would make every effort to drink at this bar and harass them. He called Orson's father whiskey dick and fabricated stories about sex with Orson's mother. Orson told Haley several times to stop, once even shoving him, but Haley wouldn't let up. Instead of getting angry about this, Orson's father would put his head in his hands and weep: the insults were relentless and humiliating and Haley was too well-known around town for anyone to try to stop him—as the owner of a Jiffy Lube, he was one of the richest people for miles. So one night when Haley was screaming at his father over the sound of "Heartbreaker" on the jukebox, Orson went outside to smoke, stole Haley's car, and drove it into a ditch two miles out of town.

"I spent a week locked up. My family could barely afford my bail," he said. "And then the judge let me come here, probably because I'm white." He raised his eyebrows and sighed heavily. "That's why I'm, you know, doing this thing with you. Because I also have a ten-thousand-dollar fine to pay."

"My parents have a lot of debt from my ophthalmologist visits," I offered. I was immediately embarrassed when I said this. We hadn't addressed my eyesight all summer.

"Yeah, you get it," he said. "You're not American if you're not in debt to someone."

I was incredibly grateful then: not just for the fact that he didn't press deeper into my nightmarish open secret, but because he was my friend. Because he had, of his own volition, come into my life.

At the end of the summer, we were made to stand in a line in the mess hall, bookended by four menacing counselors on either side. Kimborough surveyed us from a distance behind Sledge, who walked up and down our line, seething.

"You think you're going to just go back home to your parents and pretend this never happened?" he asked. "Well fuck that, and fuck you for thinking that. You are criminals. If you don't change your lives, you will be in prison or dead before you turn twenty-one. Most people your age, they have bright futures ahead of them. You? You have no future if you don't fix yourselves. You have no future whatsoever."

Kimborough made us pray for forgiveness from God and then we were dispersed back to our cabins, where we packed our belongings and the counselors distributed our phones and wallets. Orson and I were dropped off at the combination train and bus station, left to sit in the cavernous head house and deal with a flood of text messages from our parents. We had over $5,000 between us, and Orson counted out my share.

"That's going to go a long way toward those bills," he said.

"Don't you want more?" I asked. "To pay off the fine?"

"No, no," he said. "Just keep it. You need it just as much."

I pocketed my share reluctantly.

We sat in silence, the kind of warm, placid silence shared by two people who know each other intimately and are about to stop knowing each other intimately. We checked our phones and looked at our feet. Then Orson grabbed my phone from my hands and punched in his number.

"Text me anytime," he said. "I'll always respond."

An automated voice announced that his bus was departing in ten minutes, and he stood, smiling, his arms wide. "This is the last time I'll be able to do this for fifteen hours," he said. "The last time I'll be able to extend to my full wingspan."

"Cherish it," I said. "Cherish it, sir, colonel, sir."

"Yes, sir, lieutenant, sir," he said, and turned from me, jogging in the direction of his terminal.

My train wouldn't arrive until later that evening. I made a pillow of my backpack and lay across the bench, reading the part of *The Brothers Karamazov* where Mitya is trying to find money to woo Grushenka. I got through ten pages and fell asleep, and when I woke up the head house was nearly deserted and the moon was visible through the massive skylight. I pulled my phone from my pocket and texted Orson's number: *colonel, sir, it is 19:24 and i am still in the fucking train station, sir.* I watched my screen for a text back and then pocketed my phone again, trying to read. But I couldn't: the words blurred with my anxiety. I couldn't stop imagining Orson on his bus, reading my text disinterestedly and turning his phone off. I pulled my phone out of my pocket and checked again: still no response. He had obviously read my text and decided to ignore it. He hadn't expected me to text the number at all. It was a fake number, even, a mean-spirited prank—that's what the whole summer had been, a long-form attempt to get me to like him, to worship him, to think he was important. And he was. He absolutely was, but he was too important for me, too intelligent. I was gullible, small, foolish. What had I been thinking? Why would someone like Orson ever want to be friends with me?

And then my phone buzzed: *that sucks, sir, lieutenant, sir. but at least you're not on this shitty bus, sir.*

My breath leapt into my throat. I texted back as quickly as I could: *that was easily the worst summer of my life.*

yeah man, what did that even do? i don't feel reformed or whatever.

haha nope. neither do i.

but we were making MONEY.

yeah we were.

we should do that again sometime.

My heart thrummed.

§

Ingrid was valedictorian of her senior class, a size two, a volleyball player, a future biochemist. She'd been accepted early decision to Stanford. Her Tumblr avatar was a picture of Sailor Moon grabbing her cheeks in joy, stars in her eyes, pigtails twirling above her head. The most important thing about Ingrid—to me, at least, though maybe not to her—was that she had 20/20 vision. She wasn't real, and I wanted to be her.

On the family computer, I made Ingrid reblog photos of handsome boys and cute cats. She visited various forums, posting makeup advice, gushing about Neutral Milk Hotel, making Jane Eyre puns. She started accumulating friends, who insisted on DMing her and asking her about her personal life. How long was her hair? How strict was her school? Had she ever been to Disney World? Did she have a boyfriend? I loved answering all the questions, loved making Ingrid seem even more perfect than I'd conceived of her. She would never get busted for a hustle because she'd never needed to hustle. It was exhilarating to pretend I was someone who'd never needed to hustle.

When I returned from Last Chance, my parents' only option for my senior year was a Catholic high school run by nuns who were unsparing in their discipline. We had regular locker inspections and the classrooms were run like dictatorships, a nun at the head speaking poor Spanish or fumbling her way through the history of the Civil War, watching us carefully. We were to keep our hands on our desks at all times. If the nun couldn't see our hands, we were ordered to stand up and submit to a frisking conducted by grave-faced "classroom aides" who were not unlike the Last Chance counselors. Having lived through Sledge, the place wasn't difficult to master. I faked illness and broke into the lockers of skittish kids to steal their Adderall, which I sold at a high markup. I hacked into a nun's Facebook account and posted that she was having a yard sale, which attracted a swarm of people to her property before she could take the status down. I managed to affix a dildo to a crucifix, which bought me a month's detention. It was mickey mouse stuff, but I still took pictures of everything and sent them to Orson, trying to impress him.

i miss the free market of high school he wrote back to me. *i'm bored.*

He'd graduated and moved out of his parents' house into an apartment, which he financed by selling weed. Being a full-time dealer didn't suit him: he had to interact with understimulating burnouts, he had to constantly think about obtaining and pricing drugs he'd never use, his days were dictated by the texts of others. He told me several times that he knew he was destined for something more than just dealing drugs. Something more exciting, more lucrative.

at least you're making money, sir, colonel, sir I texted back, but I was still worried. The idea that he was bored and alone pained me. I texted him a photo of a license plate in the Catholic school parking lot that read GDGTSIT. *god really gets it* I wrote.

He texted me back a photo of himself in a white T-shirt, a cigarette dripping from his lips, smiling half-heartedly. I saved it.

Ingrid actually did have a boyfriend, she told her friends. He was about 5' 10" and had messy hair and was incredible in bed. Did Ashley and Sarah and Allie want to see him? LMAO of course they did. I DMed them the photo of Orson. *We were at a party when I took this LOL* I wrote. The responses came in:

Oh my godddd he is so hot!

Ingrid hun i am NOT surprised he's such a babe he's probably smart too.

Honestly if he wasn't yours i'd stealllll him

He's a really private person I wrote. *He was kind of worried abt me posting that pic. I told him it was just my friends :p*

I kept "raking lawns" after school so I could slowly pay my parents the money I'd gotten from Last Chance. I found a McMansion I liked, red brick with a slate roof and a two-car garage, and took a picture of it from the street. This became Ingrid's family's house, and I uploaded the photo to Tumblr with the caption *home sweet friggin' home.* Ingrid's dad, Eric, was a doctor and her mom, Stephanie, was a business consultant. In 2000, when Ingrid was ten, they'd moved from their starter home in a less rich neighborhood to this one, where there was a homeowner's association and acre-large lawns. Ingrid had spent her childhood attending painting classes and piano lessons. She'd learned to play "Moonlight Sonata" at age eleven and was composing her own music by age thirteen.

I texted Orson the photo of the McMansion.

these assholes I wrote. *these assholes sir, colonel, sir.*

No response.

I waited for an hour, then two hours, three, four. I concluded that he'd either died or grown sick of me. I biked to the library and checked out *Mrs. Dalloway* and *Sula* in hopes that this would somehow summon him back. I stayed up all night speed-reading both. *Mrs. Dalloway* was dense in ways *Sula* wasn't, but he'd been right: each book was the contents of a mind poured out onto the page. Characters wanting things and getting things and losing things. In my teenage narcissism I imagined myself one of these characters, suffering for Orson, pleading for him, praying for him.

Days of silence. I called and listened to his phone ring. I tried not to call too many times in a single day. My sleep grew fitful. I squinted at my phone at the dinner table. I could feel my dad watching me.

"Is it time to get your prescription updated?" he asked. "I see the way you're holding your phone."

Orson had disappeared off the face of the earth and my dad had the nerve to ask about my eyesight.

"No," I snapped. "I can see just fine."

He raised his hands as though I'd just threatened him with something sharp. "Listen, I'm on your side. I just want you to be in good shape for college."

"Yeah," I said. "I want to go into massive debt so I can compete with people who had private SAT tutors and drive massive SUVs for an upper-middle-class job I don't want and won't get anyway."

My dad snatched my phone from my hands. My mom walked into the room carrying the bucket of fried chicken she'd picked up from the neighborhood KFC.

"What did I miss?" she asked.

"Ezra doesn't want to go to college," my dad said. I'd been staring at my phone for so long that everything farther than four feet away from me was smudged, but I could make out the rigid line of my dad's mouth.

"You don't want to go to college?" my mom asked.

"We don't have money for it," I said.

"That wasn't your argument." My dad's features came slowly into focus: his skin mottled with frostbite, his widow's peak, his watery greenish-gray eyes. "Your argument was basically that college is useless."

My mom set the bucket of fried chicken down on the table and turned to me. "It's not useless," she said. "Do you know I would have *killed* to go to college?"

"You wouldn't have killed," I said.

"For fuck's sake," my dad said. "You have the grades. You have the test scores."

"But I don't have the money."

"So you take out loans! Everyone takes out loans."

My mom tightened her ponytail and looked at me pityingly. "Are you worried the other kids will be mean to you, sweetheart?"

"God, no," I said, and extended my hand for my phone, which my dad reluctantly gave back to me. "I'm not worried about mean people; I'm worried about being a fucking mark."

"Language," my dad said.

"You just swore," I said.

"*You* can't swear," my dad said lamely.

"What's a mark?" My mom ran her hand through my hair, which conjured the skin shivers I'd always experienced whenever she'd done this during my childhood. When I was scared or crying or angry she'd do this. Everything was bad, and then everything was good.

"Like what they used to call a sucker," I said, quieter than before. "Like someone who gets money stolen from them or gets a trick played on them."

"College graduates aren't suckers," my dad said.

My mom kept running her hand through my hair. "Why do you say that?"

"A lot of reasons."

"You can get a scholarship," my dad persisted.

My phone buzzed in my pocket. A phone call. "I'm going to go to my room," I said. "I'll be right back."

I felt them watch me leave the kitchen and run down the hall, where I closed the door as quietly as I could and pulled out my phone.

"Hi," I said, feeling a relief so intense it was almost dizzying.

"Hey." His voice was brittle.

"Lost you for a few days there, colonel, sir." I said too quickly.

He began to cry.

"What is it?" I asked, but he just sobbed, and I kept imagining myself next to him. I was desperate to touch him, to run my hand through his hair as my mom had just run hers through mine. Anything I could do to make everything good.

"My dad," he gasped finally.

"Yeah?"

"He's dead. He had a heart attack." A horrified sob. "At home. I came back to visit—I found him."

"Jesus Christ."

"I have no idea—I don't—I have no idea why he went now instead of later."

"I'm so sorry," I said. "Orson, really—"

"No, no. It's fine," he said, waving me away with his voice. "Sorry I didn't get your texts. I was, you know, I was walking, actually. I went on a twenty-mile walk one day. It's what I do when I can't do anything else."

"I get that," I said, though I didn't.

"I loved him," he said. "I still love him."

"I know."

"He was just killing himself. For, like, years. He drank himself to death."

Silence between us. I listened to him breathing.

"How far are you from the nearest city?" he asked.

"Maybe, like, half an hour?"

"That's close. That's closer than I thought."

I realized I hadn't told him much about where I lived other than that it was a wasteland suburb bordering on a wealthy one.

"I'm out in bumblefuck," he said.

I wanted to tell him that I remembered, but that seemed somehow insulting.

"It's, like, how long of a drive from me to you?" he asked.

"Two and a half hours," I blurted. I'd done the math several times.

I knew he was smiling. "What if I came for a visit?"

§

I stopped pretending to do homework when I saw his sedan pull up, fuzzed in the distance. I sprinted down the emergency stairwell to the rotunda.

He was hunched and paler, but it was still him. His car's wheel wells were rusted and its interior was obscured by what looked like boxes and pillows. He had driven to where I lived. Driven for me.

"What's in your car?" I asked.

"That's everything I own in the world." He looked back at the car smilingly, as though it represented some kind of impossible accomplishment. "I gave up my apartment."

"What?"

"I'm moving here," he said, grinning. "I'm moving to the city."

There was no other way to interpret this. I couldn't manage to say anything aloud.

"What?" he asked, cocking his head. "You look like you're choking."

I shook my head. He pounded me on the back.

"I'm fine," I managed.

"I had to get out of there. And you're—you know, you're my best friend."

His *best friend*.

"I don't want to sell weed anymore. I want to do something bigger."

"Of course."

We extracted a small suitcase from the overstuffed car and he let me carry it upstairs, where my parents were waiting in the living room.

"The famous Mr. Ortman!" my dad said, wrapping Orson in a hug.

"Welcome, Orson." My mom offered him a kiss on the cheek. "We were so sorry to hear about your father."

Orson screwed up his mouth and looked down at the floor. When he looked back up, his eyes were watery.

"Thank you," he said.

My dad, who was always uncomfortable with displays of grief, clapped Orson on the back. "Are you hungry?"

"I *am* hungry!" Orson wiped his eyes with the back of his sleeve and slapped his inferno of a stomach, which made both my parents laugh. "And I'll help however I can in the kitchen."

They refused his help, of course, leaving us to sit across from each other at the Formica table they had bought for the "dining room," which was really just the space between the living room and the half wall of the kitchen. Orson leaned forward conspiratorially, his eyes bright, and asked me if I wanted to share an apartment with him.

"Tell your parents you're taking a year off to work. You need to save up for college."

This was a dream. I was living in a dream. "I'll need a job before they'll let me do that."

He nodded thoughtfully, his gaze straying from me to the sofa behind me. "I can take care of that," he said. "That'll be easy."

My parents had prepared a dinner of a brisket and mashed potatoes, my mom's and dad's respective specialties, the kind of out-of-budget meal they made for guests they wanted to impress.

Orson badgered them into letting him set the table—"You can't expect me to just sit here without earning my keep"—which he did with panache, folding our cheap paper napkins into mini swans and arranging the silverware as though we were preparing for a five-course meal.

"He's spoiling us," my mom said to me, still glowing. "Orson, you don't have to spoil us. This is for *you*."

"Nonsense!" He looked down his nose at her with the fake gentility of a nobleman, and she exploded with laughter. "I'll hear none of it, madam!"

My mom retreated giggling into the kitchen, and when she emerged it was with the steaming brisket, which we all applauded as though it, and not Orson, were our guest of honor.

"You'll get the first piece," she said, setting the brisket down in front of Orson.

"That hardly seems fair," he protested. "You made it, after all."

My mom blushed and my dad laughed. This was how things always should have been. Orson would lift them out of their lives of ice burn and scant tips. He would enchant them like he'd enchanted me.

"You're telling me you two have been married *eighteen years*?" He looked from my dad to my mom. "Danielle, you could be Ezra's older sister home from college."

"Oh, come on now!" she said, but she was clearly loving it.

My dad and I brought the rest of the food to the table and it felt like Thanksgiving: there was a ready-to-feast warmth in the room, a swell of anticipatory joy.

"So, Orson, what did you think of Wellspring?" my dad asked, slicing into his brisket.

Orson chewed slowly, his features knit in consideration. "Tough but fair," he said. "It really got me back to where I needed to be. My dad always said I needed to straighten up and fly right."

"You were close to your father?" my mom asked.

"Very."

My dad nodded at me. "I think that camp did a number on Ez here. He came back a skeleton."

"Well, it was either that or, you know . . ." I tried, but didn't know how to finish the sentence.

My mom, always hypersensitive to wrinkles in a conversation, put her hand on mine. "You're so strong now. Isn't he so much stronger, Dave?"

My dad nodded, chewing, and turned back to Orson. "You look pretty sturdy yourself, Orson. You play any sports in school?"

"I was a wrestler in high school," Orson said, as quickly as if it were the truth. "Varsity."

There were nods, raised eyebrows. "Very impressive," my mom said. "Do you have a sense of what you'd like to do now that you've graduated?"

"Become a teacher." He lied about this with the same seamlessness he'd lied about being a wrestler. "After learning what I learned at Wellspring, I'd really like to give back, help other troubled kids."

"What subject would you teach?" my dad asked.

Orson took another bite of brisket and chewed thoroughly. He must have known he couldn't be quick with every single answer. "English, I think. Or sociology. I haven't decided yet. One of the humanities."

"Those subjects are important," my mom said.

"Not where the money is, but important," my dad added. "My favorite class in high school was English."

"Helping kids find themselves in books—I'm not sure, it just feels meaningful to me," Orson said. "I wish I'd had some kind of model for good behavior, or at least some way to contain my angst. I think I wouldn't have gone down the wrong path then."

After dinner, Orson sprang up to help my mom in the kitchen and my dad winked at me. "He's a good friend," he said. "Very smart. He can stay over for as long as he needs."

Orson claimed he needed some fresh air so we went for a walk in the direction of a strip mall with a smoothie shop, a nearly bankrupt video rental store, and a 7-Eleven. I was embarrassed that this was the only place to walk to, that this was all I had to show him. I wanted to carry him around in a palanquin like a king, take him through marble palaces and tropical forests.

It was a curse that I was from this place, and that he found himself in it. Then I had an idea.

"Let's go into the 7-Eleven," I said. "I want to show you something."

He nodded, game to indulge me. We walked in, our skin going greenish under the fluorescent lights. We wandered the store, lifting lighters and keychains, mickey mousing around. Then I pulled an individual Hershey's Kiss out of a bin of loose Easter candy. I held it up to him.

"How much do you think this costs?"

He raised his eyebrows delightedly. "I have no idea," he said.

"Yeah, me neither," I said. "We're gonna find out."

The cashier was clean-shaven with an emo haircut and black nail polish. I put the single Kiss down in front of him.

"Can we buy these individually?" I asked.

His name tag read "Steven." He looked at me dazedly. I had intruded on his private fantasies with an incredibly stupid request. "You want to buy that just on its own?"

I looked over at Orson, who was pretending to read a tabloid with Jennifer Aniston's crying face on it. I looked back at Steven. "Yes."

"It's forty-three cents," Steven said.

I opened my wallet and made a show of looking through my cash. "Shit," I said. "Shit, I'm sorry." I produced a ten. "This is the smallest bill I have."

Steven took the bill, unable to conceal his disgust, and proceeded to count out nine dollars and fifty-seven cents. After he handed me the change, I magically found a single.

"Sorry!" I said. "I missed this. Listen, can I get the ten back and I'll give you all the singles?"

Steven began to make a calculation in his head that he clearly lost interest in, because he handed me the ten, which I added to my hand of bills. Then I counted out nine singles and slipped the ten underneath. Steven took the wad from me, looking almost curious now, and began counting what I'd given him.

"You gave me the ten back," he sighed.

"Oh, did I?"

Orson made a little snorting noise behind the tabloid that I hoped Steven couldn't hear.

"Listen," I said. "I just gave you nineteen there. How about I give you this extra dollar here and you give me back twenty?"

Steven now seemed torn between doing what I said and calling his manager. I continued to make eye contact with him, my face even, my stare maybe a little impatient. After a few seconds of this, Steven took the bills back and gave me the twenty.

"Holy shit!" Orson crowed when we were outside again. "What *was* that?"

I unwrapped the Kiss and popped it in my mouth. "I saw it in an old movie," I said, chewing.

"What're you going to do with your eight dollars?"

"I dunno. Maybe take in a moving picture show?"

He laughed—loud, resounding—and then made an effort to quiet himself when he realized we weren't yet out of the strip mall parking lot. "Maybe seduce a nice broad into showing you her ankles?"

"I do love me some gams," I said, and he broke into laughter again. There was nothing in the world like pleasing him.

TWO

My mom was perhaps more ashamed of her parents' Evangelical faith than she was of their alcoholism. Because of this, she kept all details of her religious past from me until I was ten and she mentioned on the drive home from school that she had heard about a long-running tent revival by the side of the highway. She wondered if I'd consider stopping by with her that week, maybe on our way to get groceries? I had no idea what a tent revival was, but I said yes because she was looking at me in a way that made me worried. She wore the same vulnerable expression she did whenever my dad teased her for having "silly" hobbies like crocheting or watching old movies. She didn't take jokes or rejection easily.

The tent revival was a literal striped tent visible from the off-ramp. We parked among cars with bumper stickers that said LIFE IS LIFE and GET RIGHT OR GET LOST. The hairs at the back of my neck bristled, and when my mom offered to take my hand—the kind of thing that would have led to embarrassment and hostility in any other situation—I held it close.

"I remember these things from when I was little," she said. "I always thought they were dumb."

"Then why are we here?" I asked.

"Oh, you know—curiosity." She looked down at me, and I remember seeing a rather large scab she'd picked at on the underside of her chin. "I thought it would be fun to show you how the other half lives."

When she said that, I realized that my dad didn't know about our outing and she probably didn't want him to know. I looked ahead into the tent, where the men wore khaki shorts and collared T-shirts and the women wore floral-patterned, ankle-length dresses. Everyone was white.

"How long are we going to stay?" I asked.

"Not long," she said distractedly. "I'll make sure we don't stay long."

We stood under the tent and I immediately began to sweat. It was summer and humid in a way that sucked the vitality out of me. I scratched at my knees, which were suddenly bright red from mosquito bites. Under normal circumstances, my mom would have been tending closely to me, asking what was wrong, offering me tissues or Band-Aids or a pill from the bottle of antihistamines she kept in her purse. But she was looking ahead, in the direction of a man's voice booming over a loudspeaker.

"Who loves God?" the man's voice said.

The people under the tent cheered.

"I said *who* loves *God*?"

The people cheered louder.

"Shall we go a little closer?" my mom asked, and before I could consent, she pushed me ahead. People looked at me and smiled pityingly and stepped aside for the two of us. I always got looks like these: here comes the snaggle-toothed kid in the thick glasses, in clothes he's outgrown, with a mother who looks overworked and underpaid. But I wasn't used to my mom playing those looks to our advantage.

We got to the front of the crowd, and I could see the man whose voice was coming over the loudspeaker. He stood on a wooden platform and was dressed like the rest of the men except his khakis were long and a large gold cross hung from a chain around his neck. His hair was damp with sweat and cowlicked—as he spoke he pulled at it, as if he were shocked by the power of his own words.

"I have seen some incredible things in this life," he shouted. "I have seen sinners reformed and the blind regain their sight. I have seen transvestites give up their perversions for normalcy. I have seen Jesus find a home in every corner of this green Earth." He leaned forward, and everyone stand-ing next to us in the front row leaned forward to meet him. "I have seen *miracles*," he spat into his microphone.

"Allegah!" someone screamed behind us. "Allegah propelal mientis!"

We all turned around to see a man rolling on his back on the ground, his hands clawing at the air. "Allegah! Banefsah!" he screamed.

"Don't touch him!" the man onstage shouted to a few people who were moving toward the screaming man. "God is speaking through him!"

"Allegahbanefsahallegahbanefsah!"

I looked at my mom and was disturbed to find that she was smiling at the man onstage. She was smiling while someone was having what looked like a life-threatening fit. I tugged on her elbow and she ignored me by grabbing my hand.

"Who wants to be saved?" the man onstage asked. "Who is sick and wants to be cured?"

The man on the ground stopped screaming and lay silently on his back. Several people in the crowd raised their hands, including my mom, who raised mine by default. I slid out of her grasp. The man onstage saw me do this and grinned. He stooped close to where my mom and I stood.

"What's your name?" he asked me.

"Ezra," my mom said into the microphone.

The man onstage nodded as if my mom had correctly guessed the answer to a riddle. "Ezra is 'helper of God' in Hebrew," he said. "Would you like to come onstage and help God, Ezra?"

I would not have liked to, but my mom pulled me up. She seemed en-tranced. Onstage, the size of the tent was overwhelming. There must have been hundreds of people in the crowd.

"And what's your name?" the man asked my mom.

"Danielle."

"And why did you come here today, Danielle?"

"My son—" my mom began, and then started to cry. I hadn't seen her cry in years, and I felt like the ground was giving way under me. Why had she brought me to this tent, onto this stage, just to cry in public?

The man put his hand on my mom's shoulder. "Go on," he said. "You take your time."

"My son can't see so well," she gasped finally. "He has bad eyes. He's been wearing glasses since he was a toddler."

My cheeks flushed. The man looked down at me and then back up at my mom. "Poor Ezra," he said, which I immediately resented, but I knew better than to say anything in response.

"We've spent so much we can't afford on glasses, and they barely fix his eyesight, and the doctors are worried it'll only get worse."

The man kneeled down in front of me so we were face-to-face. "We're going to pray for you, Ezra," he said. "We're going to ask God to give you your eyesight back."

I stared at my shoes. I could feel my mom's hands tight on my shoulders.

"Who will join me in praying for Ezra?" the man asked, and there was an explosion of *Yes*es. The man put his hand on my head and said "Faith! Faith, restore this boy's eyes! Faith, let this boy see again! Let the love in this tent right now give this boy the power to see God clearly!"

My mom squeezed my shoulders. Hundreds of hands were raised and waving in the air. I had never felt so humiliated in my life.

"Ezra, tell me, son. Do you feel yourself healing?" the man stooped down again to ask me.

I looked up at my mom, who gave me a barely perceptible nod.

"Yes," I said into the microphone.

"By tonight, Ezra, God will work his magic on you. Let me promise you that. By tomorrow you'll regain your sight."

The crowd cheered again.

"Go, Danielle and Ezra!" the man said, gesturing toward the audience. "Danielle, watch your boy heal. Have faith! Have faith in God!"

My mom's pace quickened as we stepped down from the stage and then slowed once we got into the audience. She moved with deliberation, and as she did people stopped her, opened their wallets, and offered her bills. They did this until we'd reached the edge of the tent. I'd never seen anything like it before.

Back in the car, my mom let me sit in front with her. She counted the money: sixty-four dollars.

"Evangelicals have deep pockets," she said, smiling at me.

"Do they always do that?"

"No." She shook her head and put the car in gear. "Only on special occasions."

§

I asked my parents if they'd let me live in the city with Orson and work a job before going to college.

"So now you want to go to college?" my dad asked.

"I've been thinking about it," I said. "Thinking about what you said."

My mom gave a little clap of her hands. "You'd be a natural at it," she said.

My dad shifted in his seat, clearly on the verge of being pleased. "I just don't understand why you don't want to go right away."

"Well, I have it all worked out," I said, and then laid out my "plan": I would work and save up for two years and then apply to colleges in the fall of 2010. The money I'd saved would probably be just enough to cover room and board, which likely wouldn't be covered by the scholarships I'd win. If I could pull this off, I wouldn't have to go into debt.

"I've already got some scholarships in mind to apply to," I said.

My dad squinted at me, smiling faintly. "So does that mean you know where you want to go to school?"

"Absolutely." I named some state schools, some liberal arts colleges, a lesser Ivy. "And there are government scholarships I can get. And scholarships through each individual school. Merit and need."

I looked from my dad to my mom to my dad again. I made sure to blink a few times and smile a little for sincerity.

"I like this," my dad said. "I knew you'd stop with all that nonsense and see the light."

"I think he's always seen the light," my mom protested. "He was just worried about money."

"I was worried about money," I echoed.

"And now he's got a solution." She ran her hand through my hair. "My smart little guy."

One month later Orson and I had broken into the basement of our apartment building and were standing in front of the electrical grid, which he planned to manipulate to restore the power in our apartment after the landlord had cut us off for failing to pay that month's utility bill. Orson surveyed the switches and wires while I stood on my tiptoes, holding a flashlight over his shoulder.

"There's this thing about you," he said to me while toggling the switch labeled "Apartment 1B." There was a small surging noise, and sounds of complaint and then instantaneous relief murmured above us. "Like people look at you—like look into your eyes—and they think, *There's no way this guy's lying.*"

I angled the flashlight higher to give him a better view of the grid. He put a finger to his chin thoughtfully.

"I don't know what it is," he said. "It's not innocence exactly—definitely not—so much as, like, I dunno. Like openness."

"Openness," I repeated, trying not to sound skeptical.

"Yeah, like, open to scrutiny." He pulled at an errant wire. "Like you've got nothing to hide. Like you invite scrutiny because you can withstand scrutiny."

"I'd like to think I could," I said. "Not just look like I could."

"Oh, of course you could." He pinched the wire, straightened it again. "There's no question you could. You have. And you will."

My arm was starting to hurt, so I switched the flashlight to the other hand.

"You know when I first realized everything was bullshit?" he asked.

"I don't."

He spun to face me and I nearly dropped the flashlight.

"It was 1998," he said. "I found out that Bill Clinton basically ordered a blowjob from Monica Lewinsky. People talked about her being a seductress or whatever, but we both know she was pressured into it by the enormous coercive power of the person who'd been placed in charge of the Western world. Can you turn that thing off for a second? I just need a break."

I clicked the flashlight off obediently. I couldn't see him—couldn't see the room, even—and so imagined we were standing inches apart on a beach as the moon rose, each of us waiting for the other to make the first move.

"I used to think the president was this superhero monk who was too busy saving lives to care about sex," he said. "I used to think the presidency wasn't a grift."

As he spoke, there was a confusion of footsteps above us: a fight, maybe, or two people dancing very poorly. "You could say, 'Oh, that humanizes Bill Clinton,'" he said over the stumbling. "But what it really does is make him someone who's fully cognizant of his power and who uses it to get exactly what he feels he deserves. And then how about that next presidency, right?"

I nodded and then remembered he probably couldn't see me either. "Right."

"That was an explicitly criminal presidency. Iraq, Halliburton, jingoism. And the whole thing about crime is it's a scarcity versus abundance kind of thing."

There were two types of criminal according to Orson: the fake and the real. The fake criminal is shaped by scarcity, a Jean Valjean–type bread stealer. The real criminal is shaped by abundance, invading foreign countries for their oil, buying penthouses, killing people who threaten their supremacy.

"The thing about capitalism," he said, and I could feel him shifting toward me and away again, "is that it wants to tell lies about scarcity. It assumes that everything is scarce for everyone, and that everyone is scrambling at all times to make things less scarce, and that the most effective scramblers are the ones most deserving of the spoils they earn, or appear to earn. Most deserving of abundance."

I nodded again, relishing the boom of his voice.

"But the ones with abundance aren't the most effective scramblers. The most effective scramblers are the guys hustling to sell vials of crack in a two-block radius of where they were born. They're sex workers who know how to cheat a dumb client out of an extra twenty dollars. They're jacking Ferraris and robbing banks and counting cards. These aren't people you'd expect to find at the top in the way, you know, you'd find Bush Jr. and Clinton. They're working hard. They're scrambling more effectively than anyone."

"Exactly," I intoned.

"If you want to spot a real criminal," he continued on, seemingly without having heard me, "you need to look for the hoarding, the abundance, the dark triad shit. Because otherwise you've got these fake-scarcity criminals. And those aren't criminals—those are the most gifted scramblers." He sighed as though his speech had exhausted him. "Okay, you can turn it back on."

I clicked the flashlight back on and he was facing the grid again, his hands on his hips. He toggled the switch labeled "Apartment 4C"—ours—and turned to the side, frowning. There was no surging noise as there had been for Apartment 1B.

"The other wires," he muttered to himself, and gestured for the scissors he'd instructed me to bring. I handed them to him and watched as he snipped two sets of wires between our switch and that of the apartment across the hall from us, wrapping the frayed copper edges of one set around the other. Then he toggled our switch again: a surge.

"We can make Hot Pockets tonight," he said, and grinned.

§

What's he thinking of majoring in? Alice wanted to know.

Ingrid had still only shared one photo of Orson—the dripping cigarette with the half-smile—but her friends were pressing for more. I hadn't yet figured out a way to take pictures of Orson without arousing his suspicion, so I'd wait until after dinner, when he'd inevitably fall asleep from devouring whole pizzas or hamburgers or cartons of lo mein, and snap photos of him sprawled peacefully across the couch, one arm behind his head and the other across his stomach. As a finishing touch, I'd leave *The Prince* or *Meditations* open on the coffee table next to him.

He's a philosophy major, I wrote. *As you can see, he studies very hard.*

More *LOL*s, more *OMG he's so cute*s.

We talked about how much boys sleep and how stupid it is. We talked about having to wake up early for freshman orientation at our respective universities. We talked about having to buy new clothes for the various climates we found ourselves in.

Alice in a private chat: *Can you give me some advice hun?*

She was always having boy trouble, and Ingrid was more than happy to help in her capacity as Orson's blissful girlfriend.

He's still not calling me back Alice wrote.

It's like he doesn't want to talk to me ever again.

And we slept together.

Like, multiple times.

I considered Alice's words. She had hazel-flecked blue eyes, visible collarbones, and high cheekbones, was uncommonly beautiful—would certainly have been threatening to Ingrid if Ingrid wasn't happily paired off—and yet she struggled with maintaining boys' respect and attention. The phenomenon was confusing, one Ingrid and Alice had been puzzling over for weeks.

Is this the one with the shoe endorsement? Ingrid wrote.

LOL no. This guy was my first crush in high school.

He goes to school in Vermont. But he came to visit me a bunch of times.

Now Ingrid remembered. *Oh right. And he's not returning your calls?*

Not a single one. It's starting to freak me out.

Well OK—first of all, do you know he's alive LOL?

Hahahaha yes he is because he goes on his Xanga.

Hahahahaaha OK good. Well I think the thing you have to do basically is to find common ground.

A brief pause before Alice typed next: *With???*

What does he like?

I dunno, like, video games?

That's perfect. Does he like Smash Bros?

ROFL yes.

OK, so get really good at Smash Bros. And get good at—what else does he like?

The Zelda games.

LMAO of course he does! Get good at those, practice those, master those.

So I can beat him at them?

No no the goal isn't to beat him. It's to impress him.

§

Tony Jr., whose father owned the pizzeria that employed both Orson and me, was throwing a party in his parents' house and invited all Tony's New York Slice employees. Tony Jr. was, like me, thin and short, but with a direct way of speaking that was disarming coming from someone his size. He could afford slightly nicer clothes than the rest of us, and he and his family lived in a slightly nicer house than any of us probably had, and he was fond of acknowledging this—not in an arrogant way, but not in an apologetic one, either.

Orson was excited for the party because he had worked a few shifts with Tony Jr. and expected it to be a bacchanal.

"I like to watch people get wasted," he said. "It's entrancing. You just see everyone coming slowly undone, getting looser and happier, until they've become their true selves and are having these conversations they would never have had otherwise."

"Don't you want to do that yourself?" I asked. "Like, haven't you ever been tempted to try it?"

He shook his head. "I don't need booze for that—I was born loose and weird and heart-to-heart-y. How else do you think we became friends?"

I couldn't tell if this was a compliment or a put-down, and the sudden indistinguishability of the two annoyed me. I stalked out of the room and then got mad at myself for being annoyed. I pulled on a pair of jeans and a semipresentable T-shirt, brushing my teeth and mussing my hair. In the next room, he did what little he needed to manifest his handsomeness.

"Do you think we would have become friends if you hadn't been born loose and heart-to-heart-y?" I called.

"What?" I could hear Kanye West's "Good Morning" beginning to play in the background.

We had to ride the train to the party, jumping the turnstiles because we were out of money, and I watched the people riding with us: the drunk girl rocking queasily back and forth with the movements of the train, the old man holding his phone at a distance and texting with his index finger, the group of teenage boys seated across from each other, exchanging insults. Orson was peaceful among them, checking his own phone on occasion but mostly looking out the window at the city, which bristled with artificial light.

Tony Jr. greeted us at the front door with high fives, and as we entered, I realized that this was the kind of party I'd missed out on in high school: crowded, sweaty, full of dangerous alcohol consumption. I made myself a gin and tonic and got a can of Coke for Orson, who immediately downed two gulps.

"You can just hang out in the kitchen or the living room," Tony Jr. called to us over the noise of the crowd. "But don't go into the dining room. My parents have a piano in there."

I could see over his shoulder the shape of a small player piano. I imagined it probably had stained keys and foot pedals whose brass shine had been worn dull. The idea that Tony Jr. was protecting this piano made me both sad for and proud of him.

We passed through the kitchen, saying hi to our coworkers and politely ignoring the people we didn't know, Orson insisting that we sit down by the food in the living room. Wanting to sit was unlike Orson, but wanting food was, so we wound our way into the living room and found a seat on the couch, from where we watched the sad dramas of the party. Arguments, almost-hookups, drunken hellos.

"Are you bored?" he asked after a while.

The question made me giddy. He could read my mind.

"Yeah, I am, actually," I said. "Do you want to go?"

"No, no. I think I want to get you another drink and me another Coke."

This hadn't been what I was expecting, but I pretended it had been. "Yeah," I said. "Thanks. That's cool."

I watched him disappear into the crowd and waited under the dim lights. More people crowded through the door and Tony Jr. welcomed them, instructed them to throw their coats on the sofa adjacent to the one I was sitting on. Eventually a girl in a jean skirt and tank top approached me and perched herself on the sofa's arm.

"Hey," she said.

I responded in kind.

"Are you, like, a friend of Tony Jr.'s?"

"I work with him," I said. "I don't know him that well."

She nodded thoughtfully. I saw that her red Solo cup was nearly full to the brim. "He's really nice."

I agreed that he was really nice.

"So I saw you walking in with this guy. Is he your friend?"

"Orson?" I wanted to say that he was my best friend, but this felt like too intimate a fact to share with the girl. "Yeah, he is."

"That's cool." She smiled. "Is he single?"

I drank the last of my gin and tonic. "He actually has a girlfriend," I said. "Do you know Ingrid?"

The girl's eyes went flat. She had lost all interest in me. "No."

"Yeah, she works at Tony's, too."

"That's cool," she said, and then looked across the room to someone who clearly wasn't calling her name. "It was nice to meet you."

It occurred to me that it was taking Orson an unusually long time to get us drinks. I abandoned my cup on the coffee table and pushed through the crowd in the living room, where I didn't see Orson, and into the kitchen, where I still didn't see him. Tony Jr. was doing shots on the kitchen island with a group of similarly inclined guys in snapbacks and sleeveless T-shirts. After he slung back his third tequila shot, I tapped him on the shoulder and asked him if he'd seen Orson.

He pointed to a screen door behind us. "He went outside," he said.

I walked outside to find a small bonfire encircled by three girls, Orson, and a guy in an unseasonable flannel shirt. The girls were lost in conversation with one another and Orson seemed to be similarly lost in conversation with the flannel guy. I walked up to them and Orson turned to me.

"Ez!" he said, and then gestured to the flannel guy. "This is Jules."

Jules offered his hand to shake. I took it limply.

"Nice to meet you," Jules said, and I nodded.

"Watch this," Orson said. He produced a cigarette from the pack in his back pocket and lit it in the bonfire, the tongue-like flames of which had risen to my waist.

Jules laughed. "That's fucking amazing."

Orson took a drag. "I have to smoke," he said. "I don't know what to do with my hands otherwise."

"You could just put them in your pockets," I offered unhelpfully.

"Jules counts cards," Orson said, ignoring my suggestion. "Apparently he's part of this blackjack team that beats casinos all over the country."

Jules tilted his head back and forth in a show of mock humility. "We *try* to beat casinos."

"Still," Orson said. "That's badass."

I smiled politely.

"We were actually just talking about card counting the other night, Ez, right?"

"Yeah we were." I arranged my face in a way that I hoped communicated boredom, but Orson didn't seem to catch on.

"Can you teach me?" Orson asked.

"Yeah, definitely," Jules said. "You wanna get my number?"

They took out their phones to exchange numbers when I grabbed my stomach and groaned.

"Fuck," I said. "I had too much. I think I'm sick."

"Dude," Jules said flatly, possibly more out of annoyance than concern.

Orson put his arm around my shoulders, a small victory. "We'll be right back," he said. "Just stay here."

Mercifully, I found that the more I thought about Orson's conversation with Jules, the sicker I became, and I was able to successfully retch in the bushes behind the house, my shoulders shaking as I did.

"You got it all out?" Orson asked.

I shook my head and then retched some more, this time from drinking the gin and tonic on a near-empty stomach. Orson patted me between the shoulders. "Why don't we go home?"

"I think that would be good," I said, coughing.

On the train ride back, we sat next to each other, staring out the window ahead of us. The tenderness Orson had evinced by the bushes was gone: he was stone-faced, rigid.

"Are you okay?" I asked.

"I'm fine," he said. "Why wouldn't I be okay?"

I shrugged.

"I thought Jules was cool," he muttered.

"Yeah," I said. "I did too."

He narrowed his eyes at me. "Did you?"

"I really did," I said, though I could tell he didn't believe me.

That night I was too anxious to sleep. I imagined Orson in the next room texting someone—texting Jules, whose number I knew he didn't have, or maybe a girlfriend I didn't know about—and realized that this was probably the case, that he was probably angry at me and wanted to communicate that anger by texting someone. I thought about going into his room to confront him, but I couldn't. I thought about texting him, but I couldn't do that, either. I pounded my bed with my fist. This shouldn't be happening. He was enough for Ingrid. Which meant I should have been enough for him. But of course I wasn't.

§

On my commute to Tony's New York Slice, I usually passed through a gentrified neighborhood dotted with cafés and boutiques designed to distract wealthy white liberals from the guilt of living in a gentrified neighborhood. One of these boutiques was called Lehigh Outfittery. Lehigh was especially intriguing to me because it appeared to sell very little—a single rack of boxy shirts, two shelves of shoes and purses (mostly leather), and a single rack of dark-hued pants and dresses—and yet it was very popular. People loved these items and kept demanding them, apparently, because Lehigh's stock rotated in terms of color but never in terms of cut.

I couldn't resist it. I'd walk in off the street and feel instantly richer. The first time I did this one of the employees, a flamingo-legged woman in a cloche hat, followed me around the store, and when I got to the rack of pants, she told me I'd have to buy something or leave. I left. The next time I walked in, I brought a black crop top I'd sewn out of cheap linen from a JoAnn Fabrics. I'd made sure to go on a day when I knew the flamingo woman wouldn't be there—from my recon, I'd learned she only worked on Tuesdays and Thursdays. I was greeted at the cash register by a middle-aged woman I'd never seen before. Her makeup contouring was so amateurish that she looked like she had a faint five o' clock shadow. When she saw me, she drew her lips into a judgmental pout. I widened my eyes, tried to look pitiful.

"Ma'am," I said, deciding that my character was a slow-witted hick who had no idea how to navigate a city. "I bought this shirt for my sister a couple months ago and she says she doesn't like it."

The woman inhaled and drew her head back like a repulsed heroine in a silent film. "Where's the tag?" she asked.

I'd managed to steal one from a shirt on the rack during my last visit. I dug it out of my pocket and held it out to her: $115.

"I'm sorry it's not attached anymore," I said. "She just told me this is her favorite shop, and I was in town visiting—"

"Her favorite *shop*?"

I nodded.

"Has she been in here before?"

"Yes, ma'am. Her name's Lucinda. Works at the bank down the street. First in our family to go to college."

The woman gestured for me to hand her the shirt. I did, and she rubbed the fabric between her thumb and forefinger, then inspected the entire thing for holes. It lacked a label, true to form for all Lehigh items. She sighed as though I'd bested her in a game of chess.

"Cash or credit?" she asked.

"Cash, ma'am, thank you. Sorry again about the tag."

She nodded solemnly and asked for my debit card to refund the purchase. I opened my wallet to dig for it when the door behind the sales counter swung open. There, against all odds, was the flamingo woman. On a Wednesday.

"Sir," she said to me, practically vibrating with righteous energy.

"Yes?"

She looked from the crop top to her fellow clerk. "Are you giving him a refund?"

The middle-aged woman waved her hands defensively, unsure what to say.

"He never bought anything." The flamingo woman narrowed her eyes at me. "I've only seen you in here once and you never bought anything."

There was another moment of tense silence among the three of us, me performing the stay-or-go calculus, and then the flamingo woman got out her phone and I realized it was time to go. I ran.

"You're banned!" I heard her shouting after me. "If you try to come back, I'm calling the police!"

When I got home, Orson was drinking a seltzer on the couch, the Bhagavad Gita open on his lap.

"We should open a store," I told him. "Like online."

"How would we afford a store?" he asked.

"We wouldn't." I sank into the couch next to him. "You see that Lehigh's place on the way to work?"

He shrugged. He was always in his head when he could afford to be, oblivious to his surroundings.

"Okay, well there's this, like, fancy clothes store that basically sells nothing and it's popular. And when I go in there I, um—" I tried to search for the words. "They don't like me, let's just say."

He snorted. "A white dude getting followed."

"They profile everyone who doesn't look like they employ a full-time nanny."

"Sounds fancy."

"It is. And it's simple. There's actually a way we could do it. To make money."

He closed the book and looked up at me. It always felt incredible to have his full attention.

"You make people think everything's higher quality than it actually is," I said. "So what if we did that online? Make shitty clothes that look sleek and simple and sell them at a huge markup?"

He smiled. "Tell me more."

I smiled back. "I'll show you."

I made an account on a site called YouCraft and uploaded a Photoshopped picture of a sweatshirt that read, simply, THE FUTURE IS FEMALE. My name was Amy Donahue and the sweatshirt was "organic Egyptian cotton" and cost $75. I spent a couple weeks toying with the SEO, commenting on other users' pages, creating various fake social media accounts from which I could share the link to our page. Then I got two orders. Then six. Then ten.

Orson looked over my shoulder as I managed the orders. "This is wild," he said. "You were right about this."

"I told you." I tried not to sound like I was gloating. "And it just keeps going."

After two months, we had fifty orders totaling $2,250. After the 30 percent cut YouCraft took for hosting our business, we had $1,575.

We added a T-shirt that read THIS IS WHAT A FEMINIST LOOKS LIKE. Amy Donahue was quickly overwhelmed by orders. Using 25 percent of our profits, we bought Fruit of the Loom sweatshirts and T-shirts, cut the tags out, screen printed them, and sent them to a handful of lucky customers. Everyone else received an email: *I'm sorry, but there was an error in processing your order. Please bear with me as I fix this.* The rationale was that someone buying a $45 T-shirt online was rich enough and shopping online enough that they would eventually lose track of their purchase altogether.

"What's Amy Donahue like?" Orson asked, doing a headstand in the courtyard of our apartment complex. I sat in the grass, pretending not to watch him as closely as I was.

"She likes expensive clothes," I said.

"No, I mean like, what's she *like*? What's the character like?"

I laughed. "Are you method acting?"

He somersaulted out of the headstand and lay on his back, looking at the sky. "Just humor me. What's this woman like?"

"She's from, like, the suburbs of a major city. The wealthiest suburb."

"So either New York or LA. Bedford or Beverly Hills."

"Right. And her husband is some kind of banking executive or consultant and she's left home alone all day."

Orson nodded. "Yeah, I see that. Is she a wine drinker?"

"Well-aged cabs."

"And she's a feminist?"

"Only for rich white women."

"So she's racist?"

"Very, but she's too respectable to admit it."

He laughed and sat up to face me. "That's good. She's got a daughter, too, doesn't she? And she keeps trying to be the daughter's best friend."

"Yeah, exactly. The daughter absolutely hates her. But her son dotes on her."

"Because he's going to be a banking executive just like his dad."

"But, like, a *better* banking executive, so it's pretty Oedipal."

"Oh, yeah, a better banking executive. One who can fuck over more people more efficiently and with less feeling."

"He's a robot. A handsome robot. His name is Charlton."

Orson played Charlton, the only model on Amy Donahue's profile. The THIS IS WHAT A FEMINIST LOOKS LIKE T-shirt was particularly tight on him, which elicited emails from curious customers: *Is your son single?*

No, Amy wrote, *he's actually headed to UCLA with his girlfriend in the fall! We're all very proud of him.* We'd decided on Beverly Hills as her home base.

Amy's "special edition" LOVE LIKE NOBODY'S WATCHING tote bag was a hit from the first day she added it to the store. People must have really needed tote bags, because they bought it in droves, faster than we could silkscreen a handful of cheap bags with the slogan. But we'd flown too close to the sun: someone with a fairly popular Tumblr account called out Amy Donahue's YouCraft profile as a scam, and we immediately folded up shop. We walked away with only $15,000 from an idea that could have earned us $30,000.

After that, we'd developed a taste for "small businesses." It was Orson's idea to mess with Bitcoin. All the rich libertarian shitheads on Reddit and

4Chan were talking about investing. I followed their conversations closely. *At last*, they all seemed to be saying, *a chance to move money around without having to use banks as intermediaries!* A way to make their money recession proof! I couldn't blame them for hating banks, but the idea of investing all their money in cryptocurrency seemed ludicrous to me. So I set up a website that essentially functioned as a Bitcoin credit union, where people would pay me dollars to become "member-owners" of an entity that could convert their money into Bitcoin using blockchain technology. Really, what I was doing was taking their money and offering them something like tokens in a video game in return, which they kept stored in accounts they set up with me and never used. They never accrued interest because I wasn't running a bank, and the member-owners never did anything with their fake Bitcoin because they didn't know how. Orson thought the whole arrangement was brilliant and began posing as a Redditor named karmapanda who was a very successful member of my credit union and making "shitloads of money" through Bitcoin. Karmapanda would share advice animal memes and *Tim and Eric* reaction GIFs about his success, and soon he had several friends interested in investing. They even set up a *League of Legends* team together and as they played, karmapanda—whose real name we decided was Greg—jumped in the chat to tell these guys about buying a Benz and eating out every night and how incredible the Bitcoin-to-dollar conversion rate was. Everything always pointed back to my fake credit union. The guys would cycle in, invest a modest amount, let their "Bitcoin" sit for months, and then try to trade it using tips from karmapanda. I had to set up trading sites that would make these guys feel like they were actually gaming the system by investing in the nascent-to-nonexistent cryptocurrency market. Eventually I had to create a character, doxxbone, who was just as successful as karmapanda. Of course, the two didn't know each other—they just happened to be successful investors through our growing cadre of cryptocurrency sites.

That ended when a verbose Irish Redditor named dirtyharry traced all our sites to the same IP address and threatened to call the police if we didn't shut down. It was an empty threat, of course—a troll like dirtyharry was likely to have a dark web presence, and so unlikely to want to deal with cops—but we decided not to risk it. It was a sad few days: our credit union was announced across Reddit and 4Chan as a scam, and karmapanda and doxxbone were banned from both sites. A few of our member-owners who'd invested in amounts over $1,000 wrote angry emails demanding their money back, but we let them go to spam. Most had been too scared to invest more than $400, $550 tops. Luckily, we'd had hundreds of investors. At the end of it all, we had $60,402 in four different accounts, and that wasn't including our Amy Donahue money.

I sent my parents $500 a month, claiming that I'd gotten a promotion at Tony's. They called me, insisting that I not waste my money on them, and I reassured them that it was a gourmet pizza place and that the night supervisor got paid $20 an hour plus tips. They believed this, never having earned more than $15 an hour themselves, and I felt bad for them. They had been denied so much for so long that they were eager to take what I offered. Some part of them must have known I was lying—they weren't dumb—but when it came to money, they couldn't afford to care about the truth.

Orson's mom accepted the money unquestioningly and told him that she was going to use it to remodel the bathroom.

"She's been lonely after my dad died," he explained. "I think she needs something to occupy herself with." I had never met her, but I'd seen her in pictures on Facebook: tall and thin, with her son's orange-blond hair, her manicure always chipped, her eyes heavy from having spent so much time in a state of grief. Privately, I thought of her as my second mother. A mother-in-law. Orson would introduce me to her someday, and we'd get along so well she'd wonder why he'd kept me from her for so long.

It was a Tuesday and we were approaching the anniversary of our first year in the city. I had worked the afternoon shift at Tony's and Orson had worked the night shift, and when he came home his eyes were narrow, his smile nonexistent, and he collapsed onto the couch with his forearm across his forehead like a Victorian housewife who'd just fainted. I followed his gaze to the moldy ceiling and then looked back at him. He sighed.

"What's wrong?" I asked.

He shifted to his side and closed his eyes. "I'm getting that feeling again," he said.

"What feeling?"

"Just, I dunno. Boredom."

My blood went cold. "Why?"

He shrugged. "It's been a while since Bitcoin and we haven't done anything."

I didn't know what to say. I'd been temporarily stalled out, unsure where to direct my energies.

In the silence, he turned to face me. "Relax, little dude," he said. "It's not, like, an indictment of you. This is just something that happens from time to time."

"You were bored before," I stuttered. "When you were selling weed." He'd been unhappy then. So unhappy he'd moved away.

"Oh, this isn't like that. This is more like a restlessness. Like everything feels mickey mouse-y."

"Bitcoin wasn't mickey mouse-y," I protested.

He tilted his head from side to side. My blood dropped another few degrees.

"We're capable of more," he said.

"Like what?" The question came out more accusatory than I'd intended.

He shrugged. "Something more personal. Something with people, actual people actually standing in front of us. I'm tired of hiding behind screens."

When Ingrid logged on that evening, she was troubled. But she didn't want to tell the rest of the girls at the risk of shattering her perfect persona. They greeted her in a chorus:

It's Ingy!

Hey babe!

We've been talking about you.

About how much we miss you.

It's been like a week.

I watched the words appear on the screen and found myself unable to contribute. I typed the beginnings of sentences and deleted them.

Hey Ingrid wrote finally.

LMAO "hey." Are you a dude or something?

Just a rough night. I settled on the easiest excuse for Ingrid's lethargy. *Lots of homework.*

I get it Alice wrote. *I've got this biochem class that's kicking my ass.*

The topic turned to homework: who had more, who hated it more, etc. I found it incredibly boring but didn't want to redirect the conversation. Ingrid did, though.

There's something going on with me and Orson she wrote.

OMG what's wrong?

Is he OK? Are you?

Are you fighting?

No, not exactly. My fingers hovered over the keyboard, searching for the right lie. *It's just that he seems more depressed. Like he doesn't want to have sex as often.*

Ughhhh I'm sorry to hear that.

That happens to guys sometimes tho believe it or not.

Yeah that happened to my boyfriend.

The girls. Ingrid could always count on the girls. It was a rare thing, to be able to count on girls. Why wasn't Ingrid honest with them more often? They were there for her. They would never be embarrassed by me, would never judge me for having the kind of problems every woman had.

There was a movement behind my left shoulder, and when I turned around I felt something like organ failure. Orson was standing behind me, reading my monitor.

"I couldn't sleep," he said. "I tried calling your name but you were engrossed."

I swallowed and tried to prepare myself for what would happen next. Eviction from the apartment, probably. A fight first, then eviction. He'd break some of my bones. He'd demand my shares of the Donahue and the Bitcoin. I'd return to my parents totally exposed. Orson would tell everyone what he'd seen. What I'd done. I had effectively ended everything I'd built in my life.

Helloooooooo

Did she leave

Ingrid Ingrid Ingrid

Helloooooooooo hello hello

Kinda rude, girl

"Seems like a supportive bunch," he said.

I nodded. I began to cry.

"So, you're Ingrid?"

"I'm sorry," I said, and took off my glasses. "I'm fucked up. I'm so fucked up. I'm sorry."

He was silent, probably reading the whole history of the chat. "You're Ingrid and I'm your boyfriend."

There was bile rising in my throat. He laughed.

"It's funny," he said. "Are they rich?"

"Some of them," I choked.

"You know which ones?"

I nodded.

"Hey, look up at me. You can look up at me."

It was dark, and my glasses were on my desk, so all I could see was his body like a bright-blue flame in the monitor light bending toward me, and all I could feel were his hands on either side of my head and his lips on mine. It was a long time before he pulled away.

§

Wc had a new plan. According to my fake ID, my name was Thornton Weston. I was a Yale-educated aspiring filmmaker who had yet to go to film school. I wanted to be the next Martin Scorsese, but I was an inveterate partyer, too drunk and high all the time to even bother thinking about continuing my education. I dressed in ratty T-shirts and black jeans because I was embarrassed by my family's wealth.

On a rainy Thursday night, I took my ID to Torrent, a club in the city center where the cover was $50. I parked myself at the bar and ordered a mai tai, pretending to be texting a crush, my mouth screwed up in the kittenish pout of a harmless gay man. As I'd expected, two strangers walked up to me, one in a tight Lycra dress and the other in cheetah-print heels.

"Are these seats taken?" the one in the Lycra dress asked.

"No," I said. "Feel free."

Cheetah print was named Selina and Lycra was named Marta. Selina had just dumped her boyfriend and Marta was treating her to a night out. They were on the lookout for a rebound for Selina.

I rested my chin in my hand, eyeing them both as though this were the most delicious piece of information I'd ever heard. I leaned forward.

"Between you and me, I'm on the lookout for a new guy myself."

They both laughed, and Selina ordered us shots. Then Marta ordered us shots, and I followed suit.

"Now we have to dance, Thornton!" Selina crowed over the music. "We're all drunk so we have to dance!"

I made a show of protesting but ultimately let them pull me onto the dance floor, where I demonstrated that I had more rhythm than I think either of them expected. They chorused *whooo*s and clapped. Dancing had always been easy for me: I was small and flexible and didn't need to see to know how to move to music. With perfect sight came self-consciousness and distance from sound—I didn't have those problems. I watched their feet close to mine, their heels narrow and delicate like spider's legs. Unlike me, they were only capable of limited movement, and this was a good thing. I spun them, dipped them, allowed them to pirouette. We attracted a small fandom on the floor, people clapping and cheering for us as we danced. When it was done and we were all sweaty and breathless, Selina and Marta grabbed my hands in delight.

"You're *so* fun, Thornton," Marta said. "You have to meet the rest of our friends."

Unsurprisingly, Selina and Marta had friends as beautiful and rich as they were, with names like Kayleigh and Hayleigh and Madison. It took a few weeks, but I was soon spending every night with them at Kayleigh's apartment, getting drunk and watching *Real Housewives* or rolling on molly and telling each other how pretty we all were. They were all young and long-haired and supple limbed but worldlier than I wanted them to be: they had been through difficult breakups with men with powerful fathers, many of whom were local celebrities. They were savvy and skeptical of all men. I was beginning to doubt my ability to implement our plan—until I met Jamie DeCroix, a friend of Marta's who joined us in Kayleigh's apartment one Friday.

Jamie was the daughter of a Wall Street hedge fund manager who had given her free rein to pursue an acting career several thousand miles away from him. She stayed in a condo her father had purchased for her and spent her money on anything that struck her fancy: coats, shoes, champagne, drugs. She was beautiful in a way that was almost threatening, and it was precisely because of this beauty that she, like Ingrid's friend Alice, struggled to maintain a boyfriend. No one felt like they deserved her, so they dismissed her, called her names, cheated on her. She needed someone who wouldn't be threatened by her beauty.

"My friend Troy's coming to town," I said one night while *The Bachelor* was flickering across Kayleigh's plasma screen. "It's actually a crazy story how I met him."

"You tell the *best* stories, Thornton," Hayleigh purred.

"I know," I said, and smiled. "I had an internship in DC my junior year at Yale, and every day I had to walk to Capitol Hill to do some stupid paperwork, and there was this busker sitting on the sidewalk. He was super sweet, and, like *super* cute, but he doesn't roll that way, of course."

Everyone laughed.

"So, like, he would always play 'Hallelujah' whenever I walked past, and I'd always give him like fifteen bucks. And one day I gave him my number and told him to call me if he ever came out here. And he just called me last night."

"Oh my god," Selina said, and looked at Jamie. "Are we going to get to meet him?"

They were. Orson had shaved his head to play Troy, and wore the desperate-to-please smile of the formerly homeless. He dressed in a Canadian tuxedo and scuffed work boots. On the first night he came out with us he stayed at the bar drinking seltzers and telling Jamie that his dad had been a violent alcoholic so he'd run away from home at fifteen. He never sized her up, never commented on how good she looked. Jamie never looked away from him as he spoke.

I hadn't known Orson could actually play the guitar, but of course he could. At Jamie's condo, he played "Hallelujah" and then covers of Katy Perry and Beyoncé—anything we threw at him he could magic into a simple chord progression—and I got so drunk Selina and Marta had to package me into a taxi and send me to the fake address I gave them. By the time I got there, I had sobered up enough to walk home, my hands in my pockets, grimacing against an unusually biting wind.

I didn't like the next part of the plan: Orson had to hook up with Jamie. It was necessary but it made my muscles knot to think about it. It would have been too awkward to ask him to be reserved, to not give an ounce of himself to her, to do everything mechanically and be done with it before she finished. I knew how it had to happen: he had to go all out. The thought disgusted me. I told myself it wasn't real with her. It couldn't be real with her. It was only real with me.

"Oh my god!" Jamie called me the next morning. "Thornton!"

"Quieter," I said, cotton mouthed.

"Sorry, oh my god, sorry," she laughed. "You must be so hungover."

"Yep, I really am. What's up?"

"Troy and I hooked up last night. It was fucking incredible."

I had to muster enthusiasm. That was key. "Oh my god, girl!"

She laughed too loudly and for too long. "I think I am literally in heaven right now. How did you *find* this *Adonis*?"

Fuck you, I thought. "I swear I just attract beautiful men," I said.

She laughed again. "You really do, honey! Like, wow!"

Orson spent every night at Jamie's and she paid for everything: new clothes, new shoes, dinners out. I missed him, but I liked seeing him in brand-name clothes when he got home every morning. And I knew he was mine during the day. I knew that Jamie would never know him like I did. How could she? To her, he was Troy, a fictional once-homeless busker who wanted to become a professional musician. Troy told Jamie that he would love to get just ten minutes in a recording studio. He could really show those producers who he was. Jamie listened to his album-in-progress, which just happened to be about a "wake-up-to-you girl" with "sun-shocked curls." She cried a little as he played. Was it about her, she wanted to know? Yes, of course it was. He was in love with her.

A few months in, he sheepishly admitted that he wanted to record in private before taking anything to a professional studio. But, unfortunately, that would require his own space and his own equipment, which he just didn't have. Jamie flashed a bleached smile and wagged her sun-shocked curls and told him it was no problem, she actually knew a place in her same neighborhood that she was considering buying anyway. Her dad wanted her to invest because renting was just throwing money away. Would Troy like to live there? She would buy it and he could stay there. She just wanted him to be happy. Troy cried. This was the first time anyone had really *seen* him. This was the first time he'd really been taken care of. He promised to love Jamie for the rest of her life.

She bought the condo, which was worth close to a million dollars, and filled it with recording equipment. He recorded a demo of his album, *Love and Grace*, and was all ready to show it to producers when he got cold feet. He began to have nightmares. He lost his interest in sex. He was depressed, and there was nothing Jamie could do to cheer him up. So she paid for therapy, and Troy was diagnosed with major depressive disorder, and he was placed on an SSRI that he cheeked and spit into the toilet.

At therapy, Orson was a model patient in every way except when it came to telling the truth. He told the therapist Troy's story and the therapist listened and offered coping strategies and asked him how those coping strategies made him feel. He told her that the deep breathing and meditation were really helping, as was the medication, but he couldn't get over how fundamentally unhappy he was in his relationship.

"I keep having this dream," he told her. "Where I'm looking in this chest of drawers for something I've lost and there's nothing in there but I keep thinking it'll turn up. I don't even know what I've lost, but I'm desperate to find it. I look and look and I never find anything. And then right before I wake up, I find this tarantula the size of my hand."

"Does it scare you?" the therapist asked.

He shook his head. "It's weirdly comforting. I let it crawl all over me, and when it bites me, I just feel this wave of relief. Like *ah, it can finally all be over now*."

The therapist doubled his dosage. He spent nights watching TV on Jamie's laptop while she stroked his hair and promised in a thin voice that he'd definitely start feeling better soon.

Then it was a waiting game. Someone as beautiful and rich as Jamie couldn't go months without sex, but she couldn't bring herself to pressure Troy into anything. He was too perfect, and she'd feel too guilty. She called me and asked if I had any advice.

"He's just, like, so sad. He's not himself. All he does is sit around and watch TV and cry."

"Babe, you know he's had a traumatic life," I said.

"But I'm giving him such a *good* life," she whined. "Why can't he just be happy?"

Of course he wasn't happy—he was stuck in that condo with her. "He's an artist. You know how artists are these, like, really complicated people? He has to be complicated to make art. I met *so* many people like him in film school."

"I guess," she sighed.

"You know what would be really good? If you took him out to the club again. He loves being around people. He's really extroverted."

But of course Troy wasn't extroverted. He sat at the bar the entire time drinking his seltzers. When Jamie tried to get him to dance, he ignored her. Fuck it, she'd had enough, she said. She had tried *everything* to help him and he was just being a depressed little shit and throwing himself a pity party. So he'd had a hard life! Everyone has hardships! For two months in the fourth grade, Jamie had been forced to wear orthodontic headgear. She'd had her heart broken by an investment banker's son at Choate. Her friends had sometimes gotten so wasted that they'd thrown up in her hair. And look what she was doing! She was trying to make something of herself! And what was Troy doing? Just sitting on his album like some kind of *loser* who has no faith in himself!

He turned to her, his eyes cold. "So that's what you really think of me?"

His glare caught her off-guard, but she was already committed to her tantrum. "I think you're acting like a child! I think you don't know how to just *take charge of your life*!"

He sighed and shrugged on his coat. "Fine, then," he said. "I'm leaving."

"Okay, fine!" she shouted, slamming her purse on the bar. "Go ahead and leave! I'm going to stay here and get my money's worth! I'm the one paying for everything, anyway!"

She shouted this to his back: he was out the door and into the night, where I was sitting on the curb at the end of the block, waiting for him.

That night Jamie got drunk and cheated on Troy with a thirtysomething loan shark who'd helped finance the subprime mortgage crisis. When she got home the next morning, hungover and ashamed, Troy was sitting on the edge of their bed, his chin in his hands. She'd been the first person he'd trusted in a long time. He'd really believed things were going to work out with her. But she'd crossed a line, and there was no going back. She fell to her knees and put her head in his lap and begged him to forgive her, to take her back, she would be better this time, she would be more understanding. No, he just couldn't trust her. She had already violated his trust once, after all—what was to keep her from violating it again? He was going to move out of the condo. No, he couldn't do that! Yes he could. He opened their closet and began to pack up the clothes she'd bought him.

She called me crying: "Thornton! Please, he's going to leave me."

Finally, the part I'd been waiting for. "You cheated on him. With someone disgusting, too."

"I didn't mean to, Thornton! Seriously, I was so fucked up and confused. Can you say anything to him? Can you help him understand that I love him?"

"I can't do anything to help him understand that," I said, trying to conceal the smile in my voice. "It was your responsibility, and you completely fucked it up. He's been hurt enough in his life."

"Oh my god, please! Thornton, please!"

"If you try to call this number again, I'll block you."

But she did call: twenty-six times. She was used to getting her way. Then the texts started coming in, to both Orson and me: *why did this happen? why did you do this to me?* So I blocked her.

We had moved Orson's recording equipment into our packed apartment and were spending the afternoon trying to steal everything from the condo that wasn't nailed down. In the midst of this, the door burst open and there he was, in leather gloves and a knee-length overcoat, his bearlike face stony: Jonathan DeCroix, her father. His eyes were narrower and lips tighter than they'd ever looked in Jamie's Facebook photos.

"Which one of you is Troy?" he asked both of us. When neither of us responded, he set his gaze on Orson, the obvious choice for his daughter.

"You're Troy?" he asked.

"I'm his brother," Orson said quickly. "Troy left town."

Jonathan DeCroix pulled off his leather gloves, eyeing both of us. He was middle-aged but muscular, clearly well-preserved. "Who's this?" he asked, gesturing to me.

"I'm—um—Troy's brother's friend," I said, and I could hear Orson heaving a pointed sigh of frustration behind me. "Alan."

"Somehow I don't believe you, *Alan*," he said. "What I do believe is that you"—he pointed at Orson—"broke my daughter's heart."

"Fuck," whispered Orson, loud enough for only me to hear, and then too quickly Jonathan DeCroix was upon him, shoving him against the wall, delivering a quick but impactful blow to his stomach. It was horrifying to watch.

"I'm sorry!" I said, hoping this would somehow fix things, but of course it didn't. Orson sunk to the floor, breathless.

"Get out," Jonathan DeCroix said. "Both of you. And give my daughter back everything that belongs to her."

So we left, Orson stooped with his arm over my shoulder, our coats stealthily packed with silverware and gold fixtures. When we got back to our apartment, I helped Orson to his bed, where he collapsed, chest heaving. I sat next to him and kissed him on the forehead.

"I'm sorry," I said.

He waved his hand at me. "It's fine. We both fucked up in the moment."

This didn't feel true, but I was grateful to him for saying it. "Can I get you anything?"

He turned on his side, wincing in pain. "Maybe some ice?"

I went to kitchen and filled a bag with ice from the freezer. I thought of him shoved against the wall, the way his face had crumpled, the look of terror in his eyes. I never wanted him to feel that way again.

In his bedroom, I held the ice against his stomach and he squeaked out a high-pitched sigh and then closed his eyes, nodding as if I'd just made a very intelligent point.

"I need to sleep," he said. "But can you—do you think you can start unloading the stuff?"

I did. In a week, we made roughly $100,000 for the recording equipment and all of Orson's new clothes and shoes.

I sent a $10,000 check to my parents that month. Don't worry about it, I told them when they texted me in a panic. I got a raise. I'm the manager now.

§

I usually went to a coffee place around the street from our apartment called The Creamery. I liked it because they were known for their heavy cream and I took my coffee beige. The baristas there knew me by name, and typically greeted me with a chorus of "Hello, stranger!" to which I shouted back, "Come on, I'm no stranger!" My favorite barista was a woman named Adelaide, who confessed to being a chronic nail biter and was involved in a polyamorous knitting circle. Adelaide was there that morning, and she smiled toothily at me and began preparing my usual.

I stood in line, checking my bank account on my phone. It was fuller than it had ever been.

"Ezra!" Adelaide called, and I retrieved my milked-up espresso from her, exchanged a few words about RPGs and knitting, respectively, and then turned around to find Jamie standing in front of me. She was paler than when I'd last seen her, her eyeliner liquid and dramatic, her hair pulled into a tight bun. She held a very small coffee with both hands.

"Hi, Ezra," she said.

I dropped my espresso and ran. I could hear her coming after me. I ran in the direction opposite our apartment. It was just my luck that we had walk signs for four blocks.

"I know who you are!" Jamie shouted after me. I could feel pedestrians turning to look at us as we flashed by. "I'm going to the police!"

I had always been fast and had honed a talent for running in traffic: no matter how mad people got at me, they'd never risk their lives to catch me. I crossed an intersection as the walk sign was flashing. She was closing the gap between us. "Police!" she shouted. "This man stole my purse!" And then she chucked her purse at me. I felt it graze the back of my head. "Police!" she shouted again.

We made it to the park and I jumped off the footpath and over a bench. Her voice got a little more distant. I was waiting for some good Samaritan to trip me or throw something at my legs but people just gawked while she called after me. I sprinted around a picnic, jumped over two dogs. I crossed the green faster than she could and then ran directly into traffic, catching a break between two SUVs. I turned to look behind me: she was so far away I wouldn't have been able to tell it was her had she not been shouting my name between heavy breaths, still calling for the police.

I went several neighborhoods out of my way to get home. When I finally walked in the door, I found Orson splayed on the couch and freshly showered, reading the Upanishads.

"What the fuck," he said. "Did you go for a run in normal clothes?"

"Jamie," I gasped. "She saw me. She knows my name."

He closed the book. "What?"

"She was at The Creamery."

"She knows your full name?"

"I don't know. I think so."

We had no choice: we quit Tony's and moved to an apartment several neighborhoods away from our old one, even farther away from the old condo. After that, we looked for new straight jobs.

One night Orson motioned me over to his laptop. I nestled my head in the concavity between his neck and collarbone and saw what he was looking at: a picture of Boyd Tower, the slate-and-glass eyesore on the river that ran through the city center.

"Isn't that place—" I began to ask.

"Eric Boyd Sr.'s," Orson said.

"That racist real estate mogul?"

He turned to me, grinning. "You forgot 'rich.'"

THREE

WHEN ORSON WAS TWELVE YEARS OLD, HIS PARENTS LIVED CLOSE ENOUGH TO his elementary school that he could walk home after the final bell. In order to get home from the school, he had to cross a busy intersection, and it was at the northeast corner of this intersection that a man named Tim sat every day. The man had the unwashed brown-pink skin of the homeless and neglected and stank of sweat and urine. He held a sign that read HUNGRY, PLEASE HELP ME GOD and held out a 7-Eleven Big Gulp cup that never had more than a little change in it. The children veered away from him when they crossed.

On September 11, 2001, Orson was let out of his seventh-grade math class early. He wandered out of the swarm of crying, panicked kids and harried teachers and over to Tim, who was sitting in his usual spot. Tim was having a particularly lucid day, and he started telling Orson about the Iraq War. He didn't call it that, and Orson didn't know what the Iraq War was, but Tim talked about being in a country called Iraq in a place called Al-Fallujah. The British had just dropped bombs on Al-Fallujah and a lot of houses were destroyed. Tim was part of a group of soldiers who had to go into Al-Fallujah and find people who were dangerous to American oil and kill them. There was a square-shaped house with a tile roof that had collapsed on one side and was still standing on the other. Tim and another soldier were supposed to go in and look around because this was something called a Shi'a household. The other soldier said he thought that everyone had been cleared out and the house was empty, so he was going to do a quick check of the upstairs and Tim could do a quick check of the downstairs.

Tim walked through the living room, where pieces of the roof had crushed the sofa and TV and the floor was covered with rubble. He checked the kitchen, which looked pretty much the same, and then another room with a long table that was low to the ground. This room was mostly rubble, and he thought he'd just have a glance and then get out, when he heard a noise coming from underneath the rubble. It was a voice, a high-pitched one. It was saying *saiedni*, which was something Tim had heard before. It meant "help me" in Arabic.

Tim felt very bad when he heard this voice, like how Orson probably felt when he failed a test or got detention for running in the hall. He started digging in the rubble, and the digging got increasingly desperate until he found the worst thing he'd seen in his life. It was a boy about Orson's age, crying. His left arm and leg had been ripped off and he was covered head to toe in his own blood. His breaths gasped and rattled, and Tim realized his ribs were broken. As the boy called *saiedni,* blood poured out of his mouth and he choked on it. The boy stared at Tim with a pained and panicked look, his eyebrows raised, his voice as loud as he could make it, and Tim felt like he was seeing a ghost. The boy said *saiedni* one more time and his face froze, scared, and Tim could tell the boy had not been ready to die—he should never have had to be ready to die—and Tim jumped back so the slab of concrete he'd lifted to find the boy fell back into place, covering him again. And then Tim's partner came downstairs and asked Tim if he'd found anyone and Tim said no, the house was completely empty.

A week later, Orson was driving to the grocery store with his mom. There were American flags everywhere: stuck onto car windows, run up poles, hanging on front porches. His parents had taped a flag in the bay window of their prefab, single-story house. Something about the flags felt foreboding to Orson, like they were the grave markers of people about to die.

His mom was busy with the grocery list, so Orson wandered off to the deli counter, where he looked at the cuts of beef his family couldn't afford. He perused the length of the counter, nodding hello to the butcher, imagining what it would be like to eat a well-done steak for dinner, when he nearly bumped into a man in a dress shirt and khakis. He looked up: it was Tim. Clean cut, with a watch and a pinkie ring, his hair trimmed to within an inch of his scalp, his beard nonexistent. He was almost unrecognizable. They looked at each other for a few seconds, Tim with an expression of horror on his face, and then he backed away from Orson and walked quickly down the baking aisle. Orson never saw him again.

When Orson told me this story, I was lying in bed next to him, my head on his chest. I could hear the inner workings of his body: his blood, his breath, his heart. He was smoking a cigarette above my head, blowing gray contrails from his nostrils.

"That's awful," I said. "It doesn't make sense. Why would someone pretend to be a homeless vet?"

"I don't know," he said, exhaling. "Maybe it's how the dude got his thrills."

"Faking like that for a couple quarters?"

"I guess. Unless his life completely turned around in a week."

We were both silent. I listened to Orson's inhalations and exhalations, imagining myself attached to him forever, a remora on the belly of a shark.

"The rich glamorize being poor," he said finally. "They think it gives you integrity or something. They think it's like noble somehow to have been poor once. It means you've earned your wealth. But that's a myth, because the poor just stay poor. No one *gets* rich."

I rolled onto my back and sighed. "People are fucked up," I added unhelpfully.

He handed me my glasses and stood. It was good to feel him, but it was even better to see him. "*We're* fucked up," he said. Then he waltzed to the opposite side of the room and came charging at the bed, doing a flip in midair. He landed inches from me. I applauded.

"I bet you wish you could do that," he said.

"Not particularly," I said.

He kissed my forehead. "You're right," he said. "You have other talents. And we can put them to use in all kinds of ways."

§

The Boyd Tower was a madhouse of marble and red carpet and crystal chandeliers, the kind of appurtenances you'd see in a movie about the ultrarich. We worked as bellhops, lugging the suitcases of conservative senators, corporate lobbyists, wealthy evangelists and their cheated-on wives into the elevators and making conversation with them as we traveled up the many floors of the building. Orson called them blood suits, as in "let's see which of the blood suits is most willing to part with his money today." Some of them tipped big to impress each other and their wives. Others were stingy, extracting fives or tens from their Prada wallets and tossing them at us in semidisgust. Orson usually got bigger tips than I did, making up stories for the blood suits about his fraternity days at some good old boy college in Virginia or South Carolina, how many girls he charmed without believing in that "*intersecting feminism* or whatever bullshit is so popular nowadays." When we were on a shift together, we became fraternity brothers. I was the bravest of all the young pledges, the only one truly willing to take a paddle to the ass for his country and God. Sigma Delta Tau had really made a man out of me, I said, and if a brother happened to be on the elevator with us, I'd get a little punch in the arm and an extra $50. But it was Orson they loved: he acted like one of them, laughed at their jokes, complimented their watches, feigned shock that their wives were over forty. In some moments I recognized a tenderness in him that I'd only encountered when we were entangled. But it wasn't real for the blood suits like it was for me—it couldn't be. He was just a servant in the palace. His kindness was like diamonds exploding from coal: yet another nonrenewable resource they were accustomed to exploiting.

Orson became so popular that he was promoted to the front desk, where he kept a mental index of all the blood suits who stayed most frequently at the

Boyd. *Mr. and Mrs. Roy, welcome back! How are the children?* and *I hope you come back to see us again, Senator Evans!* and, on the rare occasion he didn't recognize a blood suit: *Welcome to the Boyd! My name is Orson Ortman and I'm looking forward to being of service to you!* We began to notice a pattern: the more indifferent the blood suit was to Orson, the more the blood suit's wife was likely to be enchanted by him. The wives, we began to realize, were looser with their money than their husbands. I made an Excel spreadsheet of what we called "frequent flyers," couples who stayed at the Boyd a few times a month. I made sure that I was the one lugging their baggage to the elevator when they first arrived.

"You know, I shouldn't be saying this," I'd say as the husbands were digging in their wallets for my tip, "but if you call the front desk after midnight and ask for Orson, he'll bring you off-menu wine."

"Oh!" the wives would titter, their husbands having already shoved a middling tip into my hands. "Is that so?"

I'd press my finger to my lips. "You didn't hear it from me."

Inevitably, the wives would wait until their husbands were getting drunk together in the Executive Lounge to dial the front desk. Orson's voice was young and buttery.

"How can I help you tonight?"

"Oh, hi, Orson!" the women would say, likely reminded once again how different his voice was from their husbands'. "I just—well—I heard from Ezra . . ."

Here Orson would quickly lower his voice and pick up the slack: "Yes, I imagine he told you about the off-menu wine."

The women would laugh. "Am I that obvious?"

"No, no. You're just a woman who knows what she wants."

More demure giggles. The women probably hadn't felt this way since they were coeds and their husbands had brought flowers to their sorority windows. Or maybe they'd never felt this way before—maybe their husbands had never paid as much careful attention to them as Orson was in that moment.

Enter Orson with the wine, which I had bought for $10 at our neighborhood bodega, uncorked, flavored with cheap lime juice and spices, and recorked with a new stopper. We'd melted off the labels with hot water and soap, replacing them with new ones we'd doctored in my bootlegged version of Photoshop: "Vacio, Monte Triste, 1974." A thirty-five-year-old cabernet from a winery in Lisbon.

"My goodness!" the women would say when Orson brought them bottles of Vacio. "What does it mean, *vacio*?"

"Mysterious," Orson would lie. "They call it that because there was so little of it made."

"And how do you happen to have a bottle?"

He'd wink at them. "That's my secret."

This would send them into a kind of nirvana obviously forbidden to wives of conservatives, where Orson could be many things to them at once: lover, son, confidante, spy. He was dangerous enough to be exciting but tame enough to be reassuring—he gave them the illusion of risk with the safeguard of professionalism: things could only get *so far* out of hand before he'd be whisked away by someone uninteresting (me) back to his post at the front desk.

"Can I pour you a glass, Mrs. X?"

"Of course." A devilish smile. "Care to join me?"

He'd make a show of checking his watch and the women would be momentarily shaken: Had they gone too far? Was this harassment? Would their husbands find out?

"As a matter of fact, I do," Orson would say, taking a seat on the bed next to them. "They don't let me drink when I'm at work, but—"

"Oh, I won't tell!" the women would say, emboldened. "And if you get in trouble, blame me. I'll pay you a day's salary."

"Really, Mrs. X. That wouldn't be necessary."

Now the women were pouring a glass for him, a gender role reversal that was exciting for them. "Well, I'd do it for you, Orson."

Orson's turn to laugh demurely. "That's very kind of you, Mrs. X."

Of course the women wanted to know all about Orson. Where had he gone to school? (We'd decided on Duke.) What had he studied? (Finance and economics.) What kind of career did he hope to pursue? (He was currently torn between getting an MBA and becoming an investment banker or getting a JD and becoming a state senator.) They'd each have two glasses and then the questions would get increasingly personal. What was Orson's relationship with his father like? (Orson's father was his role model, a machinist and a good Christian and one of the most decent men he'd ever known.) And his mother? (She was a schoolteacher, a kind and gentle woman who did everything she could for the ones she loved.) What was his childhood like? (Orson had grown up poor but honest—his parents hardly made enough money to adequately care for him and his four siblings—and he had resolved at an early age to win a full scholarship to Duke so he could get a good job and someday provide for his family.)

"Your parents must be so proud," the women would say, smiling with their lips closed, worried that they'd stained their teeth with Vacio.

"I suppose you could say that," Orson would reply.

"How can I be of help?" they wanted to know. "In thirty years when you're a famous senator or a rich CEO, I want to be able to say 'I knew him when.'"

"Oh, well, your kindness is help enough."

They would open their purses and start counting off hundreds: three, four, five, six. "Just a little something to get you started."

"Mrs. X, I couldn't possibly accept that."

They'd stuff the bills into his hand. "Let's just say it's for the wine, then."

Orson would offer them a rueful look, fold the bills, and wedge them in his pocket. "This is really generous of you," he'd say.

"Oh, it's nothing," they'd say. "When you've become successful, this will be chump change to you."

Emboldened by their tipsiness, the women would open their arms for a hug, which Orson would reciprocate, hugging them for as long as they wanted (typically a few seconds too long), and then allowing them to hold him at arm's length and look him in the eyes.

"You really are something special, Mr. Ortman," they'd say, their own eyes wine glazed. "If you need any favors in this life—I mean *anything* whatso*ever*—you just call me up."

Sometimes they gave him a printed business card, sometimes they put their contact information in his phone, and sometimes (the best times), they gave him another hundred or two. On an average wine night, we came away with anywhere between $500 and $900.

There were, of course, the marks who couldn't be manipulated. There was a woman in her late fifties, a self-proclaimed oenophile who tasted the wine, wrinkled her nose, and asked if it was a "cheaper vintage recorked." The conversation after that had been stilted, awkward, and Orson had left her room without a tip. Then there were the women who wanted everything but wouldn't give up the money. A younger one with platinum blond hair, late thirties or early forties, flat out asked Orson to join her in bed for a grand total of $50. Another one tweaked his nipple and pretended that it had never happened, then got flustered when he got flustered and ordered him out of the room. Another one told him that she wanted to see him again every night for a month, and after that she told him she was in love with him and asked him to join her in escaping her possessive husband. On the night he was supposed to meet her on the front steps of the Boyd, ready to start a new life, he didn't show. She and her husband checked out early the next day and never came back.

Of the frequent flyers, the wealthiest were Carol and Dmitri Argyros. Dmitri was the CEO of Argyros Oil, a company whose net worth exceeded $64 billion. He'd made a name for himself as a young businessman in Greece, where he'd been an enthusiastic proponent of deregulation and energy derivatives. In America, he paid pro-fracking lobbyists to bribe senatorial blood suits to allow him to frack on Native land. He had been a close friend of Bushes Jr. and Sr., and it was at the end of Bush Jr.'s second term that he left his wife of thirty years for Carol Sneehan, the daughter of Mark Sneehan, lieutenant governor of Texas. Carol was twenty years Dmitri's junior, which put her in her early fifties around the time we met her at the Boyd.

Carol was not conservative with her money. She'd donated millions of dollars to a megachurch in Missouri whose pastor became ensnared in a sex scandal shortly thereafter. She'd funded the losing campaigns of a number of Libertarian congressmen. She'd invested in an energy drink company that had turned out to be an elaborate pyramid scheme. But none of these failed enterprises seemed to stick to her: she and Dmitri remained friends of prominent politicians and Wall Street conservatives, appeared at $25,000-a-plate galas and between the covers of *Forbes* and *Fortune*. Botox and what I could only guess was an extensive team of dieticians and personal trainers kept Carol looking young. Dmitri, on the other hand, looked every one of his seventy-two years.

Orson and I spoke often of "landing the Carol account." She'd already taken a shine to both of us, seeing me as a sort of pathetic younger brother to Orson's capable and handsome older one. She tipped us extra on top of Dmitri's flamboyant $400 or $500 tips, and whenever she'd pass through the lobby on her way to the Executive Lounge or the pool, she'd ask us both how our nights were going.

"Quite well, actually," I said on a night when Orson wasn't scheduled to work until after the cocktail hour. "How long are you in town?"

"Oh, we're around for another two weeks, dear. We own a penthouse a few blocks over but we sometimes stay here for a change of scenery. You know how boring it can get to be in one place for so long."

I nodded, though I didn't. "Have I told you about the wine?"

"No, I don't think so."

I leaned in and told her about the wine. She raised an eyebrow.

"Is that so?"

"And, Carol? I have to admit that he's been saving a bottle just for you."

That night, Orson got the call at the front desk. He went up to Carol and Dmitri's executive suite, where Dmitri was asleep in the next room.

"He's a heavy sleeper," Carol said almost immediately. As Orson recounted it later, she was looking at Orson like he was something to be devoured. "I promise he won't wake up."

Orson was taken aback: usually it took a ten-minute song and dance to plant the idea in the wives' heads that it would be all right to drink with him.

He sat, and they drank, and he ran through the script. An hour in, she asked him the question:

"Your story's so inspiring, Orson. Have you ever thought of becoming a motivational speaker?"

"I haven't," he said, genuinely surprised.

She smiled slyly at him. "My dear, people would absolutely *pay* to hear your story. They'll all want to know how they can be more like you."

"Like me?" He tried to feign humility. "I haven't done much more than become a receptionist at the Boyd."

"Well, perhaps. But you're on your way to great things. You've worked hard, Orson, and you're living the American dream. My father was a ranch hand's son and he grew up to become the lieutenant governor of Texas. That's your future, my dear."

Carol cut Orson a deal: she'd rent out the lobby conference room and provide him with an audience if he'd just come and tell his story.

"You can do it one night after you clock out, dearest. Just bring yourself—you can bring your little friend for support if you need to, of course—and tell us all what you've just told me. And maybe afterward take some questions. We'll all pitch in a hundred dollars each, just for you."

"A motivational speaker?" Orson asked me that night while we were lying spent and naked in bed. I ran my tongue over my top row of teeth, trying to dislodge a fibrous piece of lo mein. "She just wants me to tell the story of my life?"

"Your fictional life."

"Well, yeah, of course. But I mean—even if it's fiction, it's not the most notable story."

I put my head on his chest again. "Yeah, it is. It's the kind of story they like, remember? The hard work and stick-to-itiveness thing. That's the Republican wet dream."

"But I haven't made my fortune or whatever. I'm at the beginning part of the stick-to-it-iveness. It doesn't feel like the kind of thing I can pull off."

I traced his left nipple. "Maybe you could make your fortune at the talk. Maybe you could sell them snake oil."

He laughed.

"No, I'm serious. Like, they love these televangelists, you know? You could be, like, a businessman-televangelist."

He exhaled. "I guess I could perform some kind of miracle. I could make them happier in their marriages or something."

I nodded, tracing his right nipple. "Just walk in there being like 'I have the answers. I can make old women's lives better.'"

"'I'm your conference room Jesus.'"

I don't think either of us realized what we'd stumbled upon.

FOUR

THERE WAS A BUFFET OF FRUIT AND CROISSANTS ON SEVERAL TRUNDLE CARTS in the back of the conference room at the Boyd, presided over by Pilar and Tori from housekeeping, both of whom hated me and Orson because we'd disrupted their nightly routine for what Carol was calling Orson's "Secret to Happiness Seminar." Pilar and Tori had also been tasked with bringing several ice-filled steel tubs loaded with beer, hard lemonade, and purified water down from the Executive Lounge. These tubs were to serve as the open bar, though the women Carol had rounded up for the seminar were all similar to her—early-to-late middle age, trim, impeccably made-up—and would likely not have wanted to waste their calorie count for the day on a can of hard lemonade. Pilar and Tori had to dig into the ice for bottles of Fiji water and hand them out with no hope of receiving tips. When I turned to them with an apologetic look, Tori ignored me and Pilar glared.

Orson was wearing a bespoke suit Carol had bought him for the occasion—*You have to look your best, dear, so get something tailored and I'll pay for it*—and he and I had come up with a set of talking points: his God-fearing father; his saintly mother; his hardscrabble childhood in the fields of Nebraska; his brother's cerebral palsy; his passion for economics and the law; his love of the free-market economy; his mentorship of me, a former teenage delinquent. He was going to focus on the Secret to Happiness as he understood it, which was to "work hard and pray hard," and then offer a few Tenets to Live By: 1) love the one you're with; 2) don't stray from God's path; and 3) keep your eyes on your prize. He'd rehearsed the speech for me, and even though I could detect an undercurrent of nervousness it had been suitably hypnotic: it was difficult to look away from him when he spoke, and it was even more difficult not to believe what he was saying. I felt like I was listening to a real young Republican.

I sat in the front row, between Carol and Julia Warwick, the wife of a jowly philanthropist whose antisemitism was an open secret.

"Your friend is the genuine article," Carol said to me, and then smiled pleasantly at Julia Warwick. "You won't regret coming to hear him speak," she said.

"If he sounds anything like he looks, I won't regret anything," Julia Warwick purred, and Carol laughed, so I did, too.

Orson was standing behind a podium at the front of the room, shuffling a stack of index cards on which I'd scrupulously written nearly every word he planned to say. I winked at him. He smiled tentatively and winked back. Then he turned to survey the room. He was thinking about them now, not about me.

"Ladies," Orson said, and the murmuring in the room dropped a note before stopping altogether. "Thank you for coming today. And a special thank-you to Carol Argyros for organizing this event."

"My pleasure!" Carol called, and swiveled to beam at the other women in the room. "The genuine article!" she crowed.

"Thank you, Carol." Orson knit his brows, thinking. "I've had a difficult life, ladies, which makes me all the luckier for being able to stand in front of you today.

"You could say I've lived many lives. I've been a son, a brother, a student, a mentor." Here he gestured to me, and I bowed my head reverentially. "By the grace of God, I've had the privilege of being able to lift people out of difficult circumstances and set them on the right path. I've loved and I've lost, and I've done it all in the span of a couple decades. My friend Ezra, you could argue he's had it more difficult than I have."

I nodded. I could feel every set of eyes in the room on me.

"Ezra, tell me: What was the most difficult moment in your life?"

"I sold heroin to a boy younger than me," I said. "And he later nearly overdosed."

Gasps.

"Ezra, what helped you back?"

"You did, Orson. And God."

He had found me in a homeless shelter when he'd first moved to the city from Nebraska, he said, and I'd reminded him of his brother with cerebral palsy, so he'd decided to mentor me. He'd helped me off drugs, we'd gone to college, and then we'd come back to take jobs at the Boyd.

"I worked hard, ladies, and I prayed hard. And Ezra and I made it out of danger's way."

A round of applause—the first of many. I saw Orson's smile brighten, his shoulders un-tense.

He spoke for nearly an hour and I watched the women around me pull their handkerchiefs from their Louis Vuitton purses and dab at the corners of their eyes or knit their hands into impassioned fists in their laps. Then I watched Orson, his eyes bright and his limbs fluid, pacing back and forth at the front of the conference room, captivating even Pilar and Tori, who had cracked open bottles of Fiji water for themselves. It seemed as if he were the only source of light in the room, as if we'd all be left in darkness were he to stop speaking.

"Ladies," he said. "I've been working on a way to share my happiness with you. I know we're just in a conference room in a hotel, but I think this can still be a very spiritual place."

He was going off book. I tried to make eye contact with him, but he was turned away from me.

"Can I have a volunteer?" he asked, pulling an empty chair from the front row.

The room exploded with chatter, the women looking among themselves for someone willing to volunteer. Carol moved to the edge of her seat: I could tell that she, like me, had not been expecting this. When no one emerged after thirty seconds, she stood up.

"I'd be happy to volunteer, Orson," she said, to good-humored applause from her friends. "Just promise not to send me into some kind of *state*."

Laughter. Orson joined in.

He gave her his hand as though he were helping her out of a horse-drawn carriage and she joined him at the front of the room. "You all know and love Carol, don't you?"

A chorus of *yes*es.

"And you know that Carol, despite seeming superhuman with all the loving and caring she does for us and Dmitri, is only human."

Another chorus.

Carol sat down. Orson stood behind her. "I'm going to place my fingers at your temples, Carol. And I want you to just focus on my fingers, nothing else."

The room was completely silent. I wondered, half in panic and half in curiosity, what the fuck he was doing.

"Carol, this is a process called Synthesis. It's meant to cleanse you of all the things in your body and mind that trouble you. I will take these things out and put them between my hands through the power of prayer."

I watched as Carol submitted herself completely to him, leaning her head back, closing her eyes. Orson closed his. The plan the entire time had been to make them feel titillated, playing on their attraction to Orson without pointing it out directly, but this was something else entirely. Something we hadn't discussed before.

"Okay, Carol, I want you to exhale slowly. You're going to feel a little pressure in your head. Your frontal cortex is going to light up with spiritual energy. God is capable of stimulating the brain in this way."

Carol exhaled slowly.

"Say something you're afraid of, Carol."

"I'm afraid that Dmitri will get bored of me. I'm afraid that he's already gotten bored of me."

It was a stunning admission, especially in front of all her rich friends with all their socialite niceties. She was breathing deeply, Orson breathing in unison with her. "Say something else," he said, his voice's cadence similar to hers. "Say something that scares you."

"I'm afraid that Dmitri is having an affair with one of the help."

Then I saw Orson increase the pressure at the sides of Carol's head and she appeared to jump as though a bolt of electricity were traveling the length of her body. The women gasped again.

"Carol," Orson said.

Tears had formed at the corners of Carol's eyes.

"Listen to me," Orson said softly.

Carol nodded.

"Do you feel the pressure leaving your brain? Do you feel your fears leaving your amygdala and your reason returning? Do you feel God in your body?"

Carol nodded again. Tears trailed down her cheeks.

"Relax your shoulders, Carol. There is a darkness in you that I'm extracting. You're having fears that you don't need to have."

"I can feel it," Carol mewled. "My God, I can feel it!"

"Bliss is knocking on the door of your mind, Carol. Open the door. Let it in." Orson opened his eyes. "What are you scared of now?"

"Nothing!"

"Open your eyes."

Carol opened her eyes and leaned forward and gasped and sighed, and the air in the room became dense with applause.

"Synthesis brings your body and mind together," Orson said over the applause, his hand between Carol's shoulders. "The darkness leaves your body. It restores you to sanity."

I wanted to be mad—he'd done something totally unprecedented, something we hadn't discussed—but my own vision was thick with tears. How did he always get away with these incredible things? How did he fool even me?

"What *was* that?" I asked him on the train on the way home. He was inspecting the check Carol had given him for $3,000.

He shrugged and smiled at me. "Something I thought up at the last minute."

"I . . ." I didn't know what to say. I looked out the train's window at the city lights blinking past us and then looked back at him. "It was amazing."

"It's hypnosis. I watched some YouTube videos about it. The power of suggestion."

"But it could become something bigger." The lights appeared to be blinking faster. "It could be, like, the thing you're known for."

"It could," he said dreamily, and leaned back against the window. I leaned with him, feeling the night's chill at the back of my head.

"I love you," I said under my breath.

"What was that?"

"That was incredible," I said, louder. "That was really incredible."

§

Carol was a changed woman. She told Orson she was no longer worried about her husband's loyalty. And better, even: she had renewed energy for her philanthropic projects. She was going to build a Christian girl's school in Zambia. She was going to invest in a clinic in the city where obese children could lose weight. She had never felt so light or happy in her life.

"I'm having a Women of Industry luncheon at our penthouse," she told Orson. "You have to come and do the talk again. They're going to love it."

Carol and Dmitri lived in a building in the city called the Bassetter, named for an English lord who had been a loyalist to King George III. Their penthouse, like the Boyd, was marble-floored but statelier in its decorations: Carol was a collector of ancient artifacts from what she broadly referred to as "indigenous cultures," so there were wooden masks and drums with leather skins along with the crystal chandeliers and porcelain vases. The Argyroses had the entire floor to themselves, and I found myself squinting to make out the flint-headed spears and oil paintings at the farthest edges of the room.

We arrived early on the day of the second seminar. Carol wore a white pantsuit with black earrings, the overly simple uniform of the very rich.

"Boys!" she said. "You're just in time for lunch! We're having rabbit."

"I can't say I've ever had rabbit before," Orson said. "Have you, Ezra?"

"No," I said. "I can't say I have, either." I was telling the truth.

Carol led us into a dining room with a monastery-length table and black-aproned women lining the wall. She sat at the head and we sat on either side of her.

"I was just telling my friend Susan Lehigh about you two," Carol beamed. Three of the black-aproned women poured water into the cut crystal glasses in front of us and then retreated to their posts at the edge of the room. "You know Lehigh? The clothing brand?"

"Yes," I said, maybe too quickly. "I've been in a Lehigh Outfittery before."

Carol nodded vigorously. "Yes, very chic, very clean lines. I own a number of her pieces. She's a hard worker, Susan, and very troubled. She's had a very troubled life—being a CEO isn't easy on her. I thought maybe she'd be the perfect candidate for Synthesis."

Orson nodded thoughtfully. "She certainly sounds like she needs it."

"Yes!" Carol beamed at us. "Aren't you two such the dynamic duo. Batman and Robin, or Butch Cassidy and the Sundance Kid. Oh, I know—Robin Hood and Little John!"

I choked on my water and pounded my chest.

"Are you all right?" Carol asked.

"It's common," Orson said before I could speak. "He has this tracheal defect that causes him to choke sometimes. He couldn't get the required surgery when he was a kid."

Carol's face went soft. "Poor thing."

"I'm fine!" I gasped. "Really, I'm fine."

"He's fine," Orson echoed confidently.

We barely had a chance to finish our rabbit—which was gamey and bony and reminded me too much of its living form—before the women started trickling in. They were more patrician than the crowd at the Boyd had been, more Botoxed than Carol and without jewelry and husbands, all carrying handbags so expensive they didn't even have designer labels. One by one they handed their coats to one of the black-aproned women and sat down in the living room, where the overstuffed couches and chairs were grouped in a semicircle around a wooden chair for the to-be-Synthesized.

When Susan Lehigh walked in, I knew her before Carol announced her. She was brittle looking, thin in a way that was obviously unintentional but worked well for her image. Her hair was cut in a chin-length bob and dyed jet-black, so she looked like she was wearing the helmet of a Goth gladiator. She wore sunglasses, insisting that she couldn't take them off because she'd just had cataract surgery.

"I'm going to go blind in the next ten years, I can feel it," she said.

I ground my teeth. The sentence sounded like a fork scraping against the surface of a plate.

"Nonsense," Carol said dismissively. "You're in a bad mood, that's all. Just meet the boys."

Susan Lehigh shook Orson's hand tepidly. "I hear great things about you," she said.

"All lies, I'm sure." Orson smiled.

Susan Lehigh didn't laugh. She turned to me. "And who are you?"

"Ezra Green," I said, offering my hand to shake. She took it.

"Ezra," she murmured. "You look so sweet."

"Bittersweet," I said. "Semisweet at best."

She didn't laugh at this, either, just cast a weak smile from Orson to me to Orson again. "So looking forward to your show," she drawled.

I pulled Orson into the massive kitchen, where we found a place at a flour-covered table well out of earshot of the kitchen staff.

"Does she seem a little strange?" I asked.

"Who?" Orson began drawing patterns in the flour.

"Susan Lehigh."

He looked up at me. "Yes. Definitely."

"She seems suspicious, doesn't she?"

"Of what? Of us?"

I nodded.

"That doesn't matter," he said. "We'll make her into a true believer. And if we can't, then it's not our problem."

"Isn't it kind of our problem?"

But he'd already stood up and was pouring himself a glass of water from the sink. "Ez, relax. Seriously."

In the living room, Orson held court: "Ladies, welcome. Carol tells me that you are some of the most powerful women she knows. CEOs, investors. You've shattered the glass ceiling."

"I'm jealous of them all!" Carol said, her hands on her knees like a delighted child. "If only I had their business acumen!"

I surveyed the room: everyone was rapt except for Susan Lehigh, who was standing at the back of the audience, checking her watch. Each second she spent looking at the watch's face, I became increasingly sick to my stomach, nervous for Orson, angry at Carol.

Orson went through his speech, I talked about dealing heroin, the women in the living room gasped and sighed and interrupted Orson to ask questions about his noble and beautiful life. And then it came time for the Synthesis, and Carol craned her neck toward Susan Lehigh.

"Susan! We've been waiting for you," she said.

"Oh no, I couldn't," Susan Lehigh said, wrinkling her nose under her sunglasses.

Carol and the other women tried to encourage her, asking her to be Orson's guinea pig, to try something new for a change. And where a normal person would have given in, Susan held fast.

"I'd really rather not," she said severely.

So Orson Synthesized another woman, an investor in a startup Carol had also invested in, and the woman cried and shivered and the room erupted in applause. And afterward Carol invited us all into the dining room, where her chef had prepared a buffet of various meats and vegetables and fruits and cheeses. I bummed Orson's lighter and a cigarette and went out to smoke on the balcony overlooking the city. It was night and the streets were yellow-orange under the streetlights, the people on them doll-like. I leaned on the guardrail and blew curls of smoke into the air ahead of me, imagining them floating over the city like cumulus clouds. I turned around and saw Susan Lehigh closing the sliding glass door behind her, a cigarette of her own between her fingers. She leaned on the guardrail next to me.

"Do you mind giving me a light?" she asked. She was still wearing her sunglasses.

I lit her cigarette and she puffed on it with the assuredness of a lifelong smoker, turning to survey the city. "Pretty at night, isn't it, Ezra?"

I nodded, remembering that I was supposed to have grown up on the streets. "I'm used to seeing it from the alleys."

"Mm," she said, and took another drag. "What a nice change of pace for you."

"It really is," I said, feeling somehow like I was defending myself. "It's incredible, the world Orson opened up for me."

She looked at me. "I know about you and Orson, Ezra."

"What do you know, Ms. Lehigh?"

"You haven't touched heroin. And he hasn't lived that noble Nebraskan life. It's obvious, don't you think?"

I swallowed.

"You're flim-flam men," she said. "Con men."

Adrenaline pricked beneath my skin. "I'm sorry you feel that way," I said. It was a stupid thing to say. "It makes me sad we gave you that impression, because we're really not." I was babbling.

She laughed. "Relax, I'm not going to expose you or whatever it is you're worried about. I think you're both very smart. I admire what you do." She tucked a length of hair behind her ear. "You know your audience, you know their weaknesses, and you exploit them brilliantly. I'm not at all different from you, Ezra. I know people want to look good. They want to conceal their flaws, and I design clothes that do just that for people of both genders and everything in between. And I sell those clothes at prices that are quintuple the manufacturing price. And it has become a sign of sophistication and wealth and importance to own my clothes."

I nodded, panicked, and trained my gaze back over the guardrail.

"You and Orson know very well how capitalism works, and so do I." She shook her head. "That Synthesis thing. An incredible act."

"He does it through his faith," I stuttered.

She smiled. "Of course he does." She lay a hand on my cheek and I winced in anticipation of a slap. "Still so young," she said, and took her hand away. Then she ashed her cigarette on the guardrail and went back inside, leaving me standing alone on the balcony, the noise of the city impossibly far away.

PART II

FIVE

UNLIKE MANY OF THE OPHTHALMOLOGISTS I'D DEALT WITH, DR. MENGETSU didn't wear glasses. When she first looked me in the eyes, I registered a brief flash of shock. Then she looked away, consulting a clipboard.

"What are we working with, Ezra?" she said, making some inscrutable notes. She was tall and long-necked, supposedly one of the best at what she did in New York.

I knew the exact measurements of my malady by heart. "Twenty/one-twenty, farsighted, astigmatism in both eyes. Range of vision between one and ten feet."

She nodded. "So without the glasses you can't see anything closer than a foot?"

"Or farther than ten," I said, annoyed at having to repeat myself. "I have bifocals integrated into the lenses for the close-up stuff."

"Mm," she said, pitiless. "You've had vision like this all your life?"

Vision like this. "Yeah."

"No accidents? No degenerative diseases?"

I found myself longing for the careful phrasing past ophthalmologists had employed with me. *It's not so bad* and *We can get you seeing the chalkboard again*. I used to hate the condescension, but it was better than this. "None," I grunted.

She looked me in the eyes again and I fought the desire to look away. "It might be that your vision is getting progressively worse, Ezra," she said. "You've got a slight squint right now."

I relaxed my eyes only for Dr. Mengetsu's features to blur at their edges. "I can actually see pretty well right now."

"Okay," she said, as though I had told her I could shapeshift. "Let's get you over to the Phoropter and we can take a look."

I pressed my eyes into the owlish machine and listened to the progressive clicks as Dr. Mengetsu adjusted its lenses to accommodate my vision. I read *T Q R S*. I read *S I F*. I read *L Z*. I read the *E*, the friendliest letter on the chart.

"Is this better or worse?" she asked, adjusting the strength of a prism in my left eye.

"Better," I said.

"Is this better or worse?" A new pair of convex lenses clicked over both eyes.

"Better," I said.

Dr. Mengetsu made an absent *mhm* noise. I was giving the wrong answers.

I kept looking at the *E* and listened to her making notes on her clipboard. Then we continued the process: better, worse, better, worse, worse, better. She lifted the Phoropter up and took a step back. I put my glasses on and she snapped into focus.

"You're at twenty/one-fifty," she said. "Your vision is getting progressively worse."

I felt dizzy. "Why?" I knew it was the wrong question.

"There are a lot of reasons." She flipped the lights back on and I blinked, accustomed to the darkness. "This has been happening all your life, hasn't it?"

I shrugged uneasily.

"You have weak eyes, Ezra. It makes sense that as you age, your astigmatism would worsen. It happens to a lot of people, but in your case, it's magnified by the hyperopia."

"Can you stop it?"

"I can't, but you can." She smiled for the first time since we'd met. "Have you considered a screen reader? Mobility aids?"

Screen readers and mobility aids were for the blind. "I haven't, really."

"Those kinds of things can take the strain off your eyes. And you might end up needing them down the line anyway." She made a last note on her clipboard. "Give it some thought."

I got on the train and rode it farther downtown, adjusting my tie, watching the tunnel walls flash past me and trying to gauge how difficult it was to see them. The other passengers in the train car were all perfectly visible: an elderly woman reading a copy of the *Post*, two teenage girls laughing over an iPhone, a group of men in undershirts and work boots likely riding to a construction site. Wearing a suit was difficult in the high heat of July; I took my jacket off to unbutton my cuffs and roll them up. I felt weak, and no one would want to buy anything from a weak-looking person.

But I forgot that when I walked through the doors of Chalice House and saw Orson's face. He was sunlit, in a vase-shaped frame created by the shoulders of the two venture capitalists he was sitting with, the hairs on the backs of whose necks were probably prickling in response to whatever he was saying to them. When he saw me he waved, and I smiled and waved back, and it felt for a moment like he and I were meeting each other for lunch in the middle of a chaotic workday, ordering the most expensive things on the menu because we deserved them, playing footsie under the table.

"Ez!" he gestured me over. "Welcome! This is Steven and Loren."

Steven and Loren stood for me and offered small bows. Orson was smiling suavely at all of us. "This is Ezra Green, my business partner."

"We've already heard so much," said Loren, offering his hand to shake. His nose was disarmingly child-sized and his face was round and glassy like a clock's. Steven, whose eyebrow overgrowth made him look distinguished in an unappetizing way, nodded in agreement. I shook both their hands.

"The way Orson talks about you, you'd think one of these big tech companies was about ready to poach you," Steven said, clearly testing me.

"I'd never let myself be poached," I said. "Never in a million years."

Steven nodded with satisfaction. We all sat down.

"So, we've all been waiting for you, Ez, for the big unveiling." Orson drew his briefcase into his lap.

"Now, this is your technology, Ezra?" Loren asked.

"Ours," I said. "Orson designed the prototype and I developed it. He owns the patent."

"You're modest," Orson said. "You did most of the work."

He clicked open the briefcase and withdrew the Bliss-Mini, which was designed to look like the sort of headset worn by telemarketers, with an arm that wrapped around the back of the head and ended in a magnet, an earpiece containing a magnet, and an arm extending to the base of the chin that ended in a microphone. When worn, the magnets of the Bliss-Mini sat just above either of the user's ears.

Orson held the device out to Steven and Loren and nodded. "Go ahead and try it," he said.

Loren lifted it from Orson's hands and fit it around his wide face.

"So I just say, what?"

"You say, 'begin,' " I said.

"And it does what?"

"It's a process called transcranial magnetic stimulation," Orson said. "It stimulates the nervous system in a way that induces the kind of reflective state only ever experienced by Daoshi."

Steven laughed. "How do you know that?"

"We measured their brainwaves," I said without hesitation. "At Stanford when a group of them came to visit. We found that Bliss-Mini wearers unlock all the mental agility and spiritual nullity that comes with Taoist meditation without the years and years of practice."

" 'Spiritual nullity?' "

"That's right," I said.

"Begin," Loren said, and the Bliss-Mini lit up red, then green. We watched Loren's eyes widen as he watched us.

"You should be feeling a complete nervous realignment," Orson said.

"The precursor to calm, which is the precursor to memory dissolution, where you lose track of everything that was preoccupying you prior to putting on the Bliss-Mini."

"What comes after memory dissolution?" Loren asked.

"Bliss," I said.

Loren rolled his eyes up to the ceiling and then back down to the table's surface and then closed them. He smiled, his thick cheeks dimpling, and when he opened his eyes again, they were cheerful half-moons. "I can feel it," he said.

Orson nodded enthusiastically. "It feels kind of strange at first, doesn't it?"

"Almost like a tingling sensation. But I'm feeling—"

"Clarity?" I asked.

"Yes," Loren said, incredulous, as though I'd somehow guessed his middle name. "Calm."

"Do you want to try it?" Orson asked Steven.

He shook his head. "I'm more of an observer."

"Nothing wrong with the sidelines," I said. I noticed then that Orson had ordered what looked like a cabernet for Steven, Loren, and me, that no one had touched. I poured myself a glass and took a sip.

Orson leaned forward on his elbows. "So you'll be at the demonstration tomorrow, I'm assuming?"

"Well, of course," Loren said, and looked at Steven for confirmation.

Steven sighed obligingly. "I'm interested to see how this works for multiple users," he said. "I'm selective about who gets my money, but as you boys know, I'm very founder-friendly."

"We have no objection to that," I said, and could feel Orson warming next to me. His excitement was irresistible. He got like this when everything was running smoothly, when we were building on each other and things kept getting bigger and better. It was hard not to want him to myself in those moments, to just sit back and behold him glowing with happiness.

We left them with two orders of lobster and descended into the subway, where Orson briefly grabbed my hand and squeezed it, too quick for any of the fledgling day traders to see.

"That was good," he said. "I think they liked us."

We were jostled in the car so I was flush against his profile, standing on my tiptoes. The angles of his body felt good against mine. "I think you're right," I whispered in his ear.

$

In the five years since we'd met Carol, we had been able to extract more and more money from her. We spent two years visiting her and her friends in the Bassetter and then at her penthouse in New York and mansion in L.A., Synthesizing them until they wept and had epiphanies, and Carol always insisted on paying us for our services. She paid us so well that we were able to quit our jobs at the Boyd. But Orson got restless again. I hated seeing him restless.

"What do you want?" I asked him as gently as possible one night, watching him play a game of chess against himself. "What can I give you?"

He snorted. "What can you *give* me?"

I blushed. "I mean, you've, you know, figured so much out. So I want to figure something out for you. I want you to feel—I want you to feel as happy as possible."

"Okay," he said, and castled his rooks. "Okay, well—I want Synthesis to be so much bigger."

I concealed a sigh. I was hoping for once it wouldn't be about work. "Bigger how?"

"We could do it for more than just Carol and her friends. Maybe we could, I don't know—make more money off it."

"Yeah," I said, my brain beginning to fire unbidden.

"Yeah what?"

"I can make that happen."

The key was to invent something purchasable that would make people think they were being Synthesized. To do that, I needed to make us look like maverick inventors. To do that, we needed to move to the cheapest possible apartment we could find in Palo Alto, start auditing graduate classes at Stanford, and pretend to be tech-aspirants. So we found a two-bedroom I called our "little Menlo Park."

In Palo Alto, we started to meet Stanford students, whom we hung out with and convinced that we, too, were Stanford students. To make this claim more believable, we asked professors if we could audit their engineering and biochemistry and physics courses, pretending to take notes in the back row but really jotting down our future plans: We had to build something sellable, but what? And who would we sell it to?

A professor in Orson's fluid mechanics class once asked him to demonstrate his knowledge of the continuity equation to the other students. At first, Orson deflected—he was just auditing, after all—but the professor insisted that "even auditors can contribute to the classroom environment." Orson stood from his seat and walked as slowly as he could to the chalkboard, the other students' eyes on him. He wrote the words "CONTINU-ITY EQUATION" on the board. And then his hand began trembling, and the chalk snapped between his thumb and forefinger. He dropped to the floor and did his best impression of a grand mal seizure. He remembered the professor standing over him, yelling his name, while the other students crowded around. Eventually someone thought to call campus security, but by the time they arrived Orson had recovered. Still, they wanted him to come with them to the student health center so he could remain under observation for the next few hours.

"I forgot to take my Lamictal, and when that happens any amount of stress can trigger a seizure," Orson said, and when the professor raised his eyebrow questioningly, he said, "I have epilepsy."

After that, the fluid mechanics professor never called on him again.

Among the friends we made in the Palo Alto bars was Mack Wang-Orsi, who was a grad student studying mood disorders and the human brain.

Mack, unlike many of Stanford's "work hard, play hard" types, didn't mind that Orson didn't drink, and would occasionally join him in a seltzer in between rounds. Orson had claimed to cut Coke out of his diet, declaring that the impurities of sugar and carbonate kept him from thinking clearly—and Mack seemed to endorse this idea, as well as a number of the other quirks Orson and I had learned to affect to make ourselves more appealing in Silicon Valley. Orson supposedly woke up at 5:00 every morning to meditate and then took micro naps throughout the day like Einstein. I told Mack I was on an all-protein diet, allowing myself carbs only when I was coding, and that I slept on the floor next to the six monitors I kept in my office in little Menlo Park. Mack was a self-described "sneakerhead," and claimed he had his best ideas when he was wearing his $400 Adidases.

Most importantly, Mack was a nihilist and a cynic. After a few nonseltzer rounds, we discovered he'd admit to anything.

"There's no real *reason* I'm studying brain chemicals," he told us one night, absently stirring his gin and tonic. "Honestly? You wanna know why?"

"Why?" Orson asked.

"I want a private practice in the Hills. I want to not accept insurance and just, like, write Xanax scrips for bored housewives."

"Cheers to bored housewives," I said, and Orson raised his glass, but Mack didn't. He was deep in thought.

"Everyone else here has some kind of, I don't know, like, schizophrenic sister or bipolar mother or uncle they lost to suicide and they decided to *find a cure* out of their *noblesse oblige*. Like, fuck being noble, you know?"

I nodded. I knew the feeling all too well.

"So why are you here?" Orson shouted over the music. "If you don't mind me asking?"

Mack laughed bitterly. "My parents. Typical first-gen shit. I pushed myself to succeed, got in, got here, felt like a complete fucking fool." He looked up from his stirring with a crooked smile. "But they're right about one thing: Stanford means money. I figure I mortgage my existence to this place for a few years, drag myself through classes here, and then I coast."

"It's a good plan," I said.

"I think the hard work's going to pay off," Orson said.

We talked our way into Mack's lab, where he showed us biofeedback machines and epidermal heat sensors and MRI scanners. He was investigating transcranial magnetic stimulation, which was essentially the use of magnets to cure depression. He joked that he wanted to strap the magnets to his own head, maybe stimulate some of his own deadbeat cells.

"So this is the magic bullet?" Orson asked, inspecting a pair of magnetic coils that looked like old-fashioned film reels stacked close together.

"Yeah," Mack said, switching the wad of gum he was chewing to the other side of his mouth. "You want to try it?"

Orson gamely strapped on the little cotton cap and sat back in what could have been a dentist's chair while Mack positioned the coils over his head, loudly smacking his gum the entire time.

"You're going to feel something," Mack said, smiling. "Or not."

"Hit me," Orson said.

The machine hummed and Orson closed his eyes.

"Does it take long?" I asked.

"It takes a little while," Mack said. "We do it for a lot longer on depressed patients."

Orson was silent, his eyes still closed. After what felt like far too long, Mack switched off the coils and Orson's eyes popped open.

"Damn," he breathed. "That shit really does work."

"You'll feel better and better," Mack said. "Something about electromagnetic induction."

The words "transcranial magnetic stimulation" sounded intelligent and the process was just obscure enough that we could impress outsiders with our knowledge of it. Orson had grown bored of the Palo Alto bars, so I took Mack out for two rounds of drinks and told him about Synthesis and that Orson and I wanted to develop a machine that could deliver what I called "portable intracranial bliss."

"So you want wearable magnets, you're saying?" Mack asked.

"Yes." I raised my finger for another round. "And we want some kind of user interface that alerts the wearer to the state or quality of their bliss."

"Right, right." He rubbed his cheeks vigorously, possibly concerned about having lost the feeling in them.

"If you could help us with a, um, convincing model? We can pay you."

Mack agreed, so we borrowed $600,000 from Carol and paid him to design the Bliss-Mini. When it came time to file the patent, I bought him more rounds of drinks—more than usual this time. It took him a while to get drunk, but when he did, he was nearly on the floor, sloppier than I'd ever seen him.

"Mack?"

He looked up from his phone with a noncommittal grunt.

"I wanted to talk to you about the prototype," I said. "Orson and I have been doing some research and—"

He grinned and slapped me on the shoulder. "The magnets I put on a stick?" he asked.

I widened my eyes in mock surprise.

"The portable transcranial magnetic stimulator," I said. "We're thinking of calling it the Bliss-Mini."

"Yeah." He looked back at his phone.

"We were thinking Orson might file the patent, since it was his concept."

Mack leaned in close to me. On his phone's screen was a picture of a woman in a body-con dress with blond hair extensions. The app wanted Mack to swipe right or left.

"What's it gonna be?" he asked me.

"Right," I said.

"So it is!" he shouted, and swiped right. It was a match.

"Congratulations," I said.

"This woman wants to fuck me." His eyes narrowed in an attempt to regain focus. "She wants to have *sex* with me."

"Mack, the Bliss-Mini—"

"Ez."

"Yes?"

"I'm *focused* right now. I have to figure out where this woman is."

"Okay, you can do that. But, you know—we need your blessing."

"Yeah," he said, squinting at his phone.

"Yeah what?"

"Yeah you can have my blessing. You can do the patent for the thing. It's a hassle to file a patent anyway."

I tried to suppress a smile. "Are you one hundred percent sure?"

He waved his hand at me. "Yes, yes, I'm sure. I got, like, almost a million dollars and you're getting—what?"

"A patent."

"Yeah." He snorted. "A fucking patent."

By 2014, Orson and I had landed in New York with the Bliss-Mini prototype and a fledgling company, NuLife, that promised consumers desperate for a new life the soothing effects of placebo technology. We would pitch NuLife to venture capitalists hungry to sink their money into a startup. Once we had enough seed capital, we would do a reverse merger with a useless shell company—one of those zombie operations too bankrupt to afford to close down—and then go public.

We held the Bliss-Mini demonstration in Carol's penthouse. When we arrived, she was flitting from one side of the room to the other, giving the help obscure orders ("Move the piano just a little more to the left. And lower the blinds another quarter inch"), periodically pausing to watch the movers we'd hired set up the screen Mack had designed to offer "readouts" of the Bliss-Mini's data. What it really did was produce a sine wave whose crests and valleys lengthened in response to any utterance of the words "begin now," proving only that Mack had mastered voice recognition technology.

"Boys!" she greeted us when we walked in. She pulled Orson into a hug, then me. "So wonderful to see you both! And to see you doing such big things."

Orson dipped into a half bow. "None of this would be possible without you, Carol."

"Really, Carol," I added.

"Oh, you both flatter me. You're the scientists behind this whole operation." She looked at me smilingly. "You've really come out of your shell, Ezra. You absolutely radiate confidence."

Now it was my turn to half bow. "By the grace of God," I said.

Slowly, the venture capitalists filed in. There were six besides Steven and Loren, all white, all male, all dressed in suits and wingtips. They shook hands with Carol and then with us and wandered to the opposite end of the room, where the help had arranged flutes of champagne on an end table. They helped themselves and surveyed the penthouse. They clearly liked what they saw.

"Gentlemen," Orson said, clasping his hands together. "Welcome, welcome, welcome." Everyone was immediately at attention.

"We'd love for you to take a seat," I said. "If you don't mind."

They milled to their seats, champagne in hand. Orson and I remained at the front of the room by the screen, Orson holding the Bliss-Mini.

"Gentlemen," he said. "How many of you want to be happy?"

Laughter, a few raised hands.

"Be honest."

A sea of raised hands.

"Good. I do, too. And so does my partner, Ezra Green. But the human brain isn't wired for happiness. It's wired to detect threats to our well-being and respond accordingly. As a result, we are fearful, angry, jealous creatures."

Carol was standing at the back. She was too far away for me to see the expression on her face. I squinted and then remembered that I shouldn't squint and so crossed my arms over my chest in a false demonstration of machismo.

"Enter the Bliss-Mini." Orson gestured to the complex-looking apparatus behind us. "With the advanced technology of transcranial magnetic stimulation, we have created a device that will allow the wearer to effectively 'reset' their brain. Using voice-pattern recognition, the device can detect the wearer's speech and respond with therapy tailored specifically to them."

A young-looking venture capitalist with a slight walleye raised his hand. "What's the therapy?"

"Patterns of stimulation," Orson said, not missing a beat. "Based on the cadence of the wearer's voice and skin temperature, the Bliss-Mini stimulates the brain in ways that are beneficial to them and them alone."

The room was silent. I couldn't tell if this silence was good or bad. Undeterred, Orson motioned for me to sit in the seat in front of the readout screen, where he attached the Bliss-Mini to my head and adhered a few meaningless wires to the skin below my ears, to the base of my neck, and to the top of my forehead. Then he switched on the screen behind me, which began to display an x-axis stretched and compressed into a series of jagged peaks and valleys.

"This is Ezra's brain activity without the help of the Bliss-Mini," Orson said. "He's experiencing what we call negative activity, which is when fear centers like the amygdala take over."

"Begin now," I said, and with those words my sine wave's peaks and dips became curves. The venture capitalists murmured among themselves.

"How do you feel, Ezra?" he asked.

"Calmer," I said. "Relaxed."

The venture capitalists wanted to try it for themselves: Orson magnetized their brains, watching them all say "begin now" and un-tense, generating aesthetically pleasing waves on the screen. To a one, they reported feeling calmer, able to think more clearly, soothed.

"This is cutting-edge technology made portable and practical," Orson said. "This is the future in your hands."

When we were finished, I watched Orson stand at the back of the room shaking hands, accepting invitations to dinners in members-only clubs in Manhattan. He was in his element. He was happy, and I was glad to have made him happy. He could ask me to jump and I'd jump as high as he wanted. Love is a great unlocker of potential.

§

It may be surprising to learn that a reverse merger is not a difficult thing to pull off. It happens in stages, and it happens quietly, and at the end you come away with a public company. It's better than going public the traditional way, which is like trying to put lipstick on a pig.

First: find the target. I spent hours looking up penny stocks online—defunct or near-defunct companies whose shares sold for a matter of pennies—trying to find the most ignored ones. There were whole forums dedicated to this sort of thing, where finance bros would "pump and dump" penny stocks by buying up millions of worthless shares and then letting people believe the company was about to "make an announcement," leading unsuspecting forum users to buy up shares themselves. By doing this, the conniving finance bro could raise the share price by five or ten cents and make a decent amount of money when he sold his million shares. This happened with all sorts of public zombie companies: Fielding Dishes, ASO Systems, MEGA Computers. For a few months, I lurked while Johnny and Timmy and Ricky pumped money into the penny stocks and then dumped them on the heads of other forum users. The cycle was endless and unfair but remained unbroken. I struggled to understand not only why people participated in this, but why finance bros always wanted to add y's to the ends of their names.

Eventually I found what I was looking for: RSO Diamond Corp., a company that no one was willing to touch simply because it sounded so absurd. A manufacturer of synthetic gemstones located in Alabama, RSO had gone bankrupt in 2003 when it defaulted on a large loan from a major bank. The remaining shell was now owned by the company's general counsel, Lenore Louis, Esq.

Second: meet the target. After the failure of RSO, Lenore had moved to the Santa Fe area, where she was, according to her website, pursuing a career of "spiritual advisement" to a local business owner named El Sable.

As it turned out, El Sable's business was a ranch, and the ranch was located in the desert several miles from Santa Fe. Orson and I had to rent a car to get there, Orson driving while I stuck my hand out the window to feel the dry desert air, the Neapolitan strata of rock formations and the sentinel-like cacti blurry in my vision and then briefly visible. Orson was looking from the road to me to the road, and then he ran his hand through my hair.

"Enjoying yourself?" he asked.

I nodded. *As long as I'm with you*, I wanted to add.

The El Sable ranch was massive, and Lenore, in a cowboy hat and skin that looked bronzed with dust, was standing at the front gate. She rapped a knuckle on Orson's window and he rolled it down.

"Howdy," she said in an unplaceable accent. "Hope you boys aren't trying to rob us out of house and home."

"We wouldn't dream of that, ma'am." Orson smiled. "We're just looking to take RSO off your hands."

Lenore hooted a laugh. "The garbagemen," she said. "Come all the way from New York to take my trash out."

As we walked toward El Sable's house, it became apparent that Lenore and El Sable were lovers and that they had been for many years.

"His vision is my vision," she said. "I believe in the work he's doing."

"And what work is that?" I asked, imagining that it must have been nice for them to grow old together.

But she didn't have to answer. As we came closer to El Sable's house, I could see a wooden pen in which an elephant was sleeping on its side, its skin sagging and creased. Peacocks wandered around it, their feathers folded like green wedding trains behind their backs. I looked at Orson, who was smiling as if he saw things like this all the time.

"Some beautiful animals you have here," he said.

Lenore nodded, gripping the fence. "That's Sleepy," she said, gesturing to the elephant. "We call him that because he's always sleeping, even when the birds peck at him."

"He's very majestic," I mustered.

"Sable's had him for ten years. Raised him up, so he's pretty attached to him. We used to breed them here. Now it's mostly the peacocks."

Inside, the house was decorated with the sort of clay statues and woven rugs I had seen at the airport. Lenore seemed very proud of the interior, giving us a tour that ended in the living room, where a man shaped like an upturned radish was reclining on the couch. A parallelogram of sunlight shone on him from the window above him, and his eyes were closed and his head tilted back in reception of its warmth.

"Sable," Lenore said, and the man opened his eyes. "The boys are here."

"The boys," El Sable huffed, and sat up so the sun shone directly in his eyes. "Sit down, won't you?"

Orson sat down on a couch that had been upholstered with images of Native men throwing spears. I followed suit.

"Lenore tells me you want to buy RSO."

Lenore sat down next to El Sable, her legs spread in perfect imitation of his. "It's trash," she said. "Our CEO lost everything."

Orson nodded. "We realize that RSO isn't—um—the most profitable company at the moment."

"It's trash," Lenore said again. "But it's our trash."

El Sable grunted in assent.

"I'll lay this out for you," Orson said. "We have a fledgling company called NuLife that aims to offer consumers exactly what's in its name—a new life. We use the power of something called Synthesis to reorganize the consumers' thoughts from the negative to the positive."

Lenore laughed. "Sounds like brainwashing, boys."

I shook my head. "No, it's not brainwashing at all. It's transcranial magnetic nerve stimulation."

El Sable nodded thoughtfully, then looked at Lenore, then ran his hand through his thinning hair. "It's high tech," he said. "We don't really do high tech out here. We're all about being close to the land."

I could see Orson's gears turning, searching for something to say. El Sable still hadn't moved out of his parallelogram of sunlight.

"Can I ask you something?" I said.

Lenore shifted forward inquisitively, as though we were playing a game of charades. "You can ask me anything, but I may not have an answer."

"How long has Sleepy been lethargic?"

"Since he was a baby," El Sable said. "We can barely get him to move. We think maybe it's a disease or a disorder or something, but of course we can't take him to a doctor because, well, if we try to find a doctor out here, Sleepy's going to get taken away from us."

"Mm," I said. "Can we see him up close?"

El Sable brought us out to the pen, Lenore and Orson keeping their distance from Sleepy as El Sable led me to him.

"This kind of nerve stimulation is reproduceable by the human hand," I said. "But only myself and my partner are trained to do it."

"Okay," El Sable said gruffly. "I have no idea what you're talking about, but it sounds smart."

"Can I touch Sleepy?"

"As long as you're careful. He's no spring chicken."

I stood at the top of Sleepy's head, above his ears, which fluttered in response to the flies collecting around him. His tusks were yellowish and his breath whinnied through the small spout of his mouth. I brought my hands to his head and felt the wisps of his hair, the toughness of his cracked skin. I prayed that what I was about to do would work.

"You might want to stand back," I said, and then proceeded to perform Synthesis on Sleepy: incantatory, loud-ish Synthesis.

"What's he doing?" I heard Lenore say to Orson.

"Synthesis," Orson said, clearly trying to stay upbeat through his anxiety. "He's a specialist."

I pressed my hands into Sleepy's unforgiving skin, and he stirred. I massaged his head, and he stirred some more. I Synthesized him for what must have been five or six minutes, and I could feel the moment having gone on too long . . . my spectators' attention stretched too thin. But then, miraculously, Sleepy rolled off his side, wagged his trunk, and stood up in a cloud of dust. He was massive above me, and I walked next to him as he lumbered around the pen.

"Goddamn," I heard El Sable say. "How did he do that?"

"The power of Synthesis," Orson said, barely able to conceal a sigh of satisfaction. "Imagine having that in the palm of your hand, in the comfort of your home. It's like magic."

Third step: merge. Lenore signed RSO over to us the following day, in a vegan café in town, bubbling the entire time about how she'd always wanted to be a healer but her parents had made her go to law school instead.

"Goddess's work," she said. "Sable and I are very lucky to be part of it."

We processed the paperwork and kept fundraising for a few sex-filled months. I waited for Orson to tell me he loved me but he never did: just turned flips in the middle of the room and flopped into bed and laid his head on my stomach and smoked cigarettes. It was fine, I told myself. I decided I wouldn't say "I love you," either. The words were unspoken between us.

Fourth step: go public. When NuLife debuted on the NYSE, we were sitting with Carol in her New York penthouse, watching the clouds above the skyline purple with an oncoming storm, Carol and I drinking champagne while Orson drank a seltzer.

"I always knew you two would turn into businessmen," Carol said. "I knew from the moment I met you at the Boyd."

"I think we've always been businessmen, in a way," Orson said. "Isn't that right, Ez?"

"Oh yes," I said. "We were born for it."

"How lovely." I lived for the vacancy behind Carol's eyes, the utter cluelessness. "I suppose you were, weren't you? Businessmen from birth."

We had at that point spent so much time with Carol that we didn't need to pay her compliments back, could just smile and nod and say "Thank you" or "We so appreciate all your help," could ask without hesitation for more and more money.

"It really does feel surreal," Orson said, taking a sip from his seltzer. "It seems like it was just seconds ago we were hauling your luggage."

"You always had heavy luggage, Carol," I said.

She laughed. "I have to bring all my suits with me wherever I go. I have to dress up to meet the future businessmen of America."

Just as it began to thunder, Dmitri Argyros limped into the room in a silk bathrobe, the liver spots on his head still visible in the compromised light. He was recovering from a recent stroke but refused to use a walker or a cane, so he was always a little off-balance, and his face was frozen in a permanent half grimace. Carol rushed to him, offering her arm for support. Dmitri looked at us in a way that could have been inquisitive or menacing— it was difficult to tell which.

"Mitri, dearest, you remember Orson and Ezra, don't you?"

Dmitri grunted, ignoring his wife. "Who are you?"

Orson stood and offered his hand. "Orson Ortman, sir," he said. "I think we may have met once or twice before, from across the room."

Dmitri didn't reciprocate the handshake. I stood up as well. "Ezra Green," I said. "Pleased to make your acquaintance."

Dmitri looked from us to Carol. "These are those boys with the fancy machine?"

"The Bliss-Mini," Carol said. "You remember."

He wheezed a laugh. "It's not possible to make magic like that. You can't make magic like that," he said. "Not if I can't."

He shifted more of his weight onto Carol's arm and began to shuffle forward, toward the kitchen. Carol cast us an apologetic look as they disappeared through the doorway.

"He's jealous," Orson whispered to me, and I felt his hand at the small of my back. "He's the dinosaur and we're the comet."

SIX

THE UNFAIRNESS OF THE HEALTHY EYE LIES IN ITS GLOBELIKE SMOOTHNESS, ITS agile perception, its chatty relationship with the optic nerve. A healthy eye is taken for granted—can be taken for granted—by the kind of person for whom the world appears unwarped and undisturbed. Undisturbing. I've seen thousands of people like this. They walk past me in the street and scan their periphery as they move, taking for granted the fact that they can see not only ahead of them but to their left and right, interpreting this information effortlessly, relying on absolutely nothing but their vision to move from point A to point B. Meanwhile I'm snatching brief and distorted snapshots of the murky steps down into the subway or I'm listening to the sounds of my feet, which are either accentuated by wood floors and pavement or dampened by rugs and grass. I want badly to be like them but it feels like there are tectonics happening in my eyes, like my retinas and corneas are constantly sliding into and out of place. Like my eyes themselves are shrinking and expanding: hyperopia, myopia. Everything is always in chaotic motion. All I want to do is see and I've been given junk.

I woke up on the morning of our first day in Vegas and couldn't see Orson next to me, which made me sit up like I'd been shocked with a cattle prod. I blinked at the impressionistic blur of the room, whisper-shouting Orson's name. I scrambled for my glasses and put them on to see him standing on the balcony in an open robe and boxers, leaning over the railing, smoking a cigarette. He was unshaven. He looked busy with thoughts that didn't include me. I stood and slid open the door and he jumped.

"This is early for you," he said.

"It's not that early for me," I protested. He was tense: his shoulders were nearly at his ears.

I leaned against him and he relaxed. He'd been looking at the pool, which had swarmed the night before with hard-bodied people around our age in bikinis and speedos, drinking Bloody Marys and congregating in small groups for the making of banal conversation and the exchange of phone numbers. I could hear them again this morning, laughing and splashing somewhere in the blur of my vision.

"It's weird how everyone's perfect looking," he said. "Like I always thought if you were a genius you weren't supposed to be hot."

"You're a genius and hot," I said.

He laughed and dragged on his cigarette. "I don't know about that."

"I do." I motioned for the cigarette and he gave it to me. I watched his eyes move effortlessly from me to the middle distance to the extreme distance and back to me again. His perfect vision didn't feel unfair. It felt right: a gift befitting a giver.

"We don't have to go down until dinner, I don't think," I said. "We can stay in bed all day."

I tried to give the cigarette back but he motioned it away. "Did I ever tell you I smoke because I don't know what to do with my hands?"

"I think you've said it once or twice before."

"I really don't know what to do with my hands. Like, put them in my pockets? That looks suspicious. Or perverted."

"It looks like Brad Pitt in *Thelma and Louise*."

He turned to me, an eyebrow raised, and laughed. "You noticed Brad Pitt in *Thelma and Louise*?"

"I mean, yeah. It was one of his early roles."

"Did you watch it for him?"

I shrugged. "He knew what to do with his hands."

He pulled me into a hug and kissed me on the top of my head. "You're so gay," he said.

True to form, we stayed in bed for the rest of the day. There wasn't a part of me his hands hadn't yet touched, but his touch still managed to surprise me: I shivered as he capably gripped my chest, my hips, my shoulders. When he came I felt it everywhere, even in my feet, nervous system haywire, spellbound by him. We collapsed next to each other and he breathed in my ear and then pulled at the lobe with his teeth—softly, never inflicting pain unless I asked, and I never asked—kissed me on the neck where it tickled, on my shoulders and elbows. I wasn't small then, or nearly blind, or whatever I was when I wasn't with him. I was someone new—I was his.

"Never stop," I told him. "Do this for as long as we live."

When we were finished, we roused ourselves for the 40 Under 40 Gala. He threaded his tie into a half Windsor while I watched him in the bathroom mirror, pretending to be busy un-messing my hair when really all I wanted was to see him compose himself, transition from a person who'd just had hours of sex to a person who could sit scrubbed clean and civil looking at a dinner table. He arranged himself in stages: the tie, the hair, the jacket. It was intoxicating.

"What is it, little dude?" he asked.

I shook my head and went into the bedroom to retrieve my own jacket, which I'd had tailored in secret imitation of his, from the shoulders of which I rubbed dust that hung in the air like a sleepy djinn. I slid my jacket on and held my shoulders back. I looked good, or at least good enough.

The gala was held in the hotel's ballroom, billed as a "celebration of America's best and brightest young people." It was supposedly a chance to network but it was really an opportunity to dick-measure intelligence and wealth, to drop the names of the schools we'd attended and the people we'd met. We'd gotten our invite after a short *Forbes* profile of NuLife called "Bliss for Beginners," which identified Orson as the maverick inventor of an "unlikely product" and me as his "front-end developer." The piece was more a profile of Orson than of NuLife, describing his angular jaw and his all-juice diet and his sleeping and running habits. He'd mentioned in-person

Synthesis a few times to the reporter, who'd quoted him as saying that it was the "Bliss-Mini on a cosmic level."

Orson had insisted on accepting the invites to the gala because there would be real money there, people who, even if we couldn't get them involved in NuLife, would at the very least provide object lessons in how to act rich and successful. It was more his kind of thing than mine, but who was I to object? It would be good for NuLife, and more important, it would be good for him.

At the ballroom's entrance he told me we should split up so each of us could cover more territory. "You just find people to socialize with, okay? And then back in the room we confab."

"Back in the room we confab," I said, dropping my voice in imitation of his.

He poked me in the ribs. I laughed.

"This is important," he said.

"Aye-aye."

He looked at me with mock severity.

"I mean, colonel—I'll do the best I can, sir," I said.

He went left and I went right, in the direction of a small circle of what turned out to be tall and toned women engaged in a very technical conversation about thermodynamics. When they saw me coming, they awkwardly opened the circle to welcome me in.

"You're the NuLife guy," one of them said, her upturned nose like an electrical socket in the middle of her face.

"Oh my god, yes. I knew I recognized you from somewhere," another said.

"I'm the CFO," I said in a guilty-as-charged voice. "And also sort of the COO. But your conversation honestly sounded much more interesting than anything I do."

"I doubt it," the one with the electrical socket nose said, and then offered her hand to shake. "I'm Amanda."

The other three in the circle made up some flimsy excuse to go get more drinks, leaving me and Amanda to talk.

"I'm really intrigued by the Bliss-Mini," she said. "I'm a physicist and I don't understand the first thing about behavioral science. I hope you're not offended, but it always seemed so—I don't know—woo-woo to me."

I laughed, wondering how I'd bullshit my way through this particular conversation. "It seems woo-woo to me, too," I said. "Honestly, Orson is the brains behind everything. I'm just the development guy."

"So he designed the Bliss-Mini and you, like—"

"Put it into practical application," I said. "Built it, market tested it, yeah."

Amanda nodded. I couldn't tell if she was impressed or bored. "I think it's so great what you two are doing," she said. "It's like a whole new frontier."

I wanted to shuffle my way out of the spotlight, so I asked about her research.

"Oh, it's nothing interesting, really. I'm just working on the atomization and reconstitution of tangibles."

"Wow," I said, nodding as if I, too, could reconstitute tangibles. "That's very impressive."

"Not exactly. Actually, can I ask you something?"

"Shoot."

She bent her head close to mine. "Is Orson single?"

"Single?"

"Oh my god, that was weird, wasn't it?"

I didn't say anything. I was still processing the question. The fact that someone had the gall to ask it. "Yes, he's single," I hissed finally. "He's basically a monk. He doesn't do relationships or sex."

"Of course, of course," she said. "I'm sorry. I shouldn't have asked that." Then she made the little-girl face women always make when they want to talk you into something. "Can I meet him?"

I tried to resist rolling my eyes. She was a person of potential power and influence. It was better for the whole operation if he met her. But it was better for me if she didn't.

"I don't know where he is," I said.

"I can help you find him," she said.

So we walked the ballroom in search of Orson, stopping on occasion to say hello to people Amanda knew from Harvard, where she'd apparently done her undergrad and was in the process of finishing her PhD. I was on the verge of telling her that he'd probably gone outside to smoke, which I knew would make him less appealing to her, when we found him sitting at one of the tables in a far corner of the room. He was talking to someone who looked familiar in an unsettling way, as if I'd seen her once in a dream and never again. He was leaning forward on his elbows and laughing, which he always did when he wanted to please someone.

As we got closer, I realized who she was: Emily Effham, dimpled, Barbie limbed, her face heart shaped. She'd recently played P. T. Barnum's mistress in *The Second-Greatest Show on Earth*, Oscar bait that had earned her a Best Supporting Actress nomination. She'd spent her adolescence as the bored older sister on the sitcom *Getting Even*, about two divorced divorce attorneys fighting for custody of their three children. I remembered her crossing her arms and rolling her eyes on the show, her T-shirts either midriff exposing or advertising some grindcore band the writers' room secretly liked. She was beautiful even then, and even I had a hard time looking away whenever *Getting Even* came on after school: there was something hypnotic about the symmetry of her features. Now, sitting at the table talking to Orson, her lips were parted in expectation, her eyes compassionate, the smallest wrinkle between her eyebrows. Amanda slowed her walk, clearly hesitant to interrupt their conversation. I cleared my throat.

"Orson," I said, and he turned.

"Ez! Have you met Emily? Emily, this is Ezra Green. He's my CFO."

Emily offered her hand to shake. I took it limply.

"This is Amanda," I said as though I were Orson's secretary. "She wanted to talk to you about something."

Amanda, whose face had soured with disappointment, mustered a smile and said, "I just wanted to say I think you're doing great work!" Then she did a mini-bow and hurried away. I sat down next to Orson, eyeing Emily eyeing him.

"Is that who you were talking to?" he asked, nodding in the direction Amanda had run.

I nodded. "She's a physicist."

"Well, Emily's an actress." He cheated his chair out to include her in our conversation. She beamed at me.

"I know," I said, and then added lamely: "I liked you in *Getting Even*."

She laughed, nothing like the demure giggle she'd had on TV. It sounded more like crow's feet in sand. "Wow, you're bringing back memories."

"Am I?"

"Um, yeah—" Another laugh, this one nervous. "Yeah, you are."

"Emily was just telling me about this tough divorce she's going through," Orson said.

"My ex-husband Brady—it's sad—he's . . ."

Orson looked at her encouragingly, like a therapist coaxing a confession from a client.

"He's addicted to meth," she said.

"I'm sorry to hear that," I said.

"It's very sad," Orson said.

The three of us sat in silence, Orson and Emily looking at each other and me looking at them both.

"Well," I said. "We should probably get to our table. It looks like dinner is going to start soon."

"Ez, this is our table." Orson gestured to the placard in front of me, on which my name had been printed in calligraphic lettering. "That's how Emily and I got to talking. She's sitting next to us."

"Call it serendipity," Emily said, grinning.

The dinner was interminably long. We talked about nothing—in other words, about the things Emily was interested in: saving endangered species, eating clean, navigating her Hollywood social circle. Orson listened and I ate, wondering how her voice could be both soothing and grating at once. Eventually it became easier to pretend she wasn't speaking at all and to just watch her mouth moving, to imagine it detached from her face and suspended in air. A mouth without a face was nothing. I could feel Orson warming with interest next to me, the way he'd warmed when I'd told him my boring life story at Last Chance. It was insane that he could find anything she was saying compelling. My hands went numb at the nightmarish thought that maybe this was just something he did, that he flitted from person to person with warm interest, abandoning the last for the next. But that was impossible. I had years of evidence to the contrary, proving that he was mine and I was his.

At the end of the dinner, Emily got out her phone and asked Orson to type in his number, which he did obligingly. When he'd done this, she looked over at me, an afterthought.

"Ez, did you want to give me your number too?"

"Orson can text it to you," I said.

"Great!" she said, clearly relieved, and we all stood. "It was so nice to meet you both." She kissed Orson on either cheek and then did the same to me, forcing us both to humor her stupid European affectation. "I'll be out at the pool later."

When we were back in the room, I squirmed out of my jacket and shirt and lay splayed on the bed, breathing heavily from the effort and waiting for Orson to descend on me. But he didn't—instead he sat on the edge of the bed and carefully untied his left shoe. I traced his spine with my bare foot.

"So are we going to confab?" I asked. "Amanda was really weird, but she went to Harvard, so if we see her by the pool again maybe we should meet her friends."

"Yeah," he said absently.

I sat up and watched him untie his right shoe. "What's wrong?"

"I don't know." He patted the bed with his hand. "There's something weird about this."

"About the bed?"

"No, no. About our whole thing where we stay in the same room and sleep in the same bed."

My hands went numb again. "What do you mean?"

"I mean, people might think we're sleeping together."

"We are."

He looked at me searchingly. "But is that professional?"

"Professional?"

He stood up and began to pace. "If we're, you know, supposed to be running a company, then maybe it's not the best thing if we're so—I don't know—if we're so out in the open all the time. Maybe we should try to be a little more discreet."

"Why, though? Who's keeping track?"

"People." His voice hardened. "Have you ever heard of the members of a board of executives fucking each other?"

"I'm sure it's happened."

"It *happening* isn't the same thing as it being okay."

"Really?"

"Lieutenant."

I sat up, scowling, but the look of regret on his face made me soften.

"Little dude," he said.

"What?"

"I'm not saying we'd stop anything. I'm just saying that maybe we'd try to keep it from being so obvious. People talk. People notice things."

I sighed and crossed my arms as if to hide the bloody heart I was now wearing outside my chest.

"And I'm not saying there's anything wrong with"—he gestured between us—"I'm just saying that now we've got to maintain this veneer of professionalism. We've got to make ourselves look like a team as opposed to a couple."

"Fine," I said. "If you think it's best." I thought about earlier that day, Orson lying next to me, tugging at my earlobe with his teeth.

"I think I'm going to go down to the pool. I might go for a swim," he said.

He knew I hated swimming. There was no way to wear glasses while swimming. This was a betrayal and therefore a cause for panic.

"Do you have to?" I asked, cringing at how whiny my voice sounded.

"Yeah, I think I should." He began unbuttoning his shirt, though not in a way that suggested sex. "I've got to meet more people anyway." He kissed me on the cheek. "Maybe stay in and watch TV? I won't be gone long."

So I stayed in and turned on the TV, worrying about him the entire time. What was he doing? What was he thinking? Who was he talking to? I was so consumed with thoughts of him half-naked turning flips into the pool while future world leaders looked on that I didn't realize I'd been watching the hotel information channel for fifteen minutes, a woman's sterile voice informing me over and over again that each room was equipped with an ice-making machine and a minibar. I turned the TV off, turned off the lights, and took off my glasses. Then I wedged myself under the tight-fitted covers of the bed, pulling the bedspread over my head.

In the third grade, I'd done a report on the blind mole rat. It had felt personal at the time, and it still did. I'd learned that the blind mole rat can live for more than thirty years and is native to East Africa. Their tunnel networks can be as long as six miles, they can run as fast backward as they can forward, and they almost never emerge from underground. They prefer the dark. They do not naturally select for beauty because they can't see each other. Their teeth are huge, shaped like chopsticks but with more structural integrity. They can bite through virtually anything, and this is how they dig their tunnels.

I'd been subterranean from my first day at Last Chance. I was better underground, anyway. I was in my element there. If the aboveground world didn't want me, then I'd one-up them: I'd find my own dominion and I'd rule over that place. I'd best them all at their dumb game, including Mengetsu. Seeing isn't believing. *Knowing* is believing. I knew that Orson was in love with me. I knew this about him as surely as I knew that I was in love with him. I was used to lying my head on his chest and listening to the blood churn into and out of his heart. I was used to feeling his lungs' expansion and compression. I knew him better than anyone knew him—better than his mother did. If the aboveground world was playing some kind of game with me, trying to trick him out of wanting me, then the aboveground world would lose. I would win. I knew this without question when he finally came back, slid the length of his chlorine-soaked body into bed next to mine. I would always win.

§

Emily's ex-husband, Brady Gifford, was the star of the *Pardner in Crime* franchise, in which he played a rogue cowboy-detective who was solving crimes for the FBI while simultaneously on the run from them. According to an interview he'd given in a two-year-old issue of *Vogue*, he'd met Emily at a party where she seemed to be the only "real" person.

VOGUE: So was it one of those love at first sight things? Like you saw her from across the room and just knew?

GIFFORD (laughs): Not quite. She actually came up to me and asked me point-blank if I was feeling as lonely as she was. It was this party in the Hills for someone neither of us had much to do with. We spent the rest of the night talking and—yeah, maybe that's when I knew.

VOGUE: You're fifteen years older than Emily. Has that age difference ever proved difficult for you two?

GIFFORD: No, actually. Emily's extremely mature for her age and I'm extremely immature for mine.

VOGUE: Sounds like a match made in heaven.

GIFFORD: You could say that.

I didn't read the rest of the interview because I had no interest in anything Brady had to say, only in what people had to say about him. I found headlines about him drunk and belligerent at clubs, asleep at the wheel of his Hummer on Sunset Boulevard, getting arrested in front of a tapas bar. He wasn't the picture of an addict: his torso was a muscular inverted triangle, his shoulders broad, his chin carpeted with a thick beard. The only things that betrayed his true state of affairs were his rangy hair and the graying whites of his eyes, which the telescoping lenses of the paparazzi captured nicely. He looked weirdly dignified being led into police cars, never sneering at the cameras, just keeping his eyes on his feet.

And then there were the pictures of Emily leaving her Hollywood mansion or her Brooklyn brownstone in sunglasses that bulged from her face, her sweatpants tucked into her boots, her mouth puckered with worry.

Emily Effham seen walking through Manhattan without Brady Gifford, looking stressed

Are Brady Gifford and Emily Effham finally calling it quits?

Emily Effham on her husband's drug problem: "No comment"

The divorce was nasty and highly publicized: Brady was draining Emily's fortune with lawyer fees, refusing to sign anything for months. He spent those months in his bathroom injecting meth and cocaine, overdosing twice. Emily admitted to *People* that she feared for his life and wanted more than anything for him to get help. I could tell she just wanted him well enough to sign the divorce papers.

Orson and Emily texted for several days after Vegas. He always texted her when he thought I wasn't looking—and I wasn't; he was out of my range of vision. But I could feel him go quiet. I could hear the pads of his fingers on his phone's screen.

Meanwhile, NuLife moved into a rhomboid office building in Manhattan, and it was in this rhombus that Orson and I spent most of our time building a company. We hired an accounting department, a marketing department, a sales department. We retained expensive counsel. We assembled an executive board, most of them hands-off venture capitalists with a few seats reserved for Carol and her friends. The three hands-on people on the board were Jack Delpy, a former broker with the talent to transition into management; Walter Renhauser, a Boston brahmin type who was fond of injecting cash into warm and promising corporate bodies; and Elaine Corman, who had been on the executive board of a textile manufacturer and wanted to enter what she called the "startup game." I'd handpicked all of them knowing what would attract Orson to each: Delpy's malleability, Renhauser's desperate need to be hip, Corman's slipperiness. I liked Corman especially. She wore her hair in rigid curtains at either side of her face, a cut that was almost defiant in how unflattering it was, and allowed her back to form a thirty-degree angle with her chair during our first in-person conversation, her hands in her lap, so it looked like she was about to bow to me as we spoke. She seemed bitter in a way that I recognized as originating from having once been poor, and that made me like her even more.

The final hire we made in New York was Brianna Voorhees, a recent Harvard MBA who would play the role of our executive assistant, basically a multipurpose secretary and legal liaison whose starting salary should have been $80K, but which I made $90K because she had adult braces and that endeared me to her. In her interview she'd talked about how much she wanted to impress her family with her business acumen after they'd lost their life savings trying to sell products for Amway.

"I'm smart enough to know what I want," she told me in the interview. "And I think I know what you want, too."

"What do we want?" I asked.

"Not to look stupid."

I laughed and recrossed my legs. She had me there.

At our first board meeting, Brianna sat at the end of the table taking notes, surrounded by executives. I sat at the head next to Orson, who stood, unfastening the button of his Versace suit jacket in a single smooth movement, making me twinge with arousal, and addressed everyone cheerfully:

"Friends, welcome. I'm calling you friends. Why am I calling you friends?"

Eager smiles and silence except for the sound of Brianna's fingertips on her laptop's keyboard.

"I'm calling you friends because NuLife is a family," he said. "Friends and family go together. It would be weird to call you all uncles, aunts, and cousins, wouldn't it?"

General laughter.

"Friends." He began to pace. "I am really, really honored that you all saw fit to jump aboard our ship. I want you all to know that. We had humble beginnings, and we've been very lucky to see a lot of growth in the past few months—exponential growth, if I'm being honest—and it's thanks to efforts like yours. Give yourselves a round of applause."

We all applauded, no one taking their eyes off Orson.

"Now, shall we start doing what we came here to do? Who's got thoughts for me? Who's got ideas?"

More silence. Delpy sat forward in his seat.

"Can I start by saying that I'm really grateful to be here?" he said. "Really just glad to be on board."

Renhauser rolled the irregular crenshaw of his head over his left shoulder to take in Delpy's eager face and then rolled it back toward Orson. "I'd like to second that," he said.

Elaine remained silently tilted at her thirty-degree angle.

"Accessibility," the marketing director said. "How do we sell the Bliss-Mini to people of all ages? Do we provide a mood-tracking app to bring in the health-obsessed millennial crowd?"

Orson screwed up his face. "Millennials are too broke to be health obsessed," he said. "Remember 2008?"

The marketing director shrank. "Right," he said.

"We haven't spoken about our projections for the international rollout," someone else said.

"That's because we're in the midst of the American rollout," Orson said. "I want us to be thinking about the *technology itself*. What's the next generation of the Bliss-Mini going to look like?"

"The next gen? Aren't we still focused on the first gen?"

Orson frowned and tilted his head from side to side, as if this person had actually made a salient counterpoint. "Yes. But we stay competitive by thinking ahead, don't we? That's kind of simple stuff to understand, isn't it?"

"I was actually just thinking," Elaine said. "I was thinking about Dexter Ellhorn."

Orson laughed. "The moon colony guy?"

"What about Dexter Ellhorn?" I asked.

Elaine smiled tersely. "He has a lot of visibility. With his company STARS especially, and it might be good for us to contract him to develop an, um, enhanced version of the Bliss-Mini. The next generation. Sleeker, more capabilities, that whole thing."

She looked at Orson, her face a tabula rasa.

"Dexter Ellhorn is an interesting idea," Orson said, visibly warming. "He has a ton of government contracts, doesn't he? Would we even register on his radar?"

"I can find out," Elaine said.

"If I could—" Brianna began, but Delpy made a shushing noise and she bit her lower lip.

"That'd be good, Elaine," Orson said.

I watched Delpy and Renhauser watch Elaine type a note to herself on her phone with her index finger. It was of course forbidden to ask her how old she was, but I put her at forty-eight.

After the meeting, in Orson's office, he and I sat across from each other with our feet on his desk. He seemed somehow longer limbed than usual, his face flush and radiant, and when I looked out the window behind him it was hard not to see him as part of the skyline, a colossus in his own right.

"She's smart," he said.

"Elaine?"

"Yeah."

"I'm glad you like her."

"*You're* the truly smart one, lieutenant." He slid his feet from the desk and sat up straight. "You know how to hire personnel."

I wanted to keep silent and bathe in his radiance but there was something tugging at the edge of my happiness. "The thing about Dexter Ellhorn, though? I mean, how would he update the Bliss-Mini technology?"

"What do you mean?"

"I mean." I looked around the room, suddenly self-conscious at the thought that we were being bugged. "It's not really technology in the first place, is it?"

Orson laughed and waved the idea away. "It doesn't matter," he said. "This isn't about the Bliss-Mini."

"But—well—but the whole thing about NuLife is we make the Bliss-Mini."

"Yeah, maybe for now. But I have plans for something bigger. I haven't even told you yet."

I swallowed. He was going rogue again. "Something bigger than a well-funded tech startup?"

He laughed; I laughed. It was impossible not to smile with him. "Yes. The Bliss-Mini is sort of the appetizer to the main course. It's some magnets in plastic, you know? Let Dexter Ellhorn pretty it up."

"What's the main course?"

He leaned in close and looked about to speak, but then he kissed me. It lasted just long enough for me to forget what we'd been talking about. When he sat back he whispered: "I'll tell you soon." Then he stood, and in the kind of voice he used when other people were listening, said: "I'm going to go visit marketing. Gotta course-correct for that shit in the meeting today."

I nodded and watched him leave the room. I crossed my legs in the chair and began speculating about the main course. While I was doing this, I heard his phone buzz at the far corner of his desk. I hadn't noticed he'd left it. I thought I could see Emily's name on the lock screen. Without thinking, I grabbed it, and when I was prompted to enter a password I typed in his mother's birthdate: 121656. It worked—I knew it would—and I opened the text app, where sure enough there was a new text from Emily: *hey how u doing??* She'd last texted him three weeks ago, when she'd written *that's funny* and he'd responded *glad you think so.* The thing she'd found funny was a GIF he'd sent of a dancing rabbit. I scrolled back up through their conversation: Emily often initiated but my heart sank to find that he did, too, more frequently than I would have liked. At least they talked about the same nothing they'd talked about in Vegas: Hollywood, split times, kale. Except sometimes Orson talked about NuLife in a way that sounded both hopeful and conspiratorial. It was nothing he hadn't said to our executives already, but the problem was he was saying it to *her*.

I deleted her new text without deleting the thread and then locked the phone. Why had I never done this before? Because I didn't want him to think I didn't trust him. I would always trust him—there was no doubt in my mind—but he was texting Emily, or had been, and that created a dilemma. Because of this dilemma I deserved a look at his phone. That much was fair. It was important to always be sane and fair. One day when we were married, we would show each other text threads and laugh at the pathetic people set on cracking the impenetrable shell we'd built around ourselves.

It had begun to rain and the skyline was gray and hazed with mist. I put my feet back up on his desk and folded my hands over my stomach and closed my eyes. The room, the rain, my shoes on the desk: everything felt good. Everything felt like money.

SEVEN

Orson's main course turned out to be hands-on Synthesis. He wanted face-to-face time with powerful people whom he could Synthesize out of their minds and become friends with. This would result in connections with even more powerful people, and this would result in the opportunity to make even more money.

"Think of it this way," he told me over Chinese in the condo I'd rented on the Upper West Side. "People get intrigued by the Bliss-Mini and then we promise them an experience a thousand times more powerful if they come see me in person. And who's got the money to come see me in person? Rich people."

"Right," I said. My mind was whirring again: I could actually feel my head getting hot.

"It's like the thing with Carol. One powerful person gets hooked, and then they tell their friends, and then eventually a lot of them are hooked. And we can have, I don't know—we can make it like a retreat. And have classes for them to take. Does that sound like something?"

He was sitting opposite me at the kitchen table. I wanted to take him to bed even though he was stuffing his cheeks with lo mein. He seemed totally unconscious of me looking at him, which made the situation even more irresistible.

"It definitely sounds like something."

"I knew you'd like it," he said. "You like stuff like this."

"I'll figure out the nitty-gritty," I said. I touched the tip of his foot with mine and he caught my foot between his and pulled. I nearly slid under the table. "Jesus Christ."

He laughed. "Figure it out," he said. "And I'll do you."

I lived for the moments when he wasn't preoccupied with the "being professional" bullshit. I couldn't have known those moments would be numbered.

So we needed a second headquarters. I decided it had to be something rustic, someplace people would describe as "close to the land." It had to feel like a retreat without all the sweat lodge and spa impedimenta. On a day Orson wanted to spend in the condo chain-smoking and reading the Tao Te Ching, I went into the office and found Elaine in front of her monitor, slowly clicking and scrolling with her mouse in a way that I found touchingly quaint. I knocked on her open door and she looked over her glasses at me, her face invitingly blank as always.

"Do you mind if we talk?"

She gestured to the chair in front of her desk. I closed the door and sat down.

"You're from upstate, right?" I asked.

"Utica."

"What's it like up there?"

She shrugged. "It's a lot of nothing."

"Did you ever get out to the Great Lakes?"

"Every summer. My parents had a house on Lake Ontario."

"Was it pretty up there?"

She made a *where is this going* face. "I mean, sure. As pretty as you'd expect it to be."

"How pretty could I expect it to be?"

"I don't know, Ez."

"Do you want to come to lunch?"

She looked from her screen to me as though the decision were difficult. "I could spare forty-five," she said.

We set out in the direction of Tribeca, Elaine's walk a considered plod. She was one of the few people I'd met whose stride I wasn't constantly scrambling to match. I ushered her into Sam's, a favorite deli of mine, where we were seated a considerable distance away from the window. It was understandable. Me with my bifocals and Elaine with her haircut and Danskos: we were a pathos-inducing couple, the kind of people who didn't really invite business.

I ordered a Reuben and she ordered a bowl of coleslaw. I folded my hands and smiled at her, trying to look the appealing salesman.

"We need to open a second headquarters," I said. "A place where people can come to get hands-on Synthesis."

"Hands-on Synthesis?"

"It's something Orson does—like a, you know, spiritual encounter. I can do it, too, just not as well as him."

"Okay." It was clear she didn't want or need to know more.

"This place has to be kind of classy. And it can be businesslike. But also spiritual."

She spread her hands on the table, inspecting her nails. "That's a lot of things for it to be."

"Can you scout locations with me? I need a New York native to come help me get the lay of the land."

"What would I get for it?"

I smiled. "How about a three-week paid vacation this winter? Around Christmastime?"

"I know some places that might be nice."

We were served our food. Elaine actually tucked her napkin into her shirt collar before eating. She didn't live like an executive. She commuted in a Honda Accord and wore a plastic poncho when it was raining and a beanie and knit gloves when it was cold. If I knew her better the situation would have been a Pygmalion one: I had been practicing dressing rich for almost five years, and it would have been my pleasure to take her someplace wealthy and woman-y where I could sit on a settee in front of a bunch of dressing rooms and tell her with brutal honesty which outfits she should wear and how she should do her makeup to go with each. She could get less rectangular glasses and get rid of the bangs. She would be a project I'd take on out of the kindness of my heart. I took a micro bite of the Reuben and chewed it on one side of my mouth like someone with rotten molars.

"How are your kids?" I asked.

"Good. Luca's turning seven and Georgie's ten."

"Seven and ten," I said knowingly, as though I had any experience with kids other than having once been one myself.

"Yep. Real handfuls."

We were sitting close enough that I could see a dusting of dandruff at the base of her part. I loved her way of being in the world, even if she dressed like a troll. I wanted to tell her that she was my favorite, but then there was a painful drumbeat behind both my eyes and she slid out of focus. The lights in the ceiling were haloed and extraterrestrial looking. I felt sick. I grabbed the edge of the table.

"Ez?" I heard her say.

I could feel that both my eyes were very wide open but I wasn't taking in any visual input. It was like my optic nerve had suffered an electrical surge. "Fuck," I whispered, praying she couldn't hear me.

"Ez," she said. "What's wrong?" There was real feeling in her voice, the first instance of it I'd detected from her since I'd met her.

I put my fingers to my temples and shook my head. "Nothing," I gasped. "I get headaches."

"This looks like a bad headache."

"I get migraines."

"Do you want to leave? Do you need a doctor?"

"No, no. Let's just—give me a minute, maybe?"

I could feel her tensing. I could feel other people looking at us. Miraculously, the drumbeat ceased and the kaleidoscope of the room collapsed back into focus. Among the things in focus was Elaine, who was looking at me worriedly.

"Is that normal?" she asked.

"Completely normal," I said, but I must have done a bad job of hiding how scared I was, because she put her hand on mine.

"Luca gets these whanging headaches," she said. "We give him Excedrin."

She squeezed and then withdrew her hand and I looked at my sandwich, somehow seeing in the marbled rye the untamed waves of Orson's hair. I took another bite.

§

Upstate New York was, like the city, a place that would be necessary but difficult for me to get used to. Elaine and I drove along the lakefront meeting various landowners and real estate agents. In the car, I did most of the talking, Elaine interrupting only to announce that we'd arrived at our destination. Once the New York State resident lumbered out of their clapboard shanty to meet us, I fell silent and she began talking. We were from a corporation called NuLife, she told them, and we wanted to set up a retreat. It was true enough, but she said it in such a clipped staccato that it sounded like a lie.

Orson gave me carte blanche to buy whatever I wanted, so we settled on twenty-five acres just outside of Oswego. We'd build a place that looked like a giant farmhouse but wasn't, and the lake—deep purple at night, glaucous blue in the day—would be in our backyard. I texted photos to Orson, in some of which Elaine posed next to massive pine trees or on the beach for scale.

looks hot af he wrote back. *the place i mean, not elaine.*

We broke ground on what Orson decided to call the Farm a few months later. I didn't question the name, though I suspected it had its origins in Last Chance, that naming a piece of his nascent empire the Farm would be Orson's ultimate middle finger to Sledge and Kimborough. I hired an architect to design the place, I paid the day laborers, I bribed the county to let us build what could be construed as a hotel on land that wasn't zoned for it. I brought Carol out to see the work in progress, told her that she was our inspiration, extracted more money from her.

"What will you boys think of next?" she mused as she cut the check. "I don't know how to keep up with you two."

"We just want to make the world a better place to live in," I said.

"Can I come stay when you're finished building?"

"You can be our very first guest. On the house."

When we'd finished building, Orson announced his intentions to head-quarter himself at the Farm, in the farmhouse. He told me that I would be the business liaison, handling things in the city and traveling to Oswego whenever I was needed. Which meant I wouldn't be spending every night with him.

"You're better at the business stuff, little dude," he told me. "I just have the ideas—you know how to implement them. That makes sense, right? If I just focus on the Synthesis part? You can run things in New York? You have my permission to do literally anything you want. Not that you need it."

I imagined this and the professionalism thing as a test of our love, a kind of Héloïse and Abelard situation. Absence makes the heart grow fonder. So he wanted to spend time apart—I could spend time apart. I could spend months apart, thinking about him, fantasizing about my head on his chest. I could buy things for him in New York and bring them to Oswego, things that matched his increasingly expensive tastes: shoes, cologne, an unreleased iPhone. And when we were in the same place, I'd cook him dinner like I had in little Menlo Park, all the meat-and-cheese stuff my mom and dad used to make that his body metabolized so fast he never seemed to have eaten it. There would be an end to the distance eventually, of course. I imagined a big wedding on a beach or a cliffside, all the people we knew in attendance, his mother crying, my parents sitting next to each other holding hands like they did during par-ticularly affecting movies. It would happen. He only had to say when.

$

Dexter Ellhorn had a lumpen face, a pinched nose, small blue eyes, and the feathery hair of a newborn. Like Mack Wang-Orsi, he was a sneakerhead, and he showed up to our New York office in a pair of velour Nikes and a style of tracksuit that had been made popular by a recently disgraced rapper.

"What's good?" he asked as I shook his hand, and then repeated the question to Elaine, Delpy, and Renhauser before we all sat down. The boardroom in which we were having the meeting was our smaller one—Elaine called it "intimate"—reserved for people who didn't want to be seen by average employees. We hadn't had to use it yet: Dexter was the first celebrity we'd had in our office.

"We're thrilled you were able to come out here to meet with us," I said. "We're huge admirers of your work."

Renhauser, who clearly sensed that this might be an opportunity for him to shine, straightened his posture. "The turbotrain you designed in Chicago is really incredible. My sister lives there, and she says she takes it from the suburbs to the Loop every day."

Dexter nodded with obvious false modesty. "Thank you. That's actually one of my favorite things I've done."

Renhauser sat back, pleased, like a grade school student who had guessed correctly on a test.

The door opened: Brianna attempting to look at least five years older in a boxy gray skirt and scoop-necked blouse. I'd spent very little time with her at that point. She'd mostly been an unobtrusive ghost at the ends of tables, recording everything that was being said, occasionally interjecting for clarification. Boldly, she sat down directly next to me and opened her laptop.

"Sorry—I'm running just a little late today," she said. I noticed that her desktop background was a picture of her and a big-chested older woman who must have been her mother. They stood with their arms around each other on a porch with graying eaves, a sick-looking dog at their feet.

"That's fine," I said, and turned back to Dexter. "If you don't mind, I think we're all ready to dive in."

Everyone nodded except Elaine and Brianna, who was busy typing.

"What did you think of the model we sent?" Delpy asked, his arms crossed over his thin chest.

"Really nice, definitely really nice." Dexter flicked a bit of lint from his shoulder. "It really has a calming effect."

"That's great!" Delpy said, arms coming uncrossed, and then looked at me for approval. I offered him none. "We're glad," he added, quieter.

"So basically what this thing does is it stimulates nerves in the brain to calm people down?" Dexter asked.

"And deliver them into a state of bliss," I said. "We call it Portable Intracranial Bliss."

"Mm," Dexter said, and tented his fingers. "So it kind of only has one function right now."

"One big function," Renhauser added defensively.

"One function," Elaine echoed.

"Right. Well, the first direction I'd go with this, honestly? Make it a multifunction product. I'd give it predictive abilities. Maybe tell the user a few different things about themselves they don't already know." He sighed thoughtfully, as though we were extremely lucky to be in his presence. "Not health stuff—there are tons of apps for that—but behavioral stuff. Like, 'What should I do on this day to make my life better?'"

"Wouldn't that be health stuff?" Delpy asked.

Dexter frowned. "Not necessarily. You've got this voice recognition technology, right? How about people speak to it and it speaks back?"

I felt Brianna tapping my shoulder, leaning in next to me.

"Ez, can I talk to you in the hall?"

The question was so unexpected, such an overstepping of bounds, that I didn't know what to say. "After the meeting," I told her, and watched her face fall.

We had legal draw up a contract for Dexter to sign and he hunched over it, pen nearly touching paper, and then looked up at me.

"I want a clause in here," he said. "That Orson has to do a photo shoot with me."

I shifted in my seat. "A photo shoot?"

"For Maskelyne and STARS. I'm developing drones for both companies, domestic and combat. I want the *New York Times* to do a profile about the two of us when this whole thing gets up and running. About this partnership."

"With Orson?" I didn't like the idea of Orson posing with drones. Or with Ellhorn, who seemed prematurely possessive of him.

"He's already a recognizable face in the tech world. Everyone's talking about him—you know that."

Of course I knew that. "I'll ask him."

Dexter shook his head. "Uh-uh. I need approval right now or else I'm not gonna sign."

I could feel the executives' eyes on my back. "Fine," I said. "I'll make it happen."

"Great!" He signed gamely: his signature was weirdly elegant, the outline of a *D* encircled by an arc that suggested a planetary orbit. "This is going to be really fucking cool, you guys."

We stood to shake hands when Brianna tapped me on the shoulder again. "Ez?"

"Yes, yes," I said, trying not to sound too affable, and waved as Dexter and the executives departed, Elaine bringing up the rear with her steady plod. "What is it?"

Brianna waited for me to sit down and then opened her laptop. "I think I missed a few notes from the beginning?"

"You didn't miss anything," I said, annoyed.

"Oh, right—okay. I guess then, um, I guess I might just want to ask you a question?"

I made a *get on with it* motion with my hand.

"Um, I hope I'm not speaking out of turn, but it's about Dexter. He doesn't really deliver on the things he promises. His companies are all in debt to each other: Maskelyne owes STARS money and STARS owes NeuroTech money and NeuroTech owes Maskelyne money."

"How do you know this?"

"I did some research on it at Harvard. He came to talk once and I, um, wanted to get some background."

"This isn't Harvard, though. This is the actual business world."

"Right, right. I just thought it was a little worrying. I just wanted to say something about it."

I snatched another glance at the picture of her and her mother on the porch only for her to lower her laptop's lid guardedly. "I get that you're really smart," I said. "And you work really hard. And I'm glad you're here—really. But, like, you need to not question the motives—"

The drumbeat again: agony behind the eyes. I winced and tipped forward in my seat until my head was between my knees. The carpet had been smeared to look like a black-gray abyss. I blinked fiercely as if this would make any difference. The pain seemed to echo in my ears.

"Ez!" Brianna called as if from the adit of a mine. "What's happening? Are you okay?"

I couldn't manage any words this time. I sat up uneasily, grimacing, and tried to look at the place where Brianna was supposed to be. I felt something in front of my face: her hand. My eyes must have gone glazed.

"Can you see me?" she asked, her voice pitched with worry.

"Of course I can," I wheezed. "Obviously I can." I turned away from her. "Stop the thing with your hand in my face."

"Sorry. You don't look well, though."

"I get migraines," I said. "It's nothing to worry about. Can you just give me a minute, maybe?"

"Yes." She stood. "Of course."

I listened to her pack up her laptop and walk out of the room, her heels stabbing the carpet's Brillo surface. I balled my fist and pounded it on the table, as if this would deactivate whatever was happening, and when that didn't work I tried digging the heels of my palms into my eyes, but that just seemed to make it worse. It felt like my eyes were about to explode. I staggered from the table to the front of the room and fished my phone out of my pocket, but I couldn't see it, much less the keypad, so I threw it across the room as if it had been the source of my pain. I heard it hit the wall opposite me and I felt tears dripping from my jaw and I was amazed that my eyes, ruined as they were, could still cry. I leaned against the wall and slid to the floor and pulled my knees to my chest and cried, suddenly returning in humiliation to the tent revival, the way the preacher had stooped down to address me, the money in my mom's hand. And then I blinked my eyes open and the pain was gone. The room was back in focus.

I found my way back to the table, wiping my eyes with the back of my bespoke sleeve, and asked myself what Orson would do in a situation like this. The answer was that he wasn't the kind of person this kind of thing happened to. Which meant that I needed to be the kind of person this kind of thing didn't happen to. I needed to be like him, and the only way to do that was to make this not happen, or to grit through it when it did, and eventually it would stop—it had to stop—and I would be free.

§

Mengetsu's office had been remodeled since I'd last visited, the wallpaper a distracting tessellation of a set of pastel squares, the lights deafeningly bright, her slow-blinking secretary sheltered from us patients by a sheet of fiberglass. The clock on the wall behind me was loud, and I tapped my foot as fast as the second hand moved, scrolling through NuLife's social media aimlessly, not to digest anything of value so much as prove to myself that I could still see my phone's screen. I had an unread text from my mom asking how I was—it seemed impossible to respond truthfully given where I was and what I was there for. The people waiting with me had bandaged eyes or eyepatches or wore wraparound sunglasses, their heads inclined in the direction of the ticking clock. I could tell from a quick survey of the room that these people didn't dwell in my underworld: they were all bewildered, newly blinded, unaccustomed to the dark. The mole rat doesn't acquire its defects, it's born with them. That made me different from them.

The secretary called my name and led me back into the exam room, where I sat in the intimidating chair until Mengetsu came in, her face stern as always, my chart in her hands.

"You're back," she said.

"For a checkup," I said.

She closed my chart and sat down across from me. "Did you try the screen reader?"

"Works great," I lied.

"What about the mobility aids?"

I tilted my head from side to side. "Some of them."

She narrowed her eyes at me. "What's wrong, then?"

"Headaches. Sometimes my vision gets blurry. I don't know what it is."

She crossed her legs. I felt immediately as though I'd said the wrong thing. "Headaches?"

"Like a pressure behind my eyes. Or in them."

"Has anyone ever taken a look at your eyes with a tonometer?"

"I don't know what that is."

She looked momentarily at the floor, then back up at me. "Come with me into the next room."

We walked to a room that contained a machine that looked like a sophisticated device for the gouging of eyes. I was supposed to sit in the chair and slide my face into a kind of brace directly in front of what looked like the lens of a miniature microscope.

"That's what I'm talking about," she said. "Go ahead and sit down."

I did, removing my glasses, and she instructed me to keep both eyes open as wide as possible. Then she sat behind the microscope and a flash of UV-bright white passed across my left eye, then my right. She did this a second time and a third, and by the time she was done all I could see was the afterimage of the light, which dissolved to resemble blue spots in my vision. Even with my glasses on again, I couldn't see anything.

"I need to do one more thing," she said. "We're going to take pictures of your eyes."

Now another massive machine with a head brace, but for this one I just needed to look at a simulated wheat field—or at least what I thought was a wheat field, all I could really see was grainy yellow beneath generic sky blue—and keep my eyes open as the machine made little clicking noises.

Back in the exam room, Mengetsu waited for me to sit down before speaking. It was unlike her to be courteous, which worried me.

"Ezra, you have abnormally high intraocular pressure," she said.

She swiveled to the computer at her desk and pulled up an image of what looked like a molten orange planet shot through with bright red rivulets. At its center was a small yellow orb. She dragged her mouse around the image, moving it from left to right.

"This is your eye—your optic nerve, to be specific. This at the center"—she waved her mouse around the yellow orb—"is not normal. This is what we call glaucomatous cupping."

I nodded and thought of the mole behind Orson's right ear.

"People like yourself, people with severe hyperopia, are much more likely to develop glaucoma than the rest of the population."

The mole behind his right ear was irregularly shaped. It looked kind of like the state of Ohio.

"The yellow here, this is only going to get bigger. Do you see what I'm saying?"

"Sure."

"You have glaucoma."

This felt like a hurtful and inconvenient thing to say, and I wanted to tell her that but my phone rang. It was Orson calling.

"I have to take this," I said.

"Ezra, you could go blind."

"Just give me a second."

I left the exam room and went into the hallway.

"Hi!" Orson crowed. He sounded buoyant, and I found myself breaking into a smile. I asked him what was up.

"Ez, this is—you've got to come see this. Where are you right now?"

"New York."

"What's going on?"

I looked around—Mengetsu was behind me, and I stepped forward as though this would remove me from her line of sight. "I'm at the doctor's," I said. "Just getting a checkup."

"Clean bill of health?"

"Clean bill of health."

There was a voice in the background, a woman's squawk, and Orson said, "Just leave it where it is, thanks."

"Who's that?"

"Emily. She flew out here for the week. She brought all these Holly-wood people. They're all—" I could tell he was choosing his words care-fully. "They're all very excited about Synthesis."

My hand tightened around my phone. "Wow. That's great."

"Isn't it? There's this guy who's a two-time Academy Award winner. He was in that biopic about that dude from Queen. Not Freddie Mercury."

"Brian May," I said. "*Please Stop Me Now*."

"Yes! That's it! Old dude, but he's really sweet. Really excited about our project. You really should come up here, Ez. We need all hands on deck anyway."

"I can. I can definitely do that."

"Okay, I have to go, it's getting kind of busy here. Call me later, when you're back from the doctor's. I'll be free."

He hung up. Mengetsu was still standing behind me.

"I'm going to prescribe some eye drops," she said. "It's called Lumigan.

You use them twice a day to reduce the pressure in your eyes. Just put them in when you wake up and again before you go to sleep."

"Okay," I said, feeling my phone buzz in my pocket.

"Ezra, I'm asking you to take this seriously."

"I will," I said. "I'll get the eye drops."

I had her phone in the prescription to a pharmacy in Midtown, where I knew I'd be obscure, but when I got there the place was unusually crowded. I got in line behind an old man in a newsboy hat and let my gaze wander, too preoccupied with Mengetsu to occupy this liminal time with my phone. She was self-righteous, I decided, pleased with her bona fides, pleased with what I assumed was her perfect eyesight. She didn't even wear contacts—people who wore contacts always blinked a bit more than people who didn't—so how could she call herself an expert? What did she know about the underworld? She wanted me to put a bunch of luminousness in my eyes so I could get hooked and be the kind of pathetic asshole who inclined his face toward the very loud clock in her waiting room.

I waited half an hour until it was my turn to collect my prescription and then shoved the bottle in my coat pocket.

§

I told myself I was bringing Brianna to the Farm in case I had any ideas I needed her to transcribe, but really it was because I didn't want to go alone: the thought of seeing Orson and Emily together again made me feel dizzy with anger. My mind was moving faster than I could keep pace. Something about knowing she'd be with him inspired me to think as far ahead as I possibly could.

We arrived by Hummer limo to find Orson sitting on the back patio encircled by a group of celebrities. He was gesticulating like someone who'd just survived a natural disaster and wanted to describe its scale. When he saw us, he waved, and the faces of various people I recognized from movies and TV turned and smiled benignly at us, all of them looking small under their alpaca blankets.

"Friends, do you know Ezra Green? The CFO of NuLife? And this is our executive assistant, Brianna."

A chorus of hellos. Brianna waved, her smile tight over her braces, clearly stunned to be in the presence of so much star power.

"We're talking about the power of being," Orson said. "The inherent strength we get from just *being*."

"We're learning a lot," said someone who'd been in a movie about a dying fly fisherman.

"I've actually never learned so much in my life," said someone who'd starred in a thriller about a high school teacher whose dead father possesses the body of one of her students.

"I'd expect nothing less," I said, putting my hand on Orson's shoulder, and just as I did the patio doors swung open and there was Emily.

She wore a beige bodysuit that perfectly described the curve of her hips and her tapered thighs, over which she'd zipped a black fleece hoodie. Her hair was in a tight ponytail high at the back of her head and her feet were lost in a pair of chunky fur-lined boots. She'd dyed her hair red, and it looked incredible with her skin.

"Ez!" she said, and rushed to hug me. "How was the trip up?"

"Fine," I said. "This is Brianna."

"I'm a hugger," Emily said, and before Brianna could say anything in response, she'd wrapped her in her arms.

"Why don't you spend some time with us?" Orson said. "You two can grab some blankets and share your wisdom."

"I don't know if I have wisdom—" Brianna began.

"We have to go inside and send some emails," I said. "I have something I need to work on."

It was true: I'd been struck with an idea in the moment, looking at the eager-faced celebrities cocooned in their alpaca. I walked past Orson and his coterie, my face flushed, Brianna trailing me like an obedient dog. I'd designed the inside of the farmhouse to have a massive multipurpose living room which segued into a kitchen and a dining room that annexed a foyer into which descended a quasi-ballroom staircase. We climbed this staircase up to a hallway lined with rooms that had been turned into offices. I ushered Brianna into the nearest one.

"Pretty impressive," she mustered. "Down there."

"Yeah," I said, pretending to be preoccupied. "We need to do a little work quickly."

This seemed to deflate her, but she did her best to conceal it, pulling her laptop out of her satchel and sitting down at the desk. I leaned against the wall, my hands behind my back.

"I want you to find, like, some organization for delinquent youth."

Brianna nodded, opening her laptop.

"I want you to write to them and say you're Orson Ortman's executive assistant and offer them a free tour of the Farm." I spun my hand next to my head, trying to encourage my own thought. "Make it, like, a contest. Say we can pay for one of them to come here if they write a good essay about something—we'll give them a prompt. It'll be for the parents. Like, 'How Could Your Child Benefit from Synthesis?' Or 'Tell Your Child's Life Story.' They can stay at the Farm for a night and receive Synthesis from Orson Ortman."

"Will they, um, know about Synthesis?"

"Probably not. Describe it as a bold new treatment for behavioral issues. Talk about the Bliss-Mini. People know about the Bliss-Mini, but it's too expensive for most of them right now. Talk about how, like, the treatment at the Farm is one thousand times more effective than the Bliss-Mini, and we're offering it for free."

"Right." She was typing quickly. "Got it."

"Send that out and then come downstairs."

I left her typing in the office and found Orson and the celebrities in the dining room, being served dinner by the kitchen staff. The meal was strictly vegetarian, a new preference of Orson's: he claimed animal proteins interfered negatively with the body's ability to receive Synthesis. He was the only one at the table who wasn't wine-hazy. Emily was sitting next to him, inclined toward him, her forehead too close to his.

"It's Ez!" he said, and Emily jumped back at the suddenness of the interjection. "Welcome to dinner. We're having kale soup and corn bread."

The only place to sit down was between the fly fisherman and an actress who'd transitioned from daytime TV to indie romantic comedies. I did so resentfully, and was served what looked like greenish gruel and a dense hunk of corn bread.

"Ez, we're talking about the TED Talk I'm planning on giving," Orson said. "About the spiritual power of being and admitting to your wrongs."

He was getting more and more speaking engagements by the week. This talk, about the nebulous "power of being," was especially appealing to the exceedingly dumb.

"It's a new feature of Synthesis," the fly fisherman said. "He's trying it out on us."

"I honestly hadn't heard of it before," an unfamiliar-looking woman Emily's age said. "I'm so grateful Emily brought me here."

"Ez, this is Sasha, my best friend." Emily tilted her head toward the woman, who wore dangling earrings and had the neck and face of an egret straining to catch a fish. "She's a Broadway star."

Sasha waved the compliment away, the bones in her wrist visible from across the table. "I'm just trying to break into film," she said.

"You're modest," Emily said, and looked around the table for confirmation. Everyone nodded and murmured encouragingly. "Isn't she modest, Ez?"

"She's modest," I said, and ate a spoonful of the gruel.

"So I think I want to delve deeper into this idea of being as a function of knowing oneself," Orson said. "Did you all kind of get a sense of what I was saying outside?"

"Absolutely!" crowed the former daytime TV actress. "I totally got a sense of it."

"So what I want is for everyone to have unique and special access to both the worst and best things about themselves. I want people to get to this yin-yang state that's the precursor to total bliss."

Brianna walked tentatively into the dining room and Orson motioned for her to sit down, continuing his speech without addressing her.

"I want there to be no major separation between being and doing. I want being to *become* doing."

"That's beautiful," said a man who had recently voice-acted in a kids' movie about talking garden gnomes. "I'm still trying to wrap my head around it."

"*I'm* still trying to wrap my head around it," Orson said, and everyone laughed.

"Orson, if you don't mind," Brianna said. "I just wanted to—I just wanted to take a moment to say something."

"Of course," he said. "We're all ears."

The whole table turned toward Brianna. Emily wore a vapid half-smile and twisted around her finger a strand of strawberry hair that had escaped its ponytail. I could tell Brianna was overwhelmed—of course she was. She was speaking out of turn again, acting green as always. I wanted to support her as much as I wanted to silence her.

"Sorry to do this in front of everyone," she said. "But I'm just a little concerned about Dexter Ellhorn. I don't know if he's, you know, the most—I don't know if his brand is consistent with ours."

"What do you mean?" Orson asked.

I frowned at her but she didn't look at me.

"I just, um, worry about trusting him with the next gen of the Bliss-Mini."

The guests stirred a little, returned to their gruel, clearly embarrassed at having been let in on what should have been a private conversation.

Orson steepled his index fingers at his chin and smiled. "I respect your opinion, Brianna. I really do. And I'm certain that what you have to say is very insightful."

"I don't doubt it either," I said. "But we've already signed the deal."

"I've heard Dexter Ellhorn wants to establish a colony on the moon," the former daytime TV actress said. "I think his work is very advanced, very interesting."

"It's just that all his companies are in debt to each other—"

"Brianna," Orson purred. "Do you think we could talk about this some other time? Maybe over email? I so hate to interrupt you, but we were just in the middle of talking about something else. And this thing you're bringing up, it's really more business. Do you know what I mean?"

Brianna swallowed and nodded.

When we were finished eating, I dragged myself upstairs to administer the Lumigan. My eyelids fluttered in protest as I tried to get the sticky solution in one eye, then the other. It ended up running down my cheeks, and I wiped it away with a towel, leaning over the sink and trying to see myself in the mirror, or at the very least see the mirror, but that was futile even without the Lumigan smudging my vision. I searched for the bottle on the countertop and then felt it tip over, faster than I could catch it, and a stickiness trickled through my fingers and into the sink. My hands were covered in it.

"Fuck," I said, quick and hard like I was spitting gristle out of my mouth, and washed my hands off. Then I felt for my glasses and put them on, blinking furiously. The whole thing was absurd, a waste of time, completely beneath me. I waited for the liquid to leak out of my vision and then left the bathroom to go back downstairs, where the celebrities had moved into the living room. Sasha was sitting on the couch and Orson stood behind her with his hands at her temples, clearly preparing to Synthesize her as everyone looked on. Brianna sat on the sectional apart from them, chastened, her laptop in her lap.

"You're going to feel a slight blissful sensation," Orson said to Sasha, and everyone laughed.

Sasha nodded. "I'm ready," she said.

I walked down from the stairhead, careful to be quiet, watching as Orson

Synthesized Sasha. She kept her eyes closed and her hands in her lap. He spoke in the same soft hum he always used, seemingly unconscious of his eager onlookers. His eyes were closed, too, but his brows weren't knit like Sasha's were. When he was finished, Sasha's eyes popped open as the rest of the group applauded.

"How do you feel?" Orson asked.

Sasha looked from Orson to me to the rest of the group. She seemed briefly stunned, the bearer of a secret too embarrassing to admit.

"I—I'm sorry," she said. "I honestly don't feel any different."

"You're not letting it sink in," one of the celebrities said.

"You have to give it a moment," I said.

Sasha looked down at her hands and then over her shoulder at Orson. "I really don't think anything happened. I don't think it worked on me."

Orson smiled gently. "It works on everyone, Sasha. You're just not ready to receive it."

"I'm not ready?" Her voice shook.

Orson paced from behind her to the front of the couch. The celebrities' gaze followed him. Emily put her hand on Sasha's shoulder and whispered something consoling too quietly to hear.

"Synthesis is as much about the recipient as it is about the Synthesizer. If the recipient—the Synthesized—isn't willing to receive the energy, the essence of their *being* reflected back at them, then Synthesis will be left with a roadblock. Stopped up, halted. The Synthesized will become the Un-Synthesized, which is a painful thing to be."

Emily looked up at Orson as though he were a doctor who'd just given her friend a poor prognosis. "Is there something she can do?"

Orson nodded. "Of course. She just needs to practice willingness."

"What if I can't?" Sasha asked uneasily, and the room's attention focused pointedly on her.

"Well," Orson sighed. "You may just never be able to benefit from any-thing we have to offer. And let me say, that's a sad, sad place to be in."

Sasha put her head in her hands, trembling with tears, and Emily put her arms around her friend's shoulders, reassuring her that she wasn't broken, that there was still hope for her. The rest of the celebrities either rushed to comfort Sasha or stood to pepper Orson with questions. How could they practice willingness? How could they avoid such an—um—*unfortunate* outcome? I kneeled in front of Sasha, putting a hand on her knee.

"Sasha," I said. "You really don't have to worry. You can work at this. You can be okay."

"Listen to Ez," Emily said. "He knows what he's talking about."

"I'm just scared," Sasha wailed. "I don't know what's wrong with me."

"Nothing's *wrong* with you," I said. "You've just hit a bit of a roadblock. A temporary one."

She was still shaking, but she seemed to be listening.

"We can give you a Bliss-Mini," I said. "You can come here and try Synthesis again. You can do all kinds of things to fix the problem, right?" I looked up at Brianna, who was staring dumbly in our direction.

"Right!" she chimed in. "Yes, right, you can definitely turn this around!"

"Everyone knows you can turn this around, Sasha," I said.

"Thank you," she gasped. "That—I—that means a lot."

One by one, the celebrities repaired to their bedrooms, Emily walking Sasha upstairs and Brianna following them, peppering them both with more words of encouragement. It was just Orson and me in the living room, the soft clamor of the staff cleaning up in the kitchen behind us. Orson sat cross-legged on the couch, his arms draped over the frame.

"Pretty great, isn't it?" he asked.

"Yeah."

"And these people are, like, small-time. Except for the Academy Award winner I guess. But Emily knows some real heavyweights. She can get us connected up pretty well."

I wanted him to talk quieter and I wanted to put my head in his lap, to look up at the stubble covering the bottom of his chin.

"There's a lot of money in this," he said, whispering now.

"What do you think about the thing Brianna was saying?" I asked. "About Ellhorn?"

Orson drummed his fingers on the frame. "I think it was a whole lot of nothing. Who's she to be worried about anything we're doing?"

"Well, it sounds like she did some research at Harvard—"

"So you're listening to Ivy League assholes now?" He cocked his head at me. "I thought we weren't about that anymore."

"I mean, no—"

"Then let's not be about that." He smiled and shook my shoulder. Then he stole a look upstairs, a look at the kitchen, and leaned forward to kiss me. It was brief but soft, and I couldn't help but close my eyes for it.

"I'm going to turn in soon," he said, breaking away to stand up. "If you want something to drink, whatever, the staff you hired is pretty damn attentive."

He took the stairs two at a time and I watched him go, aching for him, resisting the urge to follow him. Things were not the way I wanted them to be but they wouldn't be that way forever. They *couldn't* be that way forever. What had I done, after all? I'd given him the Farm, and his farmhouse, and the opportunity to hobnob with these semifamous people who loved him. His life would be less lush without me, less resplendent. There was no doubting that.

Something buzzed on the couch: his phone. It must have fallen out of his pocket. I picked it up, saw that he'd just received an email from Delpy, and put it in my own pocket. He'd want his phone by his bedside, I knew. He always looked at it first thing in the morning.

I climbed the stairs, whisper-shouting his name, careful not to disturb the sleeping guests. He didn't call back to me. I began checking in empty offices, and when I didn't find him in those I climbed to the next floor. All the doors were closed except for one at the end of the hall, which announced its openness by projecting a sliver of orange-ish light into the hallway. I could hear Orson's voice in conversation with a woman's. I got closer and recognized Emily's faux-innocent lilt. I stood at the edge of the doorframe to find her sitting in a chair in a tank top and a pair of Spandex shorts so small they could have been underwear. Orson stood behind her, fingers at her temples. Both their eyes were closed. He was Synthesizing her, and I watched her shoulders tense and relax as he instructed her to reconstruct this or that thing about her past, to merge the good with the bad. He was different Synthesizing her than he had been with anyone else: he moved slower, spoke more deliberately, laughed gently as she jumped at his touch. There was something very wrong about it, something that made me want to stop it, but I couldn't, because it was clear that would make him unhappy. So I wordlessly set his phone down on the carpet in the doorway and left them alone in the room, locked in a Synthesis so intense and magnetic neither of them noticed I was there.

EIGHT

REAL ESTATE DEVELOPER CHUCK ENNER, THE FATHER OF DELINQUENT YOUTH Jeremy Enner, wrote an essay about watching his adolescent son set fire to the dining room rug. He went on to say that fifteen-year-old Jeremy had been expelled from three schools and spent six weeks in a juvenile detention center for punching his history teacher in the mouth.

We are at the end of our rope he wrote. *We have tried all sorts of expensive therapies for him but are finding no relief. When we learned about NuLife and this contest, my wife and I knew we had to put our hats in the ring.*

Chuck Enner won our contest. I made him submit photos of Jeremy, whose cowlick and snarl suggested that he wasn't accustomed to sitting for pictures, and Brianna plastered them all over our website and social media. Jeremy Enner, whose parents had exhausted every form of behavior modification therapy available, would be receiving revolutionary treatment on the Farm. Specifically, Synthesis administered by Orson Ortman, one of the foremost experts on behavior modification therapy in the country.

We flew the Enners out from North Dakota and drove them to the Farm in a cavalcade of SUVs. Orson and I stood at the front doorstep to greet them while cameras flashed. The five of us posed together: Chuck rooster-necked and square-shouldered, his wife, Priscilla, slim and blinking like a panicked saluki, and Jeremy freckled and dead-eyed, clearly furious that he'd been forced to be a part of this.

Inside, away from the cameras, Orson asked Jeremy if he was feeling ready to spend twenty-four hours on the Farm. Jeremy looked Orson up and down, clearly taking in his jean jacket and work pants—an "approach-able" wardrobe I'd picked out for him that morning—and snorted.

"Yeah, I'm ready for your New Age bullshit," he said.

Chuck smacked Jeremy on the back of the head, which was horrifying, so I quickly turned away to meet Priscilla's pleading gaze.

"Jeremy can't help it," she squeaked. "We try *so hard*, but he can't help it."

"I'm sure you do," I said, and then turned to Jeremy. "It's going to help you," I said softly. "I promise."

Jeremy made a noise that sounded like he was about to hock a wad of spit, but he hocked nothing, just crossed his arms and looked at Orson, who hadn't stopped smiling.

"Let's get started," Orson said.

We ate a banquet lunch with the Enners, the kitchen staff serving meat for the first time in the brief history of the Farm. Jeremy and his father loved ribeye, and both devoured theirs with quiet precision. Jeremy clearly pos-sessed all of Orson's metabolic gifts without any of his tendency to scarf. But Orson didn't scarf: he barely ate. The Enners listened as he explained Syn-thesis and the Bliss-Mini and the Bliss-Mini 2 (currently in development), clearly distracted by the beauty of the farmhouse, which I'd had redecorated in reds and golds specifically for their visit (red and gold being Jeremy's fa-vorite colors). When Jeremy was finished with his ribeye, he slouched in his seat and began somewhat vigorously kicking Chuck's shins under the table.

"Don't kick your father," Priscilla said.

"Fuck you," Jeremy said.

Chuck stood, rounded the table, and once again smacked Jeremy on the back of the head. I jumped. Jeremy didn't move, just stayed staring into the middle distance with his arms crossed. Priscilla began to cry.

"It's like this every day," she said. "These two just fight all the time. Jeremy won't let up."

Jeremy smiled wickedly at Orson. Chuck's face was stony. He, too, could have benefited from some behavior modification therapy.

"Can I borrow Jeremy for a minute?" Orson asked.

"Go ahead," said Chuck. "Borrow him for a fucking decade."

Orson brought Jeremy out onto the patio, leaving the rest of us to finish lunch. Chuck ate his steak sternly while Priscilla glanced from her plate of asparagus to the patio.

"You have a kid and you dream of, you know, meeting his first girl-friend, sending him off to college, visiting his first house," Chuck said, de-clining to look up from the neat row of cubes he'd made of his steak. "Never in my wildest dreams did I think any of this was going to happen."

"He's our only child," Priscilla added, and began crying again.

"Frankly? I've given up. I've tried everything with him. He responds to nothing. Not doctors, not shrinks, not us. Nothing."

"What's he doing?" Priscilla asked. Orson and Jeremy were sitting across from each other on a pair of Adirondack chairs, Orson gesticulating like he had with the celebrities. Jeremy seemed to be enraptured.

"It's the precursor to Synthesis," I said. "We always do an individual assessment before beginning the treatment."

"Strap him to a bed and run electrodes through his head for all I care," Chuck said.

"Chuck!" Priscilla looked more stunned than angry. "How could you say that?"

Chuck shrugged. "How could he behave the way he does? It's one of the world's greatest mysteries."

"Mrs. Enner," I said. "I encourage you to focus on your lunch while Orson's working. If he sees us watching, your son is likely to lose focus."

Priscilla nodded resignedly and continued picking at her asparagus.

We finished eating, the kitchen staff cleared the table, and I gave the Enners a tour of the farmhouse, pointing out the small details I'd put in place to appease Jeremy: a Paramore band poster, red carpeting for the stairs, boxes of sugar-dusted chocolate Pop-Tarts in the lazy Susan.

"We want him to feel at home," I said.

Chuck grunted. Priscilla's eyes watered yet again.

We finished to find Orson and Jeremy in the living room, Orson standing with his arms crossed and Jeremy sleeping peacefully on the couch.

"He told me he was exhausted," Orson said. "He said he hasn't gotten a good night's sleep in years."

"He has night terrors," Priscilla said.

"Is this sleeping a good thing?" Chuck asked.

"Yes," I said, and Orson nodded along with me.

The twenty-four hours progressed quickly. I entertained the Enners while Jeremy received hours of Synthesis followed by several small vegetarian meals with Orson. The two took long walks on the property, talking about god knows what. There was a noticeable change in Jeremy: he seemed more serene, a little drowsy even, and his hostility toward Chuck dissipated. At the end of the stay, Orson dismissed the kitchen staff and he and Jeremy prepared gazpacho and served it to us in porcelain bowls. As he brought his parents' plates to the table, Jeremy kissed his mother on the cheek and squeezed his father's shoulder. Chuck placed his hand on Jeremy's, crying as freely as his wife had.

"You're back," he said, craning his neck to look into his son's eyes. "My little boy is back."

The Enners tried to insist on paying us but we refused.

"All we ask is that you point any other needy kids in our direction," Orson said.

A month later, Jeremy was hitting Chuck and setting fires again. He needed more therapy. Chuck called with a proposition: could he bring his family to the Farm for an extended stay?

"Absolutely," I said. "Of course, there would be a cost to stay in the farmhouse. And we can't house you indefinitely."

"No, I mean—I want to build a house close to your place, a few miles out of Oswego. Jeremy can get treatment and then we can try and integrate him into the school there."

So Chuck built a house, a four-bedroom ranch we nicknamed The Enner House, and paid $20,000 a month for Jeremy to be Synthesized by Orson. Soon, Jeremy was able to complete his junior year at the high school in Oswego. Jeremy's success was highly publicized, and word got out to other families of delinquent youth. Chuck built more Enner houses for families who were willing to relocate to the space between the Farm and Oswego, so that soon there was an entire Enner Village and Orson and I needed more Synthesizers.

It was my idea to develop Synthesis Certification. Future Synthesizers would progress through five levels: Beginner, Apprentice, Craftsman, Master, and Superior. Each level cost $30,000 to complete, $25,000 if the Synthesizer could recruit a friend, $20,000 if they could recruit two. Only the most skilled Superiors selected by Orson were allowed to conduct Synthesis on others. These Superior Synthesizers would be fully employed by the Farm for their services. Chuck and Priscilla were our first full-time Superior Synthesizers.

What began as a "holistic treatment" for troubled rich kids became, as I'd predicted, a trend for rich people of all stripes. Orson had been right that Synthesis would attract wealthy people and their wealthy friends, but he hadn't thought clearly about how to rake them in. People who possessed fortunes cared about the health and well-being of their scions, whose job it was to keep their money immortal. A derelict scion meant mismanaged money, which meant that Orson and I could position ourselves as the handmaidens of that scion's rehabilitation as well as the guarantors of the family's financial security. And we didn't have to spend all our time trying to harpoon a bunch of uber-rich white whales: this worked on everyone from people as wealthy as the Argyroses to upper-middle-class people like the Enners who had the money to move out to the Farm and were willing to go into debt to take the Synthesis Certification. The uber-rich would write us checks for our "research" while the still-rich-but-less-so functioned as our bread and butter. Within a year, the Enner Village had become an Enner Town. Bliss-Mini sales inclusive, we were turning a profit in the hundreds of millions. And that didn't include the money people were regularly donating to the Farm in the name of "scientific advancement." Orson was brilliant at getting people to invest money and recruit their friends to invest even more money with the promise that they'd see some kind of material or spiritual return.

The celebrities came back in droves. Going to the Farm and studying with Orson was the answer to a wide variety of spiritual questions such as *What is there left to strive for now that I'm rich and famous?* and *What can help me kick this cocaine habit?* and *What can help me look younger?* They were photographed walking through Manhattan wearing Bliss-Minis, appeared on talk shows singing the praises of a round of Synthesis with Orson. Some of them even bought Enner houses and spent months on the Farm at a time, walking among the less-famous with zero compunction, so that divorce attorneys from Schaumburg, Illinois, mingled freely with three-time Academy Award winners in a rich bouquet of people who were giving us money. Our profits increased exponentially by the month.

Of course Emily was there, too, in eyelash extensions and baggy sweatshirts that emphasized her twiggy frame. She worked her way through the Synthesis Certification, thankfully leaving to shoot a film in Quebec before she reached the Superior level. She was, as always, a "hugger," a hanger-on, a self-appointed ambassador of the Farm to Hollywood, a lurker in the living room and on the patio and in the hallways. Whenever she ran into me, she asked in a saccharine chirp how I was doing, what I'd been up to, whether I was stressed or overworked. I grunted monosyllabic answers and waited for her to whisk herself away to her next premiere or cameo, which she always did.

Orson was profiled in major magazines and made several TV appearances. It was so satisfying reading about him and watching him onscreen: this was him at his least bored, his most happy. He wanted to be adored and here the world was, adoring him. He spent weeks flying around the country, which meant we saw each other rarely, but it also meant that he saw Emily rarely, too. And of Emily and me, who was it who had built a kingdom for him? Who was it who made him happiest?

In a rare instance when we were interviewed together, on a morning talk show, Orson told the host that if people were going to praise him, they might as well praise me first.

"Because Ezra's the brains behind this operation."

"Is that so?" the host asked, her lipsticked mouth puckered questioningly. "Ezra, what is it you do?"

"I make it possible for Orson to shine," I said.

"Come on," Orson said, pretending to punch my shoulder.

"Really?" the host asked.

"Yes, really. I keep him fed and watered, keep stuff running behind the scenes. Basically, I do what I can to keep pace with a once-in-a-generation talent."

"Sweet words from NuLife's CFO," the host said, turning to the audience.

"True words," I corrected. "All true."

§

STARS was headquartered in Florida, where Dexter Ellhorn was from, and when the helicopter carrying Orson and me descended onto Dexter's tarmac, I could already feel how thick the air was with heat. Dexter greeted us wearing yet another tracksuit, this one paired with a thin gold chain; he held out an identical one for Orson.

"For the photo shoot," he shouted over the thwack of the propeller.

"Thanks," Orson said, inspecting the chain. "Glad the profile's happening."

"Absolutely. Ez, it's been too long."

It hadn't been long enough. "How are you feeling about the 2.0?"

"Never felt better." He cracked his knuckles loudly. "How are you feeling?"

"I'm feeling ready to see it."

Dexter laughed and pointed to a white SUV rumbling across the tarmac toward us.

"That's my driver, Omar," he said. "You don't need to remember his name."

We got in and Omar began driving. The fat palm trees lining the tarmac appeared to be doing yogic backbends toward the sun. I rolled down my window and watched the sky, massive and equatorial, feeling like my prescription sunglasses were useless against the hot white insistence of the daylight.

"So there's going to be drones," Orson said.

Dexter's eyes creased with a smile. "Combat drones, yeah."

"We're about peace," I said. "We don't like combat."

"Oh, I know, I know. There are civilian drones, too. I just think—I think the future is with drones."

"Mhm," Orson said. I noticed he'd joined me in watching the sky.

"They deliver packages, they deliver bombs," Dexter said. "Actually, I have something I think you two will really like."

Omar dropped us off at a hangar bearing the STARS logo over its giant mouth. The inside was carpeted with a fleet of drones, still and spiderlike. The largest looked like a flying hearse. Dexter ran to stand next to it.

"This is what I was talking about, the air taxi," he said. "It can carry some real tonnage. As in multiple human beings. But it's faster and more efficient than a helicopter."

"What would you use it for?" Orson asked.

"Well, obviously it would be beneficial in a combat situation, maybe a way for medics to send injured soldiers off the field. But, domestically speaking, it could also be used to disrupt the rideshare industry." He flicked one of its smaller propellers, letting it spin lazily. "Can you imagine this picking you up in Midtown and flying you all the way to Brooklyn for a fraction of the price of a taxi?"

Orson nodded. "How many tons can it hold?"

"This one?" Dexter inspected the drone as though the answer lay in its lacquered surface. "A little over a ton, I'd say."

"Mm," Orson said dispassionately. "That's a lot."

Dexter ran to the opposite wall, where an overwhelming number of remote controls were hanging by metal hooks. He selected one of the larger ones and showed it to us, his eyebrows raised. He was determined to impress us with drones, which made me both annoyed and a little sad.

"A sophisticated remote ground control system right here, one of the better models I've designed. It can adjust for velocity, air temperature, even detect a storm front." He walked between us. "Would you mind backing toward the wall just a bit?"

We backed toward the wall and watched as Dexter typed something into his watch face. Then he looked at us brightly and said, "Okay, this is going to blow your minds."

The air taxi's propellers began to whir, and then it maneuvered itself out of the sea of its fellows with the jerky velocity of a remote-control toy car: backward, to the left, then forward and out onto the tarmac. Dexter flipped a number of switches and pressed a few buttons and the air taxi took flight, shooting several hundred feet up into the heat-thick sky.

"It's going," Dexter said, then checked his watch face again. "It's going to run a quick errand. It's on autopilot. That's another great feature of this model."

We watched the air taxi disappear over the horizon, and Dexter turned to us with a *voilà* smile. "Give it ten minutes. It'll be back," he said.

"Great," I said.

Orson hooked his thumbs in the belt loops of his jeans and wandered among the drones. I waited until he was out of earshot and leaned in close to Dexter.

"What kind of contracts do you have in the global South?" I asked.

"What contracts do I have there?"

"Orson doesn't know it yet, but I want to take NuLife international."

"Shouldn't he be having this conversation with us?"

I shook my head. "No, no. I'm the business guy, he's the ideas guy. Plus his birthday's coming up."

"So you want to take NuLife international as a—you want to take it international as a birthday present?"

"It's not just me," I lied. "The whole company wants to. We're throwing him a celebration."

"Why the global South?"

I shrugged. "It's developing, isn't it? There's money to be made."

Dexter cocked his head to one side. "I'm market testing a fleet of air taxis in South America. Urmau."

"That's perfect. Do you think you can introduce the 2.0 down there?"

"I can try. I can't guarantee it'll take."

"Just give it to the leadership. Whoever you're dealing with."

Dexter folded his arms across his chest. "That would be Genial Arroya; it's a *g* pronounced like an *h*. He's the son of Genial Sr., the president. They aren't on good terms."

"So you're working with the son?"

Dexter nodded.

"Okay, give it to him then."

"I can't just peddle your product without financial incentive."

"It's your product. too."

"Cut me in."

"You get twenty-five percent of the sales down there."

"Thirty-five."

I sighed. He had the self-assuredness of a petulant child, which made bargaining futile. "Thirty-five," I ceded.

Orson walked back toward us, clapped a hand on each of our shoulders. "What're we talking about here?"

"The photo shoot," Dexter said quickly, making a show of reading texts on his watch. "The *Times* reporter should be here soon."

Then a distant whirring: I could see a dot in the sky but none of its defining features.

"Is that the air taxi?" Orson asked, craning his neck.

Dexter looked from one of us to the other and grinned. "Yep."

The whirring turned to thwacking as the air taxi settled on the ground in front of us. Dexter did some ostentatious pressing of buttons on his watch and said, "A male tiger can weigh up to one ton." Then he opened the hatch and a white Bengal tiger stood awkwardly in the passenger compartment, purring loudly. I stepped back, heart pounding, and Orson clapped his hands together and crowed with laughter.

"This is Mickey," Dexter said. "He's totally harmless. I had the drone grab him from my place."

Mickey stepped gingerly out of the drone, and Orson collapsed to his knees and held his hand out to Mickey, who began licking it like a dog.

"See, that's the beauty of the air taxi," Dexter said. "It can be programmed to fly wherever you want using the simple GPS technology I've got on my watch." He held up his watch face, tapped it. "I don't even need the remote control. Tell me this isn't shit you want to get behind."

"We want to get behind it," I said, distracted by Orson's giggles as the tiger licked his palm.

"Can Mickey be in the photo shoot?" Orson asked.

"Hell yes," Dexter said. "You've got creative control, man. We can pose with the tiger, we can pose in midair, whatever."

Orson turned to me, gleeful, all pretense of composure abandoned. "Isn't this great?" he asked.

I smiled. His eyes were so bright it was hard not to.

"Yeah," I said. "It's really great."

§

The profile came out a week later. "Bliss Effect: The Combined Genius of Orson Ortman and Dexter Ellhorn." Orson and Dexter standing arms akimbo among a sea of mini drones. Orson flying a drone while Dexter watched. Orson and Dexter and Mickey peering out of the air taxi, hovering in midair. I speed-read the profile aloud while Orson lay in the hotel bed next to me. As usual, I had Brianna book us two rooms, and as usual, we'd completely neglected one of them. Orson was still naked from our exploits, smoking, staring at the ceiling. I was spent and giddy, a compound coursing through my system that I could only describe as *him*.

"Well that was nice," he said, extinguishing his cigarette in the ashtray next to the bed. "That was a lot of nice things at once."

"All merited."

He turned on his side and draped his leg across mine. "Maybe yes, maybe no."

His smile was tense, and there was an opacity in his gaze that gave me pause.

"What's wrong?"

"Mm," he said, and then said nothing else.

"What?"

"There's just a lot going on."

I sat up on my elbows. "Like what?"

"Like a lot." He flopped onto his back again. "I don't know what to say."

Now I could feel myself beginning to sweat. "You can say anything."

"You're not going to like it."

"Just say it."

"I don't think we should sleep together for a while."

"What do you mean." I couldn't bring myself to inflect the question.

"Well, you know—the people coming to the Farm are very traditional. They've got kids. They're straight."

"You're not straight, though."

He sighed. "But I have to play a certain role. I have to be as the people see me."

"Be as the people see you?"

"I have to lead." He fished another cigarette from his pack on the bedside table and lit it, exhaled a thick plume into the air above us. "A lot of people are looking to me to lead."

I rubbed my cheeks, trying to digest the information, but it was inorganic, poisonous. "Orson," I said.

He didn't acknowledge me. "You get it, little dude, right? The whole thing has to be, I don't know, uniform. Presentable. Convincing."

Then the awful drumbeat behind my eyes again. It felt worse than before, worse than it had in a year. I imagined there was blood dripping from my tear ducts. I tried to think of the Lumigan, when I'd last used it. I couldn't remember. I hadn't gotten my prescription refilled since I'd spilled the bottle at the Farm.

"Ez?"

I waved him away.

"You're wincing." There was a tenderness in his voice that I suddenly resented.

"I'm fine," I said.

He touched my shoulder. "What's wrong?"

I rolled away from him, unseeing, my eyes pulsing. When I tried to look up, there was only a shape that suggested the ceiling fan: everything around it was constricted by darkness.

"Fuck," I whispered.

"Ez." He sounded worried now. "What's happening?"

"Nothing."

"Something's clearly happening."

"I'm having a migraine."

He leapt from the bed. "I'll get you some painkillers."

"No. Don't do anything. Please. Just lie next to me."

He lay back down. "You don't look good," he said.

I was crying then, not because of my eyes but because of what he'd said before. Or because of both. "It just hurts a lot," I said.

Then his finger was against my cheek, collecting a tear.

"I don't want you to be upset about this. I don't want you to be hurt."

I said nothing, sniffling.

"You're cute, you know that?" he said. "Your knock-knees, your green eyes, your little snaggletooth."

I imagined he said *I love you*.

I imagined I said *I love you* back.

Instead I said, "Thanks."

"You get it about the pausing, right?"

"I do."

He kissed me on the side of my head. "I'm going to get us Cokes. Will that help? Some caffeine and sugar?"

I nodded and listened to him leave the bed, tie his robe around his waist, shuffle out of the hotel room. I turned on my stomach and pressed my face into the pillow. The drumbeat ceased and I thought of the photograph of my optic nerve Mengetsu had shown me, the inflamed yellow orb at its center. I imagined that I was lying on grass, my ear pressed to the ground, listening for movement below. I was hearing myself, maybe. I was hearing myself scrambling through a network of tunnels with teeth and claws, searching for the thing that would justify my scrambling. Why was I destined to live underground?

What was wrong with me that I couldn't have him?

§

Dexter's Bliss-Mini 2.0 debuted on the market, a thicker headset with a bunch of flashing lights and extra magnets and a touchscreen, all supposed to enable transcendental meditation and healthy eating and better aerobic conditioning but ultimately just pointing the consumer in the direction of the Farm. The 2.0 promised "upgrades" that were only available via travel to Oswego, "real-life upgrades" that couldn't be downloaded from an app store. Going to the Farm and taking some classes on Synthesis and mindfulness, etc., meant, quite literally, upgrading one's mind, enabling the 2.0 to do whatever it was supposed to be doing better. This feat of advertising was perhaps the one thing Dexter did effectively.

We began making money in a way I hadn't experienced before. Gluts of it, people swarming to buy the 2.0, people swarming to the Farm. It became a sort of trendy pilgrimage, devotees bringing camping gear and paying to sleep on our property when all the rooms in the farmhouse were occupied, hoping to catch a glimpse of Orson in the throng of people crowded around the patio whenever he emerged from the house to teach a class or deliver a speech.

I bought two houses for my parents, one in Aspen for the summers and one in Long Beach for the winters, and staffed each full-time. I tried to call my parents as frequently as possible, worried not just about being a good son but about how quickly their past-life jobs had aged them, my mom's wrists inflamed from carrying trayfuls of heavy plates and the toes of my dad's left foot dead from frostbite.

"We're doing fine, sweetheart," my mom said on the day the NuLife share price had reached $115. "If anything, we hope *you're* doing fine."

"I am." I was looking at myself in the bedroom mirror, bare chested in sweatpants, my hair folded at odd angles from a night of fitful sleep.

"Not too stressed?" My dad's voice was more distant than my mom's.

"We're worried you're stressed," my mom said.

"That whole thing about executives being stressed," I said. "It's a lie. This is the least stressful job there is. Really."

A click: they still had a landline, and my dad had picked up another phone. "Well, we're watching you, Ez. You're doing such big things and we're so proud."

"So proud," my mom echoed.

"We saw you on TV the other day, that special they did on your place in the country," my dad said.

"The Farm."

"Yes. And they showed footage of Orson teaching a class."

"He's always had a face for TV, Orson," my mom tittered.

My dad heaved a comic sigh. "Your mother has a crush on your best friend."

"I do not!"

I turned back to the mirror and blinked, my image sliding in and out of focus like an amoeba on a microscope's tray.

"Well, we wanted to say we thought you were looking very handsome, but we noticed—um, I think I noticed a bit of a squint," my dad said.

"And you always got that squint when you were having trouble in school, with the chalkboard," my mom said.

I sat down on the edge of the bed, my body rigid. "This isn't school," I said. "I'm not looking at a chalkboard."

"We're trying to say, Ez, that maybe you need to go back and get your eyes checked." My mom sounded timid.

I could feel my scalp tightening. "You're always on about the eye thing. As if it really matters. You made money off it, Mom."

"What?"

"That time you took me to the tent revival. You made, like, fifty bucks."

"I don't remember that."

"Tent revival?" my dad asked.

"She took me to a fucking tent revival," I said, now unable to stop myself. "And she basically pimped me out. Said I was going blind."

"I never did that, honey."

"What the hell are you talking about?" My dad coughed: he always coughed when he was nervous.

"Ask her," I said. "Ask her about it. She'll tell you."

"We just don't want you to run into problems with your vision," my mom pleaded. "When you let these things slip, there can be consequences. That's all, sweetie—"

"I have to go," I said, and hung up on their midsentence stutters. As soon as I did, I wanted to dial them back and apologize. But I resisted. Let them sit in the mansion I'd bought them and wait for my next call. I'd done plenty for them.

It was around that time that I stopped wanting to pay taxes. Too much paperwork, too much money that could be better put toward Orson's happiness. I spent time in the Upper West Side condo that I'd stopped renting and bought outright, manipulating NuLife in my mind like a Rubik's Cube, trying to figure out the right set of moves that would make everything come together pleasingly. I knew Elaine could help make this happen to my satisfaction.

It was a Saturday morning, which meant most people would be out of the office except Elaine, whom I found staring impassively into the blue-white glow of her monitor.

"What are you doing?" I asked, and watched her try to disguise how startled she was.

"Shareholder emails," she said. "I've been here since dawn." As if she were responding to an accusation.

"You don't have to do that," I said. "Just forward them to me."

She nodded, and I watched her diligently forward each of them, blinking slightly as her mail application made its whooshing "sent" noise. Then she swiveled in my direction.

"Glad the 2.0 is doing so well," she said.

I leaned against the wall, hands in my pockets. "It was your idea."

"It was my idea to hire Dexter," she corrected. "It was you guys who really made it work."

"No, not really. It was all you." I walked to her desk and sat on its edge. "You have to stop pretending this place is a boys' club."

"It kind of is, isn't it?"

"Not really, though, because you're the one coming up with the best ideas."

She swiveled to face the skyline, unmoved by my flattery. I lifted both my feet off the floor so I was sitting perched like a child.

"Elaine, I think you should be making more money," I said.

She kept looking at the skyline.

"I need your help with something and I want to pay you for it."

"What is it?"

"Could you turn around?"

I worried I'd said it like an order, but she obliged, her pale face inclined obediently toward me.

"We've got to—I need you to, um, underreport to the IRS."

"Hide money, you mean?" It wasn't the question I'd expected her to ask.

"Yeah. I'm planning on expanding to other markets. Other countries."

"So you'll need some cushioning."

I was surprised by how well she was taking this.

"Yeah, actually. And I'll also need you to take out a loan from Deutsche Bank. Two billion. They're pretty aggressive lenders, so use a special purpose vehicle. We just need as much, um, cushioning as we can get for this."

"How much do you want me to hide?"

"Like twenty-five percent of profits."

She nodded thoughtfully. "What do I get?"

"Ten percent of the twenty-five."

She flipped a straw-like curtain of hair from her face. "Fifteen, please."

I smiled. "Sure thing."

$

Genial Arroya loved the 2.0 and was excited to be the "ambassador of Nu-Life" in his country. After Dexter introduced us over FaceTime, I spent hours with Genial on the phone talking about our corporate philosophy, the potential for expansion to Urmau, the serious health benefits the Bliss-Mini and Orson's spiritualism presented for the Urmanese.

"You are smart, Ezra," he told me. "Smartness like yours—it's something I like to have on my side."

He insisted on seeing the Farm, so I offered to fly him out on March 28, which just so happened to be Orson's twenty-eighth birthday. A golden birthday called for gold streamers, gold balloons, gold-framed photos of Orson on TV and in magazines hung throughout the farmhouse. Hundreds of NuLifers flooded from Enner Town onto our property, bearing, per my instruction, candles we would light at night to spell Orson's initials. In honor of Orson's lifelong sobriety, there would be no alcoholic beverages served, though this was pro forma: all NuLifers refrained from consuming mind-altering substances in an attempt to be closer to Orson's "spiritually unified" state. So we set up a sparkling cider fountain and rows upon rows of buffet tables. The place was busy, vibrating with activity that made me sure of myself, happier than I'd been in a long time.

Genial's helicopter landed in the grass a little too close to the farmhouse, and he emerged in a linen suit with the straight-toothed smile and flawless skin of someone whose privilege extends from cradle to grave. His only humanizing detail was his tightly curled hair, which had, over the course of the flight, come free from its gel like a poodle's fur drying after a bath. He wrapped me in a suffocating hug and then held me at arm's length.

"It is incredible to meet you, my friend! And on this special day!"

"It's a very special day," I said, squeezed in his grip. "We're glad you're here."

The NuLifers were camped out in small circles on the property, all wearing white and gold for the occasion, quoting among each other lines from Orson's TED Talks and Farm-exclusive speeches. They barely registered Genial and me as we made our way among them, Genial murmuring excitedly as he spotted the celebrities he knew from dubbed imports of American movies. When we got to the patio, I sent one of the staff to get Genial a gin gimlet—his favorite drink, he'd told me—the only one to be served on the property in a long time, a special exception for our foreign visitor. We sat in a pair of Adirondack chairs and Genial surveyed the acres of assembled NuLifers.

"Ezra, this is really beautiful, the thing you have here."

"Well, thank you. That means quite a lot."

"It means quite a lot to *you*, Ezra, and Orson, and to me. It means a lot for all three of us." He frowned. "My father, you know—he is not a nice man, not a good man."

A member of the staff with a face like a basset hound brought him his gimlet, which Genial took from the tray without a word of thanks.

"Thank you," I said as the staff member disappeared back into the farmhouse. I realized I couldn't remember his name.

"When I was a child, he would take his belt and whip me," Genial continued, his gaze focused somewhere in the middle distance. "On the back, on the legs. I have the scars from it."

And then he took off his jacket and unbuttoned his shirt, his muscles taut and ropey, and turned so I could see his back. It was covered in wormlike raised scars, some traveling the length of his neck to his waistline. I shivered. He put his shirt back on, leaving it unbuttoned.

"I'm so sorry," I said.

"No, no. Don't be sorry. My life was that way and then it became what it is, and now I am thankful."

"I suppose that's good."

"Yes, it is good. My father, after he became rich, he ran for president saying he is a socialist, but now he is not that way. He is a . . . what's the English word I'm looking for?"

"Capitalist?"

"No, no. The other one."

"Oligarch? Tyrant?"

"Yes! That is the one. Tyrant. He is controlling the country: who can come in, who can leave, what can we import, what can we export. He makes the schools teach about him, he makes the women stay at home, the men must serve in the army when they are young. People are very unhappy."

"That's awful."

"Yes, it is not like America. Here you are free, you are inventors! This is why I love NuLife, because it brings freedom and happiness. Do you know the Daroqol? Has anyone told you about them?"

I shook my head reluctantly. I wasn't keen to undertake an in-depth survey of Urmanese politics on Orson's golden birthday.

"They are the secret army who will fight against my father. You need no such thing in America."

The sun had nearly set. I checked my watch: fifteen minutes until Orson was supposed to arrive. I stood up and cupped my hands around my mouth.

"Hey, folks!" I called as loudly as I could. Everyone in front was suddenly at attention; I couldn't see if the ones in back were or not. "We're at T-minus fifteen! I need people to stand up and get in formation, please!"

The NuLifers darted expediently across the lawn, lighting their candles and assembling themselves into what we'd determined to be two large Os. Genial looked delighted.

"What is this?" he asked.

"His initials," I said. "He'll be able to see them from the helicopter."

Genial clapped his hands. "You are such a very nice friend!"

I heard it before I saw it: the helicopter's propeller descending through the air, the NuLifers exclaiming, Genial applauding as though he'd just seen the final routine in a Broadway musical. I ran out onto the lawn toward the helicopter, larger even than Genial's, and waved my arms, shouting "Happy birthday!" as loudly as I could.

The hatch opened and Orson emerged, wide-eyed, stubbled, grinning, wearing a blazer and sneakers with tongues so puffy he couldn't possibly have laced them up. And then behind him: Emily, her lips enormous with collagen, her fake eyelashes like a caterpillar's bristles.

"Holy shit," Orson said, pulling me into a hug. "Did you arrange all this?"

"Yeah." I eyed Emily over his shoulder.

"Ez, this is so beautiful," she said. "It looked so beautiful from the helicopter."

The NuLifers were chorusing "Happy birthday, Orson!" so loudly that he had to raise his hands to calm them down.

"Friends!" he said. "Thank you for this! Honestly, you don't know how lucky you make me feel!"

The applause was thunderous as we made our way to the farmhouse, where Orson stood in front of Genial and I on the lip of the patio and raised his hands again.

"A birthday is an occasion for reflection!" he shouted. "It's an occasion to think about the unity of the various components of the soul, the ethereal vessel that's transporting us through years and years of our lives."

Crazed cheering.

"I have been blessed in this life in many ways, but chief among them is the opportunity to be of service to you, to be reminded daily of the various hearts and souls that comprise this community, that make me want to *be* as I *do* instead of just *do* as I *be*."

Laughter: this was one of his many catchphrases. I squinted to try to see the NuLifers but couldn't make out any details, so I imagined them vacant-eyed in their white and gold, crawling out of their tents to kowtow to him, hair greasy, children on their shoulders. I'd given him so much, and *they* were the blessing?

"Please, remember this moment as you move through the story of your lives and remind yourselves to stay spiritually sound!"

"We'll never forget, Orson!"

"We love you!"

"There is no doing-as-being, only being-as-doing!"

"Thank you!" Orson called into what had become an inky and impenetrable dusk. There was another swelling of applause and then the NuLifers abandoned their positions and wandered toward the buffet tables, waving excitedly to Orson as they passed the patio.

"Bravo!" Genial said, standing from his Adirondack. "Orson, bravo!"

"This is Genial Arroya," I said. "The son of the president of Urmau."

"Very pleased." Genial's smile made half-moons of his eyes. He offered his hand to shake and Orson took it.

"A pleasure to meet you, too," Orson said. "Genial, this is my friend Emily."

Emily offered her manicured hand and Genial kissed it, making her giggle. Orson had introduced her. He had considered her worthy of an introduction.

"Orson, the Bliss-Mini—I am so impressed," Genial said. "I want to help you sell it in Urmau."

Orson looked at me in disbelief.

"Happy birthday," I said weakly.

"This is too much!" Orson shook me by the shoulder. "Ez, this is too much!"

I collapsed into an Adirondack.

"He is tired," Genial said. "He planned this whole day, and then we have been speaking for a long time. Maybe you and I can go inside and talk more?"

"Of course," Orson said. He turned to me and Emily.

"We'll be fine out here," she said, sitting down next to me.

Orson mussed my hair. "Holy fuck, little dude."

When they were gone, I summoned a member of the staff and ordered my own gin gimlet. I deserved a special exception as much as Genial— perhaps more.

"One of the same, please," Emily said. "Well, the same but with lime."

"A gin gimlet already has lime," I snapped. Three exceptions was too many.

"Oh right! I'm so silly. Extra lime, then."

I leaned back and pretended to be very interested in constellations I couldn't see. Emily crossed her slim legs.

"Really, Ez, you're so generous," she said.

"Thanks."

"We had no idea. We just spent the whole day shopping in SoHo."

"Sounds fun."

"It was! Orson has a flair for fashion. I didn't know that about him, did you? He always dresses so modestly."

Of course I knew that about him: I'd helped him cultivate it. But before I could say anything, she cocked her head at me admiringly.

"You probably know him better than anyone in the world. Better than his own mother."

I shrugged.

"Ez, can you tell me something?"

"Mm."

"What's Orson like? When, you know—god, I feel like a little kid— when he likes someone?"

My heart began thrumming. "He doesn't like anyone," I said, too quickly. "He's basically a monk. He's not interested in relationships. He doesn't like people crowding him."

"Oh." She traced an invisible pattern on the arm of her chair. "Well, then maybe I'm confused, but I don't think I am? Because he and I—well, we've had some intimacy."

"Intimacy," I repeated, feeling the same threat of organ failure I'd felt years ago, when he'd discovered Ingrid.

"Yeah." She giggled. "On the helicopter, too, we um—we made out for a while."

My head grew hot like an overworked hard drive. What was the angle here? What was the plan? Or was there one?

"Sorry if this is TMI," she said.

"It's not TMI."

"You are literally probably the most generous person I've met in my life." She grabbed my hand in hers: it was cold in the manner of all appendages attached to people with little body fat. "I want you to know that if you need anything from me—honestly, *anything*—I will do my best to help you."

If he saw something in her—and I couldn't bear the thought of him seeing something in her—it was the feline tilt of her eyes, the unmitigated kindness of her face, the obvious enthusiasm she had for being alive.

"I'll let you know," I said.

"Oh good!" she crowed, and squeezed my hand. "I honestly think you and I are going to be really, really good friends."

§

Orson flew to Rezopol, Urmau's capital, a few days ahead of me. I took the extra time in New York to hammer out the terms of our Deutsche Bank loan with Elaine, how exactly we'd structure our debt within the special purpose vehicle. The loan would finance the Urmanese expansion, which would inflate the share price, which would please shareholders, which would mean, ultimately, much more money.

The heat in Rezopol was honey thick, and smelled of both exhaust and eucalyptus. I flew first class because Orson had chartered the private jet, and the airport was clogged with middle-class people flying across the country for a national holiday. It took me almost half an hour to make my way to ground transport. When I got there, I could see Genial's Jeep, Genial and his driver in front and Orson and Emily in back. Orson had brought her with him.

"Ezra!" Genial held my face and kissed me on either cheek. *"Felice annõovyani!"*

"Felishe anyo vienni," I stuttered in response, which made him laugh.

"Good, wow, you already speak Urmanese like a native, impressive!"

"You made it, little dude," Orson said, pulling me into a hug and kissing me on the forehead in a way that still managed to be bro-ish. "How was the flight?"

"Comme ci comme ça," I said.

Emily cackled. "Ez, oh my god, you're a polyglot!"

We merged with the traffic leaving the airport and Genial turned in his seat to face us, buoyant like a child thrilled to have the privilege of riding up front.

"Ezra, if you are not too tired, we are going straight to the place where we will build the NuLife Center."

"It's on the beach," Orson said. "It's really incredible."

"The first of many of the NuLife Centers," Genial added. "We will have many of them here, right, Ezra?"

I nodded. We were on the highway, moving fast, and I was beginning to feel carsick.

"So, Genial, your dad has been president for how long?" Emily was shouting over the wind. She had neglected to pull her hair into a ponytail and it was blowing chaotically all over the back seat, itchy strands slapping me in the face.

"For only five years," Genial shouted back. "And now he is trying to stop the next election."

"What's his stance on NuLife?" Orson asked, his voice more audible over the wind than anyone else's.

Genial winked impishly at us. "Oh, he doesn't know about it! But what will he do?"

I frowned. This was a new development. The kind of thing that could get us kicked out of the country.

"He doesn't know about it?" Orson asked.

"Yes, but he doesn't know about many things. I keep many things from him. What is the old expression in America? *The future walks.*"

"The future marches on," I shouted.

"Yes! We march on, here in Urmau, past him. Soon everything will march on, yes?"

We exited the highway into a small town of clay houses bordering the ocean, the shine of which was fulminous. At the southernmost end of the beach was a plot of land that could have contained a large hotel. We debarked the Jeep and stood on the beach, Genial positioning himself at the water's edge.

"This is the place!" he said.

The sun was overwhelming, so I looked at my feet, and when I looked back up, I found I could only see shadows, my eyes flooded with UV, my vision constricted. I took a few deep breaths and waited for it to pass but it didn't. Orson's shadow took off its shoes and rolled up its jeans and waded into the water, and Emily's shadow kicked off its sandals and did the same, shrieking as Orson's shadow picked her up and spun her around.

"What do you think, Ezra?" Genial's shadow asked.

"It's very bright," I said without thinking.

"Oh—yes. Your eyes?"

I blinked. "No, no—I mean, the sunshine is beautiful," I said quickly. "It's the perfect place. I'm thinking, maybe, like, fifteen more locations like this?"

"Fifteen! Wow! Yes, if you have the capital, I am always happy to have more."

I shrugged, trying hard to keep looking at his shadow and not at my feet. "I'm thinking we'd sell Bliss-Minis, train people in Synthesis, distribute Orson's teachings, employ a bunch of people to do all that. And we'll probably outsource the manufacturing of the Bliss-Mini to Urmau."

"Wonderful, Ezra, it's wonderful!"

"But is your father going to dislike this?"

Genial's shadow shook its head. "No, no. This is one thing he doesn't care so much about, foreign industry coming here, failing, succeeding, more often failing. He lets me worry about this. When he finds out about NuLife, what will he do, because it will already be so successful, right? He will not care."

I nodded. "Whatever works," I said. "As long as we can all turn a profit."

"The light and the life to Urmau!" Genial said, wrapping his arm around my shoulder. "This is part of our national anthem. *Luce do vita suo Urmau!*"

"The light and the life," I echoed.

I hadn't seen Emily's and Orson's shadows approaching us. Emily grabbed me by the arm, breathless. "Come on, Ez," she said. "Let me take you into town and buy you a *banta*. It's a banana cheese sandwich."

"You have to try it." Genial said. "It is one of our traditional foods. Let her get you one."

"They're delicious," Orson said.

Genial smiled at Orson and jerked his head toward the ocean's southerly swell. "Yes, Orson—let me walk with you up this beach. There is a rock up there in the shape of a big thumb; we can climb it."

In town, I regathered my senses of color and detail. The spray of freckles across Emily's nose was visible, as was her hair's intermittent sun-blond. Her stride was long, and it was difficult to keep up with her—not that I wanted to, but I felt I had no choice. She pulled me toward a ramshackle storefront whose awning read *"Banta Tienta."*

"This is going to be good," she said. "More authentic than in the city."

We stood at the counter, Emily trying to parse an inscrutable chalkboard full of variations on the *banta* and me imagining Orson climbing a huge rock face, plummeting to the beach, shattering his spine.

"Two regular *banta*, please," Emily said to the bored clerk, who shook his head at her English. She held up two fingers and said, too loudly: *"Banta."* The clerk rolled his eyes and disappeared behind the counter.

"It's great, isn't it?" she cooed. "Like a tropical vacation."

"It's not a vacation if it's for business," I said.

"Technically yes, it's business, but I'm still having fun."

"You're not here on business."

"You're right," she conceded, and kicked the floor's chipped white tile with her sandal.

"There's actually no reason you're here." I couldn't stop myself.

She looked at me, big-eyed. "I'm just keeping Orson company."

"Sure," I said. "We all are."

The clerk handed us our *bantas* and we left the *tienta*, Emily devouring hers instantly. It seemed unfair to me that Emily should have the same metabolism as Orson. I took a bite of mine. It was delicious, which was disappointing for reasons I couldn't explain.

"Are you okay, Ez? You seem upset about something."

"I'm not upset."

"Because honestly, if you are, you can always talk to me."

I spun on my heel to face her. "I'm not fucking upset, okay? Stop asking me if I'm upset!"

"Okay." She tucked her chin into the concavity of her chest. "I'm sorry."

"Look," I said, softer, embarrassed. "Orson's climbing up a rock face shaped like a big thumb. Maybe you and I should be worried about that."

"He's pretty athletic," she said, still meek. "And Genial's there to watch him."

She didn't care, did she? She never would.

We walked south on the beach, toward the thumb, only to encounter Orson and Genial walking back toward us, Orson's hair mussed appealingly.

"How was the *banta*?" he asked me.

I told him it was good, and Genial clapped me on the shoulder, and Orson grabbed Emily's hand and pulled her to him. He pecked her on the cheek and she made a face like she was in the midst of a good dream.

"Oh, look at the lovebirds, Ezra," Genial said. "It's beautiful, yes?"

I gritted my teeth and nodded.

§

At night, we sat on the deck of the pool behind Genial's mansion, Orson turning flips off the diving board while Genial, Emily, and I split two cases of Urmanese beer.

"I am wondering what he will invent next," Genial said, scratching his bare chest. "How does such a mind develop?" He clucked and looked at the stars. "A real American."

"You're giving us too much credit," Emily said. "We Americans are actually quite average."

"No, do not—man, what are the words?—sell yourself to the river."

"Up the river," I said.

"Yes! Up the river!" He pointed at me. "Ezra always knows the expression."

Orson blew us all a kiss mid flip and then made a vertical line of his body, barely disturbing the water's surface as he entered it. Emily shrieked with pleasure and ran across the deck to dive in herself.

"Do you think it is good, the Daroqol?" Genial asked me.

"The resistance army?"

He nodded. I shrugged.

"We should really stay out of politics. NuLife's just here to rejuvenate the economy."

Genial took a long pull from his beer. "Yes," he said. "I think it is very good for NuLife, the left wing. I think it is good for the people who want something different."

"Is that a large portion of the population?"

"Yes, many. Including me." He laughed. "We want the future to finally come to Urmau."

Orson lumbered out of the pool, followed by Emily, who snatched her towel from her chair and pulled it around her shoulders like a flimsy cape.

"I should go in," she said. "I'm freezing."

"Yes, of course," Genial said. "Emily, let's both. A long day, right, boys?"

"Not too long," Orson said. "You have a beautiful country, Genial."

Genial thanked him and kissed us both on either cheek. Then the two walked back toward the mansion, evanescing into a dark patch of succulents.

I opened another beer and realized I was on the verge of being more than a little drunk. Orson was straddling his beach chair, looking up at the sky.

"It's the clearest sky I've ever seen," he said. "Like ever in my life."

"Yeah," I said, and sucked on my beer. "It really is something."

"Apparently there are different constellations down here," he said. "Carina, Centaurus, Crux."

"Crux?"

"It's just a cross." He searched the sky and then pointed. "You see right there?"

Of course I couldn't—at that point, even the patterns of the brightest stars were beyond my perceptual ability—but I made a good-faith effort, squinting in the direction he was pointing. "Sort of," I said. Then, as gently as I could: "Why is Emily always with us?"

"Hm?" His eyes were still on the sky.

"She was at your birthday party. She came here with us."

"Why not?"

"I just don't get it." I could feel the heat rising in my chest. "What's the point?"

He turned to me. "There's no *point*. She's just another person who believes in NuLife's mission."

"NuLife's mission?"

"Yeah." He turned back to the sky. "You've been weird about her since you met her."

"I wouldn't say that."

"Do you not like her?"

I downed the rest of my beer in a few gulps, stalling. "I mean, she's fine."

"It sounds like you don't like her."

"Why does that suddenly matter, whether or not I like her? It certainly hasn't mattered before."

"Look, Ez, it's simple: she's an ambassador of peace. She's helping us help people."

I laughed sharply. "You seriously think we're helping people?"

"Yes, I do, actually. I think we're doing good work in the world. At least I am."

Every muscle in my body was tight. "I'm the one working while you're prancing around pretending to be god."

Silence: he narrowed his eyes savagely. "At least I'm not going blind."

All my breath caught in my throat.

"You do a shitty job of hiding it, Ez."

"Fuck you!" I howled, and lunged at him. We landed in the grass, and he wrestled himself on top of me, pinning me to the ground. Then he replaced his hands with his knees and I writhed under him. He shoved his phone in my face.

"Look," he said. I could barely see the screen, but I knew enough to make out Emily's soft lower lip, the V of her thighs, a naked areola.

"She wants me," he said.

"Then go fuck her!" I shouted.

He stood up, sneering, and stormed into the house. I didn't watch him go. I was breathing shallowly, crying, my arms aching where he'd kneeled on them. I cried until I couldn't and then turned onto my stomach and put my ear to the ground, listening for vibrations from the underworld.

PART III

NINE

His name was Karl Rothenberg. He was forty-five but his face was uncreased and his eyes were a twinkling, babyish blue that made him look forever like a child on the verge of disclosing a secret. During a guest appearance on *Crazy Money*, he revealed to the host that his hair had gone white when he was twenty-two, and the host had remarked that it contrasted well with his "very dark" eyebrows. He wore Armani suits and loafers and was never seen in anything more casual than a suit jacket and a button-down that most people would have to take out a second mortgage to afford.

He called himself an "activist investor." He managed a hedge fund worth $3.4 billion, and he considered it his responsibility to raise the share price of corporations he thought were doing good things and destroy the share price of corporations he thought were doing bad things. His champions described him as the unsung hero of Wall Street. His enemies called him a market manipulator. He had identified NuLife as a corporation that was doing bad things and had shorted us to the tune of $1 billion. The stock price was finicky after that, plummeting and then rising and then plummeting again.

"You look good on camera, people like you, you're affable," the *Crazy Money* host said, and Rothenberg crossed his legs so his ankle rested on his knee. "Do you see yourself as someone who can make major waves in the market on the basis of personality alone?"

Rothenberg chuckled. "No, I see myself as someone who uses facts to determine who's doing the right thing. I'm trying to act in the most honorable way possible."

Brianna and I stood in my office watching the *Crazy Money* broadcast, watching Rothenberg smile self-effacingly into the camera.

"He's really smug," Brianna said. "The way he sits. Who crosses their legs on TV?"

A picture of Orson appeared in the upper-right-hand corner of the screen. "So now you're taking on Orson Ortman, the boy genius whose company NuLife is becoming an international phenomenon," the host said.

Rothenberg sat forward thoughtfully. "Yes, I am, Jim. And I'm doing that because I think Ortman's a fraud and his entire operation is a pyramid scheme. He develops this 'technology' that's supposed to 'synthesize' you, whatever that means—we can't tell if the technology even works. Meanwhile, Ortman's making these outlandish promises that he has yet to deliver on—and then he goes upstate and starts this cult that's this recruit-your-friends kind of thing where all the money's ultimately flowing toward him."

"What about his team? He's got some of the brightest minds in innovation on board."

"You mean Dexter Ellhorn? I thought he was making rockets for the president to shoot into space?"

The host laughed. "Yes, Ellhorn. But what about Ortman's right-hand man?"

A picture of me appeared where Orson's had vanished.

"Ezra Green is either the Dick Cheney behind this whole thing or the world's most useful idiot."

"Do you want me to turn this off?" Brianna asked.

"No, I'm fine," I said. "Turn it up, actually."

She grabbed the remote.

"Could this just be the folly of youth?" the host asked, louder now. "Both CEO and CFO are still in their twenties, after all."

"No, Jim, this isn't *folly*. This is a criminal operation. I've already gathered some truly damning evidence against NuLife, and I intend to expose the corporation for what it is."

"See what you can dig up on this guy," I said to Brianna.

I stayed in the office long after everyone left, first finishing paperwork, then playing PC games that reminded me of childhood. Get the POV character into the castle, then get him to defeat the ghosts. Send the race car around the track until it crashes. Brianna stayed at a desk on the floor within sight of my office, answering emails and typing up expense reports until I finished playing, at which point I summoned her. Then I described what I was in the mood for and she nodded curtly and vanished, at which point I started playing the PC games again.

No longer than an hour later she reappeared with someone who looked twenty-one, strong jawed in black jeans with a crossbar in his ear, and handed me her wallet, which I peeled apart to reveal a bag containing a few bumps of coke.

"Thank you, Brianna," I said, and she left, and the twenty-one-year-old grabbed the coke from me and did a bump, and then I did a bump, and then he took his shirt off and I took my shirt off.

Sometimes I went to parts of town where I knew I wouldn't be recognized, and the sex was quick and messy in the bathroom stalls of bars and clubs and, just once, a department store. Few if any questions were asked. I always offered to pay, which torqued some people off. I should never have offered to pay.

People reported that Emily had relocated from her mansion in LA to the Farm, where she and Orson were sharing a "modest home" together. There was a photo of it: an Enner house not unlike any other Enner house, a split-level with a garage and a garret and a bay window in the living room—I'd been in hundreds of them before but had never imagined that Orson and Emily would share one. In the photo, the two of them stood in their driveway, Orson in a black-and-red flannel with a full beard and Emily in leggings and a fleece jacket, her hair a tawny brown—quite possibly her natural color, but there was no way of knowing—her cheeks rouged from the Oswego cold.

There were other photos of them too: leaving clubs hand in hand, attending galas, posing with other celebrities. I read the tweets about them:

It's L. Ron Hotboy and Lady Barnum

Do they milk cows on the Farm? Or just investors?

I think of him as a fancy millennial Koresh

Honestly if he looks like that all the time I want in on the hustle

I began building the NuLife Centers in Urmau and employed thousands of Urmanese in the manufacture of Bliss-Minis. For every Urmanese Nu-Life Center I opened, I opened one in the States, until most major U.S. cities had brick-and-mortar places where people could buy their Bliss-Minis and have them repaired. They could take crash courses in Synthesis or be Synthesized by "Superiors" we employed for $50K a year. The Synthesized paid the Synthesizers, who in turned paid us, and all this money trickled back up toward corporate, toward me, sitting in my office in New York losing patches of my vision to the flawed machinery of my eyes. Every time I had an attack—and they became increasingly frequent in 2017—it felt like things got a little dimmer.

I couldn't stop loving him. I funneled money into the Farm, and more and more people gave up their lives to live in Enner houses and take his cure. On her weekly visits to the property, Brianna took videos for the corporate Instagram of Orson Synthesizing people, or of him sitting at the heads of eager circles and instructing people to repeat his words back to him, or of Emily leading people in some kind of obscure dance ritual. There were tents on the property, hundreds, people either visiting for a few weeks or waiting for their Enner houses to be built, people who wanted so badly to be close to Orson that they'd forfeited almost everything for the chance to glimpse him emerging from the farmhouse, dressed in a work shirt and jeans and sandals, his arms spread wide. "Good morning, friends!" he'd bellow. "Who's ready for a day of healing?" And his devotees would roar with enthusiasm. They cut him checks directly—they couldn't resist it—and it was with some of this money that he ran the Farm. The rest came from me.

I spent a lot of time with my forehead on my desk, blinking into the cavern formed by my head and shoulders, trying not to think of him. I would be working peacefully—holding meetings, or squirrelling away money in tax havens with Elaine, or obsessively monitoring the share price—and then I'd think of Orson with Emily and I'd have to put my head down because my mind would swim and my vision would flood with silver sparks. I thought of them sleeping in the same bed together, of Emily listening as I once had to the soft whinny of a snore he'd acquired since adolescence, of them waking up next to each other in the morning and smiling at the potential of a new day. Eyes locking, kissing, morning sex. It felt time and time again like I was being hit in the chest with a softball. Was this really what he wanted—a woman? I was sure he hated me after the fight in Urmau, but I knew he still needed me. The Farm couldn't run without me, and I imagined he wished that it could. Maybe he was fantasizing about pulling up anchor and drifting away from me and my white-hot neediness, my gut-turning weakness, my imperfect teeth and impossible-to-conceal pigeon toes. He knew me better than anyone else, which meant he saw clearer than anyone else all the awful things about me. The idea made me seethe. What if I had been just another means to an end, and that end was Emily? I started keeping a thermometer in my office so I could take my temperature: I was either too hot or too cold. My joints throbbed when I moved. My body was a strange and hostile place to inhabit; it felt like the entire thing had gone the way of my eyes.

On a morning when I was working my way through the most recent profile of Orson in GQ, Brianna walked into my office clutching her notebook to her chest like a shy girl in a teen drama.

"What is it?"

"There's kind of a commotion," she said. "In the lobby."

"What?"

"There's a guy down there who says he knows you? Who's asking for you?"

"What guy?"

She opened her notebook and read the name from a page: "Mack Wang-Orsi."

I looked down at my feet under my desk.

"What's he saying?"

"He's saying he needs to talk to you. Security has him."

I shook my head. The day had barely begun. "Bring him up."

Brianna's eyes widened. "Are you sure? He's acting really—he's acting kind of violent. Like yelling and stalking around."

"Just have security bring him up," I said. "It's best if you do."

Mack had aged considerably in four years: his hair was as silver as it was black, and he'd gotten a new set of glasses that magnified the pale gray wedges beneath his eyes. He was dressed in the hoodie and jeans of the Zuckerbergian douchebag and he was clearly trying his best to take measured breaths.

"Do you want me to stay?" Brianna asked, slouching beneath the combined weight of Mack's and my gazes.

"Just stand outside," I said, and smiled at Mack. "I don't think we'll need security."

I gestured for him to sit down but he stayed standing, so I stood.

"It's good to see you again," I said, and opened my arms to offer him a hug.

"Fuck you," he said.

I shrugged and sat back down. "Okay," I said.

"*Fuck* you," he repeated. "You fucking little crony, you little henchman. You feel good sleeping on top of your piles of money at night?"

He began pacing. I watched him.

"How can I help you, Mack?"

"I want the patent. I want the money."

"You gave that up in 2013."

He narrowed his eyes. "You got me drunk."

"I didn't do anything. You gave it up of your own volition."

"You fucked with me."

"You've always had a drinking problem."

"I swear to god." He put his hands on my desk, leaned in close to me, his wan face rigid with anger. "If I don't see a real cut of your profits—the stupid profits you're making off this stupid thing—I'm going to tell everyone what the Bliss-Mini really is."

I raised an eyebrow. "What's the Bliss-Mini really?"

"It's nothing," he shouted. "And Dexter Ellhorn made it into a fancier nothing! And all you fucks are getting rich off it!"

"Do you think everyone's going to believe you when you tell them the Bliss-Mini is nothing?"

He shrugged, kept pacing. "I don't give a fuck. It's the truth."

"Right." I flipped over my copy of GQ so Mack wouldn't see the picture of Orson in his $15,000 suit. "But who are people going to believe?"

He ignored this question, jabbed his finger at me. "I'm coming for you. I want five hundred million dollars. I'm going to sue you."

"Okay," I said. "We'll have to ready our lawyers."

He sneered. "You're a fucking fraud, you know that? You're fake. Everything you've done in your life is fake. Everything you've done in your life is to suck *his* dick, and everyone's going to find out, and you're going to be behind bars."

I felt myself blanch, but I didn't uncross my feet on top of my desk. "I'm sorry you feel that way," I said, my voice trembling more than I would have liked it to.

"I don't *feel* any way. I know the truth. I was in on the ground floor. Pay me or I'll tell everyone about your bullshit."

He shoved the door open and stormed out and Brianna walked in, still clutching her notebook. "Ez?"

"I'm fine," I said.

"He was yelling."

"People get mad. When you get successful, people get mad." My voice was shaking.

"Do you need anything? Do you need coffee?"

"No, no." I gestured for her to sit down and she did. "I don't like yelling, is really it."

"Who does?"

"No one," I said decisively. "Except for Mack Wang-Orsi."

She offered a tight-lipped snort. The silver sparks were back in my eyes. My vision dimmed and then brightened and dimmed and then brightened.

"I shouldn't have let him up," she said apologetically.

"I'm the one who gave you the okay." I was feeling suddenly small, like Sledge was ordering me to do push-ups. "What if you have a problem," I said, "like my headaches, but you don't believe in Western medicine?"

Brianna sat forward in her seat: this was clearly her wheelhouse. "Gold flakes in my cereal," she said. "Actually, you know what's better than that?"

"What?"

"Microdosing. It's where you give yourself, like, tiny amounts of LSD or shrooms every other day. Like a few micrograms. Not enough to trip, just enough to feel good."

"That would be good," I said. "Can you get me some?"

"Yeah, of course."

Brianna looked smilingly at me, attentive, maybe a little worried. I wondered what it would feel like if I told her why Mack was angry.

"Ez?"

"Yes?"

"Are you okay?" And as if she'd read my mind: "Is there something you want to tell me?"

"No," I said quickly. "Nothing."

§

I sat under the desperately bright lights of the *Crazy Money* set, a makeup artist brushing my cheeks with foundation and then plucking the napkin she'd tucked into my shirt collar from my neck. The executive board had decided I'd go on *Crazy Money* to address Rothenberg's allegations against NuLife. I was by then a veteran of asinine talk shows, getting booked on all the B-gigs Orson was too busy to attend. What was one more?

The host sat at the table across from me, poring over a set of index cards on which he'd made notes for our conversation. I had no index cards of my own. I didn't need any.

The cameras started rolling. A producer motioned for me to smile.

"We are joined today by Ezra Green, CFO of NuLife," the host said.

"Nice to be here," I said into the solar-quality lights.

The host turned to me. "Ezra, your company stands accused by activist investor Karl Rothenberg of fraud and criminal mischief. What do you have to say in response?"

I laughed. "I'm afraid that's impossible. We built our corporation from the ground up, using cutting-edge technology and the power of spiritual healing. Frankly, it appears to me that Mr. Rothenberg is just jealous of what we've got. We're valued at four billion dollars now, which is more money than he's managing. And he doesn't seem to have any actual evidence to back up the claims he's making about our company."

"Biting words from our prodigy CFO." The host smiled in the direction of the cameras, and I blinked, my own smile nearly thwarted by the sting of the lights. "Some people find it strange that your corporation is attached to this—what is it called?"

"The Farm," I said.

"Right, this 'farm.' Why do people need to flock to this place to get Synthesis done when they could just wear the Bliss-Mini?"

"Well, like I said, we're a company that also believes in hands-on spiritual healing. And we're a family." I flashed on Orson's face as I said this, and my hands felt numb. "We don't believe in distinctions between ourselves and our consumer base. This is why we have this place where . . . where people can interact directly with our CEO and benefit from his spiritual expertise."

"This business model—it's totally unlike anything I've ever seen."

I nodded. "It really is unique, to be sure. At NuLife, we pride ourselves on our uniqueness and innovation."

"But is it sustainable?"

I had no idea what he was getting at, but I'd learned by then never to ask for clarification. "We've projected this thing out. People actually *want* to make the trip to the Farm, more and more people as time goes on. Think of it like a retreat, just attached to a truly incredible product."

The host nodded, covertly inspecting his index cards. "What about Dexter Ellhorn?"

"What about him?"

"There are some investors who think he's all bark and no bite."

"Oh, believe me—Ellhorn's got plenty of bite."

The host laughed artificially. "Well, we've seen a really great response to the 2.0. No one can deny that your numbers are shooting up."

I tried to affect a humble smile. "We know how to do business."

"Even your detractors have got to admit that's true." He turned back to the cameras. "Folks, this is Ezra Green, CFO of NuLife. Ezra, thank you for your time."

The cameras and lights shut off and the host vanished from the table. I wandered off set to the all-purpose dressing room, where I found Karl Rothenberg standing at the door, waiting for me. He was, as always, impeccably dressed and clean-shaven.

"They always lob softballs at the corporate oligarchs," he said, grinning.

"And you're not a corporate oligarch?"

He straightened his tie, elongating his neck as he did. "No, I'm a man of the people. The very rich people."

I pushed past him into the dressing room and he followed me in, closing the door behind him. I tried to ignore this, dabbing at my makeup with one of the baby wipes from the container on the vanity.

"It was a good segment, though," he said.

"Why are you here?"

"You didn't see? I gave an interview right before you." I looked at him and he raised his hands defensively. "Not about NuLife."

"And you just, like, hung around here after?"

"To watch yours, yeah. See how you did on TV."

"I've been on TV before."

"Never to defend yourself against me."

I turned back to the mirror and continued to dab.

"I think you're well-spoken. I think you're smarter than Orson."

I flushed.

"Do you get out a lot? In the city?" he asked.

"Not really. I mostly just work."

"Let me take you for a drink."

I caught his reflection in the mirror: his hands were in his pockets and he was smiling broadly, a smile entirely unlike the terse grin he always wore on TV.

"Why would you want to take me out for a drink?" I asked. "Aren't I the enemy?"

He shrugged, still smiling. "I believe in knowing thy enemy."

I performed a quick cost-benefit analysis: he hated us, we hated him, drinks would make him vulnerable, they'd also make me vulnerable. He might tell me something I needed to know, but of course I might tell him something he needed to know.

"I get it," he said, as if reading my mind. "You're worried."

I said nothing.

"Listen, I believe in fighting a fair fight." He eyed me up and down. "We don't have to talk business. Aren't you a little bit curious what the big bad wolf looks like tipsy?"

I told myself I'd be performing recon, so I went with him to a hotel in the Bowery where he bought me sidecars and the stools were so high that my toes barely grazed the ground. He undid his tie and unbuttoned the first button of his shirt and the gel in his hair gave way to a small cowlick. He drank old fashioneds and did most of the talking: about how annoying everyone was on Wall Street, about the fakeness of Harvard MBAs, about the petty expectations of investors.

"You're so healthy looking," I said three drinks in. "Are you one of those finance guys who, like, runs every day at five in the morning? Or does push-ups whenever you're about to leave the house?"

"You got me. I've got a punching bag at my place." He mimed a few uppercuts. "You get all your anger out and you get to look at all the lucky bastards enjoying the park."

"You've got a place on the park," I said, my brain feeling glazed. "That means you're truly an asshole."

He laughed. I tried to stay alert. All good spies always stay alert.

"This Synthesis," he said. "How does it work?"

I shook my head. "You said no business. You said I wouldn't have to say anything about business."

"It's not business," he protested.

"It is. It definitely is. I know you're a devious fuck but just—I don't know—just let me enjoy the drinks before you try to take me for all I'm worth."

He sat forward on his stool, eyes bright. "Then just Synthesize me. You don't have to explain it. I just want to be Synthesized."

I sucked on the orange wedge from my sidecar. "I'm not going to do anything of the sort."

"I'll pay you."

"You couldn't pay me any amount of money."

"Okay, then I'll buy you another drink."

It felt like a matter of minutes before he was paying for a room and we were going upstairs together, me feeling light and loose-limbed and him moving with a directness I wasn't accustomed to seeing in him, but then again I was accustomed to seeing him sitting in chairs behind desks and calmly making financial predictions on TV. In the room, he took off his jacket and kicked off his shoes and sat on the edge of the bed, palms up-turned at his sides.

"What do I have to do?" he asked. "For you to Synthesize me?"

I sat down across from him and started laughing, making no effort to stop.

"Just tell me a memory that really sticks out to you," I said.

"My wife shutting the door in my face the April before we got di-vorced," he said. "No, okay—forget that. How about you sucking on that orange wedge?"

I opened my eyes. His were open too, blue as the hottest part of a flame.

Afterward, he curled against me in bed, and I could feel the front of his body against the back of mine, the cold tops of his thighs and bony knots of his kneecaps.

"I'm sorry," he said, and bit my ear. "I don't want to take you for all you're worth."

"You don't have to."

"I feel like I do, though. Because it's blood money."

I pulled his arm under mine and around my torso. "Can I ask you a question?"

"Anything," he said.

"What do you do to make yourself not in love with someone?" I flipped to face him, or rather the blur that was supposed to be him.

"What do you mean?"

"Like, if you've loved someone for a long time—how do you force yourself out of love?"

"Oh, Ez." He kissed my cheek. "You're so young, aren't you?"

"Not really. I'm twenty-seven"

"Trust me, that's still young." He brushed a strand of hair from my face. "That's very, very young."

§

A few weeks after my *Crazy Money* appearance, I had to speak at a Captains of Industry dinner that was being hosted by a financial magazine, the kind of thing that gave very rich people an excuse to assess one another and exchange pithy and confusing insults at the buffet. The invitation had originally gone to Orson, but he was busy on the Farm with something called Wholeness, a two-week-long retreat for people interested in "reconciling the bad with the good." Devotees had swarmed the Farm in record numbers: aerial photographs showed the property's entire square footage covered with tents and people and Porta-Potties. It stayed this way for days, looking like a perpetual music festival.

I'd brought Brianna with me to the dinner, which I could tell would be interminable from the moment we stepped foot in the banquet hall. The place was crowded with adults in expensive evening wear wandering among the tables and making conversation that was hostile in its politesse. There were a few people my age, mostly tech brats who had invented dog-walking apps or Bluetooth devices that curated workout playlists or community workspaces for lonely freelancers. The kind of people whose offices had beer on tap and Ping-Pong tables in "lounges." The kind of people who were, in other words, dumb and earnest, who actually believed in the fulfillment of the American dream.

Brianna and I took our seats and I looked at my phone uselessly, wondering if Orson had texted me—our texts since the visit to Urmau had been curt and professional—but I had no new notifications. Not even the daily hello from my parents, which I alternately ignored and responded to, giving them as little information about what was really going on as possible. Brianna was scanning the room, for who or what it was impossible to know, and when I pocketed my phone she leaned in close to me, clearly anticipating what I was about to say.

"Did you bring it?" I asked. "I have a headache coming on." It was a lie: I was just bored out of my mind.

"Of course," she said, and slid a small gold pill case toward me on the table. "This is for the next two weeks, so just take one."

I nodded, pocketed the case, and started to make my way to the restroom. The space was choked with people standing in fraternal huddles, and if I had been taller it would have been easier to make my way around them. I was nearly across the floor when I heard a woman's voice calling my name.

I turned and there she was, cupping a glass of champagne with both hands: Susan Lehigh. She wore glasses instead of sunglasses, her eyes clear of cataracts, deep-blue irises nacreous in their shine. I could feel my pulse in my head.

"What a pleasure to see you again, Ezra," she said. "After all these years."

I wanted a way out of the conversation immediately, but there was none. "Good to see you too."

She smiled, her mouth like a bent trapeze wire. "I've been reading so much about your business. About all the work you and Orson are doing."

"It's certainly going well." I felt like a teenager again.

"It is, isn't it? Your share price just keeps shooting up and up. What is it now?"

"It's eighty-six," I said. "We're recovering from a bit of a downtick."

"Oh, isn't that wonderful." She took a long sip of her champagne. "And you keep track, don't you?"

I shrugged. "Part of the job."

"Of course. You could give me a few pointers, I'm sure." Her "me" was the vocal equivalent of a paper cut.

"I really am hearing great things," she said. "About you especially. You're the brains behind all this, aren't you?"

"I wouldn't say that." I was trying to speak carefully. "I think Orson deserves just as much credit."

She waved her hand as if I'd just suggested she take off her makeup. "Maybe way back when. But I can tell—this is all your work, isn't it? This has Ezra Green written all over it."

I didn't want to ask her what "this" was. I just wanted her out of my sight. "Good talking to you," I said. "I should really run. I have to prepare this speech."

"Oh, of course," she cooed. "Prepare your speech."

I locked myself in a stall in the bathroom and leaned against the wall, taking deep breaths. Susan Lehigh couldn't be real anymore. She belonged to another life, one in which Orson had to assuage my doubts in Carol's kitchen. One in which I had doubts at all.

I opened the pill case to find ten miniature squares of paper wrapped in tin foil. I'd never dropped acid before, and I wanted to obliterate all memory of Susan Lehigh, so I decided I'd macrodose. I put two tabs on my tongue and closed my mouth, letting them sit there for a full two minutes before I spit them into the toilet. Then I left the stall and washed my hands next to a man who'd made a fortune fracking on the Marcellus Shale.

"You like these kinds of things?" he asked me.

"Not really," I said.

"Yeah, it's a waste of time." He pulled a linen napkin from a dispenser on the counter, dried his hands, and tossed it inelegantly into the wastebasket. "Everyone already knows where everyone else stands. There's no use arranging some dumb dinner to prove it."

As I made my way back to Brianna, I saw that the emcee had taken the stage and was making a series of nothing jokes at which people were laughing vapidly. I pulled the index cards I'd prepared from my jacket pocket and began shuffling through them: introduction, joke about Orson's absence, inspirational bit about how the company got started, joke about how young I was, expression of gratitude toward the titans of industry whose shoulders I was standing on, nod to investors, another joke, close the speech. I couldn't stop thinking of Susan Lehigh, of her face like a dried flower petal, the fact that she'd be sitting somewhere in the audience, watching me. I'd cursed myself somehow. I was being punished for something. Maybe for fighting with Orson. Or not listening to Mengetsu. There was something very wrong: I'd done something very wrong, and now I had to pay.

"Are you okay?" Brianna whispered. "Do you want to rehearse with me?"

I shook my head. "Is the microdose supposed to make me feel calmer?"

"Yes. And happier. And not headachy. Is it working?"

"Oh yeah, definitely. I feel all those things."

The first speaker assumed the stage and began talking about the importance of "innovative disruption." I checked my phone again. I had no idea what I was checking for anymore. There was no way Orson was going to text me some contrite message about that night in Urmau. What would he say? That he loved me?

I raised my head and saw Susan two tables away, her heavy-lidded eyes inclined pleasantly toward the stage as if she were watching a particularly entertaining movie instead of someone very rich talking about how he'd gotten very rich. She'd draped her jacket over her shoulders like a superhero's cape, and in the dim light she looked somehow younger than she had when I'd spoken with her minutes ago. She was aging in reverse, had been since I'd met her. She'd gotten better and I'd gotten worse. Her head began to swivel toward me and I looked away. A fucking curse.

"How are you feeling now?" Brianna whispered.

"I'm fine," I lied.

She smiled, baring her braces, and one side of her face slid off her neck like runny putty. She looked like a Dalí painting. I giggled, put my hand out to touch her dribbling cheek. She didn't flinch away.

"Ez?"

"Yep?"

"You're okay, right?"

"Oh yeah. Very good."

I took my phone out again, its face just as runny as Brianna's, the little characters beneath the apps like sigils etched on a glass bottle's surface. This was unbearably funny for some reason. I bit my lip and looked up to see a literal zoo. The couple at the table next to us had tusks—or else gave off the vibe of having tusks—and everyone at the table behind us was covered in hair that exposed only their mouths and eyes. The idea that Brianna and I were at a furry convention crossed my mind, and I snorted with laughter, attracting the annoyed glances of some of the animals. Brianna's fursona was a duck, her bill or else the idea of her bill mouthing the words *Ez can you try to keep it down people are looking*.

The duck's admonishment made it even harder to keep it down. I bent over so my head was between my knees and laughed a deoxygenated laugh, thinking of how stupid it was to have been afraid of anything or anyone in my life ever. I was a captain of industry. There was industry, and I was one of the captains of it. I imagined myself standing at the prow of a ship like Kate Winslet in *Titanic*, Orson behind me, our skin green to indicate either that we were seasick or that we were lucky or that we were in a cartoon that was very moving and photorealistic but still a cartoon. I gasped with laughter.

"Ez," Brianna quacked, her head next to mine under the table.

I sat up. Several animals in our vicinity were staring at me, their sensibilities offended, their long and hairy necks all taut with judgment. Not laughing at this would be perhaps the most difficult challenge the night had presented me yet. I swallowed and said, "Sorry. I'm really sorry." But apologizing was funny, too, so I put my head down on the table, my shoulders quivering, and mouthed *I'm so fucking sorry* into the tablecloth.

"Um, Ez." Brianna's hand was between my shoulders, shaking me. "What the fuck is going on?"

It was the first time she'd sworn at me. Brianna swearing. Brianna sweating. Brianna swooning. All impossible.

"Stop it," she whispered. "Please, stop it."

"Okay." I sat up, drawing an exaggerated, tai chi–kind of breath. "Yes, okay, I am totally centered. I am totally at ease and meditative and mindful."

"How many, um, headache pills did you take?"

I held up two fingers.

"Oh my god, Ez, you're supposed to take one at a time."

"And *you* could get fired for giving your boss drugs," I grinned. "For giving your boss not-good drugs."

I was looking at her seized-up face but also not looking at it, the thing I was not not-looking at being the emcee, who was saying "And now we welcome NuLife CFO Ezra Green to the stage."

Applause. I rose from my seat, the stern gazes of the nearby offended animals on me, the appreciative gazes of the far-off, non-offended animals on me as well. I bowed so deeply that it must have looked like a swan dive and walked onstage, waving as though I were about to be presented with an Academy Award. Ez 1, Emily 0.

The emcee offered the podium to me, clapping politely as I navigated the stage, whose floorboards described a rough-hewn smile. I tried very hard not to look or laugh at this. I grabbed the podium with both hands to steady myself—I was feeling less than seaworthy—and made no effort to withdraw my index cards from my jacket pocket. I couldn't see the audience but I imagined Brianna was in there somewhere, looking as stricken as I'd left her.

"Innovation," I yelled.

The audience was quiet, rapt.

"Innovation," I said, quieter. "Is often just cheating. Do you know what I mean? Innovation is often just pretending you have something that you don't.

"I have a hard-luck story, actually, like a lot of you people. I grew up biking from my parents' cramped apartment to neighborhoods with big houses and raking their lawns for pennies an hour. I told myself I would definitely live in a house like that someday, and now I live in two houses—two houses and a condo—that are much bigger. But that's not the point of this, is it? It's *industry* and *innovation.*"

I stumbled a little, the stage moving under my feet like a hostile carnival ride. Someone in the audience shouted something about me being drunk.

"Don't worry," I said. "I haven't had anything at all to drink. I'm just trying to cure this headache problem I have. I get migraines. Who gets migraines?"

I couldn't tell if people were raising their hands or not. I pressed on.

"Being in a state of constant competition and stress can cause the body to deteriorate. But you know what really deteriorates? Your sense of, I don't know—your sense of scale. Everything gets so much bigger and bigger that it's hard to remember being small. You all know what I mean. You're innovators.

"So say you have a product, right? And it's magic. But you *imagine* the magic. You being the consumer. You imagine it and that's how it works. It's wishful thinking but you can sell it. You being the executive. Excuse me—the *innovator.* Did you know I can actually sell anything? I could take my shoes off right now and sell them to you."

I bent and began unlacing my shoes. I got the right shoe off and then I could feel the emcee approaching me, asking for the microphone. I hobbled to the other side of the stage, clutching the microphone in one hand and my shoe in the other.

"Would you buy this shoe?" I asked.

Murmurs from the audience.

"If by wearing this shoe you could be made whole again, would you buy it? Would you, like, set up a meditation practice around it?"

"Mr. Green," the emcee said, urgency in her voice.

I turned to her. "Let them decide." Then I turned back to the audience. "Would you buy this shoe?"

Some *yeses,* some *nos,* some bewildered laughter, some noises of disgruntlement. The stage lights pulsed like dying stars. I could see galaxies in them. My eyes began to tear up, either from their beauty or from the strain it took to look at them.

"Honestly? I think you would buy this shoe. It's how our brains work. I could tell you *anything* about this shoe, literally anything, and if I told it to you in the right way, you'd believe it. That's the power of suggestion. That's how much we want to believe in innovation."

I sat down at the edge of the stage and I could finally see beyond the lights. What I saw was an abstract impressionist rendering of an audience, shadow creatures seated at shadow tables, and what looked like a centaur standing up with a centauride on his arm and the two of them walking away in shame and anger. I could feel this shame and anger as clearly as I could feel my own happiness. It was a happiness so intense that it was disorienting, spangly and shiny, both palm-of-the-hand compact and too big to be contained in the room.

"Susan, this whole thing is dedicated to you, this whole speech. You're my inspiration."

I turned around and tossed the microphone back to the emcee, who didn't catch it, and slid off the stage. Commotion, the emcee apologizing for me, Brianna grabbing my arm and hurrying me out of the banquet hall.

"What was that?" she asked, all propriety vanished.

I struggled with my jacket, giggling again, this time at the literal halos of the lobby lights, at the darkness encroaching on my vision.

"I had to say it," I said.

"Ez, please—I need you to give me the tabs back."

I obediently fished the gold case from my pocket and put it in her hand.

"We have to do damage control," she said.

Behind me: a voice, elegant, reverse aged: "Ezra."

We both turned. Susan Lehigh emerged from the banquet room door into the lobby, her heels clicking, her smile inquisitive.

"Very impressive," she said. "And sweet of you to dedicate that to me."

She was fuzzing in and out, her image overtaken by something like the static on an old television screen.

"We're just on our way home," Brianna said, her voice thick with fake apology.

"Yes, go get some rest," she said. "Good night, Ezra."

"Good night," I said. "I'm not afraid of you."

And then Brianna dragged me out the door.

§

I got a text from Orson: *come to the Farm.*

I took a company helicopter, Elaine picking at her cuticles across from me, flicking the dry and twisted ribbons of skin onto the floor between us.

"Your lifestyle has to be aspirational," she said.

"There's nothing about my lifestyle that's aspirational," I said.

"I mean there is, there's an essential part that is: you're very rich. People want to know how they can get very rich like you." Her gaze wandered out the window, where there were unremarkable clouds suspended in an unremarkable sky. "So give them something weird, something more marketable than losing your mind at a banquet. Maybe you should get your dogteeth removed and replaced with silver ones or eat only shellfish or do a triathlon."

"Can you see me doing a triathlon?"

She looked at me lazily and then looked back down at her cuticles.

I checked the share price on my phone. It was down 5 percent since the dinner.

"This isn't anything you can't recover from," she said, reading my mind.

The thrill of being in the same place as Orson, of knowing I was about to see him, was tempered by the fact that I knew I'd done something wrong, and both at once made it difficult to know exactly how I was feeling as Elaine and I made our way through the throng of Wholeness attendees sprawled across the property. They picked at the grass or offered us flowers or sang a song I deduced was about the "divine love" between Orson and Emily. Many of them were unbathed, and the stench was invasive: I imagined it clinging to my suit, melting the moisturizer from my skin. Elaine went so far as to hold her nose.

"Doing that makes you look like you hate them," I said.

"I don't care," she said. "They smell disgusting."

The farmhouse was crowded, too, but with cleaner devotees. Chuck and Priscilla Enner were hosting some kind of meditation session in the living room, and when they saw me, they waved, Priscilla instructing her students to "take a solo plunge into the abyss" for five minutes.

"Ez, it's been too long since we've seen you up here," Chuck said. Since devoting his life to the Farm he'd grown his hair out and lost what appeared to be half his body weight, likely the result of the kitchen staff's strictly vegetarian fare.

"I don't know if you've heard, but Jeremy's off to Georgetown in the fall," he said, beaming. "He took a gap year to teach English in Japan."

"Wow," I said. "That's really something."

Priscilla embraced me. "We've missed you, Ez."

"Good to be back," I mumbled, and introduced Elaine.

"Uh-oh!" Chuck said. "We're getting a visit from corporate. Do you like our crunchy ways?"

Elaine surveyed the room. "I've seen crunchier," she said.

Chuck clapped her on the shoulder. "Do you want to meditate, Elaine? Do you want to join us in our little circle here?"

I nodded in encouragement and Elaine sighed and began to remove her Danskos.

"Where's Orson?" I asked.

Priscilla pointed upstairs. "I think he's having some kind of meeting. I'm not sure what's going on. But I know he's expecting you."

My pulse quickened. What did he want to do with me?

I climbed the stairs and knocked on the door to his office. There was some kind of brief scuffling, some arrangement of bodies and furniture, and then he opened the door, his shirt partially unbuttoned, the cuffs of his jeans rolled down over his ankles. Emily sat behind him in one of her bodysuits, strands of hair dripping from her ponytail. To my surprise, he smiled.

"Ez. Come in, little dude."

I walked in, closed the door, and leaned against it, cowed.

"Hey, Ez! So good to see you!" Emily waved as though we were hundreds of feet apart. I ignored her and watched Orson, who had begun pacing, practically bouncing whenever he turned on his heels.

"So I saw the video of you at Captains of Industry," he said.

I swallowed.

"And I have no idea what you were on but it was honestly superb."

I could feel my brow unfurrowing. "Superb?"

"Yeah, I mean, you said so succinctly what I've been trying to say, what I've wanted to say during all of Wholeness. About the power of the mind. And the persuasiveness of the innovator. It was just beautifully spoken. It made me honestly kind of nostalgic for the old days."

And for a moment it was the old days again, his smile wide and kind and expectant, waiting for me to fill him in on some autobiographical detail or build on his punchline or chop the head off a chicken. He put his hands on his hips and stood in front of me and I wanted to kiss him, or at the very least hold him, but the unspoken distance between us remained. The old days were the old days and this was now.

"I'm glad you liked it," I said.

"It was really inspiring," Emily said.

"It really was." Orson got close enough to me to muss my hair: his touch was warm. "Do you want to stay for the day and help out? Take a break from New York?"

"That would be nice."

We were met with applause at the stairhead. There were camera flashes, repeated requests to be told what to do. Orson shouted above the adoration: "Live each day as if it were the next one!"

The words were repeated back loudly, and as we descended the steps and walked through the living room the NuLifers stood aside to let us pass, silt permitting the progression of a stream. Some even reached out to touch Orson, which didn't seem to bother him.

The reception outside was even louder than it had been inside. The lawn bordering the house had been trod into a thick mud, and we waded through it to get to the front of the crowd. I didn't even care that I was destroying a pair of loafers: I just wanted to follow Orson, to be as close to him as possible.

Orson picked up a bullhorn sitting on the patio's edge and spoke into it. "Friends! Can you listen to me for a moment?"

The din settled like dust. Orson gestured to me. I smiled timidly.

"This is Ezra Green. Do you all recognize him?"

Some scattered cheers, mostly restless confusion.

"He's the CFO of NuLife. He's a very, very wise person. He happened to give a speech the other day about the *very* things we're talking about here at Wholeness." He turned to me. "Ezra, would you be willing to reprise your performance?"

I took off my jacket and rolled up my sleeves and Orson handed me the bullhorn. Then I repeated what I could remember of my speech. I even took off my shoe again. When I finished, the applause was head splitting.

"Ezra Green!" Orson shouted as loudly as he could over the noise.

Emily stood between us, applauding eagerly for me. I'd outdone her. I'd commanded his audience.

"Okay, friends," he said. "You've heard some words of wisdom. Now spend some time meditating on them. We have plenty of work to do."

A final and energetic round of applause. Orson grabbed Emily's hand and led us to the side of the farmhouse, which was still slippery and wet with mud but offered us some degree of privacy.

"That was genius, Ez," he said.

"Thank you."

"True bliss looks like magic from a distance," he intoned, and I winced at the fact that he was repeating one of our corporate slogans. But at least he was repeating it to me.

"I think the human-to-human stuff is what really works," Emily said, inspecting the muddied bottom of her sneaker. "Right? Because the Bliss-Mini doesn't?"

Orson shot her a look.

Emily lowered her sneaker and inspected the other one, clearly oblivious of her trespass. "It's nice to lure people in, but what really gets the work done is the Farm, right?"

She looked up.

"What are you saying?" said Orson.

"Well, that the Bliss-Mini never worked. I tried it. It's not real. Didn't you tell me that, babe?"

Orson crossed his arms. "I never said anything like that."

I bit my lip and stared wide-eyed at my feet, wanting to spare Orson the humiliation of having to make eye contact with me. *This* was his idea of a confidante? A partner? Someone who would expose him so unthinkingly, right in the middle of Wholeness?

I raised my gaze to find Emily looking from me to Orson, obviously confused. "I'm sorry. I just mean, like, with my ex-husband, there were a lot of leaps of faith. Leaps of faith I really shouldn't have taken for him. But I believe in taking leaps of faith for you. I understand your vision."

"Ez, will you excuse us?"

I nodded and waded away from them, toward an explosion of hydrangea bushes. I could still hear them talking, and I didn't want to be out of earshot, so I dipped behind one of the bushes, crouching muddy in the mulch.

"What's your problem?" I heard Orson say. "You have to embarrass me in front of Ez?"

"Embarrass you?" Emily's voice was a hiss. "Embarrass you in front of *him*? What does it matter?"

"It matters. It's principles. He and I worked very, very hard to make the new Bliss-Mini a reality."

"I thought Dexter did that."

"Ez and I hired Dexter to do that. And for you to just, like, imply that it's fake? It's outrageous."

"It is, though! You basically said it!"

"I *never* said that." Orson's voice was frigid, controlled. "I said it was *in development*. I said we needed more time."

"The model's on the market, though. What more time can you take?"

"How many times have I Synthesized you?" he asked. "How many times have I tried to get you to see that this is about making peace with the bad and ushering in the good?"

"Honestly, when you talk like this? It makes no sense. You're not really saying anything. You're just spouting corporate nonsense."

I could hear the agitated squish of their feet in the mud.

"It basically sounds like you don't trust me," she said. "It sounds like you trust him more than me."

"And what if I do?"

My heart almost beat out of my chest.

"I'm your literal girlfriend."

"And he's my best friend. And business partner. I've known him longer."

"You sleep with me. You've told me all your secrets."

He sighed noisily. "What do you want me to say? This is just how things are."

"Fuck you," she said, and then there was an Orson-sized thud, a shallow splash. "Fuck you, Orson!"

I watched as Emily ran past me crying and then craned my neck to see Orson sitting on the ground, covered in mud, looking both perplexed and furious. I watched him stand and run after her, calling her name in the tone an adult would use to appease an unruly child.

I leaned against the side of the farmhouse, laughing and crying until the undersides of flowers and the tangle of branches were a chaotic blur. So I was sitting in a suit in the mud after giving an acid-washed speech to a bunch of unclean weirdos. So Emily and Orson were sleeping together. What did it matter? Orson trusted me the most.

TEN

EMILY CAME TO OUR NEW YORK OFFICE WITHOUT CALLING AHEAD, DIS-traught. She wore a pink jacket and pencil skirt with black trim: Givenchy's attempt at a business suit for people who'd never had to work a day in their lives. Her hair was gathered under an unflattering sun hat, and she held her matching pink clutch close to her stomach.

"Ez," she said once Brianna had let her into my office, and then turned around to stare at Brianna standing at attention in the doorway.

"You can leave, Brianna," I said.

Brianna nodded and vanished.

"Oh my god, Ez. It's the worst thing." She sat down in front of me.

I eyed my monitor, where I could see an unopened email from Elaine, likely about bookkeeping. Emily held the back of her hand to her eyes, clearly beginning to cry.

"Do you want Brianna to bring you a tissue?" I asked.

She nodded. "I think so."

I texted Brianna, who came back with a handkerchief and left again, shooting me an inquisitive look I didn't reciprocate.

Emily dabbed her eyes and shook her head. "I had a fight with Sasha," she gasped. "She told me she hates Orson."

I rolled my eyes. "Emily, he's a public figure. We can expect some people to hate him."

"She said he *humiliated* her. She doesn't believe in Synthesis."

"What does it matter? She's just one person. And that was years ago, anyway."

She gasped sharply. "It's not just her. She found this woman on the internet who's, like, obsessed with him. Jamie DeCroix."

My eyes widened. Jamie.

"She said—Jamie I mean—that Orson did something bad to her? Like, slept with her and then scammed her forever ago? She wants to MeToo him." Emily keened and hid her head in her hands. "I told her that's my boyfriend she's talking about. She just wants to *drag his name through the mud*!"

"Is Jamie's dad a hedge fund manager?" I asked helplessly, praying now that there was more than one Jamie DeCroix.

Emily nodded. "He's supposed to be one of the best ones in New York. Like, all the articles start out 'Jonathan DeCroix's daughter, Jamie.'"

My heart dropped into my stomach.

"Well," I said, trying to remain calm. "This happens sometimes, Emily." I turned to my monitor and typed in Jamie's name. *Jezebel. Vulture. Vice. Marie Claire. New York* magazine. How had I missed this?

"When did it start?" I asked.

Emily heaved another gasp. "Like, today. Sasha told her to come forward." She scowled. "I've never been betrayed like this by anyone ever in my life."

"People see success and want to shoot it down," I said, my voice shaking. "You and I both know Orson isn't like these scumbags who are getting flamed by this movement. Which is, of course, a very important movement."

Emily nodded. I wanted to deal with this immediately. I wanted her gone.

"You know the best thing you could do right now? You could go back to the Farm and if any press come by, you could tell them that the allegations aren't true. Because they aren't, right?"

"Right."

"Orson needs you more than anything right now."

"Yes." She nodded again. "That's a good idea. That's smart. You're always so smart, Ez."

I resented having to send her back into Orson's arms, but it was the only thing that made sense in that moment, the only thing that could protect his reputation. I watched her leave and then ran to Elaine's office, where she was typing away at her monitor as always.

"Did you hear about it?" I asked.

"Of course I heard about it."

I screwed up my mouth. "Why didn't you come to me?"

She tilted her head from side to side. "Because I *just* heard about it. And you were in your office with Emily."

I sighed exasperatedly. "The door's always open to you, Elaine."

She turned to me and folded her hands in her lap. "What do you want to do about it?"

"I don't know." I began pacing. "He needs to give some kind of a presser, doesn't he? He needs to address it directly?"

"Giving a presser makes it look like he's taking it seriously. It makes the accused look guilty."

"Okay. Then what does he do?"

"We let him talk to the people on the Farm. And then we go after Jamie."

"What is there to *go after*? She's a nonentity."

"She's a scam artist, isn't she?" Elaine smiled. "Her father is one of those guys who invests in stock that would skyrocket if we went under. I looked him up. Rival companies. He's in cahoots with his daughter."

My breathing slowed. "So we seed it?"

"Exactly." She turned back to her monitor, opened a new window. "We seed it. And we hope it works."

§

It was agreed upon that I would always go to Karl's place instead of the other way around, and that every time I would give the doorman $500 to say nothing about my comings and goings. It was good to be desired—to be idolized by desire—but really we'd created a situation that had too much weird velocity: if we quit, there was nothing keeping us from ruining each other's lives. We were both sleeping with the enemy, which would play about as well on Wall Street as being openly gay. If we kept going, we could each guarantee the other's silence.

He'd greet me at the door dressed down, which was an alien look for him. Cable-knit sweaters or a long, untucked shirt or a T-shirt with a Clash or Cure logo. He'd always say something like, "A temptress: you certainly look the part," and then let me in, asking me if I wanted the chenin blanc or the verdicchio he had chilling in his fridge. I'd flop down on one of his sectionals and lose myself in something uninteresting on my phone, waiting for him to circle back with a pair of full glasses and kiss me on the crown of my head, ask what was so interesting. I'd lie and claim I was doing work (I was rarely doing work), and then let him kiss me on the ear, the neck, etc.

"My wife and I had an agreement," he told me once. "We could see other people as long as we didn't tell each other about them. This was after maybe two years of no sex."

I closed one eye and then the other. There were blind spots in my periphery then, small ones that never went away. Darkness's encroachment had become less of a reaction to stress and more of a steady inevitability.

"But she couldn't deal with that, even. She said it was damaging Tucker, even though it was her idea. She said it was ruining his concepts of masculinity and fatherhood to have me in his life."

He turned on his side, draped an arm across my chest. "They went to Australia. She wanted to get as far away as possible, from me and from everything I own. She didn't account for the fact that I manage the portfolios of people who control half of Australia's GDP."

"Apparently the ancient Greeks could determine your temperament based on the first thing you see when you close one eye," I said.

He laughed hesitantly, clearly offended that I'd changed the subject. "That's bullshit."

"No, I swear." I closed my left eye and squinted at the ceiling through my right, trying not to be disturbed by the irregularities in my vision. "If I notice the whole ceiling first, I'm choleric. If I notice a part of the ceiling, like the fan, I'm melancholic."

He closed an eye in imitation of me. "I'm seeing the windows," he said. "Phlegmatic."

"The ancient Greeks weren't noticing things in a penthouse."

"I mean, for them it was like, 'Do you see the whole temple first? Or just a Corinthian column?'"

"So what does it mean, if you see the whole thing versus just a part of it?"

I shrugged. "I have no idea."

"I still think it's bullshit." He hooked his chin over my shoulder. "Say something that makes sense."

"I have a sanguine temperament."

"No, something real. About me."

"You have a sanguine temperament."

He rolled onto his back and sighed sharply. I didn't look at him, just kept opening and closing my eyes.

"Do you hate me?" he asked.

"I don't hate you. I just don't like people who think I'm a criminal," I said.

"I don't think you're a criminal. I think you're wrapped up in something bigger than yourself. I think you're getting carried away."

"So I can't make my own decisions?"

"I didn't say that."

I picked up my phone off the bedside table and opened my email. There was something from Brianna with the subject FWD: YOU MIGHT WANT TO SEE THIS!!!

He was curled against me, his mouth at my ear. "Do you love him?"

My thumb hovered over the unopened email. "Who?"

"Orson."

"No," I scoffed. "Of course not."

"Then why are you so loyal to him?"

"He's my friend."

"There are no friends in our world," he said. "There are starfuckers and master manipulators and sociopaths, but there aren't friends. And isn't he getting MeToo-ed, anyway? Do you really want to be sailing on that ship when it sinks?"

"I don't know what to tell you."

"Then tell me everything." He kissed my temple. "Let me take him down and you can split the windfall with me."

"Why would I even think of doing that?"

"Because I've taken a billion-dollar short position. The payout will be huge. And you can walk away from all the bullshit."

I opened the forwarded email. It was from Mack's lawyer – an impressive lawyer – informing me that Orson and I were being sued for $500 million for the theft of Mack's intellectual property. I stared at the words, trying to digest them, as if by reading them repeatedly I could make the problem go away.

"What's wrong?" Karl asked.

I closed my phone. "Nothing."

He crawled over me so his hands were at my hips and began kissing my stomach. "You're so cagey," he said.

"I'm just acting in rational self-interest. You know how that goes."

"Mm." His lips traveled from my navel to my chest.

"We just finished."

"So why can't we start again?"

"I shouldn't."

I slid out from under him and he sat up on his heels and watched me as I got dressed, his mouth a troubled crease in his face.

"Where are you going?"

"To work."

"When will I see you again?"

I looked at him naked, small-seeming. I bent to give him a kiss.

"I'll come back soon," I said. "I'll text you."

He nodded and frowned.

Outside, I called Brianna.

"This is ludicrous," I said, assembled in a clot of pedestrians preparing to cross the street. "He's actually going through with this? He actually thinks he can take us on?"

"Apparently."

"I'm not giving Mack Wang-Orsi five hundred million."

"Of course not."

"Go after him," I said. "You have carte blanche to do whatever it is you feel you need to do to get rid of him."

"Aye, aye," she said, and hung up.

I walked through the park, past the lithe joggers and the dog walkers and the people on midmorning dates. Who went on a midmorning date in the park? Who would want to expose themselves to the judgment of the city's bored rich? Probably people who wanted to prove their perfection. I looked down at my feet: a spot was forming at the upper-right-hand corner of my right eye. It was pinprick-big but annoying, easy to interpret as a gnat or a grain of hair. I blinked and it stayed. I had been getting appointment reminders from Mengetsu that I was ignoring. She'd even written me personally asking that I come in for a checkup. Brianna was supposed to keep that stuff from coming across my desk; she probably thought she was doing me a favor by sending it through anyway. I didn't want to sit behind the Phoropter again and watch the lenses twist and click in front of me. I didn't want to read the big *E*. I especially didn't want to get any more bad news. I'd had enough already.

§

In the winter of 2017, right around the Urmanese new year, Orson met the Dalai Lama. Carol and some of her friends were well-connected with the

Lama's media team, and they'd done something called "strategic outreach," which resulted in the Lama flying to Oswego with four placid, bald monks and meeting the genius behind NuLife. Orson had been in the midst of a self-described "creative hibernation," during which he limited his contact with the outside world—including Emily, it seemed—and brooded over the Farm and the future and NuLife in a room in his Enner house. We were texting very little then, which was painful: I couldn't bear to send messages knowing he wouldn't respond, but I couldn't bear to not send messages at all, so I sent little *hi*s and *hey*s and emoji hearts every few days, letting him leave me on read, which was almost as good as hearing back from him. When he took a brief break from his hibernation to meet the Dalai Lama, he was swarmed by the hungry NuLifers who'd been waiting for his return. I didn't want to be among them—I didn't need to swarm—but I did want to see him, even if it had to be from a distance. I flew up to the Farm unaccompanied and took a seat in the auditorium that Orson had ordered built for cold-winter gatherings, watching as he and the Dalai Lama sat together onstage, Chuck Enner between them.

"Your Holiness," Chuck Enner said, his wet-looking tangle of hair obscuring his gaze in the Dalai Lama's direction. "We are honored to be in your presence today."

The Dalai Lama laughed impishly and said, "Maybe it is me who is honored!"

They spoke for two hours, Orson about his vision of "world transcendental peace," which would be achieved through the popularization of Synthesis, and the Dalai Lama about how he admired Orson's commitment to bringing Buddhism-like principles to the West. Orson and the Dalai Lama held hands and looked into each other's eyes like lovers and Chuck Enner said something about how this meeting would usher in a "new generation of NuLife" and the children in the audience would "talk about this with their families for decades to come." There were several standing ovations and some mischievous grins from the Dalai Lama and prayer-bows from Orson, but what was most remarkable was the fact that the whole thing was happening at all. That some beautiful kid who'd hotwired a car in 2007 was being kissed on the forehead by the living Buddha ten years later. It was exactly the sort of thing I'd always wanted for him.

Genial called me two days after the Dalai Lama left the Farm, while I was lying on a bed in an Enner house mere yards from Orson but unable to talk to him because of his continued hibernation, my glasses on the bedside table next to me, the room so dark and its objects so borderless that I was almost completely blind. I could answer my phone without seeing it, which I did as soon as it rang, not expecting to hear Genial's voice.

"Ah, Ezra!" He sounded shell-shocked.

"How can I help you, Genial?"

"Ezra, I am wondering, did you watch the news yesterday?"

"No, we've been busy on the Farm. The Dalai Lama—"

"Yes, okay, I am sorry for interrupting, but I wanted to tell you that something very good that is also very bad has happened."

"What's that?"

"Ezra, I don't think we should speak about this on the phone. Can you come to Urmau?"

"Come to Urmau?"

"Yes. Can you come soon?"

"Hold on."

I put my glasses on, sat up, and opened my laptop. Wincing at the screen's brightness, I searched for "Urmau."

As we were all gathered in that auditorium watching the Dalai Lama tell Orson that he was the savior of the West, Genial Arroya Sr. had been receiving intel that the Daroqol had kidnapped the minister of the interior, brought him to a hideout in the countryside, and were demanding social reforms in exchange for the minister's safe return to Rezopol. The minister of the interior happened to be Genial Sr.'s grade school best friend, but this didn't stop Genial Sr. from sweeping the countryside in search of the hideout, finding it, and bombing it. The Daroqol living there were killed, as well as their wives and children. The minister's wire bifocals were found twisted among the blackened remains of the hut in which he'd been held hostage. The incident, which occurred within days of the new year, tipped the country into civil war.

"Oh shit," I breathed.

"Yes, Ezra, you see it now? Ha, I thought a very important businessman like you is always reading the news."

"Not this week."

"But you see it now?"

"Yes, I do."

"Maybe you can come with Dexter?"

"Dexter? Why Dexter?"

"Eh well." I could almost hear him shrug. "He is the big inventor for the new Bliss-Mini, maybe he can do something for the image of NuLife."

"Why not Orson?" I asked, knowing full well he'd never come.

"Ezra, listen, I am sending you something, okay? Look at your phone."

I put my phone on speaker and read the text Genial had sent me, a story from an Urmanese website he'd run through Google Translate. The accompanying photo was of Orson giving a lecture on the Farm, a stock photo I'd seen circulate through a number of subpar news outlets. The headline:

Orson Ortman, A Capitalist Villain.

"What's this?"

"It is *Cinqvero*, one of our conservative newspapers. They do not like NuLife because it represents capitalism, and they want my father's communism."

"And your father?"

"Well, how do you say this? *The tide switches*."

"The tide is turning."

"Yes, Ezra—" He cut himself off. "We cannot continue this conversation on the phone."

"Why? Are you being tapped?" I realized what an absurd question it was after I'd asked it.

"Come to Urmau," he said, and hung up.

§

Jamie DeCroix, still incredibly beautiful, sat cross-legged with Sasha on a morning talk show, both of them serious-faced, Sasha holding Jamie's hand in a visible display of support. The host was a woman with large hair and even larger lips, her expression one of pity and compassion. Jamie began to choke words out.

"He lied to me," she said, and Sasha squeezed her hand tighter. "He told me that his name was Troy, and he let me believe that he was going to marry me. And then he—" She trembled with tears. "He took me for all I was worth."

I sat cross-legged in front of the plasma screen in my office, positioned close enough that I could see without straining. I was bowing into and out of a butterfly stretch. My body was stiff with tension.

"Everything?" the host asked.

Jamie nodded.

"It wasn't *everything*," I said to the TV. "It was some clothes and a synth and forks."

The host turned to Sasha. "Was it hard for you to hear Jamie's story?"

"Yes, it was," Sasha said, and began rubbing Jamie's back. "I think Orson Ortman is a master manipulator who is especially adept at enchanting vulnerable people. He embarrassed me in front of a group of my friends. Reduced me to tears."

"You were the one who started crying," I said. "Orson didn't make you cry."

"Tell us more," the host said.

Sasha recounted the whole episode, embellishing it from beginning to end. Orson had coerced her into getting Synthesis, which she had never wanted. He had instructed her to disclose damning details about her past—not true—and had then asked the other party guests to criticize her—also not true.

"The point is, it doesn't work," Sasha said. "This Synthesis. It's just smoke and mirrors."

I snorted, and bent deeper into the butterfly stretch.

"We asked scientific experts to weigh in on Synthesis and the Bliss-Mini," the host said. "Here's what they had to say."

Cut to a dweeb in a cheap suit jacket whose hair was matted to his forehead. He was introduced as Dr. Desmond Filmore, professor of psychology at Rutgers University.

"We have no evidence that Synthesis is anything more than an elaborate placebo," Dr. Filmore said. "The same with the Bliss-Mini technology. We have tried to replicate both in a lab setting and are unable to determine whether those things alone, or merely the suggestion of them, yield actual results."

Cut back to the host, who was nodding in response to Dr. Filmore. Jamie was crying now, and Sasha, mic off, was mouthing words of comfort. I bent into the stretch again.

"Sasha and Jamie, how would you like to see Orson Ortman brought to justice?"

Jamie was still crying, but Sasha, whose mic had been switched back on, was quick with a response: "He should be stripped of all his wealth, and he should be sent to prison."

I turned the TV off. After Jamie and Sasha came forward, there had been a few disgruntled NuLifers who'd defected from the Farm and were talking to the *National Enquirer* and *The Telegraph*. But Elaine and I had seeded evidence against all of them: This one was an alcoholic, this one had abandoned her family, this one was cheating on his wife. The most aggressive seeding was done against Jamie. We found a photo of her, wide-eyed and visibly coked out, emerging in a mink coat from a Chelsea hotel with a rumpled-looking man on her arm: "DeCroix daughter known for her partying." And then there was the dirt on Jonathan DeCroix himself: insider trading, cloak-and-dagger business deals, a lost night in Tokyo in 2011. It made me feel good to expose him after what he'd done to Orson all those years ago.

Most of the same publications that had run Jamie's "brave" story also ran ours—journalism was about getting both sides, after all—and eventually the public was split: a vocal group of feminists who wanted to take Orson down, and an even more vocal group of NuLifers and Bliss-Mini owners and celebrities who wanted to support him.

He paused his hibernation once more to appear on a talk show with a host who was famous for having interviewed everyone from Katharine Hepburn to O.J. Simpson. The host wore a boxy pantsuit while Orson, smiling placidly, wore his humble work clothes.

"Orson, I want the truth," the host said, steepling her fingers under her chin. "Are the allegations true? Did you scam this young woman out of house and home?"

Orson grinned beatifically. "No," he said.

"Then why are these people coming forward against you?"

He looked from the host to the camera, his lips thin and pink in the beard he'd grown during his hibernation. "I love everyone I meet. I honestly do. Even the people who don't like me, who think I'm somehow untrustworthy or repulsive. And those people have a right to their opinion. Of course they have a right to their opinion. I can't help what they think. But I can say with confidence that I've never acted in bad faith. Not that I'm perfect—of course not—simply that I strive to be the best version of myself I can possibly be. And if that doesn't appeal to some people, then so be it. I wish them happiness anyway."

Emily made the rounds of talk shows. I made the rounds. We did this without anyone telling us to: there was never any question that we would. Sometimes we went together, CFO and girlfriend, me forced to sit in her cloud of Yves St. Laurent perfume and listen as she clutched the hem of her skirt and cried and described Orson as the best person she'd ever met, someone who was incapable of hurting anyone, someone to whom she'd entrust her life. I said basically the same thing but more measured—I, unlike her, had to hide my love—and the hosts ate it up. Everyone was used to loving Orson. Nobody wanted to stop.

§

Although Dexter had given each of the NuLife executives an air taxi as a Christmas present, claiming they were faster, more efficient, and better for the environment, he never traveled in one himself. We flew to Urmau in his private jet, Brianna working on her laptop in the cabin ahead of us and Dexter and I sealed off from her by a velour curtain.

"I have plans for a 3.0," Dexter said. "Something that we could debut in a few months."

I turned from the window, out of which were wads of pinkish-gray clouds, to meet his eager gaze.

"I'm listening," I said.

"I'm thinking that it could be a sort of helmet, a whole-head device that the wearer could use as, like, an experiential tool. Like virtual reality."

"How would that work?"

"Well." He pursed his lips thoughtfully. "There's a way to use VR as a tool for self-help. I was thinking how it might be interesting if we gave the user the opportunity to network with other Bliss-Mini users, to have sort of like a therapeutic encounter where they could describe their experiences. Maybe even watch videos of what's happening on the Farm. And, you know, the option for in-world purchases."

I raised my eyebrow.

"Yeah, like—they can *buy* Synthesis classes in the helmet. They can attend Synthesis classes even if they're far away. It'll increase the customer base because, you know, not everyone can drop everything and get to the Farm."

"It sounds good," I said, distracted by a rip in one of my cuticles and then the thought of Orson in his hibernation. "When could you have a prototype ready for market testing?"

"I don't even need to market test this one. I think we can roll it right out, as long as I have your blessing."

Brianna pulled the curtain aside, sticking her head into the cabin.

"The pilot says we'll be landing in ten," she said.

"Thanks," Dexter said, waving her away without making eye contact.

Brianna looked at me searchingly. She was obviously wondering whether she was going to be treated as another staff person who functioned solely to update us on minutiae. I frowned and gave a little shake of my head. She sighed and disappeared behind the curtain.

Urmau appeared beneath us, a patchwork of cities and farmland abutting a kilometers-long strip of leathery-looking beach. We landed on Genial's tarmac, which was lined with soldiers dressed in gray military fatigues, wearing AK-47s and armbands bearing the colors of the Urmanese flag: two red stars against a white background. They all looked to be in their late thirties or early middle age, their stocky legs shoulder-width apart, thickly mustachioed like Genial's father. They stood at attention as we debarked, one of them even offering his hand to Brianna, who took it and said something to him in Urmanese.

"You speak Urmanese?" I asked her, waving to the mirage-like blur of Genial as he hurried down the landing strip.

"It's not hard to learn," she said. "There are no noun declensions. You just need to know the tenses, and then it's a matter of learning all the genders and vocab."

"How many genders are there?"

"Hello, my friends!" Genial said, jogging up to us. He was smiling as always, but the lower left corner of his mouth sagged, making him look like he'd suffered a mini stroke. As if suddenly conscious of this asymmetry, he folded his bottom lip over his teeth and rubbed his chin. Dexter pulled him into a bear hug.

"Too long!" Dexter crowed. "We missed you, man."

"Yes, thank you, it has been too long, hasn't it?"

He kissed Brianna's hand and then put his arm around me. "Dexter, we will talk later? They will take you two to the house? I need to speak with Ezra right now. Privately."

We set out across the tarmac, walking among the soldiers, all of them engaged in the project of patrolling the near-empty tarmac by jogging around its perimeter and flashing their AK-47s at one another.

"This is new," Genial said morosely, gesturing to the soldiers. "All this."

"I can see that."

"My father put this army everywhere. They are in the streets now, here in Rezopol, at my house, in the countryside. Everywhere. They are watching."

I nodded, starting to dislike the idea of talking about the soldiers within earshot of them. As if reading my mind, Genial dropped his voice to a whisper.

"My father says he wants no more foreign business here. He wants no capitalism here."

"No capitalism?"

"Yes, he told me that this foreign business I brought, it is what radicalized the Daroqol." He dropped his voice even lower. "He does not know, Ezra, that I am on the side of the Daroqol. But I am worried he expects it."

"Suspects it?"

He ignored me, his voice shaking. "The right are mad about NuLife—they say Orson is trying to colonize us like Spain in the sixteenth century. My father wants NuLife out of the country, but many of the left love it. So now the Daroqol go to the centers and get the teaching and use it for—it is their philosophy of combat."

I raised my eyebrows. "What?"

"Yes, Synthesis? The good and the bad? They see all the videos of what

Orson does on the Farm. This is what they are doing every day before they fight the Urmanese National Army. It is their spiritual anthem. They think of Orson as the leader."

"Holy fuck."

"Yes, holy fuck. And the UNA, they will go to the centers and shoot the Daroqol and the bystanders. They will bomb them."

"They're destroying the NuLife centers?"

I must have spoken too loudly, because Genial dropped his voice even lower. "Yes, it is bad, I know—I did not think this would happen."

If the Urmanese NuLife centers weren't turning a profit, we couldn't afford to pay back the Deutsche Bank loan, much less with interest.

"Genial," I said.

But he was still deep in his own thought. "Ezra, you are my friend, yes?"

"Yes, but—"

"Then I will tell you this secret. In my home, I am hiding many Daroqol." He looked at me wild-eyed. "We have a plan to kill my father."

"Genial."

"Listen, Ezra—we will do it quickly, it will be a coup, and then I will become president, and the country will be free."

"I don't think that's a good idea."

He squinted upward suspiciously, as though the sky itself were bugged. "We must do it soon, before my father finds out, Ezra, and before there is any more war." He turned from the sky back to me: the crease at the corner of his mouth seemed to have grown deeper. "It will be very good for us. And very good for NuLife."

"But from what you're saying the centers have already been destroyed."

"Yes, maybe some of them, but when I am president, they will be allowed to build even bigger and grow, and the people will love them. If you can put a little more money in, then you can get even more return from them, Ezra."

"And this would be if the coup is successful?"

Genial nodded. "It is not as difficult as it seems."

I squinted down at my sneakers, too boxy and thick for the heat. "I can't just, like, cosign an assassination."

"No, no. Please, not so loud."

"Sorry."

"I am not saying you, Ezra, will do anything. I am saying only the things that you will benefit from." He raised his voice. "Now you are tired, maybe? Shall we go back to the house and sit by the pool, go for a swim?"

§

Downtown Rezopol wasn't as I remembered it: parts of the city had been cratered by bombings, and UNA soldiers stood at nearly every corner, smoking or playing cards, too distracted by their conversations to take note of the passersby, all of whom hurried past with stricken looks on their faces. We drove through the city center toward Genial's mansion, Dexter doing something unknown and complex looking on his phone, Brianna watching with me as the city rolled past. Last time I'd been to Rezopol, it had been with Orson, so that Orson's presence seemed somehow welded to its beauty—with him gone, there was no reason for the city to keep functioning. We stopped for a light on a corner where one of the fifteen NuLife centers had been built. This one had clearly been Molotov cocktailed, though not so much that it had lost its structural integrity, and draped over its sagging facade was a banner bearing a photorealistic drawing of Orson. He was looking upward and waving as though saying hello to angels. The Urmanese above his portrait had been translated into English below it: "*Urmau, welcome to the New Life!*"

I was thinking about the fact that Genial was planning to kill his father, and that to get back in Dexter's jet and return to America, which was what I wanted to do, would likely anger Genial, seriously jeopardize the health of NuLife in Urmau, and leave us to default on a $2 billion loan. There didn't seem to be a correct way to proceed. Or there was, technically speaking, but I would lose money if I proceeded that way.

When we had reached the outskirts of the city, Dexter looked up from his phone like a diver coming up for air and craned his neck to see out the window, which happened to frame an empty lot in which a group of shoeless and a few shirtless children were playing a game that involved pitching pebbles back and forth using palm fronds.

"Stop here," Dexter called to Genial's driver. "Can you pull over?"

"Is there a problem, Dexter?" Genial asked.

"It's just a spur-of-the-moment thing," Dexter said, running his hand through his mealy hair. He turned to me and Brianna. "Do you guys want to get out with me?"

We pulled over to the curb and Dexter emerged from the limo, followed by the rest of us. Genial surveyed the children with a sour look on his face, and when they caught sight of us and came running, he turned his chin up in disgust. They were screaming something that sounded like *deener pourfair*. They opened their palms at us, jockeying among themselves for the spots on the faded grass closest to us. The larger ones pushed the smaller ones down only for the smaller ones to stand right back up, their palms out again, completely undeterred.

"They want money," Genial said, looking defeated. "My apologies, really."

Brianna nodded at me pointedly so I opened my wallet, placing an Urmanese *dynere* in each child's hand. They pocketed the money, murmuring a few eager fragments of thanks in English, and then outstretched their hands again.

Genial groaned and spat on the ground. "Insatiable."

Dexter had extracted one of his suitcases from the limo's trunk and was rummaging in it. He finally produced three spidery mini drones and their corresponding remote controls, carrying them toward the children like a nest of baby birds. The children flocked him. He squatted in front of them.

"I've been waiting for some very special kids to give these very special gifts to," he said loudly, as if his volume could compensate for his inability to speak Urmanese.

"There aren't enough for all of them," I said, though no one appeared to hear me.

"These are *drones*," Dexter said, and then looked at Genial for a translation. Genial shrugged.

"They have cameras in them," Dexter continued. "You can make them fly high above the ground and the cameras will take pictures of everything the drones see."

One of the taller children pulled a drone gingerly from the pile in Dexter's hands and inspected it, clearly uncertain how this could be a justifiable substitute for money. Dexter handed the child the remote control and indicated which buttons the child would need to push in order to make the drone fly. The child nodded, clearly ill at ease outside the you-get-my-money/you-don't-get-my-money dichotomy. Dexter put the other two drones in the hands of the two next biggest children and stood back, smiling proudly.

"Now you can fly those, or you can take them to the stores and sell them," he said. "For more money than anybody could give you on the street."

The children stared at him.

"Okay, Dexter, thank you," Genial said, guiding Dexter back to the limo. "It is very nice of you." He turned severely to the children. "*Dichee graz*," he commanded them.

"*Graz*," the children said halfheartedly.

Back in the limo, Dexter crowed about the defense contracts he was using to develop new drone technology. I watched out the back window as the children manipulated the drones, pressing buttons, one of them figuring out how to send hers flying. My phone buzzed: a text from Orson. I scrambled to read it.

can i get your opinion on something

I bit my lip. *yeah absolutely*

i'm thinking of marrying Emily

what? My fingers were almost too numb to type. *when?*

i don't know. sometime next year.

I felt dizzy. All I could do was ask questions.

where?

on the farm. it's picturesque

why do you want to marry her?

because it's a good idea

do you love her?

yes.

A wedding. There was going to be a wedding. Something putrid in my gut: grief. I had imagined things differently, of course, but why? All signs had always been pointing to this. What wretched part of me had clung to hope, snagged on a vision of him in a tuxedo under a trellis for *me*, not her? I'd been torturing myself. Or rather, he'd been torturing me.

I closed my eyes and when I opened them, Genial's mansion was pulling into view. Brianna smiled at me expectantly.

"Everything all right?" she asked.

I told her everything was perfectly all right. She mimed pulling her face into a smile as though she had fishhooks stuck in the corners of her mouth. I shrugged noncommittally, my heart racing. Orson was going to marry Emily.

Genial's mansion seemed dimly lit and cavernous, a marked difference from the sunny hive of staff and foreign dignitaries and socialites who'd filtered in and out when we'd visited before. Genial himself was frenetic, walking backward ahead of us as we wandered through the foyer. He took me aside, sending Brianna and Dexter upstairs.

"I should show you what has changed here," he said as we walked through the foyer and into the living room. "Please, follow me?"

In the kitchen, he opened the door to his wine cellar and switched on the light. Voices rose from the damp darkness, men's voices engaged in bored conversation and muffled disputes. What sounded like the clanking of the butt of a rifle, the shifting of boots on the ground. A few steps down and I could see them: twenty or thirty Daroqol, deep in conversation or lost in smartphones, devices I realized I'd never seen a UNA soldier carrying. Genial shouted something to them in Urmanese and then gestured to us.

"A visitor," he said slowly, as though he was teaching them English. "From NuLife."

A chorus of cheers, even some kisses blown. Genial said something in Urmanese which inspired one soldier, dressed in a shirt bearing a Nike swoosh, jogging pants with a weed leaf motif, and mud-layered boots, to call up to us: "Thank you, Americans!"

I nodded and waved.

"Okay, we will go back up." Genial pointed to the stairhead. "Now you have seen them. Now we will go for a swim."

Before Genial could say anything else, I was up the stairs to the second floor, forgetting the Daroqol in favor of my text conversation with Orson, Genial calling after me that I should get my trunks on and my drink order ready. I flopped across the bed in my room, still staring at my phone, wondering what I could possibly type in response to *yes*. There was no telling him about the situation I was currently living through—I would be an idiot to risk texting any of that information—but there was nothing else to say, nothing that wouldn't make me look like I was desperate for him to change his mind. Like I was desperate for him. Why was he doing this to me? Why was he battering me? I blinked, and tears ran from my eyes into my ears.

A text from Elaine: *i've been watching the news.*

it's fine I wrote back. I considered telling her where I was, but then thought better of it.

She called and I sent it to voicemail.

you have to take my calls Ez.

i don't have to take them if i'm busy.

the situation looks hairy enough that we should be worried.

we'll work something out.

what are we going to "work out"?

elaine i can't exactly text the details to you.

The text bubble percolated, then vanished, then percolated again. Finally: *why? is it legal?*

jfc yes it's legal.

i don't trust you.

you have to. i'm paying for your kids' college.

The bubbles percolated once more and then disappeared for good. I opened my contacts list and scrolled to Karl's name, my thumb hovering over the call button. I pressed it. He picked up on the second ring.

"You always text," he said. "You never call."

"I felt like calling."

He made a soft, shapeless noise that sounded like purring. "What's wrong, Ez?"

"Nothing's wrong."

"Okay, well, there's something in your voice that's telling me otherwise."

I cleared my throat.

"You don't have to pretend to be unfeeling and macho," he said. "You're the least macho person I know."

There were still tears dripping into my ears. I wondered if he could tell over the phone. "I'm in Urmau," I managed, stupidly. "And I'm bored."

"Bored in Urmau?"

"They worship Orson down here."

"I'm sure they do."

I sighed. I wanted to be desired again, and to be desired I'd have to lie. "I miss you."

There was a pause, a consideration. "Say it again," he said.

"I miss you."

"Do you really?"

"Yes."

"What do you want? Do you want me to turn my phone camera on?"

"I don't know."

He laughed, not unkindly. "Should I fly down from New York?"

I hesitated, then remembered how Orson had battered me. "Yeah."

"When?"

"As soon as you can," I said. "We can get a hotel."

Another pause for consideration. "I have a meeting with a major investor in two days. But I could push it back."

I waited for him to say something else, and when he didn't, I said: "You can do anything you want."

"To you?"

"Yeah."

I could hear him smiling. "Good," he said. "That's what I like to hear."

§

Karl was strange in shorts and a floral button-down, looking entirely out of place and pale among the massive succulents that lined the streets of Rezopol. He met me at the steps of the hotel, watching me behind his sunglasses as I squinted to see him through the midday brightness. The blind pinpricks at the corners of my vision throbbed as though electricity were attempting and failing to pass through them, exposed spots in my eyesight's drywall where loose wires had burned themselves dim. He carried his leather suitcase past me and into the lobby.

"Are you checked in?" he asked.

I nodded. "Let's go upstairs."

On the bed, he massaged my shoulders, his voice in my ear.

"I know what you're doing here," he said.

"Do you?"

"I know it's bad."

"Then why did you come?"

He nestled his chin in the pocket between my neck and collarbone. "Because you're a sweet little twink with big eyes and soft hands and you look even cuter when I mess up your hair."

I tilted my head forward, sighed with pleasure in spite of myself.

"You run a criminal operation," he said. "You falsify documents and hide money and cheat people out of their investments."

"I don't do any of that."

"Yes, you do." He kissed me on the neck. "But you don't do it because you want to. You do it for him."

"I'm not anyone's servant."

He began unbuttoning my shirt from behind. "I have intel, Ez. I have people who are telling me things."

"Who?" I kept my voice as neutral as possible.

He eased my shirt off over my shoulders. "People who know. Why would I tell you?"

"Because I'm a sweet little twink."

He laughed. "Orson's the grifter and you're the genius. I said it, you can quote me."

"You just came here to insult me."

"I just *complimented* you." He ran his hand through my hair the way Orson used to. "Do you know how to take a compliment?"

I pulled away and shook my head. My face was warm. I regretted everything. "I was just missing you."

"And I was missing you." He moved closer to me, his voice softer. "Ez, I really was."

I sat still, bare chested, gripping the edge of the bed.

"You're special to me," he said.

"I know," I said.

He let out a loud laugh, a kind of squawk, and began kissing my shoulders. His hand was hot and damp and low on my stomach, creeping over my navel.

"There aren't many people who are special to me."

I began thinking of all the people who were special to me, imagining them standing in a room shoulder to shoulder. There weren't many of them, and Karl wasn't one.

"Same," I said.

His hand went deeper, beneath my belt. I gasped and he exhaled heavily.

"Do you like pain?" he asked. The question had never been asked of me before. Meaning Orson had never asked it.

And it turned out I did, or at least I thought I did. He pinched the sides of my chest where my skin stuck to my ribs. He called me names. He slapped every part of my body below my neck red. We merged in more ways than I could count and then separated, merged and then separated, and I closed my eyes and imagined he was someone else doing something he had never done before, and that when it was over, he would hold me.

We sat across from each other on the bed, our legs folded under us.

"Give up NuLife," he commanded. "Give up the ruse."

"There's no ruse."

"Give it up," he said, his eyes narrowing. "You little bitch. I'm telling you to give it up."

I couldn't tell if we were play-acting anymore. Did business really turn him on this much? I stared at him impassively. His wolf-white hair stuck up at odd angles, and there was a small scab at the bottom of his chin where he'd nicked himself shaving.

"If you don't give it up then I'm going to make you give it up."

"You can't."

"I can," he said, and slapped me across the cheek, hard.

I closed my eyes and when I opened them the room was Vaselined and hazy, my vision blinking on and off. I looked at his outline and willed my sight to right itself but it didn't. And then everything went black, and a breathtaking pain set in behind my eyes, like they'd been pierced with spikes.

"Ez?" he said, urgency in his voice. "Fuck, Ez, I'm sorry. Did I hurt you?"

I looked left, right, ahead, head heavy with pain. I could feel sweat gathering at my hairline. "I'm fine," I said.

"You don't look fine."

Gingerly, I lay back on the bed. How the fuck was I going to get out of this? I could feel him looming over me, his face pointed at mine.

"Are you in shock? Are you concussed?"

"Would I be talking to you like this if I had a concussion?" I snapped.

"I don't know. I don't know. I've never had this happen."

I laid my forearm across my throbbing eyes. "Did you do this to your wife? Maybe that's why she left you."

He sat back. "No, I never did this to her."

I sighed jaggedly, removed my forearm, blinked into the darkness. "Just put the pillow under my head," I said, pretending I was seeing the ceiling. "I just need to lie down here a minute."

Like an eager helpmeet, he wedged the pillow under my head and lay down next to me. I began to sweat again. Soon I'd have "rested," and then I'd have no excuse.

"I've never gotten rough like that before," he said timidly. "It's always something I wanted to try."

"Well, you tried it."

"You told me to."

"Not like that," I said. "Not in the face like that."

"I'm sorry." It was good to hear him plead. It took my mind off the pain. "I'm really sorry it happened."

"Tell me how sorry you are."

"Really, really sorry," he said, an uptick in his tone. "It was really, really bad."

"What was bad?"

"What I did."

"It was disgusting."

"Yes, it was."

"It was uncalled for."

"Definitely."

"So what are you going to do?"

I could feel him turned toward me. "Punish myself."

I nodded. "Finish without me. Finish alone."

"Yes, sir," he said excitedly, and slid off the bed.

"Go into the bathroom," I said. "Go fuck yourself in there."

He padded into the bathroom, where I could hear him working on himself vigorously, and as he moaned, I opened my eyes and to my relief I could see the ceiling again, the chairs and étagère full of decorative pottery across from me. But now the blind spots had grown bigger: chunks of my vision had vanished entirely, and what was left was out of focus. The pain had subsided but wasn't gone entirely. Karl gasped loudly and I sat up into the blur, felt for my shirt on the bed (it was white, and had blended in with the sheets), grabbed my glasses from the bedside table (they did little to improve my situation) and started getting dressed. I saw his shape come out of the bathroom, felt his dismay.

"You're leaving?"

"I have to," I lied. "I have a conference call."

"But I pushed everything back for you."

"Some things can't be pushed back."

I stood up and fumbled with my pants. I could feel him watching me, which made me fumble more.

"You don't look good," he said. "You look dizzy."

"I'm fine."

"I don't want you to go yet," he whined. "I want to have my Ez and eat him, too."

"I'll be back," I said.

"When?"

"I don't know. Tomorrow." My eyes were blinking out again. I tried to move faster.

"What if I do something?" he asked, sounding desperate. "What if I blow the lid off NuLife because you abandoned me?"

"I doubt you will. You haven't yet."

In the lobby, I teetered around like a drunk, squinting at my phone. I could make out black marks squirming across the screen like ants crawling over spilled sugar. I found my way to the concierge's desk and held my phone out to the shape behind it.

"Can you call Brianna Voorhees for me?" I asked. "She's in this phone."

I could feel the skepticism of whoever it was in front of me, but they obediently called Brianna and handed me back the phone. I listened to it ring—a little long for Brianna—and was about to hang up when she answered.

"Where are you?" she asked.

I told her the name of the hotel. "I need you to pick me up and take me to the emergency room."

"Are you okay?"

"I'm fine. I just—I need to go to the emergency room."

I was in a taxi with her what felt like minutes later, listening to her making demands of the driver in Urmanese. I pretended to be looking at my shoes.

"What is it?" she asked, and put her arm around my shoulders.

It might have been her breath, which was warm and citrusy, or her impressive mastery of Urmanese, or the sisterly softness of her body next to mine, or a combination of all three. I talked.

"I have glaucoma," I said, half-audibly. "It sometimes flares up."

"Jesus. Why didn't you tell me?"

I made a show of looking her in the eyes, which I couldn't see. "You can't tell anyone," I said. "I'll fire you if you tell anyone. I'll make it very hard for you to get hired again."

"I won't tell anyone."

"You really can't tell anyone."

"I swear I won't."

My jaw felt rigid. I shouldn't have told her. I shouldn't have threatened her. I felt her hand on mine.

"I'm glad you told me, Ez. I'll keep it secret." There was an unwavering smile in her voice despite everything I'd said.

I rolled down my window: we were stopping somewhere that smelled like honey and eucalyptus. Brianna got out first and then opened my door, helping me out by the arm. Sliding doors opened with a pneumatic hiss and we walked into a room frigid with air-conditioning, full of people in what sounded like various states of distress. Brianna sat me down and then I heard her speaking Urmanese again, far away, as rapidly as the native speaker she was talking to.

"It's just a ten-minute wait," she said when she returned.

Next I was in some kind of examination room, bright with sunlight, and a man's voice was saying something in Urmanese, to which Brianna responded, and then the voice, wet and jowly, asked me in halting English: "What is the problem, Mr. Ezra Green?"

I looked at the ground. I couldn't say it.

"His vision," Brianna said. "He has glaucoma. He's having an attack."

I felt a thumb on my forehead, tilting my head so the doctor—still only a voice—could get a better view of my eyes. I let my head tip back helplessly.

"We will look with the penlight? Is this okay?"

I nodded. Light flooded my vision in my left eye and then dissolved into a red-orange halo, leaving me even more compromised. The same thing happened in my right eye.

"Is it with pain?" the doctor asked.

"Yes," I managed.

"Very bad?"

"It comes and goes."

The doctor said something to Brianna in Urmanese and then left the room. I felt her at my side.

"He's saying he can treat you, but you may need surgery in the future. He's going to give you something he called acetazolamide and then he'll give you a beta blocker."

"What are those things?" The table I was sitting on felt like it was getting progressively colder. I was scared.

"It's just medication you take, like pills." She put her hand on my shoulder. "It's fine, Ez."

"I can't see anything," I said, trying to keep it under my breath.

"Did Mengetsu say this would happen?"

I shook my head and turned in her direction. "I'm going to beat this." I tried to iron the wrinkles out of my voice, dispel the fear.

"I don't think you can beat something like this."

"I do," I said.

The doctor came back in and handed something to Brianna. "Mr. Green, I am giving your wife the medications. Every day twice a day, both of them."

"I'm, um—" Brianna began to say.

"She's not my wife," I said. "She's a friend."

"Okay," the doctor said warily. "Put your hand out, please."

I felt two pills drop into my hand.

"You will go back to a doctor you see in America," he said. "These symptoms mean you will need to get surgeries for glaucoma."

"Does he need them right now?"

"No, no." The doctor walked to the opposite side of the room. "His eyes have lost vision enough, but they are not losing more now. Only eventually he will need it."

On our way to Genial's, I took the pills and waited for my vision to be restored. I swayed back and forth with the erratic movements of the taxi, feeling Brianna swaying next to me, listening to her respond to the driver's questions, presumably about directions, and then about Genial. Where was Orson? What was he doing right then? Were he and Emily in bed together, beautiful together? Had he asked her to marry him yet? Had she said yes?

Was I ever going to see him again? As in *see* him: the details of his face, the little knots of his double-jointed knuckles, the veins in his ankles?

He trusted me, that was true. But maybe he trusted me too much.

§

The plan was Genial would invite his father to dinner under the pretense of brokering peace between NuLife and the Urmanese government, and then he'd kill him. Dexter, Brianna, and I would attend this dinner as representatives of NuLife who regretted the divisiveness our corporation had caused among the Urmanese people. We'd insist that we wanted to reboot our brand to be consistent with Genial Sr.'s vision. We would talk, Genial Sr. would listen, and as the conversation wore on, he'd drink more and more *picanto,* a corn-based Urmanese soup, which Genial's staff would have dosed with ricin. When he dropped dead, the Daroqol would be unleashed from the basement to secure the mansion against Genial Sr.'s security detail, which would be waiting outside as they always were whenever he entered a building deemed safe enough for him to spend time in alone. This whole operation would send a message to the Urmanese right that the Urmanese left had triumphed, and that Genial Jr. was the rightful president of Urmau.

"Only you and the Daroqol know this," he told me on the afternoon of the dinner. "You cannot tell the other two."

"Why?"

"Ezra, I do not know these people as well. They will compromise this."

"How can you guarantee our safety?"

"It is easy," he said. "I will have an armed Jeep to take you to the jet. You put your things in it ahead of time, they will leave theirs. The Jeep is in back with the driver, always in back. The Daroqol will take you."

"We'll be shot at."

He smiled. "No one will shoot at you, Ezra, okay? Nobody wants to kill a white person, especially not an American one."

Genial Sr. accepted his son's invitation, claiming that it was good NuLife had finally *vice ao santoro* (literally: "seen the path") and decided to collaborate with the Urmanese government on building a stronger communist nation. It was difficult to know whether he really believed what he was saying, but all that mattered was that he was coming, and that Genial Jr. had given his father no reason to suspect that this might be a bad idea.

My eyesight had improved save for the widened blind spots, and I was able to see myself in the mirror in my suit, tie my tie, comb my hair. How do you dress for an assassination? Orson had always said it was better to overdress than underdress, that the overdressed just looked like they'd made an honest mistake while the underdressed looked like they had nothing. I brushed my shoulders like he'd taught me to.

A text from Elaine: *there's a shareholder meeting next week.*

I squinted at my phone. *i didn't forget.*

they're going to want to hear good news about urmau.

they will.

i hope you're being proactive?

i'm being proactive.

can you take a call?

not on this phone.

Percolating bubbles. *get a burner for god's sake.*

I told her I would and switched the phone to airplane mode. It was actually a fairly good idea; I didn't know why I hadn't thought of it sooner.

Downstairs, the table had been set for five, and Genial was already seated at the head, flanked by Brianna and Dexter. Brianna wore a floral shift and Genial a button-down with a similar pattern. I was indeed overdressed.

"Welcome, Ezra!" Genial shouted, as though we were in a stage play. "Take a seat, please."

Brianna was smiling at me encouragingly, the way a caretaker would at her disabled charge, and I resented it but there was nothing I could do. I sat down next to her and watched Dexter twirl his gold-plated salad fork.

"This is the shit," he said to no one in particular. "This is the *life*."

The doorbell rang orchestrally and the hall to the foyer bristled with staff. Then there was the sound of boots on marble. Genial Sr. emerged into the dining room in what looked like combat attire. Genial, with his thin face and delicate frame, hardly resembled him: Genial Sr., or what I could make out of him when he got close enough, had fat, clay-like cheeks, eyes so large their whites were visibly gelatinous, and a prominent mustache. His forehead under his army cap was heavily wrinkled, and as he surveyed the gilded china on the dinner table he sniffed deeply as though he were planning to discharge a wad of spit and phlegm. Next to him stood a birdlike bald man in a pair of Ray-Bans, arms folded across his chest in what appeared to be an insufficient imitation of the larger man in front of him. Genial stood, and the three of us followed suit.

"Father," he said. "It's been long."

Genial Sr. said something in Urmanese, which he promptly translated for our benefit: "Very nice to see a full table."

"These are the people from NuLife." Genial gestured to us. "Dexter Ellhorn, he is the inventor, and Brianna Voorhees, she is the assistant, and this is the CFO." He clapped me on the shoulder. "Mr. Ezra Green."

Genial Sr. shook hands with each of us, and the birdlike man followed suit. "Manuel Demarco," Genial Sr. said, angling his chin toward the birdlike man. "The minister of the interior."

Manuel smiled smugly, clearly proud to be the blown-apart minister's replacement. I saw Genial's lips tighten: Manuel hadn't been accounted for, was clearly a fly in the ointment. We all sat and the staff promptly filled our wineglasses. I watched them as they did, recognizing the look of urgency on their faces, the need to fulfill an inconsequential obligation to the powerful and indifferent. It had been a long time since I'd felt that way.

"So you're planning on revamping NuLife," Genial Sr. said, looking directly at me. "My son tells me you regret this whole thing with the Daroqol."

"That's right," I said. "We want NuLife to become whatever you want it to be."

Genial Sr. sat back in his seat and spread his hands across his thighs. "We want it to be for the people," he said.

"We have the power to ban it if you don't make it for the people," Manuel said.

"Of course," I said.

Genial Sr. said something to Manuel in Urmanese, both of them looking at me as he spoke. "What do you think it means, Mr. Green, to be 'for the people'?" Genial Sr. asked.

"It would mean that the state benefits from the corporation," I said. It occurred to me that there was no clear path to follow in this conversation. That we could—and probably would—end up talking in circles.

"I think your views are fundamentally at odds with what we want to achieve in this country," Genial Sr. said. "You are like Facebook or Twitter. You are a colonizing force, and you're spreading dissent."

"Father," Genial said lamely.

"I wouldn't say all that," Dexter said. "We have a lot of capital at our disposal. You're fighting a war, aren't you?"

Manuel turned uncertainly to Genial Sr., who nodded.

"Won't you need defense weaponry?"

"We're listening," Manuel said.

"I don't think—" Brianna cut in, snatching a look at me before she spoke, her voice shaking. "I think that may be a little inconsistent with our brand, don't you, Ezra?"

I shrugged. "What does 'inconsistent' mean, really?"

Everyone stared thoughtfully at their plates, pondering the meaning of "inconsistent."

"I think it means," Brianna tried, "that we are more focused on peace than we are on war."

"Right," Dexter said. "But we can *do* war if we need to."

Where was the *picanto*? When was this going to be over with?

Genial Sr. turned back to me. "The fact that you are profiting off Urmanese optimism troubles me," he said. "We want people to be optimistic about the state, not foreign business."

"We can make that happen," I said. "We can refocus our branding. We can synergize."

"Yes," Genial chimed in. "Synergize." His tongue fumbled the pronunciation—he'd clearly never spoken the word in his life.

"What does it mean, *synergize*?" Manuel asked.

"That we can use NuLife to encourage fealty to the state," I said.

Genial Sr. nodded approvingly. "That's a very nice idea," he said. "A very smart idea."

"NuLife definitely makes people love America," Dexter said. "So we could make it work for Urmau."

Brianna looked lost.

"How do you disassociate NuLife from America?" Genial Sr. asked. "This is what I'm skeptical about."

I didn't have to come up with an answer: the *picanto* was served. As the staff retreated to the edges of the room, I wondered if Manuel's had been spiked too. It occurred to me that I was about to witness a death—possibly two—and that I was insufficiently prepared. I imagined Genial Sr.'s lips turning blue, his globe-like eyes bulging out of his head.

"Ezra tells me he is prepared to pay you one hundred million *dynere* to stay in Urmau," Genial said.

We hadn't rehearsed this, but I went along with it. "That's right," I said.

"Add to that a few hundred rockets," Dexter said. It was hard to tell whether he actually believed what he was saying.

"Anything to rejuvenate the brand in Urmau," Brianna said, finally getting it. She stuffed a too-big forkful of salad in her mouth.

Genial Sr. took a sip of his soup and Manuel followed suit. Genial watched them nervously, scratching his cheek with his empty hand.

"Delicious," Genial Sr. pronounced, smiling at his son. "You have a better chef than I do."

"Only the finest," Genial said, and looked at me as though I were the chef myself. "It's right, Ezra?"

"Only the finest," I echoed.

The conversation stalled as we ate and were poured more wine. I entertained the thought that this dinner would last forever, that I would grow old and die at Genial's giant dining room table. And then Genial Sr. began coughing.

"Comrade," Manuel said, shaking him. "Comrade, what is it?"

Genial Sr. made a squawking noise and flapped his hands as though he were trying to take flight.

"He is choking!" Manuel looked up with panic in his face. "There is something in the soup!"

Dexter stood up, announcing that he knew the Heimlich maneuver. Genial motioned for him to sit down. Manuel looked from Genial to Genial Sr., eyes widening. I gripped the edge of the table.

"You fucking worm," Manuel hissed, and reached into his jacket, but then something pierced him between the eyes and his body went slack. My ears rang: I couldn't remember having heard anything, but I must have, because it felt like fluid was dripping from my ear canals. Genial was standing next to me, shaking, holding a gun that seemed too large for him. The top of his head was in a blind spot so I had no idea what his expression was. The staff were screaming, or at least looked like they were screaming. Dexter was screaming, too. Brianna had a look of horror on her face. Genial Sr. was trembling, gasping, the veins in his massive neck bulging.

I heard something that sounded like "Go!" and Genial was pushing me in the direction of the Daroqol, who must have filed out of the wine cellar at the sound of the gunshot, and I either mouthed or screamed "Come on!" to Brianna and Dexter, whose traumatized faces were angled toward mine. Genial said something that was too muffled by my tinnitus to understand, but he was smiling perversely, like he'd just won a colossal game of king of the hill. We were out the door and he was behind us, still saying muffled things, the Daroqol brandishing their AK-47s, and because I couldn't hear and could barely see I had no idea the UNA were upon us until they were, shooting at those of the Daroqol who weren't flanking us. I climbed into the Jeep, Brianna after me, Dexter after her, his sneakers nearly falling off in his haste, and we watched as the Daroqol and UNA fell to the ground behind us. Genial was still grinning, clearly proud of himself, still talking as he hoisted himself into the Jeep, talking and talking until his eyes unfocused and he fell from the Jeep's door and blood began to pool around his head on the ground. The driver reached back to shut the door and we sped across the lawn, away from the house. I turned to look out the side window: three UNA soldiers were upon Genial—what used to be Genial—and his body was twitching as they loaded it with bullets.

There was a liquid pop in my ears and I could hear Brianna crying next to me. Dexter was looking at me like I'd betrayed him.

"What the fuck was *that*?" he asked, sounding distant.

"A coup," I replied. "A coup that went very badly."

ELEVEN

It seems now like everything I've done in my life I've done because of love, a useless, gutting love that left me devoured from the inside. The failed coup, Genial's death, Brianna and Dexter's terror: I felt these things pressing in on me from all sides. But what felt the worst was the thought of the money we'd lost and what that would mean for Orson.

It didn't seem to matter to Karl that I'd left him in Urmau in the middle of a coup. He was back in New York within days, texting me that he wanted me, that I needed to stop playing with him. I told him I would when he dropped the short. He told me that was impossible, that he had too much evidence against us. He sent me pictures of his trunk-like cock, which I deleted. His desire was thick, dizzying, distracting. But it wasn't enough. Orson was still in his and Emily's bedroom in the Enner house, claiming that he would spend the next two months in isolation in order to achieve his next "awakening." Many NuLifers were doing the same thing, dispatching one unworthy member of each Enner house to do the cleaning and get the groceries while the rest tried to think in step with Orson, to predict what he would do next.

I went up to the Farm to visit him, fighting off more splitting pain behind my eyes as the helicopter touched down behind the farmhouse. I'd obediently taken the glaucoma pills that morning, but the door to Orson's Enner house was still shifting in and out of focus, and I barely recognized Emily's face when she answered. She gave me a strangling hug and I blinked, the room sharpening around me. She'd decorated it like Carol had decorated her penthouse: African masks, mosaics made of Caribbean shells, beaded tapestries of what looked like sixteenth-century Urmanese rebelling against Spanish conquistadores.

"Ez, I'm so glad you came!" she said. "It's not the bestbestbest time in the world, but what can you do? Orson said he'd take a few minutes out to see you."

A few minutes. I hugged her weakly back, stumbling a little when she released me. She'd changed her hair once again, to my disappointment. She was a dirty blonde now, with cat-eye eyeliner and a stud in her nose. She wore a crop top despite the changing weather, and her neat navel was visible just above the waistband of her jeans.

"Can I get you anything? Do you want tea? Coffee? We have Coke, too, or just plain seltzers."

"I'm fine." Footsteps above us. "He's upstairs?"

She nodded pertly. "You can go up whenever you want."

Orson was sitting on the edge of their surprisingly modest bed, head in hands, cigarette wedged between his left index and middle fingers. He wore a furry bathrobe and slippers. He didn't hear me come in, so I knocked on the door, and when he turned to see me, his face brightened, which sent me into nostalgic ecstasy. There resurfaced tons of small memories: his teeth colliding against my lips and our subsequent laughter, his flips in the middle of the room, all the times I'd lit one of my cigarettes on the burning end of his.

He patted the bed next to him and I sat down, feeling his warmth, carefully positioning my hand as close to his thigh as I could.

"I'm glad you're here, little dude," he said.

"Me too."

He took a drag and handed me the cigarette. I took my own drag, tasting his lips on the filter.

"I should really quit," he said. "It's bad for my image. But I never know what to do with my hands, you know?"

Obviously I knew. I'd known this for years, for his whole life. I knew him better than he knew himself.

"Yeah," I said.

"You're busy in New York?" he asked.

"Well—I, um. That's actually what I came here to tell you about."

He nodded, unhearing. "People are expecting a lot of me," he said. "You start to feel the pressure in situations like this."

"I can only imagine."

"What do you think people want next?"

"I—I mean, I really don't know. That seems like the kind of thing you'd know."

"Mm." He leaned back on his hands and looked at the ceiling. "I'm thinking people want to know what happens after death."

His body was forming beautiful angles.

"Do you know what happens after death?" I asked.

He laughed. "No, not yet. But I can figure it out. A little meditating. Some solitude. They've both worked so far."

He seemed to be in a pleasant reverie, and I didn't want to interrupt it, but I knew I had to. "Have you seen the news?"

He shook his head. "No externalities."

"Right, okay. I just—" He looked pointedly at me, but I pressed on. "I just need to tell you about what happened in Urmau."

He sighed. "What?"

I told him as quickly as I could about taking part in the coup, about Genial's death and the country's plunge into chaos.

"Okay," he said. "What does that have to do with anything?"

"Well, it means we're in trouble financially. We can't make money in Urmau anymore, and we took a big gamble on it. It could affect the share price."

He waved his hand dismissively. "I hate this stuff," he said. "You were always better at it."

"I know," I said gently. "But the company's paying for the Farm. So the Farm could be in trouble."

He turned to me with a look of such pure panic that I wanted to pull him to my chest and kiss his forehead. I did the next best thing.

"I can keep the share price up, though. I can just not disclose the situation to the shareholders."

He nodded. "Yeah. But then—what if they're watching the news?"

"It doesn't really matter as long as we keep telling them we're making money. Elaine and I can make it look that way."

"How?"

I thought about explaining how special purpose vehicles worked, but I decided against it. "We can make the debt go away. Just like, you know, bide time until we're solvent again."

"When will that be?"

"Very soon," I said. "Definitely very soon."

"It sounds like a good idea," he said. "Sounds like something we would have done in the old days."

"Yeah." I wanted to say *I miss those days*. I wanted to say *I miss you*. Instead I said, "It's foolproof. I know what I'm doing."

He stood up and walked to the window, out of which I could just make out a group of NuLifers sitting around a makeshift bonfire. "They're waiting for me to say what I have to say," he said. It was hard not to stare at his profile.

"Are you really going to marry her?" I asked. I couldn't help myself.

He scratched his cheek thoughtfully. "I mean, yeah. I thought I had your blessing?"

He didn't. "I guess so."

"I really love her," he said, his gaze wandering out the window again. "I think she may be the love of my life."

The words throbbed in my gut. I decided to say nothing. He turned to me.

"That's okay, isn't it?"

"It is what it is."

He smiled. "You get it, little dude. You understand how this works. Very Zen of you."

"Yeah," I said. I imagined getting down on my knees and grabbing him around the waist. The image lasted just a moment—to think of it any longer would have been unbearable—and then I squeezed my eyes shut as though I were having another glaucomic attack. I wanted so badly to stop caring about him but I couldn't: I knew he'd always pull me back no matter how far I managed to get from him, that this would happen with an almost scientific certainty, like the sun rising or gravity rooting us all to Earth. I should have asked *What about us?* But I didn't. I couldn't. The words had been snatched out of my mouth by my own bad luck.

§

I could barely concentrate at the shareholder meeting. The idea that I could be animated for a conference room full of suits waiting for returns on their investments was impossible. Elaine kept staring daggers at me, asking me with her eyes where exactly was I? Truthfully, I was in Orson's arms, but I wasn't at the same time. I was in an armored Jeep speeding away from a bloody coup.

We told the shareholders that, in spite of everything, we were performing well in Urmau. We didn't tell them that we'd defaulted on the Deutsche Bank loan or that we'd inflated the number of shares by a few million. We didn't tell them we were hiding all our debt off the books and falsifying our quarterly earnings reports. We pretended the Farm was turning a profit instead of being propped up by money we'd fabricated out of nowhere. We told them that Orson's business model was sound, that people were actually paying for individual classes and recruiting their friends when really they were cutting checks for top-level Synthesizers, who were cutting checks for Orson. In return, Orson gave everyone "wisdom" and "prayers." Superior Synthesizers like the Enners were raking it in, and Beginners were swimming in debt. But the shareholders didn't need to know any of that.

After the shareholders had ambled out of the conference room, Elaine sat me down next to her.

"What's wrong with you?" she asked. "You were spaced out the whole time."

The blind spots were such that I had to tilt my head to see her face.

"Why are you looking at me like that?"

"I have a headache," I lied. "It hurts when I look at anything straight on."

"You need to get treated for those." There was exasperation in her voice, as though my negligence was costing her money. "They keep happening and happening and happening."

I flashed on Genial's blank face, his body jumping as the UNA fired into him. There would be no explaining this to Elaine.

"Ez, honestly. What's going on?"

"It was a rough trip."

She squinted. "A rough trip where?"

"I was in Urmau," I admitted.

"What?"

"I couldn't text you about it. I didn't have a burner."

"Were you there in the mansion? When the dictator and his son had that shootout?"

I shrugged.

"You were there?" There was a mixture of shock and envy in her voice.

"No, I wasn't," I said thinly. "It'll just be a matter of time before we're solvent again."

She sighed, clearly annoyed that we had to return to matters at hand. "This is big enough to break us."

"But let me remind you that we're not broken."

She said nothing in response, just began scrolling on her phone. Then she stopped and showed me the screen. It was an old phone, the words on the screen too small for me to read.

"Just read it out loud," I said.

"*Dear Mrs. Corman,*" she read. "*You thought you could break me by counter-*

suing. You may have forced us to drop the suit, but I haven't dropped my mission. I WILL get the money that is owed me.

I know you live in a home in Newark with a three-car garage. I know you go to the Hamptons in the summer. I know you have two kids, Luca and Georgie, and I know they go to Robert Wagner Elementary School. I know what time they get to school and what time they leave school. I know that your husband, Bill, is a stockbroker who commutes with you to New York City every morning. Two days ago, you had roofers over to do a repair. I am watching you. I am waiting for you.

Anonymous."

"Jesus," I said.

"I know it's that Mack guy. I looked him up. He has a psychiatry practice in Palo Alto. But he's not there anymore, obviously. He's gone completely off the rails."

"He's a roach under our boot. You're being paranoid, Elaine."

"He's sending emails like these to Jack and Walter, too. It's heinous."

"Why don't you forward them to legal?"

"We should be forwarding these to the police."

"He didn't send anything to me."

"I'm sure he did. You just have people who read your email for you."

She had me there. "What do you want me to do?"

"I want you to get us some security. I want you to figure out a way to lock this guy up. He's deranged."

"I don't think we can do anything unless he makes a move."

"I thought you were on my side."

"I am on your side." I shifted my gaze to my feet, which I could see better than her face for some reason.

"Call Brianna now and ask her how many emails you've gotten from this guy."

I'd given Brianna a month off work. She'd been weak-voiced since we'd left Urmau, and hadn't sounded any better over the phone.

"She's sick," I said. "She's been sick for a while."

"I just need you to do something. Please. If you can't be present at our meetings, at least do something about this."

I told her I'd see what I could do.

§

Dexter had spent a matter of months producing the 3.0, and we rolled it out so quickly that there was no time to have any kind of celebration or gala, to do anything to mark the occasion like we usually did. Dexter and I went on TV to promote it, got lobbed a few softballs by talk-show hosts who were solidly in our corner. The hosts would inevitably call plants from the audience to come onstage and try the 3.0 out, the plant stumbling around the stage in the boxy Bliss-Mini helmet, exclaiming at all the exciting things they were doing and seeing.

Within days of the rollout customer service began getting complaints. The VR technology wasn't actually VR technology: it was a bunch of fancy pictures that were barely interactive. The voice activation was glitchy. The networking feature didn't work unless users were standing within three feet of their routers. There were none of the sleek elements of the original design: the colored lights to indicate users' mood-states, the visible magnets. The whole thing was too complicated, promised too much, to coast on the placebo effect. We'd sold over 100 million units and customers were furious when they couldn't return them.

It was during the same time that Dexter disappeared, his representatives claiming that he was hard at work designing drone technology that he believed could help bring peace to the troubled country of Urmau. Really, he was putting weaponry in the hands of children who took up fighting for the Daroqol: I saw his drones on TV, the STARS logo visible on each mini machine in a photo of five kids kneeling among a collection of them, grinning toothily in their combat gear.

After several days of calling, I finally got him on the phone.

"What the fuck are you doing?" I asked.

"Bringing democracy to Urmau," he said, a smile in his voice. "You've been watching, I'm guessing?"

"That's not what this is about—you fucked us."

"Fucked you? I didn't fuck you on anything."

"On the 3.0," I said. "It doesn't work."

"Well—"

"You said you could roll it out right away. You said it could increase the consumer base."

"And hasn't it?"

I sighed sharply. "It doesn't *work*."

"It does. You're just not taking time to familiarize yourself with the technology. It's a little too bleeding edge for a lot of consumers. The 2.0 was crawling and this is running. Wait five or ten years—you'll see how ahead of the curve we are."

"This isn't about making money in five or ten years," I said. "It's about making money now."

"These things can pay dividends."

"I'm going to sue you."

His voice hardened. "I'll sue you first."

"For what? What could you possibly sue me for?"

"For not paying me enough. This whole collaboration has been one-sided. I design things for you and you give me pennies in return."

"We give you millions of dollars."

He scoffed. "Compared to what you're earning, that's nothing."

"This is insane. I can't believe you're doing this."

"I wouldn't be doing this if you hadn't started it," he said. "You're a psychopath, Ez."

"We're recalling the model," I hissed. "Our collaboration is over."

I hung up on him and called Delpy into my office. He was the youngest of the executives, the fittest, dumbly loyal, and he and his wife had no children to worry about: perfect for what I needed. He stood attentively at my desk, hands at his sides, a clueless first mate on a sinking ship. I motioned for him to sit down.

"Are you getting emails from someone named Mack Wang-Orsi?" I asked.

"Yes, actually," he said, his face collapsing into a frown.

"A lot of us have been," I said. "Are you forwarding them anywhere?"

"To the police," he said. "But they don't seem to want to do anything about it. Apparently it doesn't qualify as stalking if he's just sending threatening emails."

"What's he threatening?"

He shrugged. "Nothing specific. I think he just wants to sound ominous."

I leaned forward, getting that feeling again like the room was being bugged. "I need you to help me with something," I said. My body was coursing with adrenaline from the phone call: I knew I was about to say something stupid but I couldn't stop. "I need you to help me shake him up a little."

"Sorry, um—what do you mean?"

"We have too many people trying to fuck us," I said. "It's getting annoying. We need to, like, send a message that this kind of thing can't keep happening. We've already lost money on the 3.0, we've lost Ellhorn, and now we have the risk of this guy going public."

"We lost Ellhorn?"

"Yes," I said, watching his frown deepen. "Don't take it personally. It's his fault, not ours."

Delpy nodded obediently.

"I need you to just do a little fact-finding, okay? Figure out where in the world Mack Wang-Orsi is right now."

"I can do that. I can definitely do that." He shifted into a blind spot and I tilted my head to see his expression, which was thoughtful but nervous, the face of someone who was weighing pros and cons.

"Don't think too hard about it," I said. "Just find out where he is and tell me."

§

Delpy hired a guy named Jimmy Palugas who worked for a moving company in Queens by day and dealt in something called "locational and loan services" by night. Palugas, who was wide-shouldered and red-haired with an acne-pocked beard, would find people who owed other people money and remind the debtors of their debt. He was very good at his job, and it took him only two days to locate Mack at a Newark Holiday Inn. Mack had been traveling from there to spy on Elaine and Renhauser, both of whom owned homes in New Jersey.

Around 2:00 a.m., Palugas posed as a pizza deliveryman and was let up to Mack's room. Mack screamed like a madman as Palugas led him out the fire exit and into a company SUV. Everyone was too busy dealing with the fire alarm to notice or care. The parking lot was deserted of onlookers. And even if there had been onlookers, who would have rushed to help Mack? He was clearly drunk. Any passersby would have simply assumed he was being led off by a plainclothes policeman.

Palugas drove the screaming Mack to a clearing in the Pine Barrens where Delpy and I were waiting in Delpy's gifted air taxi, helicopter-large but faster, more efficient, and environmentally friendly. When Mack saw me, his eyes went wide.

"You *fucker*," he breathed, causing the cab to reek of cheap scotch.

Palugas shoved him into the air taxi and closed the hatch behind them. I turned from Mack to the shaky Delpy, who was manning the control: a push button and joystick setup designed for the most clueless of pilots.

"We need to talk," I said, sighing. "You've been bothering us."

"I'm going to the police!" Mack screamed.

Delpy pressed the button, maneuvered the joystick. We broke free from the ground.

"The police?" I asked over the buzz of the propellers. "You're inside a drone."

"You fucked me. You cut me out," he slurred. "You really are just a bunch of thugs and criminals. You'll do anything you possibly can to make money."

We must have been above the trees, but it was impossible to tell. I could barely see my hand in front of my face. Behind me, Mack was writhing and grunting, attempting to stomp and kick the burly Palugas, who had somehow found a way to restrain him. Delpy pulled the joystick toward him and we veered left.

"I'm doing you a favor," I said. "You've built a successful psychiatric practice in Palo Alto, but that's going to crash and burn if you keep stalking us."

More writhing, an exasperated grunt from Palugas.

"Stop sending us the letters, man," Delpy ventured. "It really is a messed-up thing to do."

"I'll send as many letters as I want," Mack hissed. "I'll do whatever I can to get the money you fuckers owe me."

I turned around, pretending to see Mack behind me. "I need you to calm down, Mack. We're taking you to New York, okay? And then you're going to have a conversation with our lawyers in the morning. And you're going to sign some papers and you're going to leave us alone."

"You're kidnapping me!" he howled again, and I winced.

"It's a small space," Palugas complained. "We can all hear you. Too well."

Delpy veered sharply to the right. I was beginning to doubt he knew his way back to the city.

"You're already being exposed," Mack said. "People hate the new Bliss-Mini. They're catching on to your fucking scheme."

"Come on, there's no scheme," I said. "We're really sorry we had to ambush you tonight, but we knew you wouldn't come with us of your own volition."

"Sorry," Delpy said meekly.

"Fuck you! Fuck you all!" Mack began banging on the window. I could hear Palugas wrestling with him. "Help!" Mack screamed. "I'm being kidnapped!"

"Jesus." I squinted out the cockpit window, trying against all odds to see the forest floor. "We're, like, at least a hundred feet in the air."

"Two hundred and fifty-six," Delpy said, pointing to the control panel.

"Two hundred and fifty-six feet in the air," I repeated. "That's really high up."

"You realize I know about you and Orson, Ezra," Mack said, a new sharpness in his voice. "You two were fucking. I know how much you love him. I could read it on your face the minute I met you. You're doing all this for him, aren't you? Because you can't get over him? And it's a shame, isn't it, because he loves that movie star?"

I balled my fists in my lap. "None of that is true."

I could hear a smile creep into Mack's voice. "It's all true. And I'm going public with it."

Delpy looked at me like I was another species and I motioned for him to redirect his attention out the cockpit window.

"Stop him talking," I said to Palugas.

I could hear the rip of duct tape, Mack's desperate protests as Palugas sealed off his mouth. Now the writhing began in earnest, Mack kicking the back of my seat, Palugas exerting himself with the effort of keeping him still.

"Honestly, Mack, I'm really sorry about this," I said. "But you're trying to extort us, you're spreading weird, salacious rumors. It's very unprofessional. Please just try to relax, okay? Until we get to the office?"

But Mack wouldn't relax. He broke free from Palugas and banged on the window again, his muffled screams crowding the cabin. Palugas restrained his arms. Mack kicked violently against the hatch. I heard a click: the hatch releasing.

The air taxi tipped and Delpy jerked the joystick, trying to right us. Palugas made a noise like he'd been burned on a hot stove and Mack's duct-taped screams grew more urgent. I turned around and could just make out the purplish night sky, the shape of Palugas clinging to his seat as the shape of Mack fell screaming from the air taxi.

"Oh Jesus," Palugas said, and began to cry.

"What the fuck?" I barked. "Why did you let go of him?"

"It was either him alone or both of us," Palugas whined.

I rammed the heel of my palm into my forehead. "Fuck!"

I could feel Delpy shaking silently beside me.

"He fell so far." The wind blowing in from the open hatch was distorting Palugas's voice. With a grunt, he pulled the hatch closed, and the sudden stillness in the cab was unsettling.

"Yes, he did," I said, a surge of adrenaline making my stomach turn.

Palugas kept crying.

"What do we do?" Delpy asked. "Fuck, Ez, what do we do?"

"This was not supposed to happen," I said to myself.

"I know it wasn't," Delpy said.

"I know you know it wasn't!" I shouted back at him.

The cab was silent except for Palugas's crying. My gears were spinning so fast I felt sick.

"We have to just go back to the office," I said, and turned to Delpy. "Just take us back to the office."

Mack's body wouldn't be found for weeks, and by then it would have decayed gruesomely, all traces of his struggle lost to his rotting skin.

§

I took a car to Karl's, paid the doorman, and let him ring me up. Karl leaned against his open door, a big, crooked smile on his face.

"Are you drunk?" I asked.

"Never been more sober in my life."

He stood aside and let me walk in, which I did, the room too dim to permit me any more than a careful shuffle.

"You have all the blinds closed."

"That's because I *was* drunk," he said. "And now I'm not." He pointed to a half-drunk Bloody Mary on the coffee table next to his sectional. "Hair of the dog."

I wandered into his bedroom and sat down on the edge of the bed and held my head in my hands. I felt him sit down next to me.

"What's the matter, baby?"

The question—both the softness in his voice and the fact that he was asking at all—made me cry, and I took my glasses off and pressed the backs of my hands into my eyes.

"I'm a mole rat," I said.

He rubbed my back. "What are you talking about?"

"I belong underground."

He kissed the side of my head. "You don't belong underground. Not any more than the rest of us."

It was too much. Everything was too much. I wanted to tell him how I was going blind, how the person I loved most in the world was marrying a vapid movie star who changed her hair every two weeks, how Genial had been shot in the head and Mack had fallen from the drone. Maybe it would make me a better person to be regretful, but it would make me an even better person to love and be loved—being loved was the mark of being truly good. I wasn't good anymore. It was possible I never had been.

"Listen," Karl said. "I'm doing the presentation next week. You know that, right?"

I didn't say anything.

"I'm basically going to give you plausible deniability. Say Orson was the architect of the whole thing, etcetera."

I continued to say nothing.

"Have you given any thought to whether you want to get out of Nu-Life?"

"I don't want to get out."

He sighed heavily. "I think you should. I'd still split the yield with you."

"How are you so sure you'll bankrupt the company?"

"Ez, come on. It doesn't take a genius. The Bliss-Mini 3.0 is nonsense. The Farm is a pyramid scheme. Get out while you still can."

"You can't prove any of that."

I wasn't looking at him, but I could feel him tensing. "But I will. I'm going to next week. Please." He put his hand on my knee. "I care about you."

I put my glasses back on and looked at him. His forehead was dented with wrinkles. He was biting his lower lip.

"There's a reason I got drunk," he said. "I'm worried."

"Worried about what?"

"How you'll respond to what I say next."

"Try me."

"I love you."

It seemed the blind spots got bigger then, my field of vision smaller. I didn't know what to say, so I said what I thought would be most advantageous: "I love you, too."

He hugged me to him, hooked his chin over the top of my head. "Think about getting out," he said. His heartbeat churned in my ear. "Please just think about it."

TWELVE

In early June, the save the date came in the mail: a picture of Orson and Emily holding hands and locking eyes, Orson dressed down in his "of the people" Farm uniform and Emily in a conspicuously lacy dress, both smiling like they'd just been informed they were immortal. They looked immortal, like Olympians, eternally beautiful and eternally young, fashioners of fire and sunlight and thunder. "You are cordially invited to the wedding of Orson James Ortman and Emily Eloise Effham on July the sixth, 2018." I hadn't known Orson had a middle name. He'd never told me.

I tore the card and the envelope in half and shoved them in one of my desk drawers as Brianna knocked on my office door. She was still ghostly, still walking with frightened, mincing steps, but had deemed herself well enough to be back on the job, sorting my emails, fielding phone calls, jotting down ideas for growth and diversification in a little floral notebook. But any confidence she'd had before Genial's assassination was gone entirely, replaced by docility and an almost motherly worry. She spent hours in my office at a time, typing on her laptop, watching as I drank or played PC games or took calls from shareholders who were growing increasingly suspicious of our earnings reports both at home and abroad.

"The FTC is investigating us," she announced.

I produced a bottle of Pappy Old Rip Van Winkle from under my desk and poured myself a $315 shot simply because I could. She watched me as I poured, her mouth gathered in one corner of her face.

"We're under investigation," she repeated.

I took the shot. "Okay." I offered her the bottle.

"No thanks." She sat down across from me. "What do you want to do?"

"Elaine and I will handle it."

"Why are we under investigation?"

"No real reason." I hiccupped. "They got suspicious because we increased the number of shares too many times."

"Is that the real reason?"

I poured myself another shot without looking at her. "Yes."

"Okay." She sounded disappointed, as though she were a child who'd been promised and then denied a trip to Dairy Queen. "But you and Elaine should be careful."

Her face—at least what I could see of it—was beautiful in a surprising way, thin with a pleasing asymmetry to the corners of her mouth, and when she lowered her eyes to look at her notebook, I experienced a jolt of resentment. Why was I surrounded by all these beautiful people? Why couldn't I be like them?

"Where are you from in Massachusetts?" I asked.

"Lowell."

"That's a suburb of Boston, right?"

She nodded uncertainly. "Why do you want to know?"

I flashed on her desktop background. "You didn't have money growing up, did you?"

She looked visibly uncomfortable. "This is weird, Ez."

"I'm just saying—" But I didn't know what I was saying. I poured myself another shot, buying time until I could think of something. "I'm just saying that we're very alike. We grew up without money. And that's the reason we got here, right? Because we wanted money."

"I wanted to do my part to rectify the gender imbalance in the—"

"You wanted money," I interrupted.

"I guess." Her eyes flicked up to meet mine. "Who doesn't?"

"Exactly." I gestured to the TV mounted on the opposite wall. "Could you turn that on? Karl's about to give his presentation."

She switched it on and Karl appeared onscreen, sitting alone on an empty stage, a PowerPoint projected onto a massive screen behind him. The slide displayed read: DEBT STRUCTURE ON THE FARM. He looked uncharacteristically flushed.

"We have learned from people who've stopped living on the Farm that they took on massive debt in order to join NuLife," he said. "There are only a few people who can make a living on the Farm, and those are the top Synthesizers. Everyone else is being constantly asked to invest in classes, in the Farm's upkeep, in something Mr. Ortman calls 'spiritual technology,' which appears to be nothing more than his wise words. People on the Farm recruiting other people to live on the Farm. It looks like a pyramid scheme, in my opinion."

A voice from the audience: "But the people doing this aren't being lied to. They know what they're getting into. Their investment is in NuLife."

"Ah—yes," Karl said. "But my point is that it's a flimsy investment."

"But aren't they all technically shareholders?" another voice asked.

"Not technically. They'd have to buy those shares separate from their investment in the Farm, which is, for all intents and purposes, a cult."

"I think it's unfair to call it a cult," a third voice said. "I don't think Orson Ortman has any malicious intent there. There's not going to be a mass suicide or a shootout or anything."

"Maybe not—"

"And if we really do think of NuLife and the Farm as two separate entities, then one shouldn't reflect upon the other in any sort of negative way," the third voice continued.

"The fact is that NuLife is extremely profitable," the first voice said. "And I'm not sure what you have to prove that any fraud is taking place?"

"We have concrete evidence," Karl insisted. "We've spoken to scientists, data specialists. We've planted informants on the Farm, people who are telling us that this stuff really, really does not work."

"Isn't that entrapment?"

"Couldn't you argue," Karl said, "that what Mr. Ortman is doing to these so-called NuLifers could also be defined as entrapment?"

"I just don't see how any of these people are trapped. People have choices. This is a free market. You can vote with your dollar for whatever type of business you want to. It doesn't seem right to police people's freedom."

"I'm not trying to *police* anything," Karl said.

"But it sounds like you are."

A fourth voice: "It sounds like you're trying to pick apart a successful business model and a frankly quite inspiring public figure for your own benefit."

"Well, if you find him inspiring, I can't exactly help that—" Karl began.

"By your terms, it sounds like any legitimate business could be described as a pyramid scheme."

And before Karl could answer: "Where's the CFO in all of this?"

"Ezra Green is, in my opinion, a pawn of Orson Ortman," Karl said, and the PowerPoint skipped ahead several slides to a graphic of the company masthead arrayed like a crime family: Orson at the top, followed by me and Elaine, then Delpy and Renhauser, all the way down to faceless gray boxes labeled "Farm residents."

"I don't really think Ezra Green is engineering anything," Karl said. "He's passive. Everyone's just doing their job except for Mr. Ortman, who invents his own rules. At best, they're completely clueless like Mr. Green. At worst, they're fleecing people while hiding behind corporate bureaucracy. A bunch of Eichmanns with stock options."

I snorted and poured myself another shot, nearly missing the glass.

"Don't you think that's kind of a harsh comparison, Mr. Rothenberg?"

"Any other questions?" Karl asked, his voice shaking.

I told Brianna I'd seen enough and she switched off the TV. I felt bad for Karl. I felt bad for myself. There were thousands of places I would rather have been than sitting in my office with Brianna, blinking through my tunnel vision as distant purrs of thunder accompanied the occasional flash of lightning outside.

"It feels like everything's falling apart," Brianna said.

"Nothing's falling apart. You'd be the first to know if everything was falling apart."

"I think I'd be the last to know."

I fixed her in my gaze. It was a little frightening to be almost drunk on top of being almost blind. "Do you want three hundred million dollars?"

"What?"

"As a bonus."

"Ez, what are you talking about? Where would that money come from?"

I shrugged and poured another shot. "You've been loyal," I said. "You've kept all my secrets."

"I have no idea where the money would come from, though."

"Does it matter? It'd come from somewhere."

She screwed up her face. It seemed like she really wanted to know where the money would come from.

"It'd come from a shell Elaine and I created to hold some assets off the books. We'd dissolve it and give you the money."

"I couldn't take that."

"Well, it's yours if you ever decide you want it."

She said something in response but I didn't hear it: pain clanged behind my eyes and my vision began to stutter. I cast my gaze around the room as if looking at the sofa or the extra chairs or the art on the walls was going to keep what was happening from happening, but of course it wasn't. There was what felt like an electrical surge—everything got very bright, radiant almost—and then everything went black.

"Fuck," I mumbled, as if we'd just lost power.

I could hear her sitting forward, could hear the motherly tone in her voice again. "What is it?"

I shook my head.

"Ez?"

I considered trying to pour more of the Pappy Old Rip Van Winkle to prove that I could still see, but it was useless. "The glaucoma," I said.

"Oh my god." She sounded like she was the one going blind. "What's it doing?"

I waved my hand in front of my face like she had years ago. "It's totally gone." It was surprisingly easy to tell her.

"You need to go back to Mengetsu. Tell her what's going on."

"It's too late for that."

"It's not too late. You remember what the doctor told you in Urmau? Are you still taking the pills?"

"Yes," I lied.

She'd hooked her arm in mine and was pulling me out of my chair. I stumbled, saw silver sparks in my non-vision.

"We're going to fix this," she said. "We're going to get you home and then I'll call Mengetsu."

I produced my phone from my pocket and held it in her direction. "Knock yourself out. The passcode's 032889." Orson's birthday.

She took it from me and began bundling me into my coat, whispering words of encouragement in her weak voice. It was useless, really. I've since realized she was right: everything was falling apart then. The blind were leading the blind.

§

I drank nearly an entire bottle of Glenfiddich the week of my surgery, not something I was planning to tell Mengetsu about, thinking of how Orson had never tasted something like this, nor had the cross-eyed experience of being slumped against a bedframe alone in an Upper West Side condo, drunk out of his mind and wondering what someone he couldn't have was doing right at that moment.

It was the longest June of my life: I'd been dipping in and out of sight-lessness for a week while Mengetsu scheduled my surgery. The next time I'd see Orson would be as the best man at his wedding. I realized I could count the times I'd seen him that year on a single hand, the times I'd texted with him on two. I hovered between hating him and wanting him, between drinking until I'd poisoned myself and getting up to make a cup of coffee so I could figure out more ways to keep expanding his empire. But things were thinning then, like a wad of gum stretched nearly translucent, and there was no way I could restore what we'd had before. There was only denial. And the Glenfiddich.

When I woke up the next morning my head felt like a bell that had been rung and was still vibrating. I could see better—miraculously—but still not well, and felt my way to the bathroom, where I threw up, and then slumped next to the toilet, where I listened to my phone ringing in the bedroom. The ringing persisted for long enough that I had to stand and stumble back to the bed, where I managed to make out the phone's accept call button. It was Karl's voice on the other end.

"Ez," he said.

"Hi." I still sounded drunk.

"Ez, you won. I'm giving up the short."

"That's good," I said, and collapsed back on the bed.

"Look, I'm sorry. To have put you through all that. But I still think something's very wrong with NuLife. I can't get them to believe it, but I know it's true."

"Sorry you think that."

"It's a house of cards, Ez."

"Mhm."

"You could go to prison."

"Could I really?"

I could hear his breathing on the other end of the line. He sounded small and panicked and pathetic.

"It's all right," I said. "You didn't lose that much money."

"I don't care about the money. I care about you."

I wanted to laugh, and I suppressed it as best I could. "Why do you care about me?"

He sighed. "Because you're funny. And you're intelligent. And weird in a cute way. And you told me you loved me."

"I told you I loved you because it was the right thing to do, not because I felt it." I saw myself saying these words from above, my vision both omniscient and 20/20. I could feel his heart smashing apart on the other end of the line.

"I have to go," he said, and hung up.

Brianna went with me to the hospital. I wore sunglasses, pretending that I didn't want to be recognized. The truth was that I couldn't see in the sun. At the curb, I got out of the car and deliberated how I should go up the stairs: Stumble on my own? Let Brianna guide me? Try some form of echolocation? Before I could decide, Brianna took my arm in hers and helped me into the lobby.

"We'll take the elevator," she said.

We were brought into the staging room immediately, where I could just barely make out Mengetsu's face, the features of which I imagined looked judgmental.

"What did you do, Ez?" she asked. "Why did you let this happen?"

"I fucked up," I said, and smiled. It was perversely fun to disappoint her.

She sighed. "We'll try to save whatever vision you've got left."

Next, I dreamed. I dreamed I was at Last Chance and I was watching Orson play soccer in the distance. He was perfectly in focus but the other kids playing with him were blurry. I didn't care about their blurriness, only about Orson's clarity. I stood up and began walking toward them, but the closer I walked, the farther away I became, until they were ant-small on the horizon and then eventually just pinpricks of light. I knew somehow that Orson was waving at me. I looked up and it was night then, and I had just come from the mess hall, and Orson was in the sky, one of his eyes the moon. The eye appeared to gape at me.

I felt myself rise to him and the sky went bright and technicolor and filled with fireworks. Orson was smiling, encouraging me. His teeth were stars. A swath of sky I understood to be his hand reached down to me and I reached up for it.

Then I was awake—or at least I felt awake—but everything was completely dark, and I was in some kind of bed, and when I touched the place where my eyes should have been there were bandages. I sat up in panic and felt a hand on mine.

"It's all dark," I said.

"I know," a voice—Brianna's—said. "It's supposed to be."

"I'm blind."

"You're not blind. You just have to be this way to heal."

I felt my eyes begin to water, my shoulders begin to tense.

"Ez, try not to cry, okay? It's bad for you if you cry."

I sniffed, and lay back on the strangely thick pillow. "What's the share price?"

I heard her fiddling with her phone. "It's 114, actually. Up a couple points."

"Does Orson know I'm like this?"

"He's at the Farm planning the wedding."

I shuddered.

"I'm sure he wishes you well," she said.

I tried and discovered I couldn't open my eyes behind the bandages. They were sealed closed. "Can I ask you something?"

"Of course."

"Can you take me out of this? Can you make this stop?"

"Make what stop? What are you talking about?"

Then there was Mengetsu's voice in front of us, asking me how I was doing. I lay back down. I didn't want to hear her.

"He's fine, doctor," Brianna said. "He was up and talking with me."

"Ez?"

I said nothing.

"You may feel a little loopy from the painkillers right now."

"I don't feel *loopy*," I said.

"Okay, there's no specific way you need to feel." There was a smile in her voice. Now that she'd blinded me, she was kinder than she'd ever been. "We were able to lower the pressure in your eyes considerably. I'm afraid you'll still have the cloudiness and tunnel vision, but at least things won't get worse. You really need to get serious about using the eye drops and taking the medication, though. You wouldn't be in this situation if you had already gotten serious about that."

"He's going to get serious," Brianna said. "Right, Ez?"

I wanted to rip off the bandages. I wanted to leave the bed. The whole thing was patronizing. Every word out of Brianna's mouth was terrifying. I didn't want any of it to be happening. I didn't want to be myself. I felt Mengetsu's hand on my foot.

"Money and power won't save your vision," she said. "You've got to stop pretending they will."

§

I convalesced in the condo, doing what any newly blind person would do: obsessing over my compromised condition as I listened to the footfalls of my caretakers, trying hard to distract myself with the podcasts and music and movies and TV and audiobooks they played for me. Elaine visited with detailed news about the share price and all the things she was doing to outmaneuver the FTC.

"I think we can only hold up for so long," she said. "It's like rain on a rusted tin roof."

I waved my hand in the direction of her voice. "So let's sell our shares while we can still make a profit."

"That's going to be difficult to do when we're right under the FTC's nose."

"I'm sure you can do it."

"I mean, I can. But it's risky."

It seemed like her voice was coming from within a cave, an especially dark place I didn't have access to. If we won this, we would both remain very rich. If we didn't, the consequences would be disastrous.

"This has always worked before, hasn't it?" I asked. "We act and then we deal with the consequences?"

"Right." Life was coming back into her voice. "We can pull this off."

"We have before."

"We always do."

"So, then, what are we gonna do when this all works out?"

"Celebrate," she said, sounding relieved. "Get the board together and go out for drinks."

"Bigger than that," I said. "The Caribbean. Buy an island or something."

"That's a lot bigger." She laughed. "I think you're right."

"Of course I'm right," I said, but I knew I wasn't.

Elaine switched on a movie about a couple plotting to rob a TGI Fridays and left me alone in the condo with nothing to do. I thought about Mack and Genial underground and Orson and Emily in bed and money and arbitrage and gum stretched too thin. I thought about scrambling versus hoarding. What Orson had neglected to tell me almost a decade ago was that scrambling, if done effectively, can lead to hoarding. I imagined myself someone respectable, someone who'd never had to scramble, someone who'd been born into a family for whom scarcity was a strange and sad thing that happened to other people. I imagined myself someone who had actually gone to college and majored in accounting or something and graduated into an economic boom and held down a middle-class job. I imagined myself falling in love with a woman who held down a similarly middle-class job and getting that woman pregnant twice and buying a house just large enough to fit my parents in the guest bedroom. And then my parents would age, and I would raise the children with the woman, putting money away in a 401(k), buying toys and clothes and college for the children. And then I would retire to a smaller house somewhere in Arizona or Florida, and the grown children would visit me and my wife along with their own children. And then, eventually, I would die, and my wife would get a payout from my life insurance policy, and everyone at my funeral would attest to the fact that I'd lived an honest life. I would never have been Ezra Green. I would never have loved Orson.

That was the problem, loving Orson. That had been the problem for a long time. I loved him and I hadn't stopped loving him and it had stayed in my bloodstream like lead or arsenic, something that should have killed me faster than it was already killing me, something that I couldn't flush out even if I wanted to, even though he'd obviously wanted me to try. I realized with horror that I would die loving Orson, that it would never end, that it was a kind of sentence I had to live out and perhaps this was my punishment for having lived at all.

My breath quickened and I sat forward in bed, feeling my damaged eyes straining not to cry. I was sick, I knew, with no desire to seek a cure.

This was how Brianna found me long after the TGI Fridays movie had ended and a new one had begun playing, a nature documentary about rhinos. I felt her hand on my back.

"Ez," she said. "Take deep breaths."

I did, and I listened to her sit down across from me.

"Should I tell your parents?" she asked.

"About the surgery? No, absolutely not. It'll make them lose their minds."

"They might want to see you. It might make you feel better."

"I don't want anyone to see me like this."

She shifted in her seat, possibly crossing her legs. "What's wrong?"

"It's too much," I said without thinking.

"What's too much?"

"The whole thing."

"What do you mean?"

"I can't tell anyone. I want to tell someone but I can't."

"You can tell me," she said. "I'm willing to listen to whatever you need me to hear."

Shoulders slumped, sitting blind in a bed far too large for me, I told Brianna everything I'd done since the day Orson and I had shown the Bliss-Mini prototype to the venture capitalists, and then everything I'd done before. I told her about Jamie and YouCraft and the sneakers in high school. I told her about Mack and Palugas and the air taxi.

"You want absolution," she said tenderly.

"Yes." I drew my knees to my chin. "I just want someone to know besides me."

"Now I do."

I felt light, almost dizzy. I thought I could see her looking at me with a knowing half-smile. There was a slight creak at the edge of the bedroom, the ghost of a presence, and for a moment I imagined Orson was with her, watching us, approving.

"Thank you," I said.

"I'll take it all to my grave, Ez." She ran her hand through my hair like Orson used to. "I love you like family."

§

On the day of Orson and Emily's wedding, my vision was still tunneled and crowded with blind spots, everything in the distance an impressionistic haze. Some things were in focus, but not many, and I often had to squint to see what I wanted to see. This was the best the surgery could do for me. This was the end of the line.

Orson sent a helicopter to bring me from New York to the Farm, which was crowded with NuLifers dressed in various shades of white. Fairy lights had been strung across the lawn under which were arranged several rows of chairs leading to a canopy. Behind the chairs was a fleet of tables numerous enough to seat most of the Farm's occupants. The nearby Enner houses had all been decorated with streamers of different colors, the occupants sitting on their stoops singing a song they'd written which I surmised was called "A Real Love" and was about the history of Emily and Orson's relationship. Some were even playing guitars and shaking tambourines. My parents had been invited but hadn't been able to come—my dad had to get his gallbladder removed—and secretly I was grateful. I didn't want them to see the Farm up close: the people in white, the weird music, the worshipful atmosphere. I especially didn't want them to see me as blind as I was.

As I walked up the lawn to the house, I could make out Orson's mother rushing at me. She was encased in a red dress with a plunging neckline, her hair tall and stiff with hairspray. She hugged me tightly and I did my best to hug back.

"Ezra," she said, holding me at arm's length. "It's been so long coming, hasn't it?"

I nodded. "You look incredible."

"Thank you, darling." She turned toward the house, which appeared to be swarming with activity. "I so wish his father was alive to see this. Look what you two have done!"

"Yeah," I said numbly. "It's really something."

She grabbed my hand and we walked up the hill and into the house, where I was repeatedly blindsided by people rushing back and forth with trays of food and place settings and more streamers. A gaggle of bridesmaids sat perched on a set of couches, laughing at a video on someone's phone. One, totally unfamiliar to me, waved and shouted, "Hey, Ez!" as I walked by. Orson's mother separated from me to help set up more chairs. I was left in the center of the room, trying to decide my next move, when I saw a man galloping toward me, a massive camera of the kind used on reality TV shows attached to his chest.

"You must be Ezra!" he shouted. "Welcome to the hive." He looked me up and down. "I'm Joseph Rhyno with a *y*, but you can call me Rhyno. I'm the cameraman for this event."

I asked him if he was getting good footage and he leaned toward me conspiratorially. "Actually, I was hoping to get some help with a few shots. Do you think maybe you could follow me into the kitchen here?"

I stumbled after Rhyno into the kitchen, where at least twelve NuLifers were at work on plates of hors d'oeuvres, a giant turkey sculpted out of tofu, and a four-tiered cake topped with plastic figurines that, on very close inspection, looked exactly like Orson and Emily.

"Could you, um, not get too close?" said one of the NuLifers, a man with a deeply lined face whose forehead was obscured by a white bandanna. "It's kind of a delicate operation."

"Of course," I said, stepping back as carefully as I could.

"Everyone, a quick announcement," Rhyno said. "I need to get an establishing shot of the kitchen here. I'm going to step back a few feet, and I want you all to pretend I'm not here." He walked backward and beckoned to me as well. Then he framed the shot with his hands. "What do you think, Ez?"

I couldn't see anything. "Looks good," I said.

We wandered around the house and the property, getting footage of NuLifers attesting to how Orson had changed their lives. We got footage of the Enners toasting the happy couple. We got footage of children running through the fields, playing a game of tag. Rhyno asked for my opinion on every shot, and I never told him that I couldn't see what he was talking about. Eventually he sat me down on the patio and turned the camera on me.

"Ezra Green," he said. "CFO and best man and best friend. What words do you have for Orson on his wedding day?"

Rhyno's face was in a blind spot. I tried not to squint. "Good luck," I said. "On everything."

Rhyno stopped recording. I could tell he was disappointed. "Can we maybe make it a little longer?" he asked. "Like a preview of your speech?"

"Sure," I said. I hadn't written a speech.

"Okay, let's try it again."

He stepped back and announced that he was rolling. But before I could say anything, a bridesmaid was springing toward us out of the house.

"Ez!" she called.

Rhyno groaned and shut off his camera.

"It's Emily," she said breathlessly. "She wants to talk to you."

The sun was glaring directly above the bridesmaid's head, making it all the more difficult to see her. "Are you sure?"

"Yeah. She said it would be quick and sorry to inconvenience you." She turned to Rhyno. "And she doesn't want to be filmed."

I begrudgingly followed the bridesmaid into the farmhouse, down one of the many hallways, into a room that had been designated Emily's, presumably because Orson was occupying their Enner house. I could only see her form sitting slump-shouldered on the bed, but as we got closer it became clear that she had been immaculately made up, her hair in ringlets gathered at the crown of her head, her cheeks flushed, her mouth soft with a gloss of red lipstick. She looked even more beautiful than she normally did.

"Ez, oh my god," she said as the bridesmaid left, closing the door behind her.

"What? What's wrong?"

She grabbed my hand and pulled me down next to her on the side of the bed. "Thank you for coming to see me. Seriously."

"It's your wedding day," I said lamely.

"I know, but you weren't obligated to." She dabbed beneath her eyes with the back of her thumb.

I shrugged. What was one more humiliation?

"Ez, seriously, I'm sorry, okay? I know you're his best friend, I know he loves you. I was jealous of you before, but I know I never should've been."

I patted her hand. I didn't know what else to do.

"I'm scared, though," she said. "And you're the only one who can help me, it feels like."

"What are you scared of?"

She gestured around her. "It's all so beautiful, you know? The Farm, the Bliss-Mini, NuLife. It's all so *good*."

"Yeah."

"What if it's too good? What if there's something I don't know?"

I shook my head. "There's nothing you don't know, Emily. Trust me."

"Sometimes I ask him a question and he gets annoyed, or he gets sad. It's like he doesn't want to share himself with me in those moments." She shuddered a sigh. "It's like how my ex-husband used to be."

"Orson's not your ex-husband. I promise."

She looked at me so sincerely that I almost pitied her. "You know it's going to be okay then, right? You know it's going to work out?"

"Yes. It definitely is."

She held my hand in both of hers and squeezed, not bothering to clear the tears from her eyes. "Thank you, Ez," she said. "Thank you so much."

§

I sat in the front row during the ceremony, Elaine and Brianna on either side of me. Orson's mother sat behind us, sobbing loudly. The officiator was a NuLifer who had gotten ordained specifically for the occasion. She wore owlish glasses and had wiry, graying hair, both of which gave her the gravitas of a minister. Rhyno circled the perimeter, filming, darting forward occasionally to get the reactions of specific guests whose faces he found interesting. The sun made the air feel still. I looked at my hands and then at Orson, tall and handsome in an eggshell suit, standing smiling under the canopy. It was my first time seeing him that day, which felt like an injustice. He could at least have called me into his Enner house, worried aloud about getting cold feet or becoming a father or whatever people worried about on their wedding days.

A small symphony of NuLifers assembled behind the rows of chairs struck up a string-and-woodwinds rendition of "A Real Love." I turned to see Emily being led down the aisle by Chuck Enner, whose muscular chest strained under a white button-down. I hadn't realized that both Emily and Orson were missing fathers, something I had in common with neither of them. It occurred to me that maybe Orson was right to love her and not me, that I'd been the one he'd had to please in order to get to Emily. That I'd been the mark.

I trained my gaze on the ground and found myself remembering Jordan Pinkerton for some reason, the look of shock on her face as her nose began dripping blood. I had ground the Sudafed and salt together that she'd snorted—I had made her believe it would be fine if she snorted it. She had frozen, wide-eyed, in the middle of the gym floor and stared at me, shocked at having been betrayed, shocked that she'd ever trusted me. What had happened to her? Had she fallen in love? Had the love been reciprocal or not? Had it been desperate? Was she now getting married herself, maybe even to the boyfriend she'd spent so many years trying to impress? Was she having any regrets?

The vows were being said and I was remembering even further back, to when I was a child and my mom had taken me to the park and my vision was 20/40. I could see the contours of clouds and the blades of grass then—yellowish closer to the woodchips and increasingly verdant farther away—and it had felt exhilarating to be away from the apartment, to be in a nice place that belonged as much to me as to anyone else. My mom had lifted me onto the swing and told me she'd push me as high as I wanted to go, and then if I wanted to go even higher she'd push me even higher. She'd told me there was no limit to how high I could go. So I'd demanded to go higher and higher, and I'd screamed with excitement as she'd called me Superman, and then when I wanted her to stop pushing I'd called down to her, "Stop!" and I'd jumped off and into the air, imagining I was flying twenty feet when really I was just flying four. I had been too small to know the difference.

"I now pronounce you—" the officiator said, and then there was the sound of someone approaching us from behind, someone yelling, "Stop!"

I couldn't see them until I could: a crowd of FBI agents swarming the ceremony, a few of them with guns, a few more telling us that we shouldn't move. There were screams, people raising their hands in panic. Elaine leapt to her feet next to me. Brianna stayed seated, watching them patiently, and that was when my stomach finally dropped.

"We have warrants for the arrests of Orson Ortman and Ezra Green." We were wanted on charges of racketeering, insider trading, an illegal pyramid scheme, wire fraud, embezzlement. I didn't listen to everything they said. I let them cuff me and watched as they cuffed Orson, his mother screaming, "My son is innocent!" They cuffed Elaine, too, and began cuffing Chuck Enner and a few of the other top Synthesizers. I couldn't see all those they arrested because my vision had fuzzed out entirely and I was being led across the lawn, up toward the house, out onto the road clogged with shapes that must have been the agents' black SUVs. I could hear NuLifers running after us, screaming our names, pleading with the stoic agents. Emily's voice rose loud and desperate above everyone else's. "Oh my god!" she wailed. "Please! Don't take them away!"

As I was being pressed into one of the SUVs, I heard Orson call to me: "Just hang on, Ez! We'll be fine!" And then an agent slammed the door behind me.

"You scumbags stick together, huh?" the agent said to me as he started the ignition. "You've got your own little kiddie circle jerk going on."

I said nothing. I tried to bring my feet into focus but I couldn't.

"You're all so young," another agent said from the passenger seat. I hadn't been aware he'd gotten in the car. "Your whole lives ahead of you. Won't have much life ahead of you after you get out of prison, though."

"Fucking cult leader scumbags," the first agent said.

I felt sick. I closed my eyes and leaned forward so my head was almost between my knees. They'd cuffed me in front, so I dug the heels of my palms into my eyes. *There*, I thought. *That's dark enough.*

EPILOGUE

THE MOST INCREDIBLE PART OF THE FBI HAVING FLIPPED BRIANNA WAS WHAT a good actor she'd been. Too shaken by the coup to continue devoting herself to the criminal operation that was NuLife, she'd agreed to wear a wire during every conversation she had with Orson and me. She'd even brought an agent into my apartment when I'd been blind, guessing correctly that my perceptual powers would be compromised by my misery. He'd been standing in the doorway as I confessed everything, filming me. The prosecution played the footage during the trial, and I listened to myself absolving myself of my sins. After that, they'd waited to take us all down at once: the wedding was the perfect occasion for a sting.

The jury deliberated for five hours before convicting us. Orson and I each got twenty years, Elaine fifteen—her husband divorced her and moved across the country with the children. Everyone else took plea bargains for narcing on us as much as possible. The judge was very deliberate about placing Orson and me in different facilities. Orson went somewhere downstate, somewhere big, and I went upstate. I told the other inmates that I'd accidentally shot a clerk while trying to rob a 7-Eleven, and this was a boring-enough crime that there was never a price on my head. I took a lot of beatings, though. And it took me a few years before I was able to master the dynamics of prison sex: the omnipresent threat of rape, the beatings-off in the shower, the occasional intrigue and romance. I did my best to dodge threats and cycled through boyfriends, the relationships ending either when they got transferred or tired of me. I did an excellent job of hiding my blindness from everyone, so much that people not only thought I had 20/20 vision with my glasses but that I had superb night vision. I had memorized the entire facility and could move through it more adeptly than most of the COs. But I couldn't read—had to pretend, in fact, that I'd never been much of a reader—which left me inordinate amounts of time for daydreaming. A day never passed when I didn't think about Orson, when I didn't simultaneously worry about and wish pain on him. I imagined him the only crier on his cell block, his cellmate threatening to shank him if he didn't shut up. I imagined him choking on the rock-hard bread in the chow hall. I imagined him getting pummeled in the yard. I wanted him to suffer, but not too much. In my dreams I would always rescue him, and he would tell me he was sorry, that if he could do it all over again he'd do it differently, that he'd have loved me. Even in my angriest, most bitter moments, I'd pray to a god I didn't believe in that he was still alive.

During the fourth year of my sentence, I was rotated onto suicide watch. A guard would wake me up at 1:30 in the morning, give me maybe fifteen seconds to throw on a shirt, and take me down to the isolation cells, where I would listen to and watch suicidal prisoners to keep them from trying anything. One night, I was in charge of talking to an eighteen-year-old kid named Tyrell who had grown up in an environment so difficult and oppressive that he could barely get out the words to describe it. He was crying as he spoke, but trying to do it quietly, and I was forbidden from touching him, so the only comfort I could offer was listening and saying, "It's okay," or, "Keep going," when he stumbled and began choking up.

"It was always some fucked up shit happening at my mom's," he told me. "With her and her boyfriend. The kind of boyfriend she had, this guy fucked her up, fucked me up."

"I'm really sorry to hear that."

"Fuck man, no you ain't. You ain't know shit about me," Tyrell shout-whispered, exhausted by then, obviously frustrated with everything.

I sat back. "Okay, well, it's true, I don't know shit about you. But I care about you."

"Don't come at me with that faggot-ass bullshit."

"I mean, I am a fag. You know that. I've told you that."

Tyrell was silent. Then he laughed. "Yeah, man," he mumbled.

"Come on," I said. "You want me to let you in on something?"

A CO's heels clicked across the floor outside the isolation block. I could hear Tyrell's heavy breathing, how he'd exhausted himself with emotion.

"I had this business on the outside. It made people, you know, true believers. It made them feel like they could be the best versions of themselves."

"So the fuck what."

"It really works. I can do it in here, you can do it with me, I'll give you a cut of whatever I get."

"Shit sounds dumb as hell."

"So let me show it to you. What else do we have to do right now?"

Tyrell sighed. "Try me," he said.

I Synthesized Tyrell. His breathing slowed and evened.

"Damn," he whispered at the end. "How'd you do that?"

Tyrell had only been out of isolation for a week by the time he'd organized my first information session in the prison library. He rounded up five guys one week, and then eight came the next, and then twelve after that. I Synthesized them all, and I gave Tyrell half the loosies, ramen, and stepped-on coke I got in return. We bought bananas and powdered milk for our oatmeal and spent our commissary money on phone calls to our mothers. Whenever fights went down, we were suspiciously absent. We took extra-long showers. We got extra helpings in the chow hall.

I taught Tyrell how to Synthesize and he revealed himself to be something of a prodigy, capable of bringing the angriest, most dangerous inmates to tears. Gang leaders and cartel members who had served so much time that they understood life on the inside better than life on the outside came to him with their problems. Soon he was earning enough on his own that we needed to recruit more people to bribe COs and organize sessions for us. More and more people wanted to learn how to become Superior

Synthesizers. NuLife spread like a virus through the facility, and for a few months I forgot about Orson—possibly because I *was* Orson.

I was woken up a little before 6:00 one morning by a CO's flashlight, which was as bright as stadium lighting and caused my cellmate, a man who'd murdered his cousin, to call me a little bitch. The CO threw open the cell door and dragged me out without letting me put on a shirt. "You're going to isolation," he told me.

"Why?" Anxiety swelled in my chest.

"Warden figured out your con, 31151. You're dealing in a lot of contraband."

"What are you talking about?"

The CO tightened his grip on the collar of my jumpsuit. "You know exactly what I'm talking about. Just like I know you didn't knock over a fucking 7-Eleven."

I said nothing, hobbling silently next to him.

"You need a little time to think about what you've done."

"How long?"

He laughed. "He didn't say. Left it up to us. Which is good, because I don't like your lying ass."

I didn't say a word about Tyrell. I prayed to the same non-god that they hadn't gotten him, too.

In the isolation block, the guard opened the cell door and snatched my glasses from my face. I heard them crunch under his boot.

"Oh shit," he said. "So sorry about that." Then he shoved me in and locked the door.

Isolation was the only place I'd ever feared for my sanity. The room was bright and barren, too small and therefore too easy to memorize: the rock-hard bed, the little steel toilet, the blank wall opposing both. I became acutely aware of my blindness because there was nothing else to do, no one else to distract me, no noise except the COs' clicking boots and the leftovers from the chow hall that arrived three times a day. I had to think or else I wouldn't be able to tell whether I was dead or alive. I thought of Orson. I imagined kissing him. I lay on the bed and then on the ground. I stopped being able to feel time passing, which meant I stopped being able to sleep. I thought of how the world had once been incredibly big and had since narrowed to a pinhead's width. I thought of swinging on the swing as a kid.

I lied and told the COs that I was suicidal, and once every night a bored and aggressive prisoner would come to "listen" to my problems. Sometimes I'd get offered a cigarette but most often I'd be instructed to stay quiet so the listener could sleep. This happened for three nights in a row until Tyrell came on the fourth. I nearly cried with gratitude.

"Man, they was talking about how you was down here, talking about killing yourself," he said. "I got them to get me on rotation minute I found out about that."

"Who'd you have to bribe?" I asked.

He waved his hand at me. "Don't matter. I just wanted to know if your ass was still alive."

"I don't actually want to die," I said.

"Hell yeah, I know that," he said. And then, in a whisper: "But don't you go saying that like you proud of it or something. Them guards gonna kick me out minute they hear it."

"Yeah," I said. "I know."

"The fuck they do with your glasses?"

"Broke them."

Tyrell sucked his teeth. "Stone-cold nazis running this fucking place."

We sat in silence for a moment, my brain swimming with self-pity and adrenaline, my body exhausted on a cellular level from countless nights without sleep. "How'd you do this isolation thing?" I asked him.

"I don't know," he said. "You just kind of let the time happen."

I tried to let the time happen, but I could feel the bonds between my neurons fraying. When the COs came by with the leftover chow, I tried to talk to them, convince them that I'd learned my lesson and would stop the con and was completely reformed. They ignored me, sometimes laughed at me, and the blindness began to take on a whole-body quality, my senses shutting down. The chow tasted like nothing, smelled like nothing. The floor and the bed stopped feeling hard: they stopped feeling like anything at all. I knew then that I was losing my mind. All I could think about was Brianna sitting by my bedside, the bandages heavy over my eyes, her hand over mine. If it hadn't been for her, I wouldn't be losing my mind. If it hadn't been for her, I would have at the very least still been in the condo, still been capable of restoring my life to what it had been before.

I wasn't sure how much time had passed when the cell door opened and a CO's voice said that I was being transferred back to the general population. Shackled, I walked haltingly next to him as he prodded me with his club, up two flights of stairs and back to my original cage, where the fuzzed shape of my cellmate was either lying or sitting on his bed.

"The bitch is back," he said as the CO shoved me into the cell and made a show of loudly securing the lock. "Oh, how I've missed you."

I slumped against the wall and sat on the ground, listening to him turn the pages of his book, calculating, like I always did, the time until my release. 5,840 days. 140,160 hours. 8,409,600 minutes. 504,576,000 seconds.

"You're thinking too loud," my cellmate said.

Time happened: wake up, the yard, lunch, TV, the library, phone calls, dinner, shower. Tyrell was released and four kids with similar backstories took his place. I was formless, a barely sentient lizard crawling from one mandated activity to the next. I couldn't do the one thing I knew how to do best. My mind had lost its agility, grown putty-like. Why bother living if I had no function?

When I was 2,921 days into my sentence, it was announced that we were intaking a transfer of roughly 300 inmates from a different facility. The announcement came when we were in the yard, while I was sitting on a bench staring in the direction of the barbed wire fence, listening to the noise of my fellow inmates heaving barbells and covertly dealing drugs around me. An arsonist who had figured out that I was blind and took pity on me had afforded me a few bumps of poor-quality coke that morning, and I was feeling a little buzzed, wishing I'd done enough to be truly high, to feel my heart slamming against the wall of my chest. A heart attack: I should be so lucky.

The COs began herding us inside and we streamed listlessly back to our cells to kill time before lunch. My old cellmate had recently been transferred after inciting a fight, so I'd had the place to myself for a few days. But I'd been warned it wouldn't be for long.

"These transfers are from another max facility, a worse one than this," one of the many COs who hated me reassured me. "You're gonna get your fag ass kicked, 31151."

But when the door to my cell opened that afternoon, it wasn't by one of the usual COs who patrolled my cell block. This one had a lighter touch with the lock, a kinder way of opening the door, and the shackled shape who walked in ahead of him thanked him politely. The CO relieved the shackled shape of his shackles and told him it was his pleasure. And then I realized I recognized one of the voices.

The formerly shackled shape—lanky, cheerful—sat down on the ground in front of me. I could feel his face angled at mine.

"Ez," the shape said.

I felt like my head had come unscrewed. I grabbed my chest as if I'd just witnessed my own death.

"Ez," the shape said, and put his hand on my knee. "It's me."

I'm not sure how—maybe out of terror, maybe out of love—my junk eyes focused perfectly. There he was: clean-shaven, short-haired, bruised and a little anemic but still him, still grinning like he had on the first day of Last Chance.

"How did you . . . ?" I asked, not knowing how to finish the sentence.

Orson laughed and shook his head. "Don't worry about it. Point is, I'm here." He squeezed my knee. "I made it."

My eyes unfocused and it was just his voice, the warmth of his hands on my face, his lips on mine. It was the kiss equivalent of birdsong. It was impossible to forget. He pulled away and sat back on his heels.

"I'm here," he said again. "Now how about we make some money?"

ACKNOWLEDGMENTS

THIS IS A PANDEMIC BOOK, AND PANDEMIC BOOKS REQUIRE A LOT OF SUPPORT to get written. I'm grateful to my immune system, the robustness of which allowed me to keep writing even after I got COVID.

I'm deeply indebted to Ross Harris, without whose input (and sales acumen) this book would never have seen the light of day. I'm so lucky to be working with Barbara Jones, who has lifted some serious weight to get this book out there—ditto Jason Richman, who has been on the train since day one.

A huge thank you to Zack Knoll, who gave *Confidence* a home and continues to be one of its most amazing and dedicated advocates. And to Carina Guiterman, who has seen this book through several edits and generously talked with me about our process in front of a truly intimidating number of booksellers. To Lashanda Anakwah, who made sure the book got what it needed at all times. To Margaret Southard and Elizabeth Breeden, who very capably kept me from rambling on, and to Hannah Bishop and Alyssa diPierro, who sounded news of this book from the rooftops.

I'm grateful for my friends at Southern Illinois University, who read early drafts of *Confidence* and offered such thoughtful feedback. George Boulukos, who read draft one and on a hike in the woods, told me exactly what I needed to hear. Jay Needham, without whose friendship in Carbondale I would be utterly lost. And my students, whose enthusiasm makes everything worthwhile.

This book owes so much to Ryan Smernoff, whose spot-on feedback utterly transformed it. A huge thank you to Dini Parayitam, Okezie Nwoka,

ACKNOWLEDGMENTS

Andrew Ridker, and all my friends who were also my very early readers—you kept me going when I had no idea what I was doing. To Jon Petto, Vivian McNaughton, and Phoebe Rusch for their ongoing moral support. And to booksellers like Audrey Smith, who make this world a better place.

A huge hug and a thank-you to my parents and extended family, who are always on the lookout for my books in bookstores and sweetly text me whenever they find them.

To Mina, Bubba, and Cowboy, who just want to love and be loved.

And to Fig Tree, who lights up my life every day.

ABOUT THE AUTHOR

RAFAEL FRUMKIN IS A GRADUATE OF THE IOWA WRITERS' WORKSHOP AND THE Medill School of Journalism. He is the author of the novel *The Comedown* and the short story collection *Bugsy & Other Stories*. His fiction, nonfiction, journalism, and criticism have appeared in *Granta, Guernica, Hazlitt, The Washington Post, The Cut*, McSweeney's Internet Tendency, *Virginia Quarterly Review*, and *The Best American Nonrequired Reading*, among others. He lives in Carbondale, where he is a professor of creative writing at Southern Illinois University.